SIREN'S
FALL

Siren's Fall

LUX RAVEN

LACONIA
PRESS

Siren's Fall by Lux Raven

Cover design by Lisa, Little Forest Cat / LittleForestCat.co.uk
Images: Adobe Stock / Shutterstock

First printing, 2025
Printed in the United States of America

Library of Congress Control Number: 2025903661

ISBN 978-1-955283-01-4 (Paperback)
ISBN 978-1-955283-03-8 (eBook)

Published by Laconia Press (Los Angeles)

LuxRavenWrites.com

For Nick...

*Your love and support empowers me to do all the
scary, difficult things I dream of doing*

Content Warning

This book is the second and final book of the Siren's Mark duology. Rest assured, the story concludes with a **guaranteed happy ending**.

Much like the previous book, this one also contains **explicit sex, alcohol use, and violence**. There are mentions of a death by suicide, though it's not depicted or detailed.

I know content warnings can be an important mental health tool. To make sure you have the information necessary to make the best decisions for yourself, I have included a detailed list of potential triggers below. If you don't need these and you'd rather avoid mild spoilers, you can skip to the next page now.

Story includes: memory loss (temporary), illness, hospitals, physical injury, PTSD (specifically, nightmares), homophobia, sexual harassment, blood & gore, emotional & physical abuse in childhood, death by suicide (mentioned, not depicted or detailed), medical gaslighting & trauma, death, and ableism.

If you have any questions about specific triggers, please feel free to reach out to me directly at luxravenwrites@gmail.com. Your well-being is important, and I want you to be able to engage with my stories in a way that feels safe for you.

1

AVA

I've spent a lot of time in hospitals dealing with weird symptoms, but amnesia is a new experience for me.

At least—I think it is.

Isn't it?

"What is your name?" the nurse asks me, eyeing her clipboard.

This seems like a trick question.

"Ava Reynolds," I reply, mentally high-fiving myself for not giving a sarcastic answer.

The man who brought me here is standing and scowling in the corner.

He seems fun.

"When were you born?" she continues.

"January 27th, 1996."

She flips a couple of pages, nods, and writes something more down.

Yes, lady, I know my own birthday.

I do know my own birthday… right?

"Where are you now?" she asks.

"The hospital," I say. The woman scrunches her face as if I got it wrong. "…in Port Charlotte?"

She pinches her lips shut and starts writing.

"Blackwell Memorial Hospital?" I add.

She begrudgingly nods. I'm not sure why she had to be all cryptic about that, but okay.

"How did you get here?" she asks.

"Um, this guy drove me," I say, gesturing to the grumpy hot guy in the corner. "I'm sorry; I didn't actually get your name."

As I look toward him, his eyes dart away to avoid my gaze. The nurse looks to him and he nods in response.

"What is the first event you remember after your injury?"

"I was sitting on a couch and um, this guy was talking to me and my leg hurt like a bitch, and I said I didn't remember who he was…"

I trail off, not knowing how to finish that. Do I tell her that we were in this totally trashed apartment and there was blood everywhere? Should I add that I was surrounded by ultra-hot people who were covered in blood? Is the pile of ash in the middle of the room a relevant detail? I mean, I may not be Einstein, but I feel like those are the kinds of things you don't share until you have the details. Like, are these people in the mafia? Am *I* in the mafia?

Are we just the worst house sitters of all time?

"Can you give some detail?" she asks.

I look at Mr. Grumpy, who doesn't seem to give me anything to work with.

"Detail?" I ask. "Um, we were in a fancy apartment and there was this cute guy with long hair…"

I hear a strange, low, almost-growl-like sound emerge from Mr. Grumpy.

What the heck was that?

"…um, and this lady came out with a bag and she got all panicked."

"Okay, that's good enough," she says, scribbling on my chart. "Can you describe the last event you can recall before this incident?"

I strain to remember. My mind feels foggy, almost as if there's a literal haze creeping in at the edges, blurring the details and obscuring others completely.

"Um, my boyfriend and I were having dinner with his parents," I say. I hear another low rumble from Mr. Grumpy.

I've really got to learn Mr. Grumpy's name.

"And can you tell me today's full date?"

"Um," I say, wondering exactly how far off my memory really is. It does seem awfully cold out for the day that I think it is. "May 6th, two-thousand-and… eighteen?"

Mr. Grumpy storms out of the room in a sudden, violent motion.

So, I'm gonna go out on a limb and guess that was wrong

ZANE

Kami is standing in the hallway outside Ava's room, combing a hand through her hair as she attempts to make herself look less like she just lost a fight to a demon. She has tidied up a bit since we arrived and her skin is just slightly stained red from the remaining traces of blood. I wiped most of it off on the way over here, but she couldn't exactly do the same while driving.

"I can't fucking take it, Kam," I say, slamming a hand into the wall and leaving a fist-sized crater in my wake.

"I was listening," she says with a sigh. "I'm so sorry, Z. We will figure this out."

She pats my back as a reassuring gesture, but it does nothing to ease the ache in my chest.

"She's gone," I say, staring at the floor tiles beneath my feet.

"She's not gone." She grabs my shoulders and shakes them. "Listen to me. That's still Ava in there. We don't know anything right now, okay? It might not even be the lethe that caused this."

"Of course it is."

"You were so sure it was your venom making her sick before, and we all know how that turned out. Ava has some weird human medical stuff going on. For all we know, it's one of those things and her memory will come back."

"Even if it is a medical thing, she could be lost for good," I say, pinching my eyes shut. I feel warm tears spill onto my cheeks.

"That still doesn't mean she's lost. You may just have to start over," she says. "Which honestly may be a good thing in your case, 'cause you fucked things up a lot."

I chuckle at the thought of the many idiotic things I did the first time around.

"For starters," she adds, "you could avoid cursing her out at Pike's this time around."

"Oh piss off," I say with a laugh.

"Why are we pissing off this time?" Kieran says as he rounds the corner. A large, gnarled scar spans across his neck, and his red shirt masks most of the residual blood from his encounter with Asmodeus.

"I thought we told you to stay in the car," Kami says, crossing her arms.

"Yeah well, I forgot. You know—lethe and all," he says, his voice hoarse and raspy from the injury to his throat.

"That's not how lethe works."

"Can you two fucking shut up about lethe??" I snap.

"Shit, Z-Man," Kieran curses. "I'm sorry, I wasn't thinking about it like that… I know you're really into this girl. I didn't mean to…"

"It's fine," I say with a sigh, sweeping a hand through my hair.

"How is she?" he asks.

"She's lost more than a year," Kami replies, seemingly knowing that I'm not up for answering the question. "She doesn't remember any of us—me, you, Zane."

"Well to be fair, I don't remember her either," Kieran says with a smile. His smile fades as he looks back-and-forth between Kami and me. "Too soon?"

Kami smacks the back of his head.

"Ow, okay," he says, rubbing his head. "My bad, just trying to lighten the mood. Have you talked to her?"

Kami looks at me knowingly and raises an eyebrow.

"Not really," I say. "What am I supposed to say?"

"Just about anything would be better than standing silently in the corner and grumbling every time she mentions a man," she says.

She may have a point there.

I look back at the door to Ava's room and sigh.

She's right. I have to talk to her.

———•———

AVA

The nurse steps out just as Mr. Grumpy walks back in. Despite his roughed-up, ragged appearance, he's still remarkably handsome. His dark, curly hair is swept back and, for the first time since we left for the hospital, his deep brown eyes meet mine.

"Hi," he mumbles, brushing a hand through his hair as he shifts back and forth on his feet.

"Hi," I reply.

What do you even say in a situation like this?

Hi, I have no idea who you are. Care to tell me why I ended up in your wrecked house looking like a Walking Dead *reject?*

"You, er, asked my name earlier…" he says with a sigh. "It's Zane."

"Ava." I realize as I say it that I'm meeting him for the first time, but he has already met me. "Oh, I mean… I guess you know who I am already, huh?"

He gives me a small nod and chews anxiously on his bottom lip.

"So, any chance you're going to explain what all that was about?" I ask.

"Which part?"

"What the heck happened? I mean, I know what you told them, that somebody broke in and attacked me and you fought with him, but we both know that's a lie."

"Is it?" he asks with a brow raised.

"You're telling me that some random dude off the street broke into a penthouse apartment on top of a building and, in the process, broke through brick walls, bled all over the house, smashed the furniture, and beat the shit out of us and your two friends?"

He smirks slightly and brings his eyes up to my own.

"I guess you are still you," he says.

"That's hardly an answer," I say. "Were we doing drugs or something? Did you kidnap me? Are we part of some kind of fight club?"

He opens his mouth to speak but I stop him.

"Don't. If you're about to tell me not to talk about fight club, I am so not in the mood."

He pinches his mouth shut and I watch as the corners curl into a subtle smirk.

"This isn't funny," I say, crossing my arms.

"You're right," he says with a heavy sigh. "I'm sorry. Er… This is complicated. Can we start with an easier question?"

"Okay. How do we know each other?"

He sits down beside the bed on a nearby chair and closes his eyes for a moment. As he reopens them again, he takes a deep breath in.

"We're together," he says. "You're… you and I are together."

Oh.

This super-hot guy is my boyfriend?

I guess that means Mike and I didn't work out, not that I'm exactly surprised. We're a lot better at fighting than we are at getting along. I can't say it doesn't sting a bit, but I'm also not entirely bothered by the fact that I'm apparently getting it on with this chiseled god of a man.

Damn.

"Okay," I say, slowly processing the information. "What happened to my leg?"

"You were attacked," he says, his eyes catching the light in a strange way, making them look almost green. "I wasn't lying about that. He, erm… caught us off guard."

"Who was it?"

"Fuck, Ava, these are your easy questions?" he asks, tugging a bit at his hair.

"Okay, fine. For now. So your friends that were with us—Kami and the other guy that kept cracking jokes—who were they?"

"Kami and Kieran, yeah—they're old friends of mine. Well, they're your friends now too."

"Were we doing something illegal?"

"No, love," he says with a chuckle.

"How did I hit my head?"

"Your head?" He grimaces and drops his head into his hands. "Did the nurse say something about the scans? Are you alright?"

"No, she said they're fine," I say, which seems to calm him slightly. "I mean, how did I get the memory loss?"

"Oh," he says. His eyes dart around as if he's trying to carefully craft his answer. "I… I… I'm not sure, actually…"

He's interrupted by a nurse tapping at the door.

"Could you confirm your address for me?" she asks me.

"Sure," I say. "It's 1822 S Wollstone-"

"Uh, no," Zane says. "Sorry to interrupt, love, you don't live there anymore. It's 2800 17th Street, PH1. Still in Port Charlotte, though, same postcode."

"Oh um, thank you," the nurse says, stepping out into the hall.

"I moved?" I ask.

"Yeah you, er," he says, pausing to bite his lip a moment. "That was our place that we just came from."

Our place?

Before I can even process the idea, a commotion breaks out just outside the door. Several voices seem to be arguing and I only catch bits of what they're saying.

"Ma'am, I'm sorry, but it's our policy to call…"

"…hell freezes over."

"…if she wants to talk to me…"

I recognize the last voice slightly.

"What's going on?" I ask, my voice loud enough to reach the hallway. "Hello?"

Zane's eyes go wide and this time they're unmistakably green as a figure steps through the doorway.

"You've got to be bloody kidding me," he hisses as he jumps straight up.

What is Mike doing here?

2

 ZANE

I've let this arsehole live for too long.

"What… what are you doing here?" Ava asks.

Mike steps further toward her but I insert my body in between them.

"That's a good bloody question, mate," I say, clenching my fists tightly at my sides.

"The hospital called me. I'm her emergency contact," he says, puffing out his chest. "They told me she has amnesia—is that true?"

"No," I snap, at almost the precise moment that Ava says 'Yes.'

Fuck.

"Wow," he says, his narrowed eyes staring me down. "You're lying to my face right now?"

Like this prick has a right to Ava's personal information anyway.

He looks Ava up and down as Kami and Kieran appear in the doorway behind him, clearly unsure of what to do.

"Jesus Christ, Ava, what the hell happened? Did he do this?" he asked, gesturing to me. "Did he hurt you?"

The suggestion alone sends bile up my throat.

"Mike," Ava says softly, sitting up more in her bed. "I'm fine, okay?"

"You son of a bitch!" Mike screams, his fist launching toward me.

My first thought is to grab his arm and snap it off. I glance behind him as his arm flies through the air, catching an expression on Kami's face that I've come to recognize as her "don't be an idiot" look.

Fuck.

She's got a point. If this is Ava's new first impression of me, I don't want it to involve me snapping this douchebag like a twig.

Fine.

I smirk as I allow Mike's fist to connect with my face. He lets out a pained shriek, pulling his hand back in a rapid motion. He stumbles back, cradling one hand in the other as he hisses and curses under his breath.

I try my best not to laugh, though I hear a small chuckle from Kieran.

"I need to talk to Ava," he says. "Alone."

"Fuck no," I say, taking another step toward him.

"It's okay, Zane," Ava says. Her voice is soft and concerned.

No. It's the exact fucking opposite of okay.

"Yeah, like she says," he spits. "It's okay."

"Uh, Z-Man?" Kieran calls, wide eyed. "Why don't you let them talk?"

I shoot him a deadly glare.

"You have no bloody idea what you're talking about, mate. Stay out of this."

"No, Z, he's right," Kami chimes in. "You need a *smoke break. NOW.*"

"The bloody hell are y-"

"Now, Z," she says, stepping around Mike and pulling me out of the room by my elbow.

What is she talking about? I don't smoke.

"Take him outside," she says to Kieran. "I'll keep an eye on Ava."

———◆———

"You better bloody explain yourself," I hiss at Kieran as he pulls me outside into the cold air.

"Smoke is coming out of your eyes, dumbass," he says with a smirk.

"What?" I ask, looking at my reflection in a nearby window. My irises are clouded black, and a deep grey smoke is seeping from the corners of my eyes. "Fuck! The Fury smoke is still in my system."

"I think your anger is triggering it," he says, sitting down on a bench and patting the seat next to him.

I roll my eyes and reluctantly sit down.

"That fucker is in there with her right now," I grumble, tugging at a lock of my hair. "How would you bloody expect me to feel?"

"What's he gonna do, Z-Man?" Kieran asks. "You think he's gonna talk to her and they're gonna walk out of there madly in love?"

I growl at him and narrow my eyes.

"From what I've gathered, the guy is a total dick and they've already broken up once. She made the right call before; she'll do it again. Plus, you've got a much better ass than that guy."

"You have a point there," I say with a smirk.

"She was awfully surprised to see him," he says, tossing his hair to the side. "To me, that was the face of a girl who isn't used to someone showing up for her."

I nod, thinking it over.

"I don't know why he did." I sigh. "Whatever the hospital staff told him, he must've seen this as his chance to get back with her. What is he saying to her right now?"

"If I promise you she'll be leaving here with you, will you calm the heck down?"

"How could you promise that?"

"Just answer the question, crabby pants."

"Yeah, sure."

"Your wish is my command, Z-Man," he says with a sly smile.

What have I just signed up for?

———

AVA

Well, that was awkward.

"Hey," I say to Mike and he takes a few cautious steps toward me.

"I'll be *just* outside the door," Kami says, staring intently at Mike. "Call if you need anything, Ava."

Mike sits himself at the foot of my bed, his shoulders slumped and his hands on his lap. He looks different, a little older, and his nose seems a little strange—thinner and straighter.

"Is your hand okay?" I ask.

"It's fine…" he says. Of course, I know that this is his definitely-not-fine voice.

Poor Mike; odds are good that he broke his hand in that punch and Zane barely moved.

"So…" I say, deciding to change the subject. "This is weird."

"No shit," he says. "How are you?"

"I'm okay. Minus the whole amnesia stuff—which is pretty weird."

"How much did you forget?"

"They told me about a year and a half."

"Wow," he says with a deep breath in. "So you don't remember... what happened?"

"Between us? No."

"Damn. What happened? Are you safe? Did he hurt you?"

His questions catch me off guard.

Is it possible Zane was the one who did this and his friends are just covering for him?

I mean, I don't really know this Zane guy, but he seemed nice enough. Then again, everyone seems nice until they're not.

"I... I don't know," I say. "Do you think he would?"

"Of course I do," he says. "You don't remember this, but he threatened me constantly when I would try to talk to you. The guy's a total nut job."

Kami pokes her head in for a second.

"Heyyy guys, just letting you know that I'm still *right outside*," she says. "Ava, let me know if I can help you with anything. I'll be just outside the door. Just right here."

She shoots Mike a quick glare before popping back out. Mike rolls his eyes.

It occurs to me she might be listening in, so I pick up a pen and pad from the stand beside the bed and write him a quick note.

Do you think they're dangerous?

I hand him the paper and he nods in response.

Of course they are. I mean, I end up in a practical war zone with a broken leg and the three of them are covered in blood. What good excuse is there for that?

First rule of any horror movie: never trust the suspiciously attractive guy.

"Zane said that he and I live together," I whisper. "What am I supposed to do?"

Second rule of the horror movie: definitely don't go back to the suspiciously attractive guy's murder lair. You do and next thing you know, you're being sacrificed to the gods by frat boys in the woods.

That is not how you get final-girl status.

"I don't know, Ava," he says with a frustrated sigh. "Why do you ask me this kind of stuff?"

He looks down at his hands and closes his eyes.

"Maybe you can stay with me," he says. "We'll see how it goes."

He always makes me feel bad for asking him anything, like I'm the world's neediest girlfriend.

Or, I guess, *ex*-girlfriend.

Then again, maybe that's exactly why there's an ex in that word. Maybe he got sick of me being a burden. Maybe I got sick of feeling like one.

"Why did we break up?" I ask, before I have time to decide whether or not I really want the answer.

Mike looks at me and chuckles.

"I'm not sure we should get into that right now," he says, gesturing with his head toward the door.

"Oh. Um, Kami?" I call.

In a second, she appears in the doorway.

"Yeah, girl?" she says.

"Would you mind closing the door and giving us some privacy?" I ask.

"Oh, uh… yeah, sure…" She reluctantly steps back, closing the door behind her.

"There," I say. "Can you tell me now? What happened between us?"

"What do you think?" he asks, shrugging his shoulders.

"That's a trap of a question if I've ever heard one."

"Fair enough," he says with a bit of a laugh. His smile slowly fades into a soft frown as his head drops and he focuses his eyes on the floor. "You cheated on me with him."

"What?" I ask, gasping at the idea. "Wha-, I… Why?"

I can't believe that I would do that to Mike.

"I don't know why, Ava. You didn't exactly give me specifics, not that I wanted them."

"When did this happen?"

"A little over a year ago," he says. "I'm not sure how long you two were—you know—behind my back. But yeah…"

"I'm so sorry, Mike."

I don't even know what else to say. I mean, I know our relationship has been tumultuous, but I can't imagine how it got to that point.

"Why would you even come to see me?" I ask. "I mean, if I cheated on you and you have this bitter relationship with Zane, why are you here?"

He sighs before scooting closer to me on the bed.

"Because I miss you," he says, brushing my cheek with his hand. "When the person on the phone said you were experiencing long-term memory loss, I thought… maybe this is our second chance. This guy is bad for you and he poisoned you against me. Maybe this is fate's way of bringing us back together."

He takes a deep breath in and winces slightly when he attempts to lean on his injured hand.

"You are special. Nobody has ever made me as mad as you do—but no one has ever made me as happy either. I know you made a mistake, and I can forgive you."

He strokes my face with his good hand before leaning in for a kiss.

Before I have a chance to respond, my body reacts for me and I lurch forward, throwing up right in Mike's face.

3

AVA

Mike jumps back in disgust. His face and shirt are covered in vomit and he frantically spits and coughs.

This may be the most embarrassing moment of my life—at least, that I remember.

Yep, I'm going to have to move. And change my name.

"I'm so sor-" I begin to say, but am interrupted by the loud crack of the door whipping open and hitting the wall. Zane's wide-shouldered frame appears in the doorway, still and rigid, like a monster out of a horror movie. His green eyes are ablaze and the bulging veins in his neck look almost black. As he steps toward Mike, I swear I see smoke swirl around his fingertips.

"What the bloody hell did you do?" he hisses at Mike, his eyes bouncing between the two of us as he tries to figure out why Mike is covered in the former contents of my stomach.

Kieran and Kami follow quickly behind, both watching Zane in nervous silence.

How did he even know anything happened? Was he watching us?

"Did he hurt you?" he asks, his voice softening slightly. "Are you okay?"

"It's okay," I say. "I'm fine. He didn't do anything. I uh… I got sick and uh…"

"You threw up on him?" Kieran interjects. He lets out a booming laugh that echoes through the small hospital room. "That's fucking perfect!"

"Fuck you," Mike mumbles.

"You're only making this funnier, bro," he says with a smirk.

A slight smile forms on Zane's face as he eyes Mike, but his body remains stiff.

"Okay, we've all had a great laugh at Ava's expense," I say. I feel my cheeks getting warmer, though I'm sure I'm already bright red.

"I'm gonna clean up," Mike says to me as he makes his way to the door. Before he can pass, Zane grabs his arm, stopping him in his tracks.

Zane's furious expression returns and his nostrils flare.

"What were you doing?" he asks through clenched teeth.

Okay, this is awkward.

"Get off of me," Mike says, struggling to pull away.

"Why were you that close to Ava?" Zane hisses. "Tell me."

"I was trying to kiss her."

Mike's candor has me stunned—though he seems to be a bit surprised himself. He has never been particularly ballsy, unless he's drunk off his ass, so I'm shocked that he's willing to tell this majorly buff guy that he just tried to kiss his girlfriend.

Kami and Kieran watch the interaction with wide eyes.

Before I can fathom what's happening, Zane punches Mike in the gut. Mike folds over and collapses to the ground.

"You bloody bastard," he growls. "You got a fucking death wish, Michael? Trying to kiss my girl? Have you well and truly lost the plot?"

Should I say something?

"You're telling me not to mess with a taken woman? Wow, that's fresh," Mike spits.

This is really uncomfortable.

Zane grabs Mike's neck and squeezes tightly. Mike's face turns bright red as he helplessly pries at Zane's hand.

"Stop it!" I say. "You're going to kill him!"

He doesn't budge or even turn around when he hears my voice. Black smoke moves around Zane's arm and around Mike's neck.

What the fuck is that? Am I hallucinating?

Kami and Kieran tug at Zane hard from every direction, which only seems to distract him a bit as thick black smoke fills the room.

Okay. It's clear that I hit my head way harder than I think I did.

I jump out of the bed to help, but my plan quickly fails as I lose my balance trying to walk on my cast. Suddenly I'm falling and the world goes black.

———•———

ZANE

"Why. Can't. I. Bloody. Control. Myself?" I groan as I smack my head against the wall between words.

"Because you're in love," Kami says with a sigh.

"I dunno what you're talking about," Kieran says. "That was dope. I wish beast-mode Zane would come out to play more often."

"I took care of Mike, by the way," Kami says. "I sent him home and he shouldn't remember anything about the incident."

"Why didn't you bloody charm him in the first place?" I ask.

"Oh yeah," she says. "Great idea, Z, that wouldn't look at all suspicious to Ava. Her ex comes to visit and then just disappears? I overheard her talking with him and now she thinks we're dangerous. That certainly wouldn't help our cause."

"Dangerous?"

My heart sinks at the thought of Ava being afraid of me. I always believed she should fear me, but I never knew how much it would hurt if she did.

"Well, Z, out of context, what would you think?" she says.

"That's what they were talking about?" I ask. "And then I came in and basically proved him right—that I am a monster. Fuck."

"That and I'm pretty sure she saw you—*ahem*—smoking."

At least the Fury smoke seems to have finally made it out of my system now.

"I know," I say with a sigh. "Not a great first impression."

"Not the best. But that's okay. You've just got to deal with Mike in a different way. Show her you're the better man."

"I kinda liked your approach," Kieran says with a smirk.

"There," Kami says. "Do you need further proof of what a bad idea that was?"

I shrug and chuckle to myself.

"I already told you, Z-Man," Kieran says. "I can handle Mike if anything comes up, okay?"

In general, leaving things to a demon isn't a great plan, but in this case, it just might be. I look over toward Ava's room and sigh.

"She's fine, Z," Kami says with a pat to my shoulder. "They said she needs rest, so we're letting her rest, that's all."

The doctors took Ava back in for another scan after she regained consciousness. They said the vomiting and dizziness could be indicative of a concussion, but they found nothing.

If she does have a concussion, though, at least I know the Siren blood in her system will heal her. Maybe it already has and that's why the doctors didn't see anything.

We left the door to Ava's room cracked. From my seat in the guest area, I can just see her through a break in the curtain. She's fast asleep, but they're waking her up every 30 minutes or so to check on her.

"Whoa," Kieran says, catching me by surprise.

"What?" I ask, expecting him to point out a hot nurse.

"I think my memories are coming back," he says. "Either that, or I have some really boring daydreams."

"Oh. Had to happen sooner or later."

"How bad is this gonna get?" he asks, gritting his teeth.

"It should be fine," Kami says. "You're not dealing with really nasty repressed memories, so it probably won't be too bad."

"What happens when the memories are bad?" he asks.

"Your body starts to feel it first. It'll give you signals, so to speak, like chills or nausea. It's like you know something is wrong deep down, before you fully understand what it is."

"Oh, there's another one," he says with a smile. "I liked that one. Oh damn, does this mean I get to revisit all the conquests I've forgotten?"

Kami rolls her eyes and looks over at me.

"I can only handle so much of him, demon or no," she says with a sigh.

"Oh, you love me. You're just afraid to admit your feelings," Kieran says. "So how fast do the memories come back?"

"Depends. It's different for everyone and it's different every time. Lethe is very hard to control. I-"

Kami looks over my shoulder and her eyes widen. Kieran follows her gaze and his mouth parts slightly at whatever he sees.

What are they looking at?

"Excuse me, is one of you Zane Smith?" a man asks from behind me.

"Er, yeah mate," I say as I turn around. "Who's asking?"

"Port Charlotte PD. We just have a few questions for you."

4

 ZANE

Two uniformed officers guide me to a small table in a small garden just outside the hospital. One officer, a broad-bodied man with a mustache, sits down and invites me to sit across from him. The other, a small woman with ash-blond hair, remains standing behind him.

I reluctantly pull out a chair and sit down.

"Thanks for taking a moment to talk to us," the man says, pulling out a notebook and pen.

Like I really have a choice.

"Is this going to take long?" I ask, anxious to get back to looking after Ava.

"I know you've got a lot going on right now, so I'll try not to take up too much of your time. We have to investigate particular types of injuries that come in here. I just have a few questions for you."

I'm hardly up for this right now, but I know I need to get this over with so I don't have the cops breathing down my neck.

"So we've already talked to your girlfriend, Ava, and got her story, so we need you to be honest with us and fill in some details."

Having worked as a compeller in interrogations for The Council, I know the script all too well. They're trying to imply that Ava told them something, but I know there's nothing to tell—not that Ava can remember anyway.

"So, start by telling us what happened that brought you to the hospital," he says.

"Ava was attacked by this guy who broke into our house. I came in and interrupted the attack, and the guy took off," I say.

I mean, technically Ava stabbed him and turned him into a pile of dust, but close enough.

"Now, the nurses told us that she suffered multiple injuries to her head, neck, and arms consistent with being physically attacked. She also has a pretty serious broken leg. We collected epithelial samples from under her fingernails, so if she scratched her attacker, we will have that DNA for comparison."

I nod.

"Do you know how those injuries happened?" he asks. The officer behind him crosses her arms and glares at me.

"Most of that happened before I got there," I say. "Except, er, her leg."

I cringe at the memory of Asmodeus breaking Ava's leg. I can still hear her piercing scream.

"You saw her attacker break her leg?" he asks.

"Yeah," I say, closing my eyes for a moment. I feel a tear run down my cheek.

"Has Ava ever broken a bone before?"

"I, er…" I say, pausing for a moment. It's obvious that they think I hurt her, just like Mike thought, and the idea alone makes me ill. "Not that I know of."

"Were either of you under the influence of any substances at the time?"

"No, er… wait, Ava was at a bar earlier that night, so she may have had something to drink. I'm not sure. I didn't really ask."

"And how did she get home from the bar?"

Shit.

Technically, she left with Asmodeus, but anyone watching would have thought she left with me.

I'm royally fucked.

AVA

"Hey," I hear a soft voice say.

I open my eyes to Mike crouching beside my hospital bed.

"Wha-," I start to say. "Are you okay? What happened to you?"

"What do you mean?" he asks.

"You just disappeared after that fight. When I came to, you were gone."

"What fight?" he asks.

How could he possibly have forgotten his fight with Zane?

I think back through everything and I begin to question it myself. Zane seemed impossibly strong and there was smoke flowing from his fingertips.

Was that real? Was it all just some sort of bizarre concussion-induced hallucination?

"You… you didn't get into a fistfight with Zane?"

"When I punched him?" he asks, raising his hand, which is now wrapped in a brace.

Maybe I did imagine it.

"Yeah…" I say. "I guess I got confused. Where is everyone?"

"You mean your *boyfriend* and his friends?"

"Um, yeah, I guess so."

"I don't know where he is, but the other two are asleep out there," he says, pointing out the door.

From here, I can see Kieran draped over a couple of chairs, his limbs tangled in all directions. It's miraculous he can sleep like that.

A nurse steps into the room and gives us both a small smile.

"Hi, I'm sorry to bother you," she says. "Would your visitor be able to help us with a few questions about your history?"

"Um…" I say, looking to Mike for confirmation.

"Sure," he says. I'm surprised by his willingness to get involved, as he usually wants nothing to do with my health issues.

"Could you confirm if this is her current medication list?" she asks, showing him a paper on a clipboard.

"Oh, uh…" he mumbles, looking over the list. "Jesus, Ava, why are you taking all this stuff?"

"I don't know. That's kind of why they're asking you. I don't remember."

He rolls his eyes and shrugs.

Yeah, I get it, okay? My health is a mess. No need to rub it in.

"That's alright," she says. "We'll try to track down your pharmacy records."

The nurse walks out and Mike turns back to me.

"Why are you here?" I ask.

"I never got to really talk to you yesterday. I wanted to finish our conversation," he says with a sigh. "Are you hungry? Do you want me to get you some food from the cafeteria and we can talk?"

"Actually," I say, eyeing a sleeping Kieran, "I'll join you. I'm really bored of being stuck in this room anyway."

———•———

The cafeteria is mostly empty, with an older gentleman sitting alone by the window and two doctors grabbing food at the counter. I sit down at an empty table and set my crutches down beside me. Mike brings our food trays and sets them down.

"So," he says. "Have they figured out your health stuff yet?"

He keeps asking me questions like I haven't forgotten everything from the past year or so.

"I have no idea."

"Oh, yeah, that's right," he says, pointing to his head. "The whole amnesia thing."

"Speaking of which," I say. "Do you know what my phone passcode is? I tried my old one but it's not working. I clearly changed it since and I can't figure it out."

"Why would I know that, Ava?"

"I dunno; I thought maybe I had told you or something."

"You forget we're broken up now," he says with a scowl.

Fair enough.

"I guess you're right," I say, spearing a piece of fruit with my fork and taking a bite.

"Well, about that," he says with a sigh. "I'd be willing to give us another shot."

"Oh."

It's the only thing I can think to say.

Of course I have feelings for Mike, but I'm hardly in a position to be making important life decisions, and the fact that he's even asking right now feels a bit inappropriate.

Over Mike's shoulder, I can see a woman in green scrubs glaring at us. I'm not sure why we've caught her attention, but she's certainly adding to the pressure.

"I don't know what to say," I say.

"Well think on it," he says. "I'm going to fill our drinks."

He grabs our empty cups and heads over to the drink fountain around the corner.

After a second, the woman in scrubs approaches me and leans on my table.

"Are you with that guy?" she asks. "The one who just walked away?"

"Mike?" I ask. "Um… we're friends."

"But you're not like, together?"

"No. Why?"

"Okay, good," she says. "He's my friend's boyfriend, so I just wanted to make sure."

What??

"He's… dating your friend?" I ask.

"Yeah, my best friend Ashley. Sorry to bother you guys, I just thought something was going on between you two."

"Oh, no worries," I say. "Nothing is happening between us and it *definitely* never will."

I'm going to kill him.

She leaves the cafeteria just as Mike makes his way back in. He sets our glasses on the table and sits back down.

"So you want to get back together?" I ask, internally seething but trying my best to seem inconspicuous.

"Yeah," he says, taking a bite of his fries. "I think it makes sense. Don't you?"

"And you're not with anyone right now?"

"No," he says. "Why?"

"Oh, I dunno, maybe because I know you have a freaking girlfriend?" I spit.

His eyes widen and he takes a heavy gulp.

"Shit," he curses under his breath.

"Really, Mike?" I ask. I do my best to stand up and storm out, but I have to grab my crutches and awkwardly scoot my chair back while hopping on one leg.

Sadly, this isn't even my most embarrassing moment of the week.

"Okay, I'm sorry you found out this way, okay?" he says, resting a hand on my crutch. "Yes, I technically have a girlfriend, but Megan and I aren't really working out."

Megan?

Oh my god… he has TWO girlfriends???

"What the hell?" I ask. "You know what, Mike—stay the fuck away from me."

I tug my crutch from his grasp and limp away. He'll have to imagine I'm stomping angrily because I can't really stomp with my broken leg.

He runs around to cut me off.

"Ava, let's talk about this," he says. "You're being dramatic."

With that, I decide to do the most dramatic thing that comes to mind—I swing my crutch forward between his legs and he drops to the ground.

Fucking asshole.

ZANE

That's the last time I actually try talking to the police. Next time, I'm cutting straight to the part where I charm them.

I walk back into the waiting area and I see Kami slumped over and asleep in her chair. Kieran's seat is now empty, so I imagine he's off chasing an attractive nurse or doctor.

I peek into Ava's room and my eyes land on an empty bed.

What the fuck?

Bloody Kieran and Kami were supposed to be watching her.

I panic and immediately scour the room.

"Kami," I call. She jumps up in response. "Ava is missing."

"Oh god," she curses, looking at her empty room. Kieran rounds the corner in too-tight green scrubs and walks up to us.

"Relax, Z-Man," he says. "Ava is just getting food."

"What the hell, mate? Why are you wearing that?" I ask.

"Oh, long story. I had to handle something in the cafeteria."

5

I sit back down on the bed and sigh.

Nothing is quite as uncomfortable as the two-inch-thick mattress of a hospital bed. Well, except maybe the chairs in the waiting room.

Zane appears in the open doorway and gives me a slight wave.

"Mind if I come in?" he asks, putting his hands in his pockets.

"Sure," I say with a nod.

He steps in and sits down in the chair beside my bed.

"So you had something to eat?" he asks softly, sweeping his hair back.

"Yeah, I-"

As I speak, a nurse steps in with a clipboard.

"Sorry to interrupt, I just need to hook you up to the equipment again," she says, grabbing some nearby wires.

She takes a few and plugs them back into the sticky sensors on my arm.

"Would your friend here be able to answer some questions for me about your chart?" she asks.

"Oh uh," I say, glancing toward Zane.

I'm honestly not sure. I've always kept my medical details pretty private, so I can't imagine I would tell my ultra-hot future boyfriend.

"What do you need?" he asks, standing up.

"I just need someone to look over and confirm her medication list."

"I can take a look," he says. She flips through my chart before handing it over to him.

"Ahh, she stopped the Lornalaprozem; it wasn't working," he says, squinting as he scans the page. "The Gabaleptin should be 20 milligrams, not 15. The rest looks right."

I can't believe he kept track of all my meds; I can hardly keep track of them myself.

He's really hot, has a British accent, and remembers all the pointless details of my life for me… Did I make a deal with the devil to make this happen?

The nurse thanks him and steps out of the room.

"Thanks for that," I say.

"Of course, love," he says, shrugging before sitting back down again.

"I usually call Jen for help with this kinda stuff but I can't get into this new phone," I say, gesturing to my phone on the side table.

"Fuck," he curses, letting his head fall backward. "Jen is going to murder me."

"Why?"

"Because you're in the hospital and it's been a couple of days and I didn't call her." He runs a hand through his dark locks.

I giggle.

"If you help me get into this phone, I'd be happy to tell her for you," I say with a smile. "Any chance you know the password?"

"No, you didn't tell me," he says.

"Damn."

It was worth a shot.

"Have you tried 5-4-60?" he asks.

My eyes widen slightly.

"That's…"

"Your mom's birthday," he says with a soft smile. "I know. You use it for a lot of things."

I use it for my credit card pin, too, but obviously I'm gonna have to change that now.

I pick up the phone and type in 5-4-6-0. The phone unlocks to reveal a photo of Zane kissing me on the cheek.

I look happy.

"It worked!" I say. "Thank you."

He nods and smiles.

A notification pops up that says: **14 Missed Calls**.

Before I can open it, I'm bombarded with text messages.

Jen

Helloooo?

Srsly r u ok?

Beeetttchhh calllll meeeee

I find myself chuckling.

At least some things never change.

"Jen is definitely freaking out," I say. "I'll text her."

"Good," he says. "Not sure how she's gonna take the news about your amnesia."

"I might wait to tell her that part in person."

"Speaking of which, when are you okay to go?"

"They said as early as tomorrow."

"Okay," he says. "Kami called some people to come clean up the house, so it should be good as new by then. If you… uh… are okay staying there…"

Am I okay living with Zane? Should I stay with Jen instead?

My eyes fall back to the image on my phone. It's as if I'm looking at a photo of strangers—a happy couple, desperately in love. The girl in the photo looks normal, with a wide smile stretched across her face.

I don't know her, but I know I want to be her.

ZANE

I set Ava's bag down in the entryway as she follows close behind.

"Holy crap!" she says, looking around as she enters the penthouse. "I mean, I know I saw this place before, but it wasn't exactly in the best shape then."

I chuckle as her mouth falls open in awe.

"How the heck can I afford to live here? Am I the grand web designer to the queen or something?"

"The pope, actually," I say with a laugh.

"Seriously," she says, walking up to the window. "This isn't an apartment, this is…"

"A Pottery Barn?"

"Exactly!" she shouts. "Like, this is too fancy. Who actually lives in a place like this? Let alone me. Did I win some sort of lawsuit? Was I poisoned? That would honestly make so much sense."

"Not that I know of," I say, smiling.

I watch as she investigates every room of our apartment, letting out a flood of curses as she opens each door. It's moments like these that make me feel like not all hope is lost. She's still my Ava.

"What the fuck?!" she shouts as she wanders outside. "There's a fucking pool!"

She continues walking out into the garden. I step forward to join her, but the melodic ring of the doorbell interrupts me.

Ava told Jen she was heading home, so it's safe to say she's about three seconds from beating down our door.

I open the door to two unfamiliar faces: a dark-skinned woman with her thick, black hair tied into a neat bun, and a slim gentleman with a goatee.

How did they even get up to our floor?

"You alright?" I ask. "Are you on the wrong floor?"

"No, we're right where we want to be," the man says with a smirk. "You're Zane, right?"

I've come to learn that people who know you before you've met them are usually not going to be your friends.

"Are you with the police?" I ask.

The man chuckles and takes a step past me in an attempt to get inside, but I cut him off.

"Going somewhere?" I ask, grabbing his arm.

"Just having a look around," he says.

"You're going to tell me who you are, and you're going to get the fuck out of my apartment."

He rips his arm out of my grasp and gives me an indignant look.

"Yeah, no thanks," he says, another smirk forming on his lips.

Shit. He's not human.

"Let's skip to the point, shall we?" the woman chimes in. "Where's Asmodeus?"

"Asmodeus?" I ask. "Why would I know?"

"Because last anyone knew, he was after you. Asmodeus always gets his target, yet you're still alive."

"Let me guess, you're Incubi?"

Asmodeus had plenty of loyal demon followers. I probably should have expected that they were going to come looking for him.

"Tsk tsk," the woman tuts. "You didn't answer our question, so why should we answer yours?"

"I did answer," I say. "I told you I don't know."

"I think you do know," she says.

"Is it possible?" the man mutters. "Could this Siren have killed Asmodeus?"

"Did you?" she asks. Her arm shoots outward and her hand wraps around my neck, pinning me against the doorframe. Her claws extend slightly into my skin and I hiss in pain.

My instinct is to fight back, but I don't want any commotion to lure Ava back inside.

"Fine, yes," I huff. She releases me and steps back.

"You couldn't have," she says. "Asmodeus can't be killed. He's a Demon King. You-… You're just a Siren—you're nobody. No, this ca-"

"Where's the girl?" the man asks, looking around behind me.

They don't have to say it—I know they mean Ava.

I haven't slept in days and I'm relatively weak following my battle with Asmodeus. I don't think I can take on two demons alone, but I have to keep them away from Ava.

"Look at that," he says. "That question certainly got a reaction. Did Asmodeus get your girlfriend?"

"Fuck off," I say, a low growl exiting my lips.

"He did, didn't he?" the woman says. "Asmodeus killed your girlfriend so you killed him?"

The suggestion brings with it the memory of Asmodeus's videos—him hurting Ava while wearing my face. Even after deleting them, I can't get them out of my head. They haunt me.

"Yes, okay?" I snap, hoping this response will get them to leave. "He killed her, I killed him. Now get the fuck out of my house before I kill you too."

They both take a step back—possibly in fear of me, possibly in disbelief.

"Alright, we're going," the woman says. "Just remember that we aren't the only ones who will come looking for Asmodeus. His brothers will find out—and you know they won't be happy."

6

I fall backward onto the couch with a heavy sigh.

Fuck.

I should have expected that someone would come looking for Asmodeus, but I didn't consider what his brothers—the other Demon Kings—might do when they find out.

Either way, I'm not about to let them know it was actually Ava who killed him. If they want a target for revenge, they've got one now, and for all they know, Ava doesn't even exist anymore.

Fuck.

I watch Ava looking out over the city skyline from the garden. It's strange to see her in these moments, because she looks like her same old self, but this girl is something different. She's the same in many ways, but she's not the girl I've grown to love. She's not the one who called me a penguin or kissed me in her apartment that night. She's not the girl I awkwardly slipped and said I love you to in a bookstore parking lot.

I miss that girl so much.

I close my eyes and place a pillow over my head.

"You alright?" Ava asks.

I lift up the pillow and she's standing in front of me with a concerned expression.

"Of course," I say. "I should really be asking you that."

"I'm great. Apparently I'm rich and I live in a penthouse with my hot boyfrie-" she says, stopping herself suddenly. Her eyes go wide and her cheeks immediately flush.

"Did you just call me hot, love?" I ask with a bit of a chuckle. I can't help but smile at her accidental honesty.

"I mean, you're what some people might think of as hot," she says, her eyes dodging mine. "Not that I do. You're not exactly my type."

My heart feels tight in my chest as she says it. I know she doesn't mean it, but it still hurts.

"God, I'm sorry," she says, rubbing her face with her palm as she leans on one crutch. "I don't mean that. Obviously, you're everybody's type—I mean, look at you."

I let out a small chuckle.

"Is that so?" I ask.

"Oh, come on," she says with an eye roll, "now you're just milking it. Yes, okay, the whole world knows you're freakishly hot. Don't go getting a big ego over it."

We're interrupted by another knock at the door and I grumble.

"I can get it," she says, hobbling toward the entryway.

"No!" I say, jumping up and stepping between her and the door.

I'm pretty sure those demons wouldn't be back so soon, but I'm certainly not taking any chances.

She gives me a perplexed look, but sits down in the armchair.

I can hear two women's voices as I head for the door. My shoulders relax as I recognize them both. I swing the door open to reveal Kami and Jen. Kami seems unusually awkward, with wide eyes and a forced smile. Jen, meanwhile, looks like a five-foot-two ball of fiery rage with clenched fists at her sides.

"Look who I ran into on the way up!" Kami says in her best enthusiastic voice. She mouths the words 'I'm sorry' as she steps inside past me.

"Hey Jen," I say.

"Did nobody think to tell me that Ava has mother-fudging amnesia??" Jen hisses, giving me a judgmental look.

"I- sh-," I mutter. "Ava told me she wanted to tell you in person."

She narrows her eyes, seemingly deciding my fate, before giving me a reluctant nod.

"Okay," she says slowly. "I guess I'll kill Ava then."

She gives me a quick hug before stomping over to Ava and giving her a lecture. Kami and I sit at the kitchen bar as I pour her a glass of wine.

"I'm sorry, I didn't know you guys hadn't told her," Kami says with an apologetic smile.

"It's alright," I say. "She'll forgive us eventually."

"How're you holding up?" She takes a sip of wine and leans on the counter, clearly exhausted from the events of the last few days.

"How do you think?" I reply. "I'm trying to be strong for Ava but it feels like a hundred punches to the gut. What am I going to do, Kam?"

"Well, the first thing you need to do is sleep. You look like you were murdered two days ago and somebody forgot to hide the corpse."

"Gee, thanks, love," I say with a sarcastic smirk.

"That's what happens when you refuse to sleep for several days straight." She raises both eyebrows as if to say she told me so.

I huff in reply.

"I'm gonna help Ava get changed out of her hospital clothes," Jen says.

"Already done killing her?" I ask with a smirk.

"Oh, not even close," she says. She heads toward the bedroom with Ava following behind her.

"Well, at least you don't seem to be the one in trouble," Kami says.

"I'm so far beyond silver linings right now."

"As I said, you need sleep. It's not healthy to go this long without sleep. I know technically you're immortal, but that doesn't mean you won't slowly go insane if you keep this up. With those bags under your eyes, you're looking more like a raccoon than a Siren."

"Once again, you flatter me."

We sit in silence for a moment, both staring blankly ahead.

She's right. I'm bloody knackered.

"Hey, what's this?" I hear Ava ask from behind me.

I turn to see her holding a long, flat wooden box.

My heart sinks.

"It was next to the photo of my mom in the bedroom, but I don't understand the significance," she continues, unhooking the golden latch and opening it to reveal a single black feather—my feather.

I glance at Kami; her eyes have gone wide with shock but her mouth is pinched in a straight line. She looks at me as though she's wondering if I'll fall to pieces right here, right now.

I just might.

"Why am I keeping a random feather in a fancy box?" Ava asks. "Is it, like, one of those old-timey pens or something?"

With every word, I feel a band constricting tighter and tighter around my chest.

"That-" I begin to say, but my voice gets caught in my throat.

"Oh that's Zane's," Kami says. "It's kind of a family heirloom. It's a very private story—you understand."

"Oh," Ava says. "Sorry to pry. I just assumed it was something of mine."

"Here, I'll put that back for you," Kami says, holding out her hand. Ava closes the box and hands it to Kami.

Kami gives me a little nod, indicating I should follow her as Jen and Ava return to the couch. Once we've made it to the bedroom, she closes the door behind us.

"Zane, I'm…" she says softly.

The weight of everything that's happened in the past few days comes crashing down around me and I collapse to my knees. I sob violently as Kami wraps her arms tightly around me.

"It's okay, Z," she says. Her voice wavers as if she's unsure that what she's just said is true.

"I can't do this," I say through choked breaths. "Asmodeus knew he couldn't kill her so he found a way to take her from me anyway."

"Maybe there's an answer. I mean, we've never tried to get a human's memory back before. For all we know, it's possible."

"You really believe that?"

I know she doesn't, but she's desperate to give me hope.

"I don't know," she says with a sigh. "Humans are complicated. Just don't give up just yet, okay?"

———◆———

AVA

"I think I just made a huge mistake," I say quietly to Jen.

There's a sinking feeling in my chest and I find myself shaking.

"It's my fault, really," she says. "I told you to ask him. I didn't know it was a super personal thing."

"He looked like I stabbed him in the chest, Jen." I drop my head into my hands and let out a frustrated grunt. "I've literally been in his house for under an hour and I've clearly just brought up some horrific family trauma from his past. What am I going to do in hour two—set fire to his grandmother's ashes?"

I find my eyes scanning the room for any conspicuous urns. Apparently that's how much I trust myself at this moment.

"It's okay, Ava," she says. "Whatever it is, Zane loves you. He really does. So you hit a sore spot; you'll get past it."

It seemed to be a little more than a sore spot. He looked devastated.

"Should I be staying with you?" I ask, my chest burning with guilt. "Was this a mistake? I can't remember anything and who knows what landmines I might run into."

"You'll be fine. This is your home. Plus if you haven't noticed, this place is baller. I don't have a pool or a view or one of those fancy little toilet things that washes your butt."

"What? Does this place have those?"

"Not that I've seen, but maybe there's a secret button."

I chuckle and she smiles at me.

I look down at my hands as they continue to shake.

I feel this clawing feeling deep in my chest. Maybe it's because I feel so guilty for hurting Zane. Maybe it's something else.

7

AVA

Jen took the past few days off to stay with us at the apartment, helping me with my memory and picking up some chores since I can't do much with a broken leg. She also made me a set of "Ava's Life Flashcards" to help jog my memory.

"Okay, next one," she says, holding up a card with her photo on it.

"Really?" I say. "That's obviously you."

She smacks me on the shoulder.

"Play along," she says with a furrowed brow. "Images are supposed to help jog your memory; I saw it on TV."

"Well if you saw it on TV…"

I get another smack on the shoulder.

"Okay, okay," I say, rubbing my shoulder slightly. "That's Jen. She likes comic books and board games."

"Aaannd…?"

"And torturing her best friend."

She swings to smack me on the shoulder, but I know it's coming and dodge out of the way.

I hear footsteps across the wood floor and turn to see Zane coming downstairs from the office. He gives us both a small wave and an awkward smile before heading to the kitchen.

"Ugggghh!" I groan, letting my head fall into my hands. "This is the worst, Jen."

"Hey, I know you don't like the flashcards but you don't have to be a bitchmuffin about it."

"No, not the flashcards," I say with a sigh. "It's Zane."

"What about him?"

"I don't know how to act around him. To him, we're boyfriend and girlfriend. To me, he's the random cute stranger who took me to the hospital. He keeps staring at me like he wishes I were the 'old me' but he seems—I don't know—defeated? It's almost like he thinks I'll never get better."

"Well you will. The doctors even said they think so," she says with a reassuring pat to my back.

"Will I? What if I don't? What if I'm stuck forgetting almost two years of my life?"

"Then we'll still love you anyway. Zane is crazy for you. He'll come around. Besides," she says, holding up a flashcard with Mike's face on it. She has clearly drawn devil horns on him with a black marker. "At least you got to get rid of this loser—twice."

I chuckle with her and lean back on the couch.

Memories of Mike come flooding through: laughing at the movies, having an awkward dinner with his parents, throwing a roll of paper towels at his head when he accused me of cheating. That pretty much sums up our whole relationship; for every good memory, there was another crappy one.

I let out another sigh. My ears are ringing and my head hurts.

"I'm sorry you're going through this," Jen says. "Your memory will come back, though. Just you wait."

"How will I even know if it does?"

"Knowing you, you'll probably start banging Zane right away."

I feel blood rush to my cheeks and cover my face with a pillow. I just hope Zane didn't overhear that or I'll officially die of embarrassment.

———

ZANE

I lie down on the bed and bury my face in Ava's pillow, inhaling her scent.

I don't know how much longer I can take this torture.

She looks at me and all I see is pity. I could be anyone in the world to her—or no one. *That's what I am, isn't it? No one.*

Jen and Ava are laughing in the living room as they go over the flashcards Jen made to boost her memory. I wish they stood a chance of working, but I know better than to get my hopes up.

My phone vibrates and I pull it out of my pocket.

"Hello?" I answer.

"Hey, Z," Kami says through the phone. "Just calling to check on you."

"Still breathing. Have you found anything to help Ava?"

"No…" she says in a quiet voice. From her tone, I can tell she's encountered more discouraging news since we last spoke. Her hope is clearly dwindling.

I'm startled by the doorbell ringing several times in quick succession.

What the bloody hell is it now?

I dart to the door so the girls don't have to get up, checking through the peephole to be sure my demon friends aren't back.

I see a man with long, dark brown hair hunched over.

So it's my *other* demon friend.

I open the door and he stumbles in, falling onto the floor.

"Hey, Z-man," he says with a forced smile, gripping his abdomen. There's blood dripping from a rather large wound, and he's holding his intestines in his hands.

"Bloody fucking hell, mate."

Jen stands up next to Ava and they both look this way.

"Kieran?" Jen asks with a gasp.

"Hey Jen, beautiful as always," he replies, grunting slightly as he speaks. "How's my little lady killer?"

"Are you-" she begins to say, starting to walk toward us. "Oh my god, you're bleeding!"

"Ahh this? It's no big deal," he says with a wink. "I'm a fast healer."

"I've got him," I say to Ava and Jen. "Jen, bring me the first aid kit from the bathroom?"

She nods as I scoop Kieran into my arms and bring him to the bedroom.

"Aww, it's like our honeymoon," he says. "You're carrying me over the threshold."

"Threshold is the front door," I say, placing him on the bed. "What the hell happened to you?"

"So good news, bad news," he says. "Bad news is I got cornered by some demons who were pretty sure I helped you kill Asmodeus."

"Shit."

"Good news is I won."

"You don't look like you won, mate," I say, shaking my head. "Why aren't you healing?"

"Well, I haven't had a proper meal in a while," he says. "A few humans will only go so far without Siren venom. They're just not strong enough."

"Why didn't you say anything?"

"Oh yeah, seemed like a great time to bug you with my problems. Plus, to be fair, I really didn't predict getting de-kidneyed by Asmodeus's lackeys."

Fuck.

If he's injured and starving, his body won't replenish itself. He could die.

Jen enters with Ava in tow and sets the first aid kit on the bed. They both look horrified.

Ava limps over to the bed and sits on the edge.

"What can I do?" she asks.

"I need you to go down to the restaurant, ask for Daniella and Eric, tell them I need them up here immediately."

She nods, pushing herself up off the bed and rushing out as quickly as she could with her crutches.

"It's gonna be okay," Jen says, sitting beside Kieran. "What can I do?"

I look at Kieran and I see that his eyes have gone all black. I'm going to have to charm Jen into forgetting that little detail.

"I'm so sorry," Kieran groans.

"What are you on about?" I ask.

In an instant, I get my answer. Kieran pulls Jen by her shirt and feeds off of her, a light white smoke passing between her mouth and his. Jen faints and falls off the bed with a thunk.

"Shit, I didn't mean to do that," he says. "She just got too close to me; I couldn't resist."

"You're lucky you didn't seriously hurt her," I snap.

"You're the one who let her get so close to me!"

"I thought you could handle it; Ava was just there!"

"Ava's not human anymore, bro!" he snarls, wincing in pain as he clutches his wound tighter. "She doesn't have that human allure."

His eyes suddenly shift back to their usual color and his expression becomes serious.

"Wait, shit, Zane," he says. "Ava's immortal now."

"Yes, I'm aware."

"No, Zane—fucking listen to me." His eyes lock with mine as he speaks slowly and firmly. "Ava's. Not. Human."

8

I awkwardly make my way through the doorway on crutches with two restaurant staffers in tow. Zane asked me to bring Daniella, a petite chef with a blonde pixie cut, and Eric, a waiter with tan skin and black spiky hair. I'm not really sure why he needed these two specifically, but there wasn't a lot of time for questions.

"Wait here," I say to them as I hobble toward the bedroom.

I stop in the doorway and both Zane and Kieran look my way. Their body language is odd and stiff and they both look at me with the same gaping expression.

"Um… I brought Daniella and Eric; they're in the kitchen. Should I bring them in here?" I ask, unsure why they're staring at me like I've got snakes for hair.

Zane blinks at me for a moment, seeming to forget the relative urgency of the situation. I look around for Jen but don't immediately see her.

"Where's Jen?" I ask.

That seems to snap Zane out of his daze and he shakes his head, jumping up from the edge of the bed.

"Jen fainted," he says, walking to the other side of the bed and lifting up an unconscious Jen in his arms. "I think she just got overwhelmed. Can you look after her while I deal with Kieran?"

I nod as he carries Jen into the living room and sets her down on the sofa. I sit down on the loveseat beside her.

"Daniella, Eric," he says to our two guests. "You two remember Kieran, right? Come with me…"

He leads them back to the bedroom and closes the door behind them. I look over to Jen, who seems to be sleeping soundly.

After a minute, Zane emerges from the bedroom and sits down beside me. He sighs and combs his fingers through his hair, sweeping a few messy strands out of his face.

"Have you called an ambulance?" I ask, and his eyes raise to meet mine.

He traces my shape as if he's analyzing me, trying to solve a puzzle of some sort.

"Daniella and Eric are…" He pauses, pinching his lips together in thought. "They both know Kieran and they will take care of him. He'll be fine."

"Do they have some sort of medical training or something?"

"They have, uh…" he says, chuckling a bit. "Kieran has special health issues that those two are both qualified to handle."

A high-pitched moan comes from the bedroom and my head snaps in that direction.

"Are they doing… what I think they're doing?" I ask, my face contorting in disgust. Zane smirks and cringes simultaneously.

"It's complicated," he says. "Don't overthink it—he'll be fine."

I keep going back and forth between thinking these people are totally normal and almost certainly in the mob. People showing up with massive injuries and refusing to go to the hospital feels like some firm evidence in the mob column.

Not really sure what kind of mob uses high-end restaurant workers as doctors, though. That is—if what they're doing in there is doctoring.

Eww.

I turn back to Zane, whose eyes are still locked on me.

What are you staring at? Is there something on my face?

"Have you remembered anything?" he asks.

"I uh… I'm not sure…"

How do you even know if your memory is coming back or if you're just reminded of something that had been stored away in your brain?

"Any particularly visual memories? Like brief video clips, one after the other?"

"You say this like you've been through this before."

He furrows his brow, waiting for me to answer his question.

"This morning," I say. "Jen showed me the flashcard of Mike and I remembered a bunch of stuff. It was a lot like what you described."

He grumbles slightly and looks me over, almost studying me. His face is stern but I see an unmistakable vulnerability in his eyes.

Before I can register what I'm doing, my hand reaches out and caresses the side of his face. His gaze holds mine and he freezes at the unexpected gesture.

I tug my hand back in embarrassment and I can feel the heat rush to my cheeks.

Oh my god, Ava, why are you touching this guy's face? Way to respect personal space. Why am I so awkward?

"I'm sorry, I…" I mumble. "I don't know why I did that… I didn't mean to… I…"

"Has that happened before?" he asks.

"You mean, am I randomly going around touching people's faces? No, that was just… okay, I don't know what that was. Let's just pretend that never happened."

"No. Have you had any strange physical feelings like that before?" he asks. "Like your body was acting on its own?"

"Um…" I say, pausing to think. "I mean, when Mike tried to kiss me, I felt really uncomfortable and nauseous and then… well, threw up on him."

"You're probably allergic to dickheads." Zane smirks and looks up at me through his lashes and my stomach flips and flutters in response.

It's very hard to try and act cool when this guy is giving me a permanent case of the butterflies.

"Probably," I say with a chuckle. I smile before doing my best fake sneeze.

"Oi, cheeky," he scolds, laughing a bit. "You're not that funny, you know that?"

"I know—I'm downright hilarious."

He stares deeply into my eyes and I feel the sudden urge to kiss him.

Why not? I mean, he is technically my boyfriend, right?

Before I chicken out, I wrap a hand around the side of his neck and lean in, pressing my lips against his.

His tense muscles instantly relax beneath my touch and he melts into our kiss, clinging to me as if I were his sole source of oxygen.

"Phew!" a voice calls. We both startle and break away from the kiss, turning to see Kieran emerging from the bedroom in just his boxers. The place on his stomach where his wound was is now seemingly repaired, albeit still covered in blood.

"That was a close one," he says with a sigh, walking over to the kitchen bar and pouring himself a glass of water.

I'm baffled by his miraculous recovery.

Should I have been going to a chef instead of doctors this whole time?

Kieran looks to Zane and me as we awkwardly fidget and do our best to not act suspicious.

"What?" he asks. "What'd I miss?"

———.———

ZANE

I lean up against the wall in the lobby of the doctor's office as I hear the distinctive tapping of Kami's heeled boots against the floor.

"Why are we meeting here?" she asks. "Is Ava okay?"

"Ava's fine. She's just in for a follow-up. What did you find out?"

"Honestly? A whole lot of nothing. I talked to every Immortal medical expert I can find and the good news is, they all seem to think she'll get her memory back over time."

"And the bad news?"

"That's all they seem to know. They don't know when or how. It's pretty rare to be the marked human mate of a Siren, rarer still to be one who has ingested lethe. They've never seen a case like hers and everyone seems pretty stumped."

"That's just bloody perfect…"

"Come on, Z," she says, patting me on the back. "This is good news! You'll get Ava back, it just may take a while. You're 200 years old; what's waiting a bit longer?"

She has a point.

"Check me out!" Ava says, emerging from the hallway with no crutches or cast to be seen.

"Hey, Ava!" Kami says. "You already got your cast off?"

"Apparently I'm a fast healer!" she says with a big smile. "I'm pretty sure that's the first time a doctor has ever said that. The only thing my body is usually good at is gathering obscure symptoms."

"Good sign," Kami whispers to me under her breath.

———.———

The sharp scent of chlorine hangs in the cool air. With each stroke, the water parts and my body is propelled forward. I thought a swim would distract me from my thoughts, but the quiet has just amplified them.

I've never been the impatient type, but after just over a week I'm desperate to have the old Ava back.

How is it that I've been alive for two hundred years and yet it feels like my whole life happened in just one?

I stop at the end of the pool and prop myself up on the edge, resting my elbows on the tile trim. I pull myself out and grab a nearby towel, running it through my hair.

An odd sensation pulls my attention and I turn to see Ava watching me through the window. Her eyes scan my body until she catches me looking her way and she quickly looks away.

So much for not being your type, eh love?

Usually it would be a bonus that I could feel her arousal, but under the current circumstances, it's a bit more of a curse than a gift.

As I walk into the house, Ava's gaze follows me and she nibbles slightly on her bottom lip.

Bloody hell.

I make a beeline for the shower and crank the handle all the way toward cold. The icy water washes over me and shocks my senses. It does a decent job of distracting me from the urges building in me—whether they're Ava's or my own.

I let out a heavy sigh.

Ava needs to get her memory back soon, because this limbo is driving me insane. She's herself, and yet, she's not. It's as if I'm cheating on Ava—with Ava. When we kissed yesterday, it only complicated things further.

I step out of the shower and pat myself down with a towel before wrapping it around my waist.

When I return to the bedroom, I find Ava lying on her stomach and reading on the bed. She's wearing tiny black shorts, black thigh-high socks, and a loose gray sweater that hangs just off her shoulder.

This woman is going to be the death of me.

"Uh.. Wha.. Er…" I stutter. My mouth has gone instantly dry and my brain has shut down. "What are y- you doing… here?"

"The bedroom?" she asks with a raised eyebrow.

"Uh…" I say, my eyes raking along her figure.

Fuck.

"No, I mean…" I shake my head from side to side. "You were just in the living room."

"I felt like it would be more comfortable," she says.

Her stare migrates down my chest and what I'm feeling tells me she probably didn't come in here just for comfort.

Come on, Zane, fuck. You're the king of control. You can handle this.

"Do you want me to leave?" she asks.

"No, I was er… just getting in the shower."

So much for being the king of control.

"Didn't you just get out of the shower?" she asks.

"Yeah, er… I did, but I like to take two showers because, um," I say, slowly walking backward into the bathroom. "You know how they say you're supposed to take multiple showers for the, uh, you know… muscle stuff to er… with the blood flow and all that."

I sound mental.

My heel hits the doorframe and I stumble slightly but regain my balance.

"Zane," she says, standing up and walking over to me. "Don't lie to me, okay? If you're uncomfortable around me, it's totally fine to ask me to leave."

"No, I, that's not it," I say with a sigh. "I just want to give you your space."

It's mostly true, although there's something else I'm more interested in giving her.

Bloody brain.

"I don't need space," she says. "I know this whole thing is weird and there are clearly plenty of details I don't understand, but we'll work it out. Are you sure I'm not making you uncomfortable?"

My mind is clouded with my own lust as well as Ava's.

Uncomfortable is not the word I'd use.

"No, love," I say. "You're just fine. It's all me. I'm just all up in my own head right now."

She takes a step closer to me and brushes a strand of hair from my face. In one fluid motion, our lips meet and she pushes me against the doorframe. I grab her by the hips and tug her body into mine, her warmth and touch igniting a fire deep in my chest.

I scoop her up into my arms, her legs wrapping around my waist as I leave a line of kisses along her neck. As I set her down on the bed, my lips find hers again, but she suddenly pulls back.

"I can't…" she says softly. Her breathing is ragged and she blinks a few times, still holding my gaze.

"Shit, Ava, I…"

"No, Zane, that's not what I meant. That's what you said when we kissed—'I can't.'"

"I didn-" I begin to say, but I pause to process what she's saying.

If she's not talking about yesterday, that means…

She remembers.

9

Zane hovers above me, his arms on either side of my torso. His eyes widen and his lips part slightly in shock.

"You… you remember that?" he asks.

"Um… yeah," I say, suddenly feeling a little bashful. "I guess when we kissed, it brought some things back."

There's a slight ringing in my ears and pressure in my head as more images flash in my head. My apartment. The doctor's office. Jen. The Pike. A rooftop.

"Whoa…" I say, letting out a heavy breath.

"Are you okay?" he asks. "What happened? Are you feeling sick?"

"I think I just remembered more."

He blinks slowly while he remains otherwise frozen.

"I felt something with you that I hadn't felt in a really long time," I hear his voice say in my mind.

The ringing in my ears becomes louder, the pressure increasing.

"Ava?" Zane says softly, stroking my cheek with his fingertips.

"I'm okay," I say, pinching my eyes shut.

He pulls back and rolls to the side so that he's lying beside me.

A barrage of images enter my mind, one after another.

My apartment. The hospital. A flicker of green eyes in the dark.

"I want you."

My eyelids pinch tighter.

"You're about to get what you want, baby."

Okay then—wow—that's a very graphic one.

My eyes shoot open.

"Are you… okay?" he asks. "What… what are you remembering?"

A smile begins to form at the corner of his lips, as if he could tell what I was thinking.

Before I can respond, more memories flicker in my vision: Zane's apartment. The bowling alley. Giant. Black. Wings.

Okay, it's official—I'm losing my mind.

"I-… I don't… understand," I mumble, massaging my temple with my fingers. I back up and lean against the headboard.

"Baby, what's wrong?" he asks. "Talk to me."

As I open my mouth to speak, more memories fog my mind and overwhelm my senses. Words, moments, and emotions hit me like waves, crashing through me.

I feel myself being pulled toward oblivion and stars begin to form in my peripheral vision. I know this feeling well—I'm about to lose consciousness.

Zane's voice echoes in my mind as I fade into the darkness.

"I can live without my wings. I can't live without you."

—⋅—

Low voices bicker in the distance as I slowly pry my eyes open.

I feel like I've slept for a thousand years.

Kami is sitting in a chair beside the bed with her legs crossed while she peruses a magazine.

"Hey there, sleeping beauty!" she says with a smile, setting her magazine down.

"What happened?" I ask with a hoarse voice.

"You took a little lethe-recovery power nap. Feeling any better?"

"Ughh…" I groan. "I feel like shit, but uh… I think my memory is back."

I rub my eyes and groggily sit up on the bed. My head hurts, my eyes sting, and my throat is raw—but I've certainly felt worse.

"Do you remember Asmodeus?" she asks.

"You mean the part where I skewered him with Kieran on an office chair?"

"That's right, you ass-kicking human, you!" she says with a smile. "You know, we should probably tell Za-"

She's interrupted by the door swinging open and violently colliding with the wall.

"Ava!" he huffs breathily, rushing to the side of the bed and dropping to his knees. "You're awake. Are you alright?"

"I'm fine," I say, leaning in to give him a kiss. His eyes widen and he freezes as my lips touch his.

Not exactly the warm welcome I had hoped for.

"You're… you…" he mutters.

"She's got her memory back, Z," Kami says.

"Miss me?" I ask with a playful grin.

Rather than reply, he grabs my face and pulls me in for a kiss, his lips melting into mine with a feverish zeal.

I guess I'll take that as a yes?

"Ahem…" Kami coughs. "If you guys want to get freaky, can you at least wait until I've left the room?"

I pull away, taking in a deep breath as Zane's eyes follow me intently.

"Sorry," I mumble, feeling my cheeks redden.

"Look at you, up and conscious!" Kieran says from the doorway, another silhouette peeking out behind him.

"Who else is there with you, Kieran?" I ask.

"You mean me?" a voice says in a familiar Irish accent. Finn emerges from behind Kieran, giving me a small wave.

"Finn!" I say. "Long time no see!"

"Same to you," he says. "I know, I've missed quite a bit. This lot has been filling me in."

I nod. I'm a little overwhelmed at the sudden crowd of people in the room, but happy to see that they're all here and okay.

"Okay, that's enough," Zane says, as if he had read my mind. "Let's keep the excitement to a minimum, shall we? Let's let her rest."

"Yeah, I bet that's what you'll be doing," Kieran says with a wink.

"Out!" Zane says, ushering everyone through the door and closing it behind them.

He lets out a heavy sigh and playfully hops onto the bed beside me, giving me a big smile.

"I thought I'd lost you," he says, his eyes watering as he brushes a strand of hair out of my face. "I missed you so much. With everything going on out there, I was starting to think you weren't going to wake up."

"Everything going on?" I ask.

His expression tenses, as if he just shared something he hadn't meant to.

"It's not important, really," he says, shaking his head.

"Yeah, that's not exactly comforting."

"There may have been a little trouble after you killed Asmodeus, but we're handling it."

"Handling what?"

"Some demons," he says with a sigh. "Those who were faithful to Asmodeus aren't too happy that he's gone. They're looking for answers, looking for revenge."

Crap. That's not good.

"Are they coming after me?" I ask.

"No," he says, shying away slightly and avoiding eye contact.

"No...?"

"They're after me."

My chest tightens at the thought.

"Why would they be after you and not me?" I ask.

"Let's not worry about that right now."

"And when do I get to worry about it, Zane? When demons try to kill you?"

"Baby," he says with a sigh. "I'm sorry to make you worry. We're working out a plan to deal with it; that's partly why Finn is here."

"Partly?"

"Well, he called to say he was back in town and was ready to help with Asmodeus. Obviously, we had some news for him on that front."

"Beat ya to it, Finn," I say with a laugh.

"Bloody right, you did," he says with a smile.

"Well my memory's back now, Zane, and I'm not going to let you keep getting away with this self-sacrificing behavior. Our priority needs to be keeping you safe."

"Well, I think that's going to be easier now," Kami says, opening the door and leaning on the doorframe.

"Eavesdropping, are we?" Zane asks, shooting her a glare.

"Then don't talk so loud," she says.

"Why is it going to be easier now?" I ask.

"Well, the good news is, according to a source of mine, the demons are finally leaving town."

"You say good news... does that mean there's bad news too?" I ask.

"The bad news is..." she says, pausing for a deep breath. "We don't know where they're going."

10

Finn and Kieran are sitting beside each other on the couch as Kami walks up and sits down on a nearby chair.

"I'm gone for about a week and you're all off getting duped by doppelgangers, killing the Demon King, getting amnesia, brawling with demons…" Finn says, popping the cap off of a beer bottle and taking a sip. "Nothing is ever boring with you lot these days, is it?"

"I could go for some boring right about now," I say, slumping into the armchair. As Ava walks past me, I scoop her into my lap and wrap my arms around her waist.

After the scares we've had lately, I'm never letting this woman out of my sight again.

"So your memory is back?" Kieran asks Ava.

"It would seem so," she says.

"Coolness," Kieran says. "Mine too. That lethe stuff is wild, isn't it?"

"That's one word for it, I guess," she says. "I don't think I'll be trying it again anytime soon."

I have half a mind to pour the rest of that bloody bottle down the drain. This whole experience has been way too close for comfort.

"Then I'm sure you'll be happy to hear I cleared every last drop from the house," Kami says.

"That's probably a good idea," Finn says, taking another sip of beer.

"So what's all this with the demons, now?" Ava asks.

"Ahh, yes, that," Kami says. "To be honest, I'm not really sure. According to my sources, they're all leaving town."

"Now, when you say all…" Kieran says.

"I mean all. They're leaving—collectively—all at once."

"Well, shit," Kieran says. "That can't possibly be good, can it?"

"But don't we want them to leave?" Ava asks.

"Sure," I say. "But it does make you wonder: why now? What happened to make them suddenly pack up and move?"

"And if they're not here," Kami adds. "Where are they going?"

She's right. It reminds me of mass animal migrations, like when the birds suddenly migrate off-season before a hurricane or when the fish disappear before a tsunami. Whatever it means, it's probably not anything good.

"Does that mean it's dangerous?" Ava asks. "What about Jen? Do we need to keep her safe?"

"It should be safer than ever in town," Kami says. "And if anything, it's probably less safe around us right now."

After the Kieran debacle, it's probably easier to keep Jen away from the house anyway—otherwise I'll have to charm her every five seconds.

"Less safe because demons are after you?" Ava asks.

"Maybe," Kami replies. "We're not sure right now, but I've been making a few calls, and it would seem that a few Sirens have gone missing."

"Missing?" I ask. "When were you going to tell me this?"

"When I thought you could handle it," she says, giving me a glare.

"This is exactly what I mean," Finn says. "Never boring."

"So what do we do?" Ava asks. "Do we have to kill another bad guy?"

"She's got a taste for blood now," Kieran says with a laugh.

I shoot him a scowl.

"No, no," Kami says. "We stay put and be vigilant for now. Nobody's coming to kill us or anything."

She says it very confidently, but I hear a hint of worry in her voice.

Deep down, none of us really know what kind of wrath killing a Demon King could bring upon us, because no one has ever done it before.

———•———

AVA

Kieran, Finn, and Kami say their goodbyes before Zane closes the door behind them. He lets out a heavy sigh and leans back against the closed door. His usually neat curls are tousled and unruly, his eyes sunken and bloodshot.

Even with his superhuman good looks, his exhaustion is obvious.

"You need sleep," I say. I hug him and rest my head on his chest.

"You're probably right," he says with another sigh, wrapping his arms around me.

"I'm right?? Uh oh…"

"Why uh oh?"

"You must be another demon because there's no chance you're Zane," I say with a giggle.

"Oi!" he says, laughing slightly. "Okay Miss Cheeky, that's enough from you."

He grabs my butt and hoists me up. My legs instinctively wrap around him and I let out a surprised yelp as he carries me to the bedroom. In a quick motion, he places me on the bed and lies down next to me so that we're both facing each other. I laugh softly as he brushes my face with his fingertips, his eyes locked on mine as a broad smile stretches across his face.

"Why are you so happy?" I ask.

"Seriously, love? You're alive, you have your memories back. What's not to be happy about?"

"Oh, I dunno, just some unexplained disappearing Sirens and the town demons going south for the winter?"

"Of all the things that scare me, those don't even crack the top ten."

"Okay, then, macho man."

"Want me to show you just how manly I can be?" he asks with a shameless smirk, wrapping his hand around my waist and pulling my body up against his own.

"Not tonight, Romeo," I say, swatting his chest. "You are officially on bed rest. You look like you've hardly slept all week."

His eyes fall slightly and he bites his lower lip.

"You have slept, haven't you?" I ask.

"I've slept some."

"Zane... what's some?"

"I tried. I got a couple of hours."

"You only slept a couple of hours last night?"

"Er... this week."

"Holy crap, Zane! No wonder you seem so worn out! Why haven't you been sleeping?"

Although that does explain why I found the TV remote in the toothbrush holder last night.

"I just couldn't," he says with a sigh. "Those first few days, I thought you were never going to get your memory back. Then, when it started coming back, you lost consciousness. I was worried. Plus, I can't really sleep anymore without you in my arms."

His eyes dodge my gaze and he chews nervously on his lip.

"Aww," I say, nuzzling into his shoulder. "You could've told me—maybe I could've helped."

"You had plenty to deal with."

"Well, you don't get to decide what I do or don't get to deal with, okay?" I say, kissing his cheek.

"Mmm-hmm..." he hums, his eyes falling shut.

"I'll get you your pajamas," I say, attempting to stand up, but Zane's arm tugs me back into bed with him. "Zane, I have to get ready for bed."

A soft purring snore radiates from his chest as Zane snuggles deeper into his pillow with a faint smile on his face.

"Zane?" I whisper, but there's no response.

I relax beside him and watch him peacefully drift into a deep sleep.

———◦———

My phone buzzes on the nightstand and I reach for it. The time reads: 10:42 am.

Crap. I guess we really slept in today.

The phone vibrates in my hand as a call comes through from the building concierge. I step out of the bedroom, treading softly across the floor to avoid waking Zane. I close the door behind me and walk out into the living room before answering.

"Hello?" I say, bringing the phone to my ear.

"Hello, Miss Reynolds?" the concierge says.

"Yes, this is she."

"We have a visitor at the desk asking for you," he says. "A Mister David Reynolds. Do you know this person? Would you like us to let him up to your floor?"

My stomach sinks and twists just hearing his name.

David Reynolds—my dad.

"Um…" I say, pausing to process what he's just told me. "No. Don't let him up."

"Alright, Miss Reynolds…" the concierge says.

"I'll come down to meet him."

11

The elevator doors open to our building's bottom floor. Everything is crisp white, from the marble flooring to the ivory columns.

A short, round man sits on a bench along the wall. He's mostly bald with a bit of brown hair left above his temples and a salt-and-pepper goatee. His ratty, olive-green pullover is notably out of place in this swanky lobby. I've never really felt like I belonged in a fancy place like this, but my dad sticks out like a sore thumb.

"There's my little girl!" he says, standing and opening his arms to welcome me in for a hug.

The thing I hate most about seeing him isn't even all the obviously bad stuff—the lying, the screaming fights, or the insults—it's these moments, when he pretends everything is fine. When he puts on his 'loving parent' act and we have to exist in this momentary state of fiction.

I keep my arms crossed as I walk up to him.

"Why are you here?" I ask.

"Do I need to have a reason to want to see my daughter now?" he asks, giving me an incredulous look. He seems to realize I'm not going to hug him because he lets his arms drop to his sides. "I tried calling, but you don't seem to be answering your phone anymore."

He acts as if he doesn't remember our last conversation, but we both know I made it very clear that I was done with him.

"That's intentional," I say. "How did you even find me?"

"I may be an old man, but I can still figure out how to look up an address on the internet."

I guess it was unrealistic to expect to be able to avoid him forever, but I hate having him anywhere near the home that Zane and I have built together. I just want to keep him in my past.

"Okay, well you found me. I still don't have anything to say to you."

"And why is that?"

"You know why."

"You're still holding a grudge over that? Get over it already."

"Get over which part, exactly?" I ask, my voice getting louder with every word. "Mom dying or you insinuating she was pathetic?"

"We should talk about this somewhere private," he says, eyeing the concierge standing at the desk.

"No. I only came down here to make sure we were clear that you're not welcome anywhere near my building. I'm not having a private chat with you. This conversation is finished."

"So you're just going to keep blaming me for something that she's responsible for?"

"Fuck you," I snap, my volume rising again. "Yeah, so she killed herself, but you might as well have done it. All your bullshit got in her head—hell, it got in mine too. You tear people down and you exploit their weaknesses. You're toxic!"

His eyes darken and his expression falls, as if someone has just flipped a switch and revealed the real man behind the facade.

"It's not my fault you can't handle…" he pauses, his eyes widening slightly as his mouth closes.

"Go ahead mate," a familiar voice says behind me, "finish that sentence."

———•———

ZANE

"And you are?" the man says, his tough exterior failing to mask his intimidation.

"Ava's boyfriend," I say, wrapping an arm around her waist. The man looks like an older, wider version of Ava's brother Dylan, and based on the conversation I heard as I walked up, it's pretty clear that this man is Ava's father.

Ava has always struggled when it came to talking about her mother's death, but I knew that whatever happened weighed on her and I knew she blamed her father. Now I know why.

"Yeah, your brother told me you had a new boyfriend," he says to Ava, almost ignoring me completely. "Mike didn't make enough for you?"

He laughs and gives me a pat on the arm.

"I'm just kidding," he says with an unsettling smile. "So my daughter is living with you here?"

Ava fidgets anxiously and her heartbeat pounds beneath her skin.

"Why are you here?" she asks him. "What do you want?"

"I had some mail I've been meaning to give you," he says, pulling something from his back pocket. He hands her a stack of papers wrapped in a thick rubber band.

"Thanks," I say, taking them from his hand.

"You have quite a lot of tattoos there, uh…"

"Zane."

"Your job okay with all those?"

"I'm not working right now, but it's never been an issue."

"Oh," he says, judgment dripping from his voice. "That explains why you can't afford a haircut."

He laughs in a way that straddles the line between friendly and insidious.

If I punch all of Ava's family members the first time I meet them, would that reflect poorly on me?

"How do you afford a place like this if you're unemployed?" he asks.

I know Americans are a little more forward, but his question seems like an overstep by any standards.

"That's really none of your business," Ava says, her muscles tensing.

"Is that so?" he asks. "You into something you don't want your girlfriend's dad knowing about?"

I can't help but chuckle at the thought. Of all the people in Ava's life, I know that he's the one I least need to impress.

"Like what?" I ask. "You think I'm an arms dealer?"

"Or another kind of dealer," he says, his eyes narrowing slightly.

"Oh please," Ava says with an unusual bitterness to her voice. "You of all people are concerned that my boyfriend is involved with drugs? Why? Do you need a new supplier?"

"How dare you," he says, sticking his hands in his pockets and puffing out his chest. "You know I don't use drugs. You're just trying to embarrass me."

I don't know, mate. Seems like you don't really need any help on that front.

"Bullshit," she says. "I guarantee you've got pills in your jacket pocket right now."

"I need my medication for my back, you know that," he says, taking a step toward Ava. I resist the urge to step between them, but just barely.

"What I know is that you're an addict and the only reason you're here is because you need money, not to deliver my fucking junk mail."

"Yes, Ava, I have trouble affording my medications, but that doesn't make me an addict. And I wasn't going to ask you for money, even though it's obvious you have plenty to spare. Because I know better than to ask a selfish bitch li-"

He's interrupted by my fist colliding with his mouth. He staggers back and touches his now-bleeding lip with his fingertips.

"This guy seems like a real catch, Ava," he says, sucking in his split lip. "Great self-control you've got there, pal."

"He's the only one who's actually welcome here," she says. I scoop an arm around her and attempt to guide her back to the elevator while he stands there nursing his injury.

"And what does he expect in return?" he shouts as we walk away. "You're not exactly a supermodel, darlin'. You think a guy with this kind of money is with you for your personality?"

I stop just before we reach the elevator and turn around. He gives me a sinister look as I walk past him to the concierge desk.

"Don't let that man in here again," I say, before turning to join Ava back in the elevator.

The doors open and we step inside. We watch as Ava's father is escorted out by security as the doors close.

"Are you alright?" I ask. She nods, but is clearly a bit shaken up.

"I take it you found my note?" she asks with a soft smile.

"Yeah: 'Ran to lobby - be back soon.' I feel like you left out some details there." She nods again.

"Oh, here you go," I say, handing her the wad of mail from my pocket.

She pulls the rubber band off and begins skimming through the pile.

"I'm sorry you had to deal with that," she says. "He's a part of my life that I just wish I could bury."

"If anyone can understand that, it's me."

"Oh boy," Ava says, holding a black envelope.

"What is it?" I ask as she opens it to reveal a black and gold card. She holds it up so I can read the text: You're Invited to Our 5-Year High School Reunion.

Oh boy, indeed.

12

AVA

Zane unlocks our front door and it swings open. He drops his keys in a bowl beside the door and sits down at the kitchen bar, pulling his phone out for a moment before placing it to the side.

"So, do you want to talk about it?" he asks, his eyes soft and questioning.

"Which part?" I ask.

"Any of it?"

I feel a knot forming in the pit of my stomach. Even though I trust Zane, I can't shake the fear that the more he knows about my broken family and all my damage, the less he'll want to be with me.

Sometimes it feels impossible to outrun my past. I thought I could get away, start fresh in a new city, and never have to deal with my mom being gone or the only family I have left being manipulative assholes who completely messed me up. Yet here I am, back in my hometown and dealing with the same old crap as always.

I sigh, sitting beside him and resting my head against the cool countertop.

I guess I'm going to have to deal with this at some point.

"I told you, my family is messed up," I say. "That was just my dad trying to get me to talk to him again so that I'll give him whatever it is that he wants this time."

"How are you feeling about it?" he asks.

"Is that your way of asking if it's okay that you punched my dad?"

He chuckles slightly before turning to me with a smile.

"No, love," he says. "I saw you fighting back a grin when I punched him, so I took that as your approval. I mean, how are you feeling about seeing him and…

what he said."

"You mean the part where he accused you of being a drug dealer?" I ask, lifting my head from the counter and giggling. "Or the part where I accused him of wanting to buy off you?"

I'm pretty sure that one seriously scandalized our concierge, because when I had said it, he looked like he got about twelve inches shorter, shrinking behind that front desk. This place was used to the kind of clientele you see on *Lifestyles of the Rich and Famous* and my dad and I were going full *Real Housewives*.

"George seemed pretty afraid of you at that point," Zane says, smirking.

"Is that his name?"

"The concierge? Yes, George."

"Of course it is. That's such a fancy kind of name. You name your kid George and they're immediately limited to jobs done in suits and tuxedos."

"Baby," he says. "I'm 200 years old. Do you think I'm not going to catch on to your attempts to change the subject?"

"Well, that's not fair," I say, scrunching my lips sideways. "You have an advantage."

"It's not supposed to be a competition, love."

I sigh and lay my head back on the bar.

"I just…" I mumble, groaning slightly into the countertop. "I get away from him and I think I'm immune to all his garbage, but then he shows up and I'm right back to letting him get under my skin again. I don't even like the guy and he still manages to affect me and tear me down."

"You know, love, we don't really get to choose our emotions," he says with a soft, empathetic smile. "Otherwise, why would we ever choose the bad ones?"

"I just don't want him to win. He says these things to hurt me, and if he succeeds—then he wins," I say, sitting back up again. Zane looks at me with a mix of pity and concern and his eyes flash green for just a moment.

When will I be able to get past never feeling good enough?

"Should I go find him and knock him around a bit more?" he smiles slightly, but his offer is definitely serious.

"Whoa there, maniac!" I say with a giggle. "Haven't you ever heard that fighting never fixes anything?"

"It fixed Mike's nose."

I can't help but burst into laughter.

"You're so mean!" I tease him, getting up and walking over to the living room so I can lie down on the couch.

"Feeling alright?" he asks, joining me on the couch.

"I'm okay. This kind of stress this early in the morning just really took it out of me."

I close my eyes for a moment and sigh. Emotional stress has never been particularly great for my health, nor has interacting with my dad in general.

Some people are just so bad for you that they drain your energy simply by being in the room.

"Do you want to talk about your mom?" he asks.

Shit.

"You… you heard that part?"

He nods his head in response.

"I…" I start to say as a tear drips from my eye. "I know I don't really talk about it… I don't know. It's still hard."

I feel more tears welling up and before I know it, they're pouring down my cheeks. Zane looks physically hurt by my crying and rushes to wrap his arms around me.

"I know, baby," he says. "It's okay."

"It's his fault," I say, my voice wavering slightly. "He always ripped her apart, criticized everything she did—just like he did to me, and to Dylan. I just learned to ignore him while Dylan became desperate for his approval. But my mom—she listened."

The tears fall faster as I burrow into Zane's shoulder and he strokes my back with his hand.

A knock at the door pulls my attention and Zane hops up to answer.

"Are we expecting someone?" I ask.

"I hope you don't mind," he says. "I invited a friend over."

Before I can reply, he opens the door to reveal Jen with a box of cookies in each hand.

"Guess who!" she says, walking inside and setting the cookies down on the table. "Aww, honey, you're crying? That stupid dickasaurus made you cry? I owe him a kick to the shins!"

She sits beside me and pulls me in for a hug.

"It's cool," I say, with a slight sniffle. "Zane already punched him in the nose."

"Oh shit!" she says with a gasp, turning to Zane. "For reals? Didn't you punch Dylan too?"

Zane gives her a slightly guilty shrug and she laughs.

"So you're the only Reynolds he hasn't punched in the face, huh?" she says with a smirk. "I mean, you better not have or I'll kick your butt, crumpet-muncher!"

She jabs a pointed finger at him in warning.

"Did you just call me crumpet-muncher?" he asks indignantly.

"Just if you hurt my girl," she says with a smile. "In all seriousness though, you're kind of my hero. I'd love to punch Ava's dad—that guy is a grade-A assface."

"You brought cookies?" I ask.

"Yep," she says, holding up two boxes. "Oreos in case you want to stuff your face with saturated fats, and really—who doesn't? And the peanut ones that help your stomach in case you make yourself nauseous on Oreos."

"You're the best!" I say.

"World's dopest BFF, that's me!"

My eye catches the reunion invitation on the side table.

"By the way, did you get one of these?" I ask, picking up the envelope.

"Oh shit," she says. "When is the RSVP deadline? I totally forgot!"

"You're actually planning on going?"

"Duh, Ava! And so are you! I am NOT going alone to our reunion!"

"Why on earth would you want to go? High school was terrible and I can't stand all those people."

"Okay, yes, high school wasn't that great, but that's the whole point! I'm so much cooler now and we've gotta stick it to all the popular kids."

"What are you talking about? You had tons of popular friends… oh. This is about Tess, isn't it?"

"Tess?" she asks, in a voice that I know very well as an attempt to feign innocence.

"Your arch enemy, mean girl, and girl you 'totally didn't have a crush on'—that Tess."

"I did not have a crush on Tess!" she shrieks, slapping my shoulder and shooting me a glare. "I'm already missing the version of you that didn't have a memory."

"How rude!" I say, smacking her with a throw pillow.

"I don't have a crush on her. I want to show that bitch that I got hot, smart, and fabulous."

Gotcha.

"So you admit that it is about Tess!"

"Okay, fine Ava, but you have to go with me and we have to show them that we're cool and hot now!"

"I dunno," I say with a sigh. "I hate this stuff."

"You can bring your hot, rich, British boyfriend," she says with a smirk.

Damn. She's good.

13

I walk up to the corner of 8th and Olive Avenue, where I see Jen waiting for me outside the boutique. It's an older brick building with well-dressed mannequins in the window.

"Hey, hon!" she says, giving me a soft hug.

"Hey!" I say.

"Okay now, you've gotta help me find something that makes everyone faint when I walk in." She takes my hand and guides me inside, then introduces me to the shop owner, Tina, who turns out to be one of her cousins.

She begins perusing the racks of clothing.

"What are you going to wear?" she asks.

"To the reunion?"

"No, to Mars," she says, sticking out her tongue. "Yes, to the reunion!"

"I don't know. I'm sure I've got something that will work. I'm not exactly as stoked about this reunion as you are."

"Oh come on, you should be even more excited than me! You've got this smoking hot boyfriend, you're a successful web designer, you no longer have braces—you've got a serious glow up on your hands!"

"Well, thanks, Jen," I say with a scowl. "Here I was thinking I wasn't all that bad in high school."

"Oh, you know that's not what I mean! I just mean that you're even better than you were then."

"Nice try," I say, playfully sulking.

"Okay, fine, you were a giant dork and so was I, but everybody knows that no high schooler has ever actually been cool anyway."

She laughs as she pulls out another dress and adds it to the stack in her arms. Pretty much every single one is a variation of black or gray.

"Whoa there, Morticia," I say. "You sure you've got enough black options there?"

"Morticia?" she asks with a hand to her heart. "I think that's the nicest thing anyone has ever called me."

She laughs and continues sifting through the racks.

"You should try something!" she says. "It's no fun to do my trying-on montage alone!"

"I'm hella broke," I say. "You forget I just got out of the hospital not too long ago and lost my memory, so I'm behind on basically everything at work and I don't get paid until I complete a job."

"I can totally front you until you get paid."

"No, no way. I don't need anything new anyway."

"Oh you're no fun!" she says with a frown, skimming the remaining dresses.

After twenty minutes of browsing, Jen heads to the dressing room with an array of black dresses in hand. I take a seat on the beige tufted bench outside and begin playing a game on my phone while I wait.

"I hate this one!" she shouts from the other side of the dressing room stall. "I'm not coming out. I look like a poorly wrapped burrito."

"Well now I want to see it even more," I say.

"Too late! Catch!" she says, as a black wad of fabric is lobbed over the stall door. I reach out just in time to catch it.

"Crap, Jen!" I say. "You gotta give me more of a warning next time!"

"Okay, then. Hanger, coming at ya!"

I ready myself just in time to catch a clear plastic hanger as it flies out of the dressing room.

"If I lose an eye in a freak hanger accident, I'm taking one of yours!" I say, looping the shoulders of the dress over the hanger and hooking it on a nearby rack.

"Sounds fair," she says, walking out in a black, high-low dress with a high halter neckline. "Too basic? I feel like it's too basic."

"Don't you already have that one?"

"Do I?" she asks, looking down. "Shit, I do."

She stomps back into the dressing room with a groan.

After a moment of shuffling, I hear a thump on the door and a heavy sigh.

"You okay in there?" I ask.

"Yeesss…" she says with a moan. "Technically."

Yeah, I'm convinced.

"Do you need help?" I ask.

"Nooo," she grumbles. "Maybe."

"What's going on?" I ask as the door cracks open.

"I'm stuck," she says, letting out another frustrated huff as I join her in the stall. Her arms are tangled above her head in a mess of black chiffon and sequins.

"Oh yeah, you're really stuck!"

"Thanks, Admiral Obvious!"

"Admiral? Don't you mean captain?"

"Nope, you got a promotion for your achievements in obviousness," she says gruffly. "Now help me!"

I laugh and attempt to tug the dress off over her head, but it refuses to budge.

"The tag said size 18," she says, straining against. "Does this look like a freaking 18 to you?"

"We'll get it off," I say, attempting to stretch the fabric stuck around her shoulder. With a quick yank, the dress loosens and I manage to pull it off her.

She drops to the floor in her bra and underwear, letting out a grunt as she sits.

"This is so frustrating!"

"What's wrong?" I ask, sitting down with her.

"I just hate trying on stuff and I…" She's interrupted by the buzzing ring of my phone. "Let me guess, Zane?"

I pull my phone out and see that it's just my pharmacy.

"Nope," I say, putting the phone on vibrate and slipping in back into my pocket. "I feel like you said that in a very pointed way. Is everything alright? Are you mad at Zane or something?"

"No," she says with a sigh. "I'm sorry. It's not you, it's me—really. I just have been thinking about this whole reunion and I just… I think of all those people we went to high school with and I still feel like a loser. I just broke up with my girlfriend, I still live in Port Charlotte, and my mom still pays my cell phone bill."

"You're not a loser, Jen," I say, scooting closer to wrap an arm around her shoulder. "You're a badass lab technician with a great life and friends and family who love you. You have a killer sense of style and you've memorized the names of every mutant in the X-Men universe, okay? Those bitches don't even know their

Beast from their Banshee."

She chuckles a bit as a slight smile appears on her face.

"You're right," she says. "I just see what you and Zane have and I want that. I want to be all cuddly and sweet with someone. And then every time I talk to my mom it's all 'When are you getting married? When am I getting grandbabies?' Ava, every single time I come home, my mom tries to set me up with her hairdresser's daughter."

"Why her hairdresser's daughter?" I ask.

"Because she's literally the only Chinese lesbian my mom knows," she says with a giggle. "I just… I don't want to show up at the reunion with no date. I worry everyone's going to ask and I'm just going to be like, 'Oh, yeah, that girl you saw on my Instagram, yeah she cheated on me and now I'm a single loser.'"

"Being single does not make you a loser."

"You know who says that? People with big, muscly boyfriends."

I wish Jen could see how awesome she is, but nobody ever really sees themselves through clear eyes.

"If you want, I can be your big muscly boyfriend," I say.

"No offense Ava, but you can hardly lift your own purse."

"Fine, then. I'm not gonna be your boyfriend now."

She giggles before standing up and offering me a hand up as well.

"Okay, scoot outta here. Emotional chat over. I gotta get sexy-fied."

I laugh as I make my way out of the dressing room. After a moment of silence, she emerges in a low-cut silk dress with half-sleeves and a fit-and-flare silhouette. She looks like a gothic pinup girl—which is precisely Jen's aesthetic.

"Alright, I look bomb in this one," she says. "Go ahead, shower me with compliments!"

"You look like Bettie Page and Elvira had the world's hottest lesbian baby."

"Damn right, I do!" she says, posing in front of the mirror.

She does a quick twirl before heading back into the dressing room.

"Do we know who else is going to the reunion?" I ask.

"I talked to Lucas and he's coming with his boyfriend," she says. "Deb is coming too, but she doesn't have a date either, so at least I don't have to go stag while my ex has a hot date. That would be seriously awkward."

"Good point."

"Paige might be bringing her brother," she says. "Oh, oh! You know who's totally gonna be there?"

"Who?"

"You remember Dave, Alex's friend? Turns out his sister is on the alumni committee and he's helping with everything."

Dave? The guy I was on a date with whose jacket I accidentally never gave back from that night out at Pike's? The guy who Zane punched in the face? The guy whose calls I've been ignoring?

Crap.

14

 ZANE

I make my way out the swinging double doors and onto the city sidewalk.

"Zane?" a familiar voice calls from down the street. I turn to see Kami making her way toward me in a gray plaid suit and red heels.

"Hey!" I say as she pulls me in for a hug.

"What are you doing here?" she asks, pointing to the building behind me. "Were you at the library?"

"Oh, uh… yeah," I say, slipping the books behind my back. "Just doing some research."

"That was smooth as sandpaper, Z." She smirks and raises her eyebrows. "Care to tell me why you just hid those books behind your back?"

Fuck. I should've known. Very little gets past Kami.

"Simple, love. Because I didn't want you to see them."

"Cute," she says, narrowing her eyes and holding out a hand.

"Alright, nosy," I say, holding out the books for her to see.

"*Autobiographical Confrontation in Pivotal Life Events*?" she reads aloud with a confused look on her face. "And… *Reunion at Murder High*?"

"Yep," I say, slipping the books under my arm.

"Okay, now I'm actually worried about you. What the heck are these about?"

"I told you, they're just some research. It's a long story."

"Research for what?" she asks. "Are you plotting a murder at a high school reunion or… okay, I don't have a joke for the other one because I have no idea what it means."

"I'm not planning a murder."

"But you are planning some other high school reunion crime?" She laughs as I shoot her a glare. "Besides, we didn't go to school so…"

"No crime of any kind."

"Wait… high school reunion… Is that what this is about? Are you going to Ava's reunion or something?"

"Maybe," I mumble. "Are you gonna make a big deal about this?"

"No, but I am going to ask why you got books to research for a reunion."

"It's just… I wanted to be prepared."

"For a party? Come on Zane, you're a Siren. We're great at social events and winning people over."

She's certainly right, for the most part. Sirens are naturally charming and social events come easy to us, whether we enjoy them or not. But the other day with Ava's dad got me a bit off my game. It was as if he didn't think I was good enough for his daughter.

Luckily, his opinion means nothing to Ava, but what if it had? It's usually a bad idea to alienate your girlfriend's father within minutes of meeting him—not that punching him in the jaw did me any favors either.

"I just want to make a good impression," I say. "I've never been to one of these before."

"Really? You've never been invited to a reunion?"

"Of course I've been invited, but it sounded rubbish so I never actually considered going. Up until recently, I've made a point of avoiding humans and these sorts of things. Have you?"

"Yep," she says. "It's fun to be someone's arm candy and have a whole room of people staring at you. I love to go with people who were nerds back in the day, because the look on everyone's faces is priceless. *Why yes, I am incredibly attractive, thank you.*' It's a blast! Plus, I never actually went to any school so I don't have to deal with the drama and anxiety."

"Interesting…" I say, pondering to myself for a moment. "Maybe you can help me… possibly with a couple things. What are you doing here, anyway?"

"Checking the bulletin boards." She points to a public posting board through the library window. "A couple of my informants don't like talking in person, so I use the boards to keep in touch."

"Are you free now, then?"

She eyes the board for a moment.

"Sure," she says with a nod, putting her hands in her pockets. "What's up?"

———·———

It's the day of the reunion and I'm fully dressed in my suit, waiting for Ava to finish fixing her hair. There's an unexpected knock at the door, and I open it to find Jen in a black silk dress. She has her arms crossed and is tapping the toe of her high-heeled shoe against the floor. A woman stands behind her in a black lace top and slim red pants.

"Jen," I say. "I thought we were supposed to meet you downstairs."

"You were," she says. "But I texted Ava fifteen minutes ago and she said she was 'almost ready' so I figured she was full of it and I should come up and get her butt in gear."

"Ava," I call out. "Jen's here! We're all waiting for you!"

I welcome Jen and her friend inside and they seat themselves at the kitchen bar.

"I'm Zane by the way," I say to Jen's friend, who I assume is her roommate.

"Deb," she replies, giving me a slight nod of recognition.

"Did she find something to wear?" Jen asks. "Or is that why she's taking so long?"

"They've been in there for hours," I say.

Meanwhile, I put my suit on an hour ago and have been sitting here for 45 minutes. Usually, Ava's not particularly high-maintenance, but she's not the problem today.

"They?" Jen asks. "Don't tell me she's bringing another date, because I swear to god if Ava has two dates and I have none I'm going to lose my shit."

"No she's…" I start to say, but am interrupted by Ava emerging from around the corner.

"Okay, sorry, I'm ready!" she says, hopping out on one heel as she slips the other on her foot.

She's wearing a bright blue, skin-tight sequin dress with full-length sleeves and a dangerously short skirt.

"What the heck, Ava!" Jen squeals. "I thought you said you weren't buying something new! I know for a fact I would remember seeing this one."

"Kami insisted I borrow it," she says. "Is it too much?"

"Too much? Only in the sense that I'm going to have to kill you for showing me up. Can we get a twirl?"

Ava does a little spin in place, revealing the dress's low, open back.

Holy shit.

I'm going to have to kill Kami for this one.

"Okay," Jen says. "I hate you. I mean, I love you, but I hate you. I'm starting to think I should've brought you as my date."

A quiet growl rumbles in my chest, but I do my best to mask it with a cough. Ava gives me a slight smirk before turning back to Jen.

"Well, about that," Ava says, "I actually can't be your date."

"Yeah, yeah, I know," Jen says. "You're all in love with the big British beefcake over here."

"No, not that. Because you already have a date."

"Deb doesn't count."

"Wow, thanks," Deb says, sticking out her tongue.

"Sorry, Deb," Jen says with a smile. "You know what I mean."

"Alright," Kami says as she rounds the corner in an ultra-tiny leopard-print dress. "I'm ready! Let's do this thing!"

Jen turns to Ava, then to me, then back to Ava.

"Okay, this is the best present anyone has ever given me," Jen says, smiling wide.

"I know, right?" Kami says, grabbing her purse. "Now are we gonna go make everyone jealous, or what?"

———

We pull into the parking lot in front of East Port Charlotte High School, a bland brick building with a browning lawn out front.

"So this is your high school?" I ask Ava as we step out of the car.

"Yep," she says. "I know, terribly exciting, isn't it?"

"I like learning about your life."

Ava gives me a quick smile before following the group inside. The school halls are lined with gray lockers and directional arrows are taped to the linoleum flooring. We follow the arrows and signs until we're greeted by a blond woman in a black dress. She's standing beside a plastic folding table covered in name tags.

"Hey there!" the blonde says to us. "Jen, Deb, hey! We have name tags pre-written for former students, so just grab yours and head on in! Feel free to grab a blank one for your guests."

The girls nod and look over the table for their name tags.

"You must be a guest," the blonde says to me. "I'm pretty sure I wouldn't forget you."

She bats her eyelashes at me and giggles.

I'm used to humans fancying me, though this woman is surprisingly forward since I'm clearly here with a date.

"I'm here with my girlfriend, actually," I say, walking up to Ava and wrapping an arm around her waist.

"Oh," she says. "That's a shame. Is your girlfriend a former student?"

"Come on, Claire," Jen says. "You remember Ava."

"Ava Reynolds?" she asks as Ava turns to her. "Oh my gosh, I totally didn't recognize you without the dyed black hair in front of your face!"

"Um… yeah, it's been a while," Ava says.

"You know, Erica's brother was asking about you earlier," she says with a wink. "You should go say hi."

My eyes narrow as I tighten my grip around Ava's hip.

Who is Erica's brother and why does he have a death wish?

"Oh um…" Ava mumbles. "Will do, thanks."

"Ava!" a man's voice calls from down the hall.

I swear to god if I turn around and see Mike's bloody face, I'm going to end him.

Ava's eyes go wide before she turns around and I follow.

"Hi Dave!"

15

I greet Dave with a small wave.

His long hair is swept back and he has grown a beard since I last saw him. He's wearing a black button-up shirt and black slacks with a white blazer.

"Long time no see!" he says, putting his hands in his pockets. "Jen, good to see you! You both look lovely!"

"I know, right?" Jen says with a giggle.

I feel Zane's arms wrap around my waist and pull me back slightly into him.

"And these must be your dates?" he asks, gesturing to Kami, Deb, and Zane.

"Oh, yeah," Jen says. "This is Kami, my date. Kami, this is Dave."

"Nice to meet you," Kami says, shaking his hand as her eyes briefly flash gold.

"And this is my roommate, Deb."

Deb says hello and shakes his hand as well.

"And this is Zane," Jen says.

"Ava's boyfriend," Zane adds, shaking his hand firmly while holding eye contact.

"Nice to meet you, Zane," Dave replies.

I'm surprised Dave is so cool with him after he punched him in the face.

"Same to you," Zane says, keeping an arm around my waist as he shakes his hand.

I raise an eyebrow at Zane and he smirks in response.

"He doesn't remember," he whispers into my ear. "I charmed him."

That makes a lot more sense, actually.

"Well, you guys should check out the rest of it," he says, pointing us in the direction of the gym. "Erica, my sister, worked on the decorations all day."

As he opens the doors, the soft thumping of bass morphs into a cacophony of loud nineties music and chatter.

The gym is decked out with blue string lights and white fabric draped from the ceiling. There's a photo booth in the corner with balloons spelling out "EPCH Reunion." In the low light it looks quite pretty, but I'm pretty sure the effect is mostly due to it being so dark.

Looking around, I see multiple familiar faces: my lab partner from Freshman year who never did his part of the projects, the kid who used to carry a briefcase instead of a backpack, the girl who threatened to beat me up in the girls' bathroom because she was convinced I looked at her funny.

Why am I doing this again?

"Jen! Deb!" a voice calls.

A woman makes her way out of the crowd and runs to greet Jen and Deb as Dave is called away by his sister. She hugs both of them before Jen introduces the rest of us.

"Paige, you remember Ava," Jen says, gesturing to me as I give her a nod. "This is Ava's boyfriend, Zane, and my date Kami."

"Whoa," Paige says, her jaw dropping as if it had been disconnected from the rest of her mouth. "You're… Ava's boyfriend?"

"Yep," Zane says, lacing his fingers in mine and giving me a quick kiss on the cheek. "That I am."

"I love your accent. Are you British?" she asks, batting her eyes slightly.

I don't know Paige that well, but she's about to get very acquainted with the back of my hand.

"Yes. I'm from England."

"That's so cool!" she says, giggling like an idiot. "Did you come here for work?"

"Uh, not exactly. Just needed a change."

"So what do you do then?"

Okay, bitch, I'm literally right here. Can you not ogle my boyfriend right in front of me?

"I'm er…" he says, pausing as he looks at Kami for a moment. "I'm a real estate investor."

I raise my eyebrows at him in surprise.

He's usually one to play down how he makes his money. Now he's calling himself a real estate investor?

"Wow!" she says. "You're just such a catch, aren't you?"

I shoot her a quick glare.

"Okay, then," Jen says, pulling me away. "We're gonna go find a table.

Nice seeing you, Paige!"

Deb breaks away from our group while the rest of us find a nearby table and sit down. Zane steps away to grab us all drinks.

"Well, that was awkward," Jen says, hanging her purse on the back of her chair.

"I don't remember Paige being quite so… strangle-able," I say.

"Yeah, that was pretty, uh… bold."

"Well, he's a S…" Kami says, her eyes widening as she stops herself halfway through. "A… citizen of England. You know how Americans feel about the accent and all. I'm just saying it's normal for us… to uh, get extra attention."

"I always forget that you're English too," Jen says. "Why don't you have the accent?"

"I technically lived in England, yeah, but I traveled a lot and lived all over. I didn't like the way people treated me when I had an accent, so I've always tried to adapt."

"That blows." Jen shakes her head. "But I get it."

I look over to Zane, who seems to be fending off another admirer at the drinks table.

"Hey, girls!" a voice calls. I turn back to see a short brunette woman with bangs and a nose ring. She's wearing a white, sleeveless, bodycon dress and matching heels.

It takes me a moment to recognize Jen's archenemy—Tess.

"Heeyyy," Jen says in her best faux-friendly voice.

"Look at you guys!" she says, her voice and posture indicating she's already a bit drunk. "Still hanging out together at the same table after all these years!"

She giggles in a way that lets us know she's not really kidding but wants to pretend she is.

"Yep, that's us!" Jen says. "And look at you! I hardly recognized you! You've grown so much—I mean not height-wise, of course."

"And who's your friend?" Tess asks.

"This is Kami," she says. "She's my date."

"Oh wow. You're so gorgeous," Tess says, turning to Kami. "I didn't think that was Jen's type."

"Aww, well my Jen is so popular," Kami replies, wrapping an arm around Jen and leaning into her. "I'm just glad she had time for me tonight. She's such a stunner, isn't she?"

"Yeah, uh… of course."

Zane walks up to our table and sets the drinks down before sitting beside me.

"Hello there," Tess says, smiling at Zane. "And you are?"

"Zane, I'm Ava's boyfriend," he says, kissing the top of my head.

"Wow," she says. "Who would have guessed you'd both do so well for yourselves."

"Yeah, I really lucked out," Zane replies with a smirk. "So how do you all know each other?"

"Well, we all had a few classes together. And Jen and I were in competition for valedictorian. I ended up winning, of course," she says, pointing to a blue sticker on her name badge that says 'valedictorian.'

"Did you print out your own sticker?" Jen asks.

"No," she says with an uneasy laugh. "You're so funny, Jenny."

Jen gives her a glare in response.

"And we ran against each other for class president," Tess adds. "Which, huh… I guess I won that one too!"

Bitch.

Jen looks a little upset, but seems to be doing her best to shake it off.

"It's funny how we all think things like class president are meaningful," Kami says with a smirk. "And then we grow up and realize how pointless and petty all this high school nonsense is, right?"

"Yeah totally," Tess says with an awkward laugh, before turning to Jen. "So what are you up to now?"

"I'm a lab technician for GenoRev downtown," she says with a smirk.

"Good for you," Tess says with a smile. "Someone needs to do those kinds of jobs. It's great that you found something that suits you."

Jen narrows her eyes, but I can tell she's wavering between being furious and on the edge of tears.

"Excuse me," Jen says, standing up. "I'm going to go use the restroom."

She walks away quickly. Even though my instinct is to go chase her or give Tess a talking to, I know Jen wouldn't want me to act like it's a big deal.

Zane pinches his lips tight and looks back to Jen as she heads out the cafeteria doors.

"And what is it that you do now, Tess?" I ask.

"I'm in medical school, actually," she says. "I did my pre-med in just three years, so I got my bachelor's in Medical Studies and am already in my second year of med school. Crazy, right?"

I'm kind of glad I didn't ask while Jen was around, because I'm pretty sure that would have upset her more. Jen's mom always wanted her to be a doctor like her dad.

"Oh, well that makes sense," Kami says. "You've got that doctor kind of look."

"I do?"

"Yeah, you know, the circles under the eyes and the pale skin—I guess you don't get much sleep."

She chuckles in response.

"That's so true," she says, uncomfortably staring at the ground before excusing herself to mingle with the rest of the crowd.

"What a raging bitch," Kami says, taking a sip of her punch. "Was she born with the stick up her ass or did someone shove it up there?"

I snort with laughter and nearly choke on my own drink.

"I might go check on Jen," I say.

"I'll come with you," Kami says.

We head to the bathroom to find Jen, several men stopping to wink at Kami or give her a wave along the way.

I open the bathroom door to Jen reapplying her makeup in the mirror. She seems to have been crying and is touching up her mascara.

"Aww, Jen Jen," I say, trapping her arms in a big bear hug. Kami joins me.

"You guys are squishing me!" she squeals. "Stop it, I'm fine, you're gonna suffocate meeee."

We both release the hug as Jen takes a heavy breath in.

"If it's any consolation, when you left, Kami basically told her she looks like a tired hag, so there's that."

"Really?" she asks. "I'm kind of sad that I missed that."

"I can go tell her again if you want," Kami says, leaning her head into Jen's shoulder.

"I'm okay," she says with a giggle. "Really, I'm okay. Let's go out there and dance."

Kami nods and the three of us make our way out to the dance floor, where the music has quieted and a commotion has drawn the crowd to gather around the stage.

"What's going on?" Kami asks.

"I have no idea," I say.

"…and I paid LJ to take my SATs!" a familiar woman's voice says over the speaker system.

We look to see Tess shouting into the microphone as the crowd reacts in gasps and whispers.

"Mrs. Carter was such a bitch, but I told her she was my favorite teacher so she'd write me a recommendation letter."

Jen's eyes widen and she gasps before breaking out into laughter.

"Oh my god," she says to me. "How sloshed is she right now?"

"Um… I would guess very."

"Also, I told everyone I kicked Hannah off Mathletes because she cheated, but I actually kicked her off because she was smarter than me and I hate sharing attention."

Jen and Kami break into what can best be described as a cackle, almost falling to the ground in laughter. The crowd continues with a mix of gasping, laughing, and booing as each new revelation comes to light.

My eyes scan the room for Zane and I see him leaning against the wall and snickering. As I walk up, he gives me a smirk.

"Did you have something to do with this?" I ask.

"Who, me?"

"So Tess just decided to bare her soul?"

"What can I say, love—the punch is proper strong."

I wrap my arms tightly around him and give him a hug.

"Thank you," I say.

"Just this once, I didn't do it for you," he says, stroking my hair. "Jen is family. Nobody fucks with my family."

16

 ZANE

Jen, Ava, and Deb sit down in a booth while Kami and I wait for our order at the counter. The midnight crowd at the burger shop is practically nonexistent—besides our group, there's just one couple sitting in the corner.

"Did you see Hannah's face?" Jen squeals. "I swear she turned eight shades of red. I'm honestly shocked that she and Tess didn't throw down."

Ava and Jen laugh among themselves.

I'm not sure I've ever seen Jen quite so happy.

"That was the most entertaining reunion I've ever been to," Kami says, leaning up against the wall and smirking.

"I have to agree," I say. "Although it's the only one I've ever been to. Thanks for the advice, by the way. I think it went well."

"Well, I told you not to say you were unemployed. I didn't tell you to charm the mean girl into spilling her guts to the crowd. Honestly, I'm kind of disappointed I didn't do it myself—that was a brilliant idea. I haven't laughed that hard in a long, long time."

I chuckle and glance back at Ava and Jen.

"I think you made Jen's night," Kami adds. "Although I'm not sure Deb had quite as much fun."

Jen's roommate—and ex—Deb isn't usually much of a talker anyway, but tonight she has been particularly quiet. Ava and Jen are both laughing their arses off, but Deb seems to be staring off into space, looking dejected. As I watch, she stands up and shuffles out of the booth before stepping outside.

"She a friend of Tess?" I ask.

"I doubt it," Kami says. "I think she's just got other things on her mind."

"Other things?"

I'm not sure exactly what she's getting at. Deb seemed to disappear for most of the night, only rejoining us at the end.

"Men are so clueless," she says with an eye roll. "I got the impression she wished I wasn't there tonight, if you get my drift."

I open my mouth to respond but we're interrupted by a loud group of men walking in and stepping up to the counter. They seem to be pretty intoxicated and are wearing dress shirts and slacks with loosened ties around their necks. Since we're just down the street from the high school, I wouldn't be surprised if they came from the reunion too.

One of the men proceeds to order for the group while the others laugh and joke at a volume best reserved for heavy metal concerts.

"Little Avaaa Reeeynoolds!" one of the men shouts, taking a couple of tipsy steps toward her table. I feel my chest rise and my muscles tense. "I used to get high with your brother behind the bathrooms by the basketball courts. Where's Dylan at, anyway?"

"Not here," she says loudly. "Sorry."

She turns to Jen to continue their conversation. The man scoffs, but seems to let it go, returning to his group beside us.

"Bitch," he mumbles under his breath. Before I have a chance to respond, he zeros in on Kami and walks up to her.

Perfect, this man is clearly going to get himself killed without my help.

"Hey babe!" he says. "Were you at the reunion? I'm pretty sure I'd remember you."

Kami rolls her eyes and laughs.

"Daaammmnnn…" his friend says, eying her up and down as he too stalks closer.

"Wow!" she says with a sarcastic drawl. "I can't believe I've attracted not one— but two—of Port Charlotte's most eligible wasted douchebags! I'm honored!"

Her eyes narrow as a devilish grin appears on her face.

In a particularly ballsy move, the second man licks his lips and steps closer to her, reaching out to grab her waist. Kami grabs his wrist and twists his arm behind his back in a swift motion. As she does, I hear Ava and Jen's chatter rapidly come to a halt.

"'Scuse me, pal," she says, her eyes now glowing gold. "Consider this a fucking museum, alright? You look, but you don't touch, or I'll break your arm. Got it?"

"Hot," he says, leaning back into her.

How bloody wasted is this guy?

He lets out a shriek as Kami wrenches his arm backward and pushes him to the floor.

"Men," she scoffs.

One of the man's friends bends down to help him. Jen and Ava appear close behind us, both looking shocked and unsure of what to do.

"Where's Deb?" I ask.

"Um… she left… She called herself an Uber," Ava says softly, looking back and forth between Kami and the man on the floor. "Are you guys oka-"

Ava's mouth drops open as two other men approach Kami, stepping well into her personal space.

"What the hell?" Kami snaps, taking a large step away from them. "Haven't you guys ever heard of personal space?"

"I just wanna say hi," one of the men says, stepping closer still as if he's about to kiss her. The other man is close behind.

She punches one in the stomach before kicking the next square in the bollocks.

"What the heck is happening right now?" Jen asks, her eyes wide as she looks at the three men laying on the floor.

The last remaining man from their group looks upon the scene with a mixture of shock and horror.

"I-" he begins to say, looking between Kami and the men before looking at me. "I'm so sorry. I don't know why they're acting like this."

One of the men on the floor grabs Kami's leg and she yelps before stepping on his hand with an unsettling crunch.

"How bloody pissed are these blokes?" I ask.

Kami gives me a stunned expression before taking several steps away from the men on the floor.

"We had a lot to drink, I guess," the remaining man says, giving me a guilty look. He pats a hand awkwardly on my shoulder. "I didn't realize we had so much."

"Don't apologize to me, mate," I say as his friends groan in pain on the ground. "Keep better company."

"You're right," he says, his hand rubbing my shoulder before gripping tightly around my bicep.

"The fuck are you doing?" I say, pulling away.

"You're just so…" he says, his eyes wandering over my body, "gorgeous."

He lunges forward with his lips pursed, but I dodge backward as he stumbles.

"We need to get the hell out of here," Kami says. "Now."

Ava and Jen both nod, wide-eyed, as we all take off toward the door. We pass a couple in the parking lot and the woman starts to chase me to the car, her boyfriend following her close behind.

We all sprint until we make it to Jen's car. Kami jumps in the front with Jen, while Ava and I get in the back and lock the doors behind us. The woman catches up and begins beating on the car door, tugging at the handle as she attempts to get in.

"You guys, what the actual frack is happening right now??" Jen screams, looking to each of us for some semblance of an explanation.

"That's a bloody good question, love," I say, letting out a heavy breath.

The woman outside the car is banging at the door and one of the men from earlier emerges from the restaurant.

"Drive now," Kami says. "Questions later!"

Jen slams the car into gear and peels out of the parking lot, breathing heavily as she drives away.

"Where the frack am I even going?" she asks.

"Go to their penthouse," Kami says. "It's the safest."

"Safest??" she asks. "What is even happening right now??"

"Something is wrong with our powers, Z," Kami says to me.

"No shit, Kami," I say.

"Powers?" Jen asks, barely keeping her eyes on the road as she looks rapidly between us. "Oh my god… Are you superheroes? Mutants? Do you have magic seduction powers like Stacy X? Or Starfox? Ava, you're dating an X-Man and you didn't even tell me??"

"He's not an X-Man, Jen," Ava says with a slight smile.

Jen looks back and forth between us and Kami shrieks as the car nearly veers off the road.

"Geez, Jen!" Ava says. "Watch the road!"

"Should I watch the road, Ava?" she replies with a snarky tone. "I've just had the weirdest night of my entire life and there are super people in my car, but my driving sucks, so let's talk about that."

"We're not super people," Kami says. "You don't see any spandex on me, do you?"

"Don't give me ideas," Jen says, squinting as she focuses on the road. "What are you then?"

Kami looks back at me and I respond with a shrug. Ava just gives her an uncertain look and Kami sighs before turning back to Jen.

"We're Sirens, okay?"

17

AVA

Jen pulls her car into the garage and turns off the engine.

"Okay, you can't just drop a bombshell like that and then let it go," she says. "Somebody start talking."

"We'll talk once we're inside," Kami says, looking around before opening the car door. "I'm not having this conversation until we're behind a locked door."

We all step out of the car and head for the elevator. Zane has an arm around my waist and Kami and Jen are just steps ahead of us. Zane and Kami have been doing their best to act as if there's nothing to worry about, but their body language is telling a different story. They walk softly but with purpose, scanning the space as if Jen and I are celebrities and they're our bodyguards.

We enter the elevator and make it to the penthouse without incident. Kami ushers us inside as Zane locks the door behind us.

"Fuck," Zane curses, slumping against the closed door.

"Okay, what the actual hell is going on?" Jen asks. "You guys are Sirens? And something is wrong with your powers and that made those randos come onto you? And you!"

She walks over to me and begins smacking my arm repeatedly.

"Hey!" I yelp, jumping away. "You're gonna hit the sick girl?"

"You bet I am!" she says in a grumpy voice. "How the heck do you not tell me you're dating a mythical creature?! I deserve to know if my best friend is banging a superhuman. Wait a minute… now that I say it out loud… I have questions."

"Jen!" I scold.

"What? I just want to know how the logistics work. Like if he's a Siren, does that mean he has-"

"No," Zane interrupts with a groan, standing up and leaning on the kitchen bar. "I don't have a fish tail, I don't have scales, and I do not have a crustacean friend."

"Duh, Zane," she says with an eye roll. "You don't think I know the difference between Sirens and Mermaids? What kind of half-assed geek do you think I am? I was going to ask if you have a bird penis."

Zane coughs in surprise as he nearly chokes on air.

"Well, that's a new one," Kami says, plopping into an armchair with a small chuckle.

"You don't just ask someone about their penis, Jen," I say with an eye roll. Zane seems to be struggling to hold back a laugh.

"I didn't ask him. Technically, I asked you."

"Alright, alright," Zane says, waving his hands in surrender. "I have a normal, human penis."

"Just normal, huh?" she says, scrunching her lips to the side as she joins Kami in the living room. "That's disappointing."

"For a lesbian, you're awfully penis-obsessed," Kami says.

Zane and I walk over to the couch and sit down. He puts an arm around my shoulders and pulls me in close to him.

"How about we talk about the more pressing issue—like those men going batshit crazy over you two?" I say.

"Yeah, what was that?" Jen asks.

"Good question," Kami says. "I've texted some friends trying to figure it out, but I haven't heard back yet."

"What's your theory?" I ask.

"Hmm…" she hums, scratching her head and chewing on her lip. "I mean, it's gotta be the pheromones, right?"

"Pheromones?"

"Yeah," Zane says. "Sirens have a bit of an evolutionary advantage—humans are naturally attracted to us via pheromones and our, uh… physical qualities."

"You mean because you guys are hot?" Jen asks.

"Yeah, that," he says with a smirk. Zane has never been much for humility.

"So your pheromones have gone crazy and are making people sex-crazed?" she asks.

"Could be," Kami says. "That's all I can thi-"

She's interrupted by the buzzing of her phone and quickly answers the call.

"Omar hey I-" she pauses for a moment, looking concerned. I feel Zane stiffen and sit upright in response. "Yeah, we're having the same thing over here. Is she with you now?"

She pinches her lips shut and narrows her eyes.

"Good," she says, pulling her phone away to look at the screen. "Oh hold on, can I call you back in an hour? I need to take this. Okay, bye."

Zane leans forward with a worried expression, but Kami holds up a finger telling him to wait.

"Hey, I-" she says into the phone, sitting up slightly. "What do you mean? Quando…"

Kami starts speaking rapidly in a language that is either Spanish or Italian. Jen looks at me, then back to Kami, trying to figure out what's going on.

"What are they saying?" I ask Zane.

"I'm not sure. My Italian is not great," he says softly, chewing on his cheek slightly. "They're talking about Sirens… someone was killed… about half an hour ago?"

"Half an hour?" Jen asks, her eyes widening. "Shit."

"Shit what?" I ask.

"Come on, comic books 101, something insane happens on the other side of the world, all of a sudden your powers are going crazy here—zero percent chance they're not connected."

Zane combs his hand back through his hair and curses under his breath.

"Okay, thank you," Kami says through the phone. "We will. Bye."

"What did they say?" I ask.

"So, Omar just had the same thing happen to him that happened to us. Nearly got accosted on his way to work," she says, looking at Zane before turning to Jen. "Omar is also a Siren."

"Yeah, that's a bad sign for sure," Jen says.

"And I just talked to my Council contact in Italy and apparently a group of Sirens were attacked and killed just outside of Naples. They think it was demons."

"Demons?" Jen shrieks.

"Shit," Zane curses, rubbing his face with his hands. "What are the odds Jen is right?"

"Right about what?" Kami asks.

"There's a massacre involving Sirens and, at the same time, all our powers go pear-shaped. No chance that's a coincidence."

"What's wrong with being pear-shaped?" Jen asks.

I'm assuming pear-shaped doesn't mean they're going to have a hard time finding jeans that fit.

"It's an expression, love," Zane says. "It's another way of saying our powers are all fucked."

"Unfortunately, I think you're right," Kami says with a sigh. "Something is definitely up. But I don't think that's the most disconcerting bit of non-coincidence here."

What could be more disconcerting than their powers being out of whack and a bunch of Sirens being murdered?

"Fuck," Zane says, letting his head fall into his hands.

"Somebody gonna let me in on the secret here?" I ask, looking back and forth between Kami and Zane.

"This isn't the kind of thing that happens all the time," he says with a sigh, reaching out to hold my hand. "Immortals don't just kill each other."

"Wait, you guys are immortal?" Jen asks, her mouth agape. Kami gives her a nod as Jen sits in stunned silence.

"But what does that mean?" I ask. "If this isn't normal, I mean… Like, obviously we know that things are going weird with your powers, but what am I missing?"

"Demons don't just ambush Immortals at random," Kami says. "And this happening now, in addition to the Sirens going missing, there's no way it's a coincidence."

"Which means…"

"This is about me," Zane says, closing his eyes and taking a deep breath in. "This is a message."

18

ZANE

"What…" Ava says, her eyes soft but questioning. "What does any of this have to do with you?"

"Because," I say with a heavy sigh, "they know I killed Asmodeus."

I sweep a hand through my hair, pushing it away from my face.

I was so caught up in getting Asmodeus out of our lives that I didn't even consider that there might be some kind of retribution coming for me if I were to succeed.

"But you didn't kill him, really," Ava says. "I did."

"Okay, hold up," Jen says, her voice shifting to an almost-scolding tone as she turns to Ava. "You *killed* someone?"

"I um…" she says, chewing on her lip slightly. "Sort of… Technically. But he was a demon and a bad guy, so…"

"A demon *and* a bad guy? Are there good demons?" Jen leans forward in her chair.

"Well, I mean…"

"Kieran's a demon," I say. Kami raises her eyebrows at my admission but I just give her a shrug.

The Immortal cat is already out of the bag, so to speak.

"No shit…" Jen says with a smirk. Her expression slowly shifts as she looks between Ava and me. "Wait, seriously?"

"Seriously," Ava says.

"Whaaaattt??" Jen shrieks, jumping to her feet. "Kieran is a literal mother-freaking demon? What does that even mean? Are we talking red guy with a tail like Azazel? Or are we talking baddie manipulating shit in the shadows à la Mephisto? Oh my god, can Kieran make me Ghost Rider??"

What the hell is she talking about? Why does she want to ride ghosts? I'm probably going to regret asking.

"You're confusing comic books and real life again, Jen," Ava says. "Kieran cannot make you Ghost Rider and he does not have a tail."

"Er, actually…" I say. "In his demon form, he does have a tail."

"What??" Ava asks, her eyes widening. "He has a demon form?"

"Oh my god, girl," Jen says. "You find out your boyfriend's friend is a demon and you don't even ask if he has a tail? How are we even friends?"

"My bad. I don't immediately think to ask about demon tails or bird penises. But that's why I have you."

"So true, but I think we've gotten off track. You killed a demon?"

"Yeah, it's kind of a long story, but when I got attacked and ended up in the hospital, that was him."

"And you killed him?" Jen asks, wide-eyed.

"Yeah…" Ava awkwardly fiddles with her fingers in her lap.

"What a badass!"

"Okay," Kami interjects. "As much as I am honestly enjoying this discussion, I do think we should get Jen home safely, and I should probably head out soon after."

"Whyyy?" Jen whines, sitting back down. "I have so many questions!"

"Because you're human. If the situation gets further out of hand, it might start affecting you."

"Why hasn't it affected me already?"

"Probably because you're more accustomed to us. You spend a lot of time around people with Siren blood, so you have a bit of immunity."

"Orrr… I'm a superhuman?" she asks with hopeful eyes.

Ava laughs and shakes her head.

"Wait… why are you guys talking about me like I'm the only human? Ava's human too…" her eyes dart between the three of us. "Right? Ava is a human… right? Why aren't you guys saying anything?"

"Sort of," I say with a shrug. "She was, but she's bonded to me. So she's not quite human anymore."

Jen leaps up and runs to Ava before smacking her arm several times. I instinctively tense at someone hitting her, but I know the gesture is intended to be playful.

"Hey!" Ava groans.

"You didn't tell me you're a freaking superhero??" Jen shouts. "I'm gonna kick your little secretive butt, missy!"

"Okay, that's enough," I say, scooping Ava up and placing her on my lap.

"I'm not a superhero," Ava says, rubbing her arm. "I don't have any powers or anything, I'm just immune to their abilities."

"Oh please! That's what someone says before their power suddenly manifests in a moment of crisis."

Ava giggles and Jen joins in, sitting beside us on the couch.

"Okay," Jen says with a sigh. "So I guess I should go home then?"

Kami gives her a nod.

"I'd walk you to your car," Kami says. "But I think that would only make things more dangerous for you."

"It's alright," she says, gathering her purse and coat as she turns to Ava. "But you and I are grabbing lunch tomorrow and I want more details."

"Kami got home safely," I say, setting my phone on the bedside table.

"That's good," Ava says, falling backward onto the bed with her arms spread. She's wearing a black tank top and matching underwear. "I guess humans aren't really that much of a threat to a Siren, are they?"

"Yeah, not really." I lay down beside her and wrap an arm around her waist. "Except this one here. This human is going to be the death of me."

Her cheeks redden as she looks up at me through her lashes.

"Who said you were allowed to be so charming right now?" she asks with a smirk.

"I can't help it, baby," I say, brushing a strand of hair behind her ear. "I can try to be less charming if you want."

She laughs and sticks out her tongue teasingly.

"Okay, then," she says. There's a mischievous twinkle in her gray eyes as she bats her lashes. "Let's see it. Be less charming."

"I could talk about having a bird penis."

She bursts into a genuine laugh and the ring of her voice sends warmth through my chest. It's my favorite sound in the world.

"Touché," she says, still giggling.

My world has certainly gotten a lot more complicated tonight, but I can't even focus on that because I'm still just so glad to have her back.

"It's been a weird day," she says.

"You're telling me."

"What are you going to do? You can't exactly go out with people getting all crazy horny over you."

I can't imagine wanting to leave when I have Ava at home, but she's got a point.

"Kami's going to reach out to a few of her contacts to find out more. There are some people who specialize in Immortal physiology who can hopefully help. Honestly, I'm not quite sure."

"Why would Sirens dying in Italy cause this?"

"Maybe it didn't cause it directly. It could just be another part of their plan."

Her eyes lock with mine.

"Can I ask you a question?"

"No," I say, giving her a cheeky smile as I tug her in closer. "Of course, baby."

"Why did you say the demons are sending you a message for killing Asmodeus?"

"Well… I ran into some demons while you were still getting your memory back. They were looking for Asmodeus and they weren't too happy. It can't be a coincidence that demons suddenly start killing Sirens."

"But why do they think you killed him and not me?" she asks, her face soft yet serious.

Oh. That.

"I might've said that I did," I say, closing my eyes for a moment. "I realized there were going to be repercussions, but I didn't want them falling on you. I just said whatever I could to avoid them coming after you."

"But couldn't they still come after me to get to you?"

She's not wrong. That's why the other part of my lie was key.

"I may have also told them you were dead."

19

As I hop out of the car, the chilly outside air pricks my skin. I breathe into my hands and rub them together in a weak attempt to warm them up, but it's of little use. Instead, I go for an awkward sprint for the cafe door as I curse the weather under my breath.

My joints are already fussy enough, but in the cold they petrify to a point that I'm just barely able to bend.

I swing the glass door open and let out a sigh of relief as I'm hit with a blast of warm indoor air and the bitter scent of coffee.

I'm just not made to live in the cold.

The cafe is relatively empty for mid-day on a weekend. Other people probably had enough sense not to come out in these freezing conditions.

I see Jen wave from a booth in the corner and I walk over to join her.

"F-f-fuck tthiss w-weatherr…" I stutter through chattering teeth as I sit down across from her in the booth.

"I'm surprised Zane didn't insist on carrying you in here himself," she says with a teasing grin.

"Yeah, that would have gone really well…"

"Oh that's right," she says, nodding. "Fair point."

Zane wasn't too keen on the idea of letting me come out to the cafe when he's trapped at home, but if he had his way I'd be wrapped in twelve layers of bubble wrap and wearing a suit of armor everywhere I go.

"How is that going?" she asks.

"Unclear. He hasn't left the house since last night and Kami is trying to make some phone calls to see what they can figure out."

"Speaking of which," Jen says, pulling a plastic bag from her purse. "I have questions."

The bag is filled with small plastic tubes and swabs and cotton pads and more little plastic zipper bags.

"That doesn't look like questions. That looks like a science fair project. If you're going all Doctor Frankenstein on me, can you at least not give me neck bolts? It's just not a good look for me."

"Oh come on," she says with a huff. "I'm a scientist and I want answers. What's so wrong with that?"

"What does your science entail?"

"Well, I already tested myself. Skin swabs, blood tests, saliva, hair, breath…"

"Geez, Jen! When did you even have time to sleep?"

"I'm an adult. I don't have to sleep if I don't want to," she says with a pout. "What are you, my mom?"

"Oh yes, that's a very adult thing to say," I say with a snicker. "So why are you running tests on yourself and why did you bring an entire lab worth of equipment with you to brunch?"

"Because I have questions that need answers, like what is up with Zane and Kami? What about my exposure to you guys makes me immune to their weird power glitching? If I splice my DNA with something magical, can I be an X-Man?"

If I know anything at all, it's that Jen can absolutely not be trusted if she thinks there is a chance that she could become one of the X-Men.

"Okay, Jen," I say, placing a hand on hers. "Slow your roll. You are not allowed to splice your DNA with anything, okay?"

She huffs and rolls her eyes, crossing her arms across her chest.

"You're no fun."

"Anyway… did you find anything with your tests?"

"Sort of." She pulls out a notebook and flips to a page with notes scribbled on it. "My blood showed slightly elevated oxytocin, estradiol, and estrogen levels, which isn't particularly informative but that's consistent with what I would expect from pheromone exposure. Looks like Kami was right about that. I've probably developed a tolerance."

"Okay…"

"I picked up traces of some kind of pheromone-like substance on my hands, but it's not a match for anything that I have an available reference sample for. So I assume that's Siren pheromone. I can't tell how it's being secreted, though. That's where you come in…"

"Oh great," I say. "You know how much I love tests. Why me?"

"Well, I have all the stuff to test you, Zane, and Kami so we can figure this thing out. I might be able to help. There are a couple of chemical antagonists that can counteract the effects of pheromones. I just have to figure out more about how they're being excreted."

This wasn't all that gross until she said excreted. Eww.

"Can we just save the mad science until after we eat?" I ask.

"Okay, fine party pooper." She puts the bag of supplies back into her purse. "But I'm getting my samples later."

Jen and I look over the menus for a moment before deciding on our choices. She goes up to the front counter to order for both of us while I wait at our booth. After a few minutes, she reappears with a coffee in each hand and a number for our table.

"They said our food will be ready in a few minutes," she says, sitting down and scooting into the booth. "Okay, so… can Zane turn into a bird?"

"What?" I ask.

"Sirens are half-lady, half-bird. So Zane isn't a lady and you both insist he doesn't have a bird penis, so where are the bird parts?"

"Don't talk so loud," I say in a hushed tone. "He has wings. No other bird parts as far as I can tell."

I mean, how would I really know if he had a bird spleen or something?

Jen nods and makes a few notes in her notebook.

"What kind of wings are we talking about? Can he fly, or is this more of an ostrich situation?"

"Um, they're big with shiny, black feathers. And yes, he can fly, or… could, I guess."

"Could?"

"Well, you remember that thing with my liver?" She nods, wide-eyed. "He cut off his wing so that he could bond to me and save me."

"Shit…" she curses softly. "That's so goddamn romantic."

"Anyway, he can't fly anymore."

"Tell me you had flying sex before he cut off his wings."

"No, you perv," I scold, trying to stay quiet. "He can't just fly overhead in a city anyway."

"Totally unrelated question—does Kami still have her wings?"

"Je-"

We're interrupted by the server approaching our table. He's a skinny guy, maybe eighteen years old, with curly blond hair and freckles.

"French toast?" he asks.

"That's for me," Jen says. He places the plate on the table in front of her and turns to me.

"And the quiche for… you?" he asks, staring a bit uncomfortably.

"Yep, that's me," I reply, waiting for him to put it down.

"I love your hair."

There are two ways that men say that sentence. Sometimes, they're just telling me that they like my purple hair and we both continue on with our days. Other times, they feel that my colorful hair is an invitation to stand too close to me and force awkward small talk down my throat before they tell me I'm pretty and try to get my number.

This one is feeling a lot like the latter.

"Uh, thanks."

"You're gorgeous," he says, still holding my food.

And there it is.

"Thanks," I say, mostly because I have nothing else to say.

He jumps into the booth beside me, unceremoniously dropping my plate onto the table as he reaches an arm around my waist. I instinctively push him off, pulling my knees up between us and kicking him out of the booth.

"What the fuck?" Jen snaps. "Don't touch her, you epic creep!"

The guy presses forward single-mindedly and Jen swings her purse hard into his head. The guy tumbles over as we both look at each other, stunned.

"Oh my god," she says. "You have the Siren mojo."

As the guy staggers to his feet, we lock eyes and seem to have the same thought—run. We bolt out of the booth and down the hallway toward the back of the restaurant. When I pass a busboy coming out of the kitchen, something seems to overtake him because he drops his tray and begins chasing behind us.

Jen runs into the women's bathroom and I follow. Once inside, she quickly locks the doors behind us.

"What the fuuuck…" she whispers. We both jump as we hear pounding on the door.

"Let me in, sweetheart!" a man says. I can't even tell which one of them it is.

"What do we do?" I ask.

"Call Zane? Or Kami?"

I pick up my phone to dial Zane, but then I realize he's affected too. He can't leave the house.

"We can't," I say, looking at Jen with a clear panic in my voice. "We can't call a Siren because they're in the same boat as I am. And we can't call the cops, because they're human and they could be affected too. What the fucking fuck are we going to do?"

"No problem," Jen says calmly. "We can't call a Siren, we can't call a human. So we call a demon."

20

 AVA

Another hit shakes the door in its frame as Jen leans against it.

"When is Kieran going to get here?" she says through heavy breaths. "I don't want my cause of death to be 'mauled by a horny mob in a bathroom'!"

"He said he was at his house, which is about eight minutes away," I say with a sigh, checking my phone. "That was three minutes ago, so we've got at least five to go."

"Great… Don't these guys give up at some point? Like, I get that these magic pheromones are making them all hot for you, but do they still work through doors?"

"I don't know! I didn't even know I had them!"

"Well you must," she says, jumping as another pound rattles the door behind her. "That sure as hell ain't normal."

"We just have to get to the penthouse," I say, breathing in and out slowly to calm myself.

"Zane's gonna lose his mind when he finds out about this."

She's right. If Zane knew what was happening, he'd want to come and handle it himself, but the last thing we need is more Siren pheromones floating around.

"Yeah, I'll deal with that when I get to it," I say with a sigh.

I feel my phone vibrating in my hand and I look down to see Zane's name on the screen. His timing is impeccable.

I don't want to worry him and make him think he has to drive over here, but I also don't want to lie. I debate letting it go to voicemail, but decide that would definitely be more suspicious, so I settle for answering.

"Hey," I say with my best voice.

"Hey, love," he says softly, an uneasiness in his voice. "Sorry to interrupt your lunch. I… erm… this is going to sound crazy, but I just had a weird anxious feeling and I wanted to make sure you were alright."

"I'm just at the cafe with Jen."

That's technically true. Well done, Ava.

"Okay," he says with a relieved sigh. "I just felt like maybe I was picking up on something from you, through the mark. You're fine, right?"

"Let me in, sweetheart!" a voice calls from outside the door, followed by a swift thunk and a groan.

Did that guy just try to body slam the door?

"Who was that?" Zane asks, his voice low with a rumbling undercurrent.

"Oh," I say nervously. "I um… I don't know. Some guy."

Also technically true.

"Ava…" he says sternly. "What's going on?"

"Well… um… it's not a big deal or anything but it would appear that maybe I might kind of sort of have the same thing you and Kami have."

"Wait… what?" he asks, sounding more confused than upset.

"The pheromone thingies," I say. "Either that or I'm just looking particularly hot today."

I giggle in an attempt to diffuse the tension, but the line remains silent.

"Zane?" I call, checking to see if he's still there.

"I can be there in fifteen minutes."

"No, no!" I scold. "We've already…"

I hear scuffling and grunting outside the bathroom door.

"Alright, ladies," Kieran calls from the hallway. "Your one-man rescue crew is here and the coast is clear."

"Is that Kieran?" Zane asks.

"Yes, see, we've got everything under control."

"Kieran is nobody's definition of under control."

Jen opens the door to a smirking Kieran with two men collapsed at his feet.

"We'll be home soon," I say. "I'm hanging up now."

Zane gives me a grunt in response that I've come to understand is the sound of him reluctantly agreeing to something he doesn't like, then I hang up the phone.

"So, anyone want to tell me why these guys chased you into the ladies' room?" Kieran asks, guiding us out to the parking lot.

"Kami and Zane's Siren pheromones are going bonkers for unknown reasons," Jen says. "And now apparently something about Ava's weird Siren bond thing is making hers go nuts too. So she attracted the lovely suitors you saw outside the door."

Kieran's jaw goes slack as he stares at Jen.

"Jen knows??" he asks, turning to me with wide eyes. "What the fuck, man? Nobody tells me anything, I swear."

"Yeah, they kind of had to tell me because I was there when Kami and Zane attracted a wild hoard of lusty humans," Jen says, pursing her lips. "I mean, god forbid my best friend tell me she's dating a supernatural creature. No, couldn't possibly just tell me—her bestie—that she's dating a guy with freaking wings!"

"Oh my god, Jen," I say with a disgruntled sigh. "Are you ever going to let that go?"

"It depends."

My instinct is to ask what it depends on, but I kind of already know the answer.

"I can't turn you into an X-Man!" I say as Kieran guides us to his truck.

"Fine," she scoffs. "Kieran, can you make me Ghost Rider?"

"Ha!" he laughs. "Not quite. If you had asked a few months ago, I could've made you into a Succubus, but that ship sailed."

"Succubus?" Jen narrows her eyes and tilts her head.

"Get in, you two," he says, opening the door to his truck as we all hop in the front. "We'll figure out how to get your cars later."

Kieran shifts the car into gear and drives out of the parking lot.

"Did they tell you much about me?" he asks Jen.

"They said you're a demon," Jen says. "And Zane said you have a tail."

"Ahhh, that's a common misunderstanding," he says with a smirk. "That giant thing in my pants isn't a tail."

"Eww," I say, sticking out my tongue. Kieran just bursts into laughter.

"Sorry, couldn't help myself," he says, still laughing between words. "Yeah, I do have a tail in my demon form. Horns too. Not gonna lie, it's pretty fuckin' hot."

"Would be a lot hotter if you were a girl," Jen says.

"I can be."

"Can be what? A girl?"

"Yeah," he says. "I'm an Incubus. We have the ability to shapeshift, including between genders. Comes in handy when I want to bone a straight dude."

"I… That…" Jen says, pausing for a moment. "I honestly don't know how I feel about that."

"I have that effect on people." Kieran smirks.

"So Incubus, that's a sex demon, right?"

"Yep."

"That makes so much sense… So you said you could've made me into a Succubus? Why can't you now?"

"Well, technically I couldn't have. We're all creations of the Demon King, Asmodeus. He could turn humans into Incubi or Succubi. That's how I was turned, but…"

"That's the guy Ava killed, right?" she says, looking to me for confirmation.

"Wow, they told you quite a lot," he says with a chuckle. "Yeah, technically it's debatable if Ava killed him or if I did, but let's just say the guy isn't doing a lot of demon-converting these days."

"Hmm…" She pulls her notebook out of her purse and jots down a few things.

"Are you taking notes?" Kieran asks.

"We're all becoming Jen's test subjects," I tease. She shoots me an irritated glare.

"Kinky," he says with a laugh. "I like it."

"It's not my fault I'm the only person here who cares about science," she pouts.

"What kind of science are we talking, here?" he asks. "Computer science? Rocket science? Uh… Okay, not gonna lie, I thought I had more sciences when I started that sentence. I'm realizing I don't really know that many types of science."

"Chemistry," she says, pulling out her bag of testing equipment. "I'm getting samples from all of you."

"Usually if a woman wants a sample from me, she takes me to dinner first."

"Not that kind of sample." Jen's brow furrows and she crosses her arms. "Although… wait a minute, that could be really interesting. I changed my mind; I'm gonna want semen too."

"You're such a romantic," he says, smirking.

Why did I ever let Jen and Kieran meet each other?

"Okay, you two," I say. "Can we cool it on the semen talk? I never got to eat but I still feel like I'm gonna hurl."

"We're just discussing science," Kieran says.

Jen grabs my arm and rubs a gauze pad on my palm.

"One down," she says, dropping it into a small plastic bag and sealing it. With a pen, she writes 'Ava Palm Trace' on the label.

"What did I say about doing experiments on me without asking?" I scold.

"Technically, I asked," she says. "I just didn't wait for your answer."

21

 ZANE

I pace back and forth across the living room, my feet rapping against the wood floor with every step. My hands twist and tug at my hair. Ava texted me telling me they were safe and on their way, but the wait has me on edge.

Why would she be affected by whatever is going on with my powers?

It's not like she has any powers; she's almost entirely human.

What am I missing?

I hear the slight click of a key in a lock and turn to the front door. Ava gives me a soft smile and steps inside with Jen and Kieran in tow. I walk swiftly toward Ava and rest my hands on her hips.

"Are you alright?" I ask, scanning her for signs of trauma. Her skin and clothing look fine and her heart rate is steady, but she smells of fear.

"I'm alright, babe," Kieran says with a smirk. "Thanks for asking."

I shoot him a quick glare and return my attention to Ava.

"I'm fine, honestly. Everything's okay," she says, giving me a tight hug and pressing her cheek to my chest.

Even when she's been through something like this, she's still trying to put me at ease.

What did I ever do to deserve this woman?

"I'm fine too," Jen says, sticking out her tongue as she hangs her coat over a chair.

"Sorry, Jen," I say. "I was getting to it."

"I'm just kidding. I know how you two love doves are."

I give Ava a kiss on the forehead before releasing her from my grasp and sitting down in an armchair. Kieran and Jen sit on the couch and I scoop Ava onto my lap.

"Alright, what the fuck happened today? Don't sugarcoat it," I say, looking at Ava, then Jen.

Jen looks to Ava for the go-ahead before she decides to answer my question.

"So, we went to brunch. Everything was good and then the server brought our plates out. He started getting kinda weird with Ava—staring at her, telling her he liked her hair and that she was super pretty… that certainly happens a lot with Ava…"

I feel my blood pressure rising and a slow heat spreading throughout my body.

I could've done without that particular detail.

"…then he jumps in the booth with her," she continues, "reaches an arm around her and gets all up in her business…"

Ava rubs a hand along my shoulder to comfort me, but it's doing little to quell the fire building in my chest.

Not only did he touch a woman without her permission, but that woman was *my Ava.*

"So Ava gives him this crazy seated dropkick that would make Stone Cold proud and the guy goes whooooosh—bam!—right onto the floor," Jen says, miming the actions along the way. "And then I'm all, 'Oh shit, you have the Siren power thing!' So we make a break for it and run until we hit a dead end in the back and slip into the women's room. And then the guys are all, 'Rawr let us in, we think you're super hot!'"

"Guys?" I ask, furrowing my brow. "I thought it was just one."

"Oh yeah, we caught another one on the way," Jen says, seemingly unfazed. "So then Ava's like, 'What do we do?' and I'm all 'Let's call Zane', but then Ava realized you've got the sexy juju too, so we couldn't. So I suggested we call Kieran."

"And they did, and I came in and sucked a bit of human soul—you're welcome," Kieran says with a wink.

"Is that what you did to them?" Jen asks.

"Yep," he says with a smirk. "Sucking is a special skill of mine."

I roll my eyes and let my face fall into my palm.

"Can we get back on track, please?" I ask.

"That's pretty much it," Ava says. "We left our cars there and Kieran drove us straight here."

I nod, trying to process everything they've told me.

"It just doesn't make any sense," I say, combing my hand through my hair.

"Why would Ava be affected? She's not a Siren. I mean, I know we're bonded, but still…"

"How does the bond work exactly?" Jen asks. "Ava mentioned you had to cut off your wings. What did you do with them?"

"Oh, I er…" I start to say, cringing as I remember the initial shock of pain. "Technically I only cut off one, but there's this fluid inside, basically a special form of our blood. The Immortal blood helps heal Ava and rejuvenate her cells. I don't know a lot more than that."

"Did you give her a blood transfusion?" she asks.

"I drank it," Ava chimes in, sticking out her tongue and shaking her head. I guess it's not a particularly pleasant memory for her either.

"Oh," Jen says. "Well that's really gross, but okay."

"Yeah…" Ava replies with a nod.

"So your blood is in her system," Jen says, turning to me. "That's simple enough, then. That just tells us that those Siren pheromones are obviously in your blood, which is helpful. Does she have any other powers that you know of?"

"No. No powers."

"What powers do you have?" Jen asks me.

"I have a venomous kiss," I say. "It makes people feel aroused, enhances sexual passion. Like an aphrodisiac of sorts. And I'm stronger and faster than humans. I can also control people by suggestion if I'm touching them."

"Okay, wow." Jen pulls a notebook out of nowhere, seemingly by magic. "That's a lot to unpack."

She writes down a few things before looking back at Ava.

"So, venomous kiss… safe to say you haven't tested that?" Jen asks.

"Uh, no," she says. "I haven't kissed anyone since Zane."

I smirk at the thought.

Damn right—because she's mine.

"Well we'll need to test that to be sure."

"No we bloody won't," I spit, my stomach clenching at the thought. Ava's hand runs along my back to calm me down.

"But we need to know," Jen says.

"She can share a drink with someone," I say. "Same effect."

"Sharing a drink?" she asks, her eyes narrowed and questioning.

"Yeah, the venom is in our mouths and very potent."

"Hmm… Okay, we'll come back to that. And signs of strength? Speed?"

Ava shakes her head.

"Still a weak-ass human," Ava says with a chuckle. Jen jots down a few more lines of notes.

"Alright, magical touch control powers…" she says, holding out her hand. "Try me."

"This is silly."

"Good friends support their friends' science experiments," Jen scolds.

"Fine," Ava says, reaching across the coffee table to grab her wrist. "Um… dance like a chicken."

"Dance like a chicken?" Jen asks, pulling her arm away to write more notes. "Really? That's what you went with?"

"What was I supposed to do?"

"I know what I'd do," Kieran chimes in.

"We all know what you'd do, mate," I say with a smirk.

He chuckles and leans back with his arms crossed behind his head.

"So it's safe to say that didn't work," I say to Jen. "Otherwise you'd be flapping your arms and squawking."

"We need a control," she says. "Your turn, Siren man."

She holds out her arm to me.

"Come up with something better than a chicken dance, though."

"Okay," I say, chuckling as I wrap a hand around her wrist. "Smack Kieran in the face."

Jen turns around and immediately slaps Kieran—hard—her palm making a satisfying thwack as it collides with his cheek. She gasps in shock over her action.

"Not cool, bro," Kieran whines, rubbing his rapidly reddening cheek.

"Whoa," Jen says, adding a line to her notes. "You're the freaking Purple Man."

"I'm what now?" I ask, tilting my head.

"Really?" Ava asks with a chuckle. "When will you learn that literally all of Jen's references are about comic books?"

Oh. Of course.

"The Purple Man, aka Zebediah Killgrave," Jen says. "Quite possibly Marvel's all-time scariest villain with the power of mind control."

"That doesn't sound like a compliment," I say.

"Oh, it's not," Jen says, pausing a moment before seeming to realize that what

she said might be offensive. "I mean, it's not an insult either. It's just, you know…
you guys have the same powers. You're not crazy or evil or, well… purple."

This is one of the only times I've seen Jen so flustered and I can't help but smile.

"No worries," I say.

"So anyway," Jen says, "it certainly doesn't seem as if Ava has any of your
other powers, which leads me to believe the attraction thing is something in the
blood. Probably a low-level effect that just makes you a bit more interesting and
attractive when working normally, like the subtle attractiveness boost a woman
gets while ovulating."

Kieran raises an eyebrow and shoots me an inquisitive look.

I'd bet good money he doesn't know what ovulating means.

"Your current levels of pheromones or hormones are likely far higher than
normal," she continues, "for reasons we have yet to determine. But scientifically
there are several avenues to dull the effects of whatever we're dealing with,
especially if we know it's blood-based."

"Kami might know more," I say. "She said she was doing some investigating
and trying to get in touch with an Anatopath—a sort of doctor for Immortals.
They can sense disturbances in the body. They can't always cure them, but they
can tell us what is wrong."

I pull out my phone to call Kami, but see that I already have a voicemail from
her. I excuse myself and step outside to listen to the message.

"Hey, Z," her message begins. "So I've done a lot of research, and I think
we know what's going on. But Z—it's bad. A Council contact called me before I
even had a chance to call them. Those Sirens that were killed? They're not being
reborn like they're supposed to. No new Sirens have been born in the last month.
The power boost we've been getting is because there's a backup in the system. Call
me when you get this."

I knew it was bad, but this is worse than I expected.

Whoever's killing Sirens, they want them to stay dead.

22

 ZANE

Twelve.

In the past month, twelve Sirens have been killed.

When a Siren dies, a new Siren emerges from Mount Thera, an island volcano off the coast of Greece. With every death, there is new life.

Until now.

Twelve.

Twelve is the number of Sirens whose deaths were permanent. The number of Sirens that we may never get back.

Their powers had nowhere to go, so the collective became stronger. These growing powers have come at a high cost.

"Z?" Kami's voice calls from the phone speaker. "You still with me?"

"Er… yeah, sorry. I'm still processing all this."

"Any ideas?"

She clearly asked me a question and I completely missed it.

"Sorry, love," I say. "What was the question?"

"Why would demons try to hurt you by doing something that would make you stronger?"

"Maybe they want to make me miserable by making it so I can't be in public without being accosted by humans?"

"I doubt that. Besides, how would they even know that would be the effect? It's not like this has happened before."

"That's a good point," I say, scratching my chin. "Maybe they didn't know at all. Killing Sirens might just be the message. They may not have expected it to make us stronger."

"Hmm… yeah. It could have been an unexpected side effect."

"Have you been able to get in touch with our Siren friends?"

"Yeah, everyone I know has responded, so we're all good there, but they're definitely having the same problems. It turns out Alek's mate David had a similar incident around the exact same time as Ava. My guess is that there was another death or—god forbid—many, and the collective power became strong enough to affect human mates."

What a bloody clusterfuck.

"What do we do?" I ask, raking my fingers through my hair.

"Well, we need to figure out how to counteract it. I'm working on finding a solution."

"Jen's working on that too. She wants samples from all of us, but she was saying we might be able to control it."

"Oh yeah, Jen's some kind of scientist, right?"

"That she is."

"Anyway, once we figure out a way to get around without causing a riot, I think we need to get closer to the action and figure this out. I've called a few Council contacts of mine and they agree they want Sirens involved in figuring this out. But with my rep, they're not too keen on letting me join the team."

"Can't blame them on that one, love," I say with a laugh. "Last time you saw Paul, you attacked him with a cheese grater."

"That bastard had it coming—he rolled his eyes at me and called me dramatic," she says with a growl.

"I'm not saying he didn't. I'm just saying that kind of behavior is not going to make you any friends."

"Well, obviously the Iron Siren knows all, because they said they'll let me investigate if you sign on too."

"Me?" I say with a scoff. "The Council wants me to investigate the Siren disappearances? Talk about a conflict of interest. I'm the one who picked a fight with the demons in the first place."

"They don't see it that way. You've always been the Council's golden boy. You can do no wrong."

"And what am I supposed to investigate in Port Charlotte? These things are going on half a world away."

"Well, you wouldn't be investigating from Port Charlotte. We'd be going home."

The Council doesn't just want me on this investigation—they want me back in London.

———•———

Ava tucks herself deep under the sheets of our bed until just her eyes peer out from the top.

"What are you doing, love?" I ask, fighting back a laugh.

"Getting cozy," she says with a soft smile. "After the day we've had, I deserve to be warm."

"You deserve everything, baby," I say, slipping beneath the covers to join her. I wrap an arm around her waist and pull her until our bodies are flush against each other.

My stomach turns with unease, but I've come to recognize feelings like this as not being my own.

"Something on your mind?" I ask, stroking her hair as she burrows into my chest.

"Are you kidding? Everything is on my mind. Between Jen's battery of tests and killer demons on the loose and crazy Siren powers going out of control, my mind is in a million places."

"I know it sounds like a lot—hell, it is a lot—but I'll keep you safe, I promise."

"I'm not worried about me," she says with a sigh. "I'm worried about you. They're after you and trying to hurt you, but I'm just a weak little human and there's nothing I can do to stop it."

She's the one made of fragile organs wrapped in paper-thin skin, and she's worried about me?

"You, my love, have never been weak," I say with a smile, pulling her chin up so our eyes meet. "Yes, you are a human, but you are the human who saved my life when you killed Asmodeus."

"I only could because he saw me as weak," she says, pouting.

"Then he learned what I've known all along: underestimating you is a dangerous mistake."

She smiles and her cheeks redden slightly.

"There's just a lot going on," she says. "I just don't want any more surprises."

"Well I'm not sure that's a realistic expectation. Our lives have been anything but predictable lately. It'll only get more complicated if we move to another country."

"Move to another country?" she asks, shooting up into a seated position.

Me and my bloody mouth.

"I'm… I mea-" I stutter, trying to stop myself from making a bigger mess of things. "I'm sorry, I was thinking that I had already brought it up, but clearly I haven't. Kami said that the Council has invited us back to London to investigate this further."

She stares at me blankly, her eyes wide.

"What?"

"We do not have to go," I say. "This is entirely your decision. I won't pull you away from your home and your life."

"And what about your home? Do you want to go back?"

"London is a beautiful city, and I loved living there," I say, reaching to stroke her cheek with my hand, "but my home is wherever you are. As long as I'm beside you, I'm home."

"Oh quit it with the romantic stuff!" she scolds, her cheeks now a deep crimson red. "I can't think straight when you're being all sweet."

"Sorry, baby," I say with a chuckle.

"I don't know about moving to London," Ava says. "But I have always wanted to go, and for the most part, I can work from just about anywhere. I would like to see where you grew up… or… I guess you didn't really grow up, did you. Where you… aged? That sounds really weird. Where you… increased in years? Okay, that's even weirder. Where y-"

"Love," I interrupt, smiling.

"Fair enough, not the point," she says. "The point is, if you want to go back to London, we could certainly go—for a while anyway."

I ponder her words. It has been a long time since I've been to London and I have missed it, but everything that comes along with this trip will be complicated, to say the least.

"I'd love for you to come to London with me."

23

Music plays on the stereo as I try, unsuccessfully, to focus on work. I've been staring at my screen for what feels like forever but I've made no progress at all. When I hear Zane come upstairs, I consider it a welcome opportunity to step away from the computer for a moment.

"Hello, love," he says, wrapping his arms around my shoulders.

"Hey," I say, leaning back into him. "Whatcha up to today?"

"Not sure yet. Still waiting to hear back from Kami."

"She hasn't called yet?"

"That's what I just said," he says curtly, pulling away.

"Okay, then, smartass," I say, spinning my chair to face him. "What's got your panties in a twist today?"

"Besides having every demon in the world trying to kill me and a breakable human girlfriend who's now attracting every creep on the planet?"

Ouch.

I get that he's under stress, but I don't see why I'm getting the brunt of his attitude.

"Thanks," I say with an eye roll.

"Oh, so now I've offended you?" he asks.

"Well, I'm not particularly fond of being called breakable and you implying that I'm a burden because I'm human."

"I can't just tiptoe around you being fragile, okay? I mean, even by human standards, you're far from hardy."

Well, fuck you very much.

"Did you come up here just to insult me?" I stand up and cross my arms.

"No, your ego is apparently just as delicate as the rest of you."

"Oh, fuck off!"

"Make me," he says, stepping toward me with a disturbing glint in his eyes.

I push his chest but he remains still and lets out a smug laugh at my failed attempt. As my eyes meet his, a hand swings through the air almost faster than I can see and collides with my face.

I stumble back in shock, just barely keeping my footing. My jaw drops in shock as the stinging sensation spreads from my cheek to my ear and jaw.

"What…" I whisper, unable to comprehend what I'm experiencing.

Where did this come from? Is this really Zane? Could Asmodeus be back?

I shiver at the thought and step backward.

"You're… you're not Zane," I say softly. "You can't be."

"Oh really?" he asks with a devious laugh. He pinches his own arm before looking back at me. "I certainly feel like me."

He swings again, and this time his fist hits my face with enough momentum to knock me off my feet. My tailbone hits the ground with a heavy thud, pain immediately radiating from the spot.

On instinct, I scrabble to my knees and begin to crawl away, but I feel a kick to my side that brings me to the ground.

"Stop!" I scream. "This isn't you!"

Another kick hits my abdomen and the sharp pain makes me gasp for air.

"No! Stop!" I yell again, trying to pull myself away.

I feel my body shaking and I clench my eyes shut, sending tears streaming down my face.

This isn't right. It doesn't make sense. What is happening to him?

The shaking intensifies and I open my eyes to see a panicked Zane hovering above me.

"Baby, wake up!" he says, his voice trembling and his eyes full of fear.

My eyes take in the sight in front of me: a shirtless, terrified Zane and a low white ceiling—the one in our bedroom. I turn my head to the right and see my nightstand and enough sun peeking through the blinds to let me know it's early morning.

Shit. It was a dream.

I let out a heavy sigh and my muscles relax.

"Are you okay?" Zane asks breathlessly.

"Yeah," I say softly. "I had a bad dream. It… it was a dream, right?"

"Why?" he asks. "Were you dreaming of an Incubus? Was it Kieran?"

"Is that possible?"

"I mean, if it were an Incubus, I would be able to feel it," he says. "It was definitely just a dream. Does that mean it was Kieran? Are you afraid of Kieran, baby?"

"No, no. Not at all. It wasn't Kieran."

"Are you sure?" he asks. "You can tell me, love. You seemed so terrified. It tore me apart to see you like that. What was happening? Who were you so scared of?"

I opened my mouth but no words came out. I couldn't tell him, my sweet and loving boyfriend, that the monster in my nightmares was the one he fears the most.

So instead, I do the only thing I can do: I lie.

"It was no one, just a creepy shadow. They didn't even have a face."

———

Jen sits across the table from me with her eyes wide and a stunned look on her face.

"You didn't…" she says.

"I did," I say, shaking my head. "What was I supposed to say?"

"No, you're right. You couldn't just tell him. Based on what you've told me, it sounds like that would've crushed him. It's just… it's a bad situation is all."

"You're telling me," I say, letting my head drop into my hands.

"He can't hear us, can he?" she asks softly, raising her shoulders slightly and looking around the apartment.

"No, Kami came and picked him up to bring him to her house this morning. They're meeting with some supernatural doctor of some sort."

"Okay, good. So do you think you're really afraid of Zane? Because if you are, I can help you get away. We can figure it out."

"No!" I snap. "I am not at all afraid of Zane. Even in the dream, I knew something was wrong. I knew it wasn't him… but…"

"But what?"

"Sometimes I have nightmares—or flashbacks—about Asmodeus attacking me when he looked like Zane."

"He attacked you while looking like Zane?? You didn't tell me that part!"

"He was a sadistic creep," I say, my jaw clenched. "He wanted me to think that Zane had betrayed me because he knew it would hurt Zane. He filmed it and sent it to Zane."

"Fucking fracking fuck, Ava," she says, her hand covering her mouth in shock. "What a son of a bitch. I'm glad you killed him, otherwise I'd have a demon to kill and these are *not* demon-murdering shoes."

I giggle as I look down at her chunky black heeled boots.

"I'm so sorry, girl," she says, shaking her head and closing her eyes for a moment. "I hate that all of that stuff happened to you, but I think these dreams are a totally normal reaction to trauma like that. He stole your boyfriend's face—that's fucked up."

"I just don't want him thinking that he's a monster, because he's not."

"I get it." Jen nods with a slight frown. "You're protecting him. I would've done the same thing."

"Thanks," I say with a sigh. "Anyway, I assume you came over for a reason and not just to hear me talk about my dreams."

"Well, the main reason I'm here is because I took a personal day to run a bunch of tests for you guys and I found several interesting things."

"Do tell."

"So, um, has anyone ever tested you for autoimmune diseases?"

"Yeahhh… I think so," I say, suspiciously. "They were all negative."

"Well, since I wanted to learn more about your body's healing, I ran a couple tests and your ANA test came back positive."

The words *came back positive* are so foreign to me that I blink slowly several times to process her words.

"What?" I ask, dumbfounded.

"I don't know which, but you have an autoimmune disease."

"You… I… I have… the test actually shows something?"

"It does," she says. "It's um… not a great thing to hear, I know, but…"

Nobody wants to have a serious disease, but at the same time, knowing that there's an official name for whatever is wrong with me is an incredible relief.

"No, Jen," I say, leaping across the table to give her a hug. "This is so, so helpful. Thank you!"

"Wow," she says, dumbfounded as I pull away. "I didn't see that as going over all that well, but I know you wanted answers. I'm glad this is a start for you."

"What else did you find?"

"Well, because your body's immune system is fighting itself, the supernatural antibody-equivalents in Zane's blood seem to be working overtime. It doesn't seem to mean much for you, but it might be having an effect on Zane's healing. I need to do more tests before I can draw any conclusions."

"You mean I'm making him sick?" I ask. My heart stops at the thought.

"No, no," she says, shaking her head vehemently. "If anything, you're making him stronger. His body replicates the healing effects in yours, but his body has nothing to heal. It's hard to say exactly what's going on, but I think it could be a good thing. This could contribute to even more advanced healing for him. At the very least, he won't be getting a cold anytime soon."

I chuckle at the mere idea of Zane with a cold. He acted like a baby a few days ago when he had to vicariously deal with period cramps. I can only imagine how he'd handle a stuffy nose or a cough.

"I'm glad being sick can at least be a good thing for once, I guess," I say.

"Anyway," Jen says, pulling a few folded sheets of paper from her pocket, "I was able to find the pheromones in the blood, like we thought. It seems to be closest to chemicals found in quails during mating."

"Quails?" I say, trying to hold back a laugh.

"Yep," she says, giggling. "You're dating a bird man. Speaking of which, we never finished our conversation the other day when Zane got all defensive about it. What are we talking? Is it unusually large? Unusually small? Barbed? Ribbed for her pleasure?"

"Eww, Jen!" I shriek. "Barbed?"

"Yeah, it's a thing. Google cat penises!"

"No, I will not Google that and neither should you or anyone else. How did you even end up… you know what? I don't wanna know. What did you find out about the pheromones?"

"Well, you're in luck, because I am the one-and-only, super-awesome Jen…" she says with a smile. "I know how to fix it."

24

 ZANE

I take a sip of tea from one of Kami's speckled white ceramic mugs before setting it back down on the coffee table.

"You alright?" Kami asks, sitting beside me on the couch with her own cup of tea in her hands.

Am I? Fuck, I don't know.

"Yeah, sure," I say with a sigh. "I guess."

"Well, I'm convinced," she says with a laugh.

"It's just… Ava just woke me up early this morning."

"Oh," she says, raising an eyebrow. "I would expect that would put you in a better mood."

She smirks at me and takes a sip of her tea.

"Not like that," I say, my eyes narrowing. "She had a nightmare."

"Oh. What kind of nightmare?"

"I don't know. She was pretty vague about it, like she didn't want to tell me. I woke up to this anxious feeling, and she was tossing back and forth, whimpering and gasping. She was mumbling 'no' and 'stop' like someone was trying to hurt her. When I woke her up, she just seemed so panicked. I hate seeing her like that. It was just like before with… with the dream about Kieran… or, technically, Asmodeus."

"Do you think it was Kieran? Or another Incubus?"

"No," I say, shaking my head. "When it was Asmodeus, I could feel everything as if it were real—because it was, really. But this, it was just a dream."

"Then what's the big deal?"

"When she opened her eyes, she was just so frightened. I thought if she saw me, she'd know she was okay, but instead, she just looked afraid. I just hate feeling like I couldn't help her."

"Well, maybe you can't."

"Real bloody helpful, that is," I say, leaning back into the couch with a sigh.

"I just mean that you can't save Ava from everything. Sometimes she's going to be scared or hurt or upset and there will be nothing you can do about it. It can be the hardest part of a relationship for anyone, but for you-"

"It's unbearable," I say, finishing her sentence.

I've never been good at accepting that some things are out of my control. And when it comes to Ava, not being able to help her just wrecks me.

We're interrupted by the chime of the doorbell.

"That must be them," she says, standing up and disappearing into the next room.

Finn agreed to pick up the Anatopath from the airport and bring her here. If Kami or I went out in public right now, it would probably cause a riot.

"You a'right, mate?" Finn asks as he walks in, followed by Kami and a tiny, gaunt woman.

"I'm good, thanks," I say, standing up to give him a hug.

"Zane, this is Galena," Kami says, gesturing to the woman who I presume is the Anatopath.

Galena is pale with long brown curls stacked in a messy pile atop her head. She's wearing a long, loose purple dress and an oversized black fur coat.

"Nice to meet you," the woman says with a nod, tucking her arms behind her back.

"Thank you for coming," Kami says. "Tea?"

The woman shakes her head and sits down in a white armchair across from me. Kami takes a seat between us and Finn sits beside me on the couch.

"Alright then," the woman says. "Let's cut to the chase, eh? I take payment up front, no small talk. I reach out, touch as needed, until I get a sense for what is wrong with you, then I tell you what I've learned. I don't guarantee solutions."

"Okay then," Kami says, furrowing her brows slightly as she pulls an envelope from her pocket. "I suppose I can appreciate a woman who gets down to business. Here's your payment."

Kami hands Galena the envelope, which she briefly thumbs through before stuffing it into her own purse.

"So you'd like me to sense the both of you, correct?" she asks Kami, gesturing to her and me.

"Yes," Kami says.

Galena reaches a hand out to touch Kami's neck, staring deeply into her eyes as she purses her lips.

"Mmm…" Galena hums. "Well, you're right. You're linked to more power than you should otherwise have. The collective power in you is more than that of a single Siren. I can sense it."

Kami blinks anxiously and looks over at me.

"I can't quite see why Sirens aren't being reborn," Galena says, squinting slightly. "I'm not able to connect to that through you."

Galena pulls her hand away and stands up, walking over to me and placing her hand on my shoulder.

"Oh…" she says, bending down slightly beside me and closing her eyes. "You're… you're different."

Bloody hell. That's never a good thing.

"Different how?" Kami asks, beating me to the question.

"So, you," Galena says, gesturing to Kami, "have the powers of multiple Sirens within you. But Zane… he has multiple souls."

"I what?" I ask.

"Shhh!" she scolds, shooting me an irritated look. "There's so much happening within you. You're… you have a mate of some sort… a bond, yes?"

I nod, if only to avoid being chastised for talking again.

"There's a line connecting you together. You must be soulmates. I can sense… her? Yes, her…" she says. "She's unique. Feels… human?"

I nod again.

"I like her," she says with a slight smile. I can't help but smirk to myself at her comment.

That's my girl. You don't even have to meet her to like her.

"She's a contradiction," Galena continues. "She's fragile but strong. Kind but forceful. It makes sense that she has a battle within her."

"What does that mean?" I ask.

Her eyes pop open and she gives me an irritated look for talking, then closes her eyes again.

"Her body is fighting itself, and fighting yours," she says. I want to ask more, but I'm trying not to push my luck. "Her blood is working against her. I've seen this before in humans—it's usually some type of disease. Your blood is working against it, though, trying to help her. It's working in you too; healing what shouldn't need to be healed."

Did Kami find the world's most obnoxiously cryptic Anatopath just to slowly drive me insane?

"You're a curious case," she continues, opening her eyes and touching my neck. I find myself growling slightly at the intimate touch, but she doesn't pull away. "The restrained Siren, with a human mate, an ill one—and your soulmate, no less. I can reach quite deep."

"Does that mean you have an answer?" Kami asks.

"There is something I can sense, but it's hazy," Galena says. "Extreme heat, but no sun. Something is in the air."

She pulls her hand away and sighs.

"I'm sorry, that's all I see," she says.

"I know you didn't promise answers," Kami says, "but is there anything we can do? At least to solve the immediate problem?"

"Yes," she says with a nod. "It may be a little… unorthodox, but I would recommend Tamarix."

My stomach sinks.

No. Fuck no.

"Tamarix?" Kami asks. "You want us to get high?"

"That's not really the point," she says. "The psychological high would be more of an unintended side effect. Tamarix will weaken the power of your pheromones and make it so you can go out in public. It will also likely make you intoxicated, yes, but it's better than the alternative."

"What's option B?" I ask, my heart beginning to race.

I fucking hate Tamarix. Plenty of immortals use it as a recreational drug, but not me. There's a reason I don't even drink in excess. I hate the feeling. I hate being out of control.

"*It's okay,*" Finn's voice sounds in my head. "*I know this freaks you out. It's gonna be fine.*"

The fuck it is.

"You're lucky I have any options for you at all," she says with a scoff.

"We appreciate your time, Galena," Kami says, "but Zane is really not a fan of feeling tipsy or inebriated. Do you have anything else you can suggest?"

"I'm sorry, but no, I don't."

A low growl vibrates in my chest.

I rather be trapped indoors for the rest of my life than have to take Tamarix just to leave the house.

I feel nauseous and anxious at the same time.

"Mate, we'll figure something out," Finn says. *"I know how much you hate it. We'll solve this."*

I open my mouth to speak, but realize there's no use. This is all she's going to give us. We're on our own.

25

 ZANE

I close the door and throw my keys onto the table with a sigh. Ava is curled up on the couch with a blanket and her laptop.

"What's wrong?" she asks, raising her brows and setting her computer to the side. "Bad news?"

"Nothing we didn't already know," I say, joining her on the couch.

Ava gives me a kiss on the cheek and I lie down on her lap. As her fingers comb through my hair, a calm rushes over me that only she seems to be able to provide.

"Well, Jen was able to help a lot," she says in a chipper voice. "She thinks she can make some sort of cure for you guys by the end of the week."

"You're kidding," I say, sitting upright.

"Nope. She's got some sort of science thing… a hormone protagonist or something?"

"I really doubt that's what she said."

"Well, whatever," she says, sticking out her tongue. "It's a sciencey thing and she seems to think it will work."

"That's incredible!" I say, pulling her in for a tight hug.

"Okay, okay! You're squishing me!"

"Sorry, love, I'm just relieved. The answers we were looking at, well… they were nonstarters."

"I'm happy to bring you some good news, then. She said it may not be perfect and we all may still have some effects of the pheromones, but people shouldn't go totally nuts on us anymore."

"That's fine by me."

"Aaaand… she had another discovery."

"What…?" I ask tentatively.

"She said that I have an autoimmune disorder."

I blink at her, stunned.

"What does that mean?" I ask.

"I mean, it's not great news. It sort of means my immune system is attacking me," she says.

"Your blood is working against you…" I mumble, repeating the words Galen had told me earlier.

"Um, yeah, I guess so. But knowing brings us closer to answers and closer to a solution."

"So what does this mean? Is there something that could help you?"

"Well, it's a lifelong illness; there's no cure or anything. But there are a bunch of treatments I can try."

"That's bloody brilliant!" I say, pulling her in for another squeeze.

"If you're going to keep squishing me every time I tell you good news, I'm going to have to start coming up with bad news instead."

"Do you have bad news?"

"No. Jen is pretty jealous that we're going to London without her, though."

"If this were a leisure trip, I'd say she could come but-"

"She knows, she gets it. Besides, Jen can't really just leave work to go on a demon-hunting adventure."

"To be clear, I do not intend this to involve demon hunting in any way," I say, pulling her chin up so that her eyes meet mine. "If we're doing this, I'll need to know you're safe at all times."

"Why are you so concerned about me? I thought the demons think I'm dead."

According to Kami, it's not just the demons. Apparently word got back to the Council that Ava was dead and she decided not to correct them. It's not that we don't trust the Council, but—no, actually, I don't trust them at all. It's best that no one knows that Ava is still around, otherwise people will have questions.

"They do," I say with a nod. "Actually, they're not the only ones. But that means that I won't be able to be with you all the time, to protect you."

"I know I'm a human and all, but that doesn't mean you have to babysit me 24/7."

"Yes, love, I'm aware."

Probably should wait to tell her that I asked Finn to come along and keep watch over her.

"You agreed to that way too easily," she says, furrowing her brow skeptically. "Are you planning on tying me to the bed when we get there or something?"

My body immediately reacts to her words, and my focus becomes clouded with lust.

Tying her to the bed certainly wasn't my plan, but it seems like a great idea now.

Ava sweeps her tongue across her lower lip and looks up at me from behind her lashes. I see the green glow of my eyes reflecting in hers.

What was I saying?

"Have you gone silent on me?" she asks with a knowing smirk.

"Are you trying to fluster me, cheeky girl?" I ask, scooping her onto my lap. Her knees fall onto either side of my legs so that she's straddling me. The sensation of her body against mine sends a rush of heat through my veins.

"Who, me?" she asks, biting her lip. "How could a little human fluster a big, tough Siren?"

With each word, she grinds her hips against me and my eyes roll back with pleasure.

This 'little human' is fucking walking Viagra.

"You-" I start to say, but she leans in to kiss my neck.

Fuck.

I try to speak again, but all that comes out is a guttural moan.

She giggles with her lips against my neck. In a swift motion, I flip us so that I'm on top of her.

"I'll take that as a yes?" she asks with a teasing smile.

"Hasn't anyone ever told you not to tempt a Siren, baby?"

"I can't help it. You're just so… temptable." She nibbles at her lower lip, pulling it in with her teeth.

"Better stop biting that lip, love, or I might bite it for you."

She leans in until her lips brush my ear, her soft breath against my neck sending tingles down my spine.

"Yeah?" she whispers. "What if I want you to?"

My every nerve ignites and our lips collide again. I dip my hand into her jeans and stroke against her panties as she moans.

"You flustered, love?" I ask teasingly.

Her eyes hold a mixture of lust and determination that lets me know I'm truly in for it now.

She tugs me tighter against her with her legs wrapped around my hips, digging her nails deep into my back. I growl as the feeling overwhelms me.

This woman is going to kill me, and I'm going to enjoy every bloody minute of it.

I feel her fingers graze the sensitive area where my wings would extend and an involuntary whimper leaves my lips. Before I can react, her nails dig in hard and a sudden burst of ecstasy rocks my body.

"Ahhhh fuuucckkkk," I moan, grinding against her involuntarily as my self-control abandons me.

In an instant, I shred her jeans, leaving her in lacy black panties and a T-shirt. She tugs down her panties as I rip off my own trousers and toss them across the room.

"I need you," she says breathily.

Don't have to ask me twice.

I race to the bedroom for a condom, slipping it on and returning to her in a time that is almost certainly a personal best. I jump on top of her, but she pushes against me so we roll onto the floor, with her straddling me.

I erupt in a slew of curses as she lowers herself onto me. She raises and lowers her hips at a torturous pace, but soon quickens and begins grinding against me.

I push the coffee table to the side and grip her arse in my hands before flipping us so that I'm now on top. I thrust hard and fast until I hear her staggered breaths and gasps of bliss. Her nails dig into my wing ridges again and I can't hold on any longer.

I'm overcome with waves of euphoria, shivering and shuddering as I collapse on top of her. I breathe for a moment until my vision clears and my sense returns, then pull myself away just enough to look into Ava's eyes.

Her expression is strange, almost shocked. Her eyes are hazy but wide and questioning.

"Something wrong, love?" I ask.

She stares at me blankly for a moment before responding.

"Your… your wings."

"Oh," I say, realizing that I've let my wings—well, now just one wing—unfurl during sex. "Yeah, well… certainly not the first time."

"No, Zane, you don't understand…" Ava says. "You… Your wings… You have two."

26

Zane pulls himself out of the pool, his skin wet and shimmering in the light of the setting sun. My eyes flow from his inked chest down to his chiseled abs and red swim trunks.

Yep. I'm officially perving on my boyfriend.

Does it even count as perving if he's my boyfriend?

He grabs an orange towel and dries his hair before draping it over his shoulders and walking inside. He pauses for a moment as our eyes meet.

"You eyeing me up, love?" he asks with a smirk.

"Wha-… I…" I stammer. "I'm not eyeing… *You're* eyeing you up."

"That was terribly convincing. Almost believed you." He laughs and raises an eyebrow suggestively, walking toward me.

"Oh shut up," I say, sticking my tongue out at him. "You're like, biologically engineered to be attractive, okay? It's not my fault, it's your darned Siren biology."

"You're immune to my powers now, love." He wraps a hand around my waist and tugs me in against his chest.

That doesn't make me immune to muscles and tattoos, smartass.

He leans in for a kiss, but we're interrupted by the ringing of the doorbell.

"Jen?" he asks with a sigh.

"Yep," I say with a half-smile. "She's supposed to be bringing our 'cure' by."

"I guess I should get dressed then." He plants a kiss on my forehead before reluctantly stepping back and heading toward the bedroom.

I walk over to the door and open it to a smiling Jen with a large paper bag in hand.

"Hey girl!" she says. "I come bearing gifts, and by gifts I mean a probably not particularly fun shot for the both of you."

"Aw thanks, you shouldn't have," I tease.

I invite her inside and we both sit at the kitchen counter.

"So what do we do?" I ask.

"Unfortunately, I'm not really trained to give shots, but the easiest place is the butt… Which is a bit awkward for everyone."

"Okay, okay," I say, feeling a bit squeamish. "So we do… that… and then what? Does it work immediately?"

"I'd give it at least twelve hours. We can test it out tomorrow."

"How?"

"I figure we'll just send you into a public place, keep watch, pull you out of there if anything goes wrong."

"What?" Zane's voice shouts from the other room. He quickly appears beside us in a white t-shirt and jeans.

"We have to test it at some point," Jen says.

"Sure, but we test it with me."

"No," she says. "Ava makes more sense as a test subject. She has less Siren blood and the effect is weaker for her, so she's a better first subject. Plus, she has human biology and this antagonist serum is based on human medicine. It could affect you completely differently."

"So we just throw her to the wolves?" he asks.

"It's fine, Zane," I say with a shrug. "If I'm the best first test, then so be it. Worst case, I can just leave and Jen will be nearby to watch out for me."

"At the very least, I'm coming too. I'm not letting you two get into trouble on your own again so you have to call Kieran."

"You can stay in the car with me if you must, caveman," she replies with a teasing eye roll.

"So, we take the stuff, then we test tomorrow?"

"Seems like a plan," she says. "I assume caveman wants to give you the shot himself."

"I think I missed something," Zane says, turning to me.

"It's a shot in the butt," I explain.

"Oh," he says. "Yeah, I'm definitely handling that. I do actually know what I'm doing on that front."

"Eww," Jen says, fake-gagging. "Talk about TMI, there, buddy! I don't need to know whatever freaky butt stuff you guys get up to!"

Honestly, with all the questions Jen has asked about Zane's penis, she can hardly claim innocence. She started it.

"I'm not saying anything dodgy," he says with a glare. "I'm a trained medic."

"You are?" Jen asks. "Is there a Siren training academy or something?"

"He was a soldier," I explain.

"A soldier? Like… in the Middle East or…?"

"Like in World War II," Zane says with a smirk.

Jen's eyes widen and her jaw goes slack.

"I am so dumb," she says, shaking her head. "Of course you're older than you look. It's just like Wolverine; how did I not realize? You don't by any chance have an adamantium skeleton, do you?"

"I didn't understand half of those words," he says, his face contorted and confused.

"Wait, if this works and we try this stuff on you, is a needle even gonna work? Like, are we gonna bend the needle or anything?"

"Actually, that's a good point." He rubs his forehead. "We'll probably have to pierce the skin first. We'll cross that bridge when we get there."

Before Jen can respond, her phone rings and she pulls it out of her pocket to answer.

"Hey, what's up?" she says into the phone, giving us an apologetic expression. "Yeah, I just stopped by Ava's on my way home."

She rolls her eyes.

"No, it's just Zane and Ava," she continues. "Why do you keep asking about her anyway? … Yeah, she's my friend, and Ava is my bestie and she's with Zane and… Why am I justifying this to you? What does it matter?"

She huffs and grumbles to herself before stuffing the phone back in her pocket.

"She freaking hung up on me!" she screeches.

"Who?" I ask.

"Deb," she says, scrunching her face. "Ever since the reunion she's been totally weird to me and keeps asking me why I'm spending so much time over here and about Kami. It's like, Deb if you like Kami fine but you don't get to act all bitchy over it."

Oh.

I was a bit worried when Jen told me she had moved in with Deb. I was afraid old feelings would surface and she'd end up hurt. What didn't occur to me was that Jen might not be the one who gets hurt.

"And you think she likes Kami?" I ask.

"I mean, why else would she be acting like this?"

Zane smirks as he pulls out a bag of chips and pours some into a bowl.

"Sure, why else?" Zane asks, giving me a knowing look.

"Anyway," she says with a sigh, "I'm gonna go home to my crazy roommate-slash-ex-girlfriend. I'll text you to set something up for tomorrow."

With that, we say our goodbyes and she makes her way out the door.

———

"Why this place, anyway?" Zane asks, nervously kneading at the steering wheel.

"I told Ava to choose someone who had never shown any interest in her," Jen says, "and apparently the people at this coffee shop have never flirted with her before."

"I'm liking this place more now," he says with a grin. His smile quickly fades and his eyes narrow. "Wait, that's an abnormal thing for you? Are people flirting with you everywhere you go?"

I feel his anxiety rising and I give him a comforting pat on the back.

"She's a woman," Jen says, "and an attractive one. You're basically doomed, buddy. Might as well accept that your lady is in high demand."

"Saying it like that is not really helping," he says with a slight growl.

"Did you just growl at me?" she asks, scrunching her lips.

"No, it wasn't at you in particular."

"How do you even growl? I thought you were part bird. Do birds even growl?"

"You and Ava are quite stuck on this bird thing, aren't you?"

"Onnn that note," I interrupt, trying to get us back on track, "I'm going to head inside."

"Wait," Jen says, pulling out her phone and holding out a Bluetooth headset. "I need to call you on this and you need to put it on."

Jen has insisted on being in my ear for this. She says it's for my own safety, but I'm pretty sure she's just playing out a spy fantasy.

I hand her my phone. While she's setting it up, I turn to Zane, who's doing his best to hide his apprehension.

"While you guys are waiting in the car, why don't you talk to Jen about your wing situation?" I ask. "Maybe she can help."

"I… I don't know…" he mumbles.

"Wing situation? Ooh, ooh! I wanna help!" she says, handing me the Bluetooth headset and my phone.

I jump out of the car, ready to get this over with, and I give them a small wave. *Okay. Let's do this.*

<hr>

ZANE

I watch Ava walk toward the coffee shop.

"So, what wing situation?" Jen asks, getting out of the car and moving into the front seat beside me.

"Oh, I uh…" I say, trying to figure out how I even go about explaining this.

"Great, that's a good sign," Jen says, talking into her phone.

Ava's inside, no issues so far.

We watch through the glass doors and windows out front. I can see Ava walking to the counter as a young man steps up to the register. I concentrate in an attempt to pick up their conversation.

"…get for you?" the man asks as I catch the tail end of his sentence.

"Um… caramel macchiato… and a bagel please," she says.

"She's ordering…" Jen explains.

"Yeah, I can hear them," I say.

She pauses for a moment before nodding and returning to listening on her phone as we watch the interaction.

"Good, now get closer," Jen says.

I feel conflicted at every step. It goes against everything within me to allow Ava to walk directly into danger, especially when I'm right here and can do something about it.

Ava steps closer to the counter until she's leaning on its edge. The man seems unfazed as he prepares her order.

As much as I'd happily relieve him of his limbs, I'm relieved I won't have to.

"So if this works, you guys are all set to go to London, huh?" Jen asks.

"Erm… yeah," I say, trying to pull my focus from Ava in the cafe.

"Is it just you and Ava, or are all the Super Friends coming along?"

"Well, my mate Finn is coming and Kami too. I haven't told Kieran yet, but I wouldn't be surprised if he invited himself along."

"Oh dang, you haven't told your BFF yet? Not cool, man," she says, shaking her head.

"To be fair, we're currently stuck at home until we solve this."

"True," she says, turning her attention back to Ava.

"Okay, final test," Jen says into the phone. "You've gotta touch him."

A growl rumbles through my chest at the thought.

If she has to touch him for this test, can't she just kick him in the shin? That counts as a touch, doesn't it?

"How the heck am I supposed to do that?" Ava mumbles into the phone.

"When he hands you your order, just brush his hand or something."

My hands tighten around the steering wheel until my knuckles turn white.

This is fine. I can handle this. I'm the bloody Iron Siren, aren't I?

I hear a slight crack in the plastic of the steering wheel, so I pull my hands away.

Not looking to buy a third replacement on that.

"So what's going on with the wings, then?" Jen asks. "Talk to me. It's a good distraction."

"I uh," I say with a sigh. "So Ava explained that I cut off my wing to save her and form the bond between us, right?"

"Yep."

"Well, the other day we uh… we were, erm… hanging out an-"

"Doing the do, got it," she says with a nod.

Fair dues. So much for my attempt at subtlety.

"Anyway, I spread my wings and they were…. both there."

"You… wait… you had both of them? Your wings?"

"Yeah, the one I cut off is back."

"But you guys heal quickly, don't you?"

"True, though… to create a new wing… it would require intense healing and power, far more than any Siren has."

"And don't you have much more power right now? With the enhanced powers and Siren deaths and whatnot?"

"I… I suppose so," I say, pondering for a moment. "'Healing what shouldn't need to be healed.'"

"Huh?" she asks.

"The Anatopath, an Immortal doctor if you will. She told me that Ava's immune system was working inside me."

"Ohh interesting. That would make a lot of sense, actually. I suspected her autoimmune issues might be enhancing your healing abilities."

"So what do I do about it? Is it fine, then?"

"I would guess you're just healing at a much faster rate, with the effects of Ava's autoimmune disease and the Siren power boost. But you might want to avoid getting too excited for a few weeks."

"What's this now?"

"You know, no bang-bang, P-in-V fun time?"

Bloody hell.

"Why's that?" I ask.

"Well, if your wings are weak or still healing, I'd keep them tucked up for now. You don't want to do anything that makes them pop out or stretch or whatever it is they do."

"Fuck that," I say. "You tell Ava that and I'll have to kill you."

She lets out a hearty laugh.

"You've got it bad, man," she says. She pauses to listen to her phone for a moment. "That's great! You can come back to the car when you're done."

"What?" I ask.

"Ava's fine. She did the touch test and the guy didn't react. She's just waiting for her bagel and then she's coming back."

"Thank fuck." I sigh and slump into my seat, watching Ava through the windows.

A man walks up next to her as she leans against a nearby counter waiting for her food.

"I love your hair," the man says, and my blood pressure instantly rises.

"Thanks," she says softly.

I straighten up in my seat with one hand on the door handle, ready to leap out of the car.

"Hey," he says. "Can I get a little sugar?"

Motherfucking…

I launch out of the car and race into the cafe. I hear Jen calling, trying to stop me, but I burst through the door before she can reach me. Ava looks surprised as she walks toward me. My eyes scan the room for her pursuer, and I find him at the same counter with a couple of paper packets in his hands.

"Did he hurt you?" I ask, grabbing Ava's shoulders and looking her over.

"Who?" she asks. "The cashier? No, I'm fine."

"No, that twat." I gesture to the man, who is now sitting at a small table.

"You dope," Jen says, huffing as she catches up to me. "He wasn't flirting with Ava."

I look back at the man as he pours the sugar packets into his coffee.

Literal fucking sugar.

Well, at least I didn't knock the bloke out.

27

 ZANE

"I've been meaning to ask you about something," I say to Jen as we stand side by side in the elevator.

"Yeah, I kind of figured that when you offered to escort me to the parking garage," she says with a chuckle. "Seeing as how you live in the nicest, safest building I've ever seen."

"That obvious, eh?"

"A bit." She shrugs. "Let me guess, you're looking for tips on how to propose to Ava?"

My head swivels toward her and I swallow hard.

"What? No. Why would you say that?"

She bursts into laughter, leaning against the elevator railing.

"Wow, for a guy who's been alive as long as you, you'd think you'd have a better poker face."

"I ha… I don't… Did you just call me old?"

"I mean, if the grandpa loafer fits…"

I shoot her a glare as the elevator comes to a stop. The doors open and we step out into the underground garage.

"So what *did* you want to talk about?" she asks.

"Ava told me about the tests you ran for her—that you said she had a positive test for an autoimmune disease. I wanted to ask: what do we do about it?"

"What do you mean?"

"I mean… I don't understand much about the human healthcare system, even less so about the American one. But it seems rather…"

"Shit?"

"Yeah."

"You're not wrong. American healthcare is pretty atrocious, even worse for women and people of color. And when it comes to people like Ava with chronic conditions or anything outside the norm, it's a downright clusterfluff."

"Clusterfluff?"

"A shitshow. A sharknado. An explosive dumpster fire of suck."

I laugh and shake my head.

"But what do we do about it? I know she's said there's nothing I can do, but… it feels like there should be something."

"Besides kicking her doctor's asses?" she asks with a giggle.

"It has certainly occurred to me."

"Well, I'm sure Ava hasn't told you this part because she doesn't want to take advantage, but there's a fast track to better healthcare that works pretty much everywhere."

"Which is?"

"Money." She shrugs her shoulders and gives me an awkward smile as we reach her car.

"Money? You're telling me I could pay for her to have better doctors?"

"Yep. It's sad but true. Wealthy people get a totally better system than the rest of us. The doctors are more capable, the waits are shorter, the tests are faster, the treatments are better. You throw enough money at something and your whole situation can change."

"Bloody hell…"

"I mean, I don't know exactly how much money you've got, but you're super old and immortal and you live in a fancy-ass penthouse, so I figure you've gotta have some fix-my-problems money."

"I do," I say with a smirk.

It's ironic, because I've spent quite a long time accumulating it, but I've never had any idea what to do with the money that I have. It's probably quite an out-of-touch problem to have. But I had no idea human health could be purchased. That's fucked up in every possible way.

"Then google 'concierge medicine,'" she says.

"So I basically bribe some doctor and Ava will get better medical care?"

"Yep. Specifically, look for a rheumatologist. It might cost an arm and a leg, but it could get our girl feeling better a lot faster."

Well that is as good as done.

———◦———

I tap my fingers against my knee as I wait for the doctor to arrive. Ava sits beside me on the couch, chewing on her lower lip as she reads her book.

"You're being weird," she says, looking up at me.

"How am I being weird?"

"You've been antsy all morning and you keep checking the time on your watch. What are you waiting for?"

"I can't get anything past you, can I love?"

"What's going on?"

"I've invited someone to stop by. The front desk sent them up just now, so they should be here mo-"

As if on command, the doorbell rings and I immediately rise to my feet.

"That's not suspicious at all," she says, watching me with narrow eyes.

Part of me considered consulting her before hiring private doctors, but after looking at the price, I knew there was no chance she'd agree to let me spend that kind of money on her. In this case, I decided it was better to ask forgiveness than ask permission.

I open the door to a team of four well-dressed professionals: two women in muted business attire underneath white doctor's coats and two more people—a man and a woman—both in fitted navy blue scrubs. The woman in scrubs is carrying a large black bag and the man has a large black plastic crate on wheels.

"Hello," one woman says. "I'm Dr. Ali, this is Dr. Singh. We're here from Modern Medical for an appointment with Ava Reynolds."

"What??" I hear Ava squeak behind me.

"Hey, you're right on time," I say, opening the door all the way and ushering them in. "Please, come in."

I hear Ava scramble to get up from the couch as the group walks in. When I catch her eye, she's giving me a furious glare and anxiously smoothing out her clothes.

"Hi, are you Ava?" Dr. Ali asks.

"Hey, yes. Hi," she says, shooting me another quick look that tells me she's definitely going to scold me for this later.

"Oh, you don't have to get up for us," the doctor says. "You can stay as you were."

"Please feel free to sit and set up anywhere you'd like," I say.

They each get to work rather quickly; one pulls out a laptop while the two in scrubs start opening up their cases and setting up various equipment. Ava looks like a deer in the headlights as she sits down and watches the scene unfold. The whole team moves in a coordinated, effortless way as though their every move had been carefully choreographed.

"I'm Dr. Ali," she says to Ava, holding an iPad in the crook of her arm as she speaks. "I'm a general practitioner with Modern Medical. Generally, we do our first meeting with just one doctor, but in your case, we know you have a recent positive ANA test that warranted further review from a rheumatologist, so Dr. Singh is also here with us to discuss more."

Ava's eyes are wide as saucers as she nods. I move to stand behind where Ava is sitting and lean against the back of the couch, my hands on either side of her shoulders.

The doctors talk with Ava for a moment before diving into medical questions. They're remarkably thorough and focused, going over every little detail of her medical records, including the test results that I had Jen send in. I watch in a combination of awe and horror as they manage to provide better medical care in thirty minutes than Ava seems to have encountered in years of failed appointments.

I had no idea just how monumental the difference could be in quality of care if you add a few zeros to the cost. I'm nearly kicking myself for not doing it earlier.

"Based on your past history of anemia, your ANA and C3 results, and your symptom history," Dr. Singh says, "I'm relatively confident that I know what's going on here. While we're here, we'll run some more tests, but barring anything too unexpected, I think we're looking at lupus."

"Huh?" Ava says.

"Has anyone ever talked to you about Systemic Lupus Erythematosus?"

"I… I think someone mentioned it once, but they said I didn't have it."

"Hmm… I'm actually quite surprised by that. You meet all the criteria quite conclusively, and I see you had abnormal C3 Complement results a few months ago. Did your doctors mention those to you?"

"I think they thought it was related to the liver issues I had with that medication."

"Hmm…" Dr. Singh scrunches her nose slightly, as if she's silently judging

Ava's past doctors. "Well, I'm not sure that would make sense, but I wouldn't be surprised if your liver failure was actually a result of your untreated lupus. Certain autoimmune complications can make you unusually susceptible to liver injury."

"Oh."

"Actually…" She squints at her iPad for a moment. "I'm actually surprised how well you bounced back from that liver episode. It's quite unusual. That part I'm not really sure about, but the body is unpredictable."

Oh, she recovered quickly alright, but due to the effects of the mark and ingesting my wing blood. Not exactly the kind of thing you can tell a doctor.

"So what are the chances it actually is lupus?" Ava asks.

"Honestly, I think we have conclusive data already. I'll still want to get blood and urine samples and a cheek swab while we're here, but it's mostly to confirm what we already know and get a better understanding of which of your systems are currently affected."

"Does that mean that's what she has?" I ask. "Lupus?"

"Yes." She says it like she's not dropping this huge news; that Ava finally has a diagnosis. That she hasn't just given a name to the monster that has been plaguing her for so long.

"Does that mean you can help her?"

"There is no cure for lupus, but there are several management options. Many people with lupus manage their symptoms and live well, and some even achieve remission and will go long periods without having any symptoms at all. It is a manageable condition and we have options. So it's going to take a while to find the right treatments and lifestyle modifications. We'll start with these tests to get a sense of the health of your various body systems and what your liver can tolerate. You said you'll be traveling for a while, but we can start with a list of some of the easier lifestyle changes and you can test those out while you're in England. When you return, we'll have the results and we can evaluate the effectiveness of what you've tried and start looking at medications or other treatments."

The rest of the appointment goes by in a hazy blur—the doctors take Ava's questions for a while, then the techs take some samples for tests. When they're all done, they pack up with the same methodical precision as they've done everything else. They say their goodbyes and I escort them to the door with several rounds of thanks.

When the door closes, Ava lets out a sound that I don't expect: a laugh.

"You're laughing?" I ask.

"I just can't believe it! I have an answer—finally. It's not this nameless shadow haunting my life. It's a real thing that they can treat and they have the tests to prove it. It's real." She launches at me and wraps her arms around my torso, squeezing tight as she rests her cheek against my chest. "I was so ready to tell you off for booking this appointment without telling me, but I can't even be mad because I'm just so relieved."

"I'm glad." I rest my chin atop her head and smile. "I'd happily pay any price to make your life better, love."

"How much did this cost, anyway?"

"You don't want to know."

And she must know that I'm telling the truth, because she doesn't even ask. *Thank fuck. She'd bloody kill me.*

28

"What's wrong with her?" Ava whispers to me.

"I heard that!" Kami says, flopping onto the armchair across from us.

"I'm… I-" Ava mumbles, looking to me for help. Kami interrupts her with a burst of laughter.

"It's fine!" she says, giggling between words. "I had to go update my passport so I am… just a little bi-"

"She's smashed," I say.

"Mashed?" Ava asks, turning to me with a confused expression. "Like… mashed potatoes?"

Kami laughs hysterically, falling over in her chair.

"No, love," I say. "Smashed. I mean, she's high."

"Because she went to get her passport? What am I missing?"

"See Zane, you always tell stuff wrong," Kami says, climbing onto her chair until she's perched on her toes. "Zane told you the Anatopath suggested Tamarix, right? To fix our powers thing. Well it's weird, but it works. So I had to update my passport today, which meant basically a whooooole lot of stupid, boring hanging around in government offices, so I had to take Tamarix to go out so everyone wouldn't be all obsessed with me."

"Tamarix?" Ava asks. "That sounds like a prescription thing."

"It's a tree, actually," I explain.

"Oh shhhhhhh," Kami says, holding a finger to her lips. "I said you're bad at explaining things, so stop explaining things already. Ava, it's a fancy tree bark, like cinnamon, but it has an effect on Immortals. Think of it as cannabis for the supernatural set. It's probably Greek because it has an x in it…"

Kami suddenly starts speaking in fluent Greek and Ava looks at me to confirm she's hearing what she thinks she's hearing. I nod.

"Wait…" Ava says. "I thought you said the Anatopath didn't have any answers for you."

Technically, I said her idea was a nonstarter.

"You know how Z is," Kami whispers loudly. "He's got issues with being in control!"

I don't have issues with being in control. I just want to be in control all the time.

"I didn't come here to be psychoanalyzed," I say with a grumble.

"My bad, Zeazy-Zeez!"

It's official: I'm never again hanging out with Kami when she's like this.

"That's one more impromptu nickname than you're allowed for the day," I say.

"Oh Zeezle," she says with a snicker, "you're adorable when you're grumpy."

"This is precisely why I'm here."

"To be adorable?"

Ava laughs. She seems to be enjoying Kami's inebriated state—which makes one of us.

"To give you Jen's cure."

Ava pulls out the small tote bag with the vial inside.

"Aww, Jen is the greatest!" Kami says. "Her cure worked?"

"Yep. We tested it yesterday and there were no issues."

"Except for the part where Zane almost killed a guy for liking sweet coffee," Ava says with a chuckle.

I shoot her a scowl, but she just smiles in return.

"This sounds like a brilliant story. I want details!" Kami cheers, jumping on the couch between us.

It's always trouble getting these two in the same room, but with Kami acting like she is right now, I'm doomed.

———⦁———

I put the pan of veggies in the oven and close the door. The doorbell rings, and I wipe the cooking oil off my hands with a paper towel before answering it.

"Hey there!" Kami says, "I just stopped by to bring back your luggage scale."

She pulls the scale out of her handbag and hands it to me.

"Oh, thanks," I say. "You all packed up?"

"Yep," she says with a sigh. "I can't believe we're going back to London, I mean, for more than just a visit."

Kami is heading out first, but we'll be meeting her there in a couple of weeks.

"Yeah, it's a bit wild," I say. "I mean, I always imagined I'd move back at some point… until Ava, that is. Had no idea I'd find my fucking soulmate in an American hospital. Now it's just…"

Home is wherever she is.

Bloody hell, that's soppy. Say something less lame.

"…I would consider living here now," I say softly.

Kami gives me a look that implies she was expecting me to say something else, but then just shakes her head and smiles.

"So is Kieran coming with us?" she asks.

"Of course," I say with an eye roll. "From the moment I told him, he wouldn't shut up about English accents and how much he wants to shag Prince Harry and his wife. Honestly, I just invited him along on the condition that we never finish that conversation."

Kami giggles and I toss some salt into the boiling water on the stove.

"Making dinner?" she asks.

"Pasta and veg. You want to stay? We've got enough for three."

"No, no. I might chat for a minute, but I'm just on the way home. I just wanted to drop that off. Is Ava home?"

"She's actually at a physical therapy appointment, but she'll be home in about half an hour."

"Aww, just look at you all domesticated!" Kami squeals, peeking into the oven.

"Oi! I'm getting proper ready to ship you out early."

"Oh, before I forget—do you have any unexpired Oyster cards from your last trip?"

"Check the bedroom dresser," I say, gesturing toward the bedroom.

The water reaches a boil and I pour in the pasta, turning it down just slightly before covering the pan.

Suddenly, I hear a loud gasp from the other room.

"Kami?" I call, rushing to the bedroom to see her standing in front of my open dresser in shock with a box in her hands.

Wait…

Open dresser?

Shit.

I open my mouth to explain, but no words come out.

"Is this… what I think this is?" she asks, gesturing to the taupe box in her hands.

She turns it around to reveal a thin gold bracelet tied in a Hercules knot.

"What else would it be?" I ask, running a hand through my hair.

"Shit, Z!" She covers her mouth and quiets her voice before shoving the box back into my drawer. "Why didn't you tell me?"

"I hadn't gotten around to it!" I huff. "I hadn't exactly expected you to come along and dig through my underthings."

"You told me to look in the dresser!"

"I meant on the dresser!" I say, pointing to a small ceramic tray on the dresser's top with some cash and an Oyster card.

She looks at me and her eyes go wide, before she smiles and launches into a bear hug.

"You're getting fucking married!" she shrieks excitedly as she does her absolute best to crush my bones.

"Calm down, love, I haven't even asked her yet," I say, fighting off a smile. "I haven't even explained to her about the bracelets or what they mean."

Ever since I bought that bracelet, it has worn at the back of my mind.

I've been to war and looked death in the face, so few things scare me.

But I'm terrified she'll say no.

29

 AVA

"What kind of weather should I pack for?" I ask, sifting through a pile of clothes on the bed as Zane sits in a nearby armchair.

"Rain," he says.

"Okay, I brought two raincoats and some boots too. What other weather does London get this time of year?"

"Other weather?" he says with a smirk. I chuck a T-shirt at him and it lands on his head.

"You're not being helpful."

"You're right, love, I'm sorry. Can I try again?"

"Fine," I say with a sigh. "What *is* the weather like?"

"Rain," he says with a serious expression, "…or mist, and sometimes fog."
I roll my eyes.

"That's London's weather, honest. You're probably going to be cold."

"And wet…" I grumble, throwing another heavy coat into the suitcase.

"Oh yes," he says, stepping behind me and wrapping his arms around my waist, "definitely wet."

He kisses my neck and shoulder as I catch on to the innuendo.

"That's not what I meant, you perv!" I say, giggling as I give him a quick smack to the shoulder.

"You really set that one up for me," he says, stepping back.

"So, London—should I bring like… nice going-out clothes or mostly normal everyday clothes?"

"You can always buy whatever you need while we're there."

"Okay, Mister Moneybags. Or I can just pack the clothes I need."

"Bring a couple of outfits for nice nights out, but mostly warm, casual clothes. I want you to be comfortable."

"But what if I need to show up one of your ex-girlfriends?" I ask with a teasing smile.

"In that case," he says with a soft laugh, taking a step forward and grabbing my ass, "you better take this with you."

"You really are a perv today!" I say with a giggle.

"Seriously, love," he says, his expression shifting to a more serious one, "you have no competition to worry about."

A knot forms in my stomach as I contemplate his words. I can't help but notice he didn't say that there was no way we'd run into his exes.

Honestly, I was kind of hoping they were all dead. That would certainly make my life easier.

"I thought you dated Sirens and a bunch of other supernaturally beautiful people," I say.

"Erm… I guess," he says, combing his fingers back through his hair and ruffling it. "I don't really think of them like that. A lot of our friends look like that."

Well, crap.

That's it—I'm officially packing my hottest clothing. I am *not* going to be the ugly human in the land of supermodels.

I search through my closet and spot the tight red bandage dress I wore to the club when we last went out.

It certainly seemed to go over well last time.

I pull out the hanger and turn around to a sour look on Zane's face.

"What?" I ask.

"That dress?" he asks, his eyebrows raised as he swallows hard.

"You don't like it?"

"Erm… of course I like it, it's just… that bloody dress… If my friends back home see you in that dress, I may have to kill them."

I giggle as I watch his eyes turn an increasingly brighter shade of green.

"Okay, no red dress," I say, slipping it back into the closet.

Of course, I reserve the right to buy an even hotter dress depending on how attractive your female friends are.

"Do you think your friends will like me?" I ask.

"Honestly, you've already met most of the important ones—Kami and Finn. I didn't meet Kieran until I lived in the States. The rest are kind of… lower-tier friends. I'm sure they'd like you, but if they didn't, I'll tell 'em to piss off. Who knows who we'll even run into in the old neighborhood."

"I forgot to ask. Where are we staying?"

"Oh," he says with a quizzical look. "We're staying at mine. I have a house there still and my property manager has been looking after it when I'm not around. Kami said she's going to get it ready for us."

Oh.

———·———

ZANE

London, England - 1967

I lean against the wall, watching strangers dance to the band playing on the stage in the corner. Men and women wave their arms in the air with little regard for rhythm or coordination. I light a cigarette and bring it to my lips.

"Where's Tara?" Kami asks, appearing beside me.

"Getting drinks," I reply.

She looks over toward Tara at the bar. I follow Kami's glance to see two men flirting with Tara.

"You're going to let some blokes chat up your woman?" Kami asks, raising an eyebrow.

"She's a Siren," I say. "If she wants them to leave, she'll make them."

"I know she's a Siren. I'm just trying to figure out if *you* are," she says with a laugh. "Seriously, how can you stand it?"

"She can handle herself just fine. Besides, what can happen here? You think she's going to run off with any stranger who fancies her?"

Would I care if she did? Honestly, I'm not sure. At least she'd be happy.

"I'm not saying she's going to run off with them. I'm just saying your reaction isn't particularly Siren-like."

"Well, that's me."

"Hey, hot stuff," Tara says, walking up with our drinks in hand.

"Hey, lovely," I say, pulling her into my side.

"Careful!" she scolds, handing me my beer. "You might make me spill."

"Dance with me?" she asks, taking a sip of her beer as she sways to the music.

"You know I don't enjoy dancing at these places," I say. "Go with Kami."

"But I want to dance with yooouu," she whines, wrapping an arm around my waist and pulling me toward her.

She insisted I come out tonight, so I did, but it's clearly not enough. I already want to go home, but I know she'll say we haven't been here long enough.

She pulls me in for a kiss and I taste a bit of Tamarix on her lips.

"Getting high already?" I ask. "How much did you have?"

"I have extra," she says with a giggle, pulling out a packet of thin brown flakes and leaning into my chest.

"Fucking…" I say, pushing her off me. "You know I hate that stuff."

"You're such a damned prig, Zane," she scoffs, hitting my chest hard with her fist and knocking the wind out of me.

"Hey!" Kami interjects, stepping between us. "Calm down, Tara."

She doesn't get it. She never gets it.

Tara wants to love and be loved. She wants to have a whirlwind romance and passion. And I try—I do. That's why I agreed to a relationship.

But the reality is, I don't have anything to give. And even if I could, I don't want to. I don't want another Ilen. I don't want another city burnt to the ground because I couldn't control myself.

What single person could be worth that level of risk?

"All I wanted to do was have a little fun with my boyfriend!" she yells. "Why can't you just let go and have some fun?"

Why can't I let go?

Because when I let go, everyone dies.

30

Nine hours and fifteen minutes.

On a plane. To London.

To me, that's nine hours and fifteen minutes of torture.

I have to squeeze my stiff joints into a tiny, uncomfortable seat that only reclines about five degrees back. Then that little fan above me will blow cold air into my face, as if the cabin wasn't cold enough.

Do they do this to torture sick people specifically, or do airlines just hate everyone?

"Boarding group A, Premier Plus members, and First Class are now boarding," a voice says over the speakers.

"That's us," Zane says, standing up and grabbing our carry-on bags.

"Aww mannn…" Kieran whines. "Why am I not sitting with you guys?"

"Because you didn't pay for your own ticket," Zane says.

"Hey! You know it'll be helpful to have me there—an undercover demon on your side?"

"I bought your way, didn't I? Don't get greedy now."

Zane and I head for the line.

Oh good. Standing. I love standing.

The line moves forward and when we reach the gate, Zane hands the attendant our tickets and passports. The woman looks them over for a moment before nodding and welcoming us aboard.

"C2?" I ask, looking at the ticket in Zane's hand. "We must be pretty close to the front. I guess that's why we get to board so early."

Zane nods slightly and smiles as we step onto the plane. It's earlier in the morning than I'm capable of functioning, so I let Zane handle the logistics while I follow behind him like a zombie. He stops and I walk directly into his back with a small thump.

"Oof," I grunt. "Why did you stop?"

"These are our seats," Zane says, gesturing to a little two-person pod of sorts in the first class section.

"You're kidding me." My jaw drops open and I stare at the seats—a set of two massive reclining chairs in their own cubicle with footrests, side tables, and full-size TV screens.

"Nope," he says, throwing the luggage into a cubby beneath the footrests as he steps inside.

"I…" I mutter, my feet unable to move. "How much did this cost? Those tickets must've been outrageously expensive!"

"They're fine. Don't worry about it."

I walk in and sit down in the chair. It's surprisingly comfortable.

Is it even possible to fly without that one weird guy next to you who aims his air-conditioning vent right into your face?

"Where is Kieran sitting?" I ask.

"Economy," he says. "I'm not made of money."

"I thought you said they weren't that expensive!"

"They're not… for you. After everything you've told me about your experience of flying, I'm not letting you be in pain for nine hours."

I raise the armrests between our seats and lean in to give him a big hug. He chuckles and I can feel the vibrations in his chest.

"So it's a good surprise then?" he asks.

"It's a great surprise," I say, giving him a light smack on the shoulder. "But you're not allowed to spend that much money on me ever again!"

"Alright, never again."

"Why do I think you've found a loophole?"

"More like twenty," he says with a laugh.

I roll my eyes and stick my tongue out at him.

"I can't believe we're going to London—in first class, no less," I say, leaning into Zane as he wraps his arms around me.

"Honestly, I can't either. It's been so long since I've been," he says with a relaxed sigh as he settles back into his seat. "I've taken a quick trip here and there, but not since we met."

"Are you excited?" I ask.

"I am."

I can feel the excitement through our bond, but it's more than that: happiness, anxiety, and—underneath it all—a deep gnawing fear.

—·—

"How was your flight?" Kami asks as she drives.

It's surprisingly terrifying to suddenly be on the opposite side of the street. I'm doing my best to not gasp every time she makes a tight left turn, but I still find myself digging my nails into the armrest.

"Um… good," I say. "Actually, surprisingly good. I was able to sleep for a while and our seats had their own massagers and a little mini-fridge full of drinks. It was wild!"

"First time flying first class?" she asks.

"Yeah…"

"I only fly first class these days. Flying in the regular seats after you've seen what first class is like… it's just offensive."

"Ehh-hemmm…" Kieran coughs in the front seat.

"Kieran's cheesed off because his ticket was economy," Zane says.

"I'm actually alright with it. The guy I sat next to was hot and had a British accent. I was so close to getting him to join the mile-high club with me."

"I'm pretty sure you can get arrested for that," I say.

"It would be worth it," he says with a mischievous smile. "Do you Brits call it the mile high club? Or is it, like, the one-and-a-half-kilometer club?"

"Why did I bring you again?" Zane asks.

"Same reason you invited, Finn, I bet. You need more bodyguards for Ava."

Excuse me?

"What?" I ask. Zane freezes, refusing to turn to look at me. "Zane?"

"I invited Finn just in case we needed backup," he says. "And I told you I won't be able to be with you the entire time. He can be with you when Kami and I can't be."

Oh good. I have a human sitter.

"I don't need to be babysat," I say, shooting him a glare. Unfortunately, he's still avoiding looking at me, but I'm pretty sure he can feel the hole I'm boring into him with my eyes.

"I know. It's just in case."

"I thought everyone thinks I'm dead anyway. Do you think someone's gonna try to kill a dead girl?"

"Even if the chances are 0.001%, I would never risk your life. Just humor me on this one, love?"

"Okay," I say with a sigh. "But if you keep acting like I'm a porcelain doll, you and I are gonna have words."

Sitting around by myself would probably get boring anyway.

"We're here," Kami says, pulling into a driveway.

I peer out the window at the red brick house, lined in green hedges with a garden out front. It's two stories with a couple of chimneys on the roof and white window frames.

"This is your house?" I ask.

"Not what you expected?" Zane says.

"It's so pretty and quaint," I say. "I feel like your style is so modern and black-and-grey, but this is so… cute!"

"Thanks, love," he says with a laugh. "I've owned it for about a hundred years. It was actually relatively modern when I bought it."

"Huh…" I say, inspecting the mansion.

"I got it all ready for you guys," Kami says. "Should be all set."

"Kami lives just down the road," Zane explains, gesturing in one direction.

We step out of the car as the boys grab the luggage out of Kami's trunk. Kami pulls out a key and opens the front door to reveal a beautiful home with freshly painted white walls and modern decor.

"Wow!" I say as Zane and Kieran enter behind me.

"Damn, Z," Kieran says. "The more I hang out with you, the more I realize I need to get me a sugar daddy… or mommy… or both…"

Zane rolls his eyes and sets the luggage down in the entryway.

"How'd you already get a photo of Ava here?" Kieran asks. I turn to see him inspecting a framed photo of Zane and me sitting on the mantle. "So much for your 'no family photos' policy."

"Policy?" I ask.

Zane and I both walk over to Kieran.

"Yeah, he always said framed photos were something only old married couples had in their house. Something you wanna tell us?"

I blush at the insinuation.

"It's nothing," Zane says, a slight defensiveness in his voice. "I didn't do it. Kami set up the house for us—she's just being cheeky. It means nothing."

I didn't think it meant anything before, but based on his reaction, I'm not so sure.

31

A sliver of sunlight peeks through the window and wakes me from my sleep. Ava's head is tucked into my bare chest, her soft breaths warming my skin.

My eyes open to the familiar brick fireplace in my London bedroom. The crisp white ceiling reminds me of home, but the view out the window reminds me we're not in Port Charlotte. It all feels so surreal.

All of the things that I never thought would happen seem to be happening at this very moment. Being in love with a human, back home in England, coming back to work for The Council, trying to prevent a war that I may very well have started myself… Ten years ago if you had told me I'd be here in this moment, I'd say you were completely mad.

Who knows, maybe I'm the mad one now.

I promised myself I'd never pull someone into my life again after Ilen. After my lack of self-control led to a massacre. Hell, that one mistake almost got Ava killed over a hundred years later.

Ava's chest rises a bit higher, then falls as she wakes.

"Morning, love," I say. She replies with a soft mewl and cuddles further into my chest, her fingers lightly tracing my tattoo.

My skin tingles as she runs her fingers along my chest and I let out a contented hum.

This is perfect.

I mean, sure, we're only here to find out why Sirens are being murdered and hopefully to prevent a war between Immortals and demons, but besides the impending doom, things are about as good as they could be.

"What time is it?" she mumbles.

"It's about…" I say, glancing at the clock beside my bed, "11 am."

"Crap, really?" she groans, flipping onto her back. "I'm soooo tired."

"You're jet-lagged, baby. Tired is to be expected."

She rolls back onto my chest and moans softly.

Well, I'm wide awake now.

"I should get up," she says with a sigh.

"I could think of a way to help you wake up," I say, grabbing a handful of her arse and pulling her closer into me.

"Is that so?" She stretches her arms and legs slightly, yawning a bit before looking up at me with those grey eyes.

"I can give you a demonstration." I roll on top of her and pin her arms above her head and she smiles.

I give her a slow kiss, my hands moving to the back of her head. I duck under the covers and plant a trail of kisses down her chest and stomach as she giggles.

"Hey dude, do you guys wa-" Kieran's voice calls.

Ava shrieks and I jump up, poking out of the covers to see a grinning Kieran standing in the doorway.

"Bloody hell, mate!" I yell. "You ever fucking heard of knocking?"

"My bad," he says with a laugh. "Don't mind me. Feel free to continue."

"Piss off before I rip your bloody limbs from your body!"

"Alright, dude!" He raises his hands defensively. "I was just gonna ask if you wanted breakfast, but it looks like you already-"

"Out!" Ava yells, throwing a pillow in his direction.

He dodges the pillow, stepping backward out the door and closing it behind him.

"Fucking tosser," I curse, falling onto the bed beside Ava with a sigh.

"Yeah, kind of ruined the moment."

"That's Kieran for you. He's proper good at that."

———·———

"Are you nervous?" Kami asks as we walk through the doors of the Council offices.

From the outside, it's a bland, grey concrete building with large windows, much like every building in Canary Wharf. Inside, you might mistake it for a posh office lobby or a government institution. The people and everything about it appear ordinary.

But appearances are misleading when it comes to The Council—they always have been. Part law enforcement agency, part concealment operation, part supernatural UN; The Council is anything but what it appears to be.

"Why? Should I be?" I ask.

I told The Council I would check in upon my arrival, so that's precisely what I'm doing. It shouldn't be a particularly dramatic affair.

"No," she says. "It's just been a while. I know you had mixed feelings about working for The Council before. Just making sure you're okay with all of this."

"I mean, it's hardly how I'd prefer to come back to London, but there's nothing I can do about the circumstances. As for The Council, they know that my participation is temporary and comes with rules. I've told them this case is the only reason I'm back and that I'm handling it entirely on my own terms."

Kami nods in understanding as we approach the front desk.

"Hello," I say to the receptionist. "I'm just here to check in with management."

The man nods and types on the computer for a minute before instructing us to sit in the corner and wait for someone to meet us. After a few moments of silent waiting, we hear the clacking of a woman's heels on the cement floors.

"Zane!" the woman says as she walks up to us. "Good to see you!"

It's Helen Dalton, a long-time Council leader I once worked under. She looks to be in her mid-fifties, with a short brown bob and a grey suit. But, as always, looks can be deceiving with The Council. She's actually a 700-some-year-old Haltija, a faerie of sorts from an ancient family.

"Helen," I say, standing up to shake her hand. "It's lovely to see you again. You alright?"

"I'm good, thanks. I can't chat long, but I wanted to come down and personally say hello and get you set up with your credentials."

She guides us into a small side room and hands over an overstuffed manila envelope. I open it to reveal cover IDs, case files, and a Council badge with my name and photo.

Here we go again.

"Is this all I-" I begin to ask, but am cut off by a sharp pain in my side. I groan and stagger back before onto a nearby chair for stability.

My mind is instantly drawn to Ava and I try desperately to sense any sort of signal coming through our bond. I pick up on something, but it's far from what

I've hoped—it's pain and panic.

Fuck.

I look up to a concerned Kami and Helen beside her when something occurs to me.

Fuck.

I need to get out of here. I need to get back to Ava. Something has gone wrong and she's in trouble. There's just one small problem—if I want to keep Ava safe, I can't let The Council know she's still alive.

"I'm fine," I say. "Weird stomach cramp. You know how it is."

"Sirens can get stomach cramps?" Helen asks.

"Yeah, sure," I lie. "Sometimes when I fly long distances, it messes with my stomach."

"Really? I'm sorry to hear that."

"Oh yeah," Kami chimes in. "Me too. Happens to me all the time."

"Well can I get you a glass of water? Or anything else?"

"No I'm fine," I say, biting my lip as I feel the panic rising in my gut.

Fuck.

This is why I left her with Kieran and Finn. She was supposed to be safe.

"I should probably get home," I say. "Sleep it off."

"Of course," Helen says with a nod. She says she'll go ahead and put my information into the computer herself and, after a rushed bit of small talk, we head out of the building.

We walk out slowly and calmly as if nothing is wrong, but Kami has clearly caught on to the urgency.

"What's going on?" she asks, upping her pace to a brisk—but unsuspicious—walk. "Is it Ava? Is something wrong?"

"It felt like I got punched in the stomach," I say.

As soon as we get past the sightline to the building, we break out into a run and I call Ava.

No answer. Fuck.

Panicked, I call Kieran and it rings for a moment before picking up.

"Hello?" I say, but the only reply is a clamoring of sounds followed by silence.

And then a scream.

32

I dig through my luggage to find my favorite ultra-soft leggings.

I really should unpack my clothes into the dresser, but all I really have the energy for is a short walk to the living room.

Rather than upending my suitcase to find a shirt, I grab one of Zane's and throw it on.

I never think of Zane as a giant or anything, but when I wear his clothes, they practically drown me and I suddenly feel like an elf.

Wait… are elves a real thing? They probably are, aren't they?

That's a question I've never had to think about before.

I walk into the living room and see Kieran sprawled out on the leather couch, watching TV.

"Good morning, Kieran!" I say.

"I got that impression," Kieran replies, sitting up and giving me a wink.

"Ugh! Way to make it creepy, man."

"It's just sex," he says with a laugh. "You humans are so bashful!"

"Didn't you use to be human?"

"Technically." He crosses one leg over the other and casually leans back. "I wasn't a particularly normal human."

It's hard to imagine Kieran living a normal human life—learning to ride a bike, going to school, growing old. Though I do like thinking of him boinking his way around a retirement home.

"What were you like as a human?"

"Psshh…" he huffs, kneading the back of his neck with one hand. "I was boring."

"But you just said you weren't a normal human."

"Yeah, I just…" he says, drifting off as his eyes look far off into the distance. "You can be both weird and boring. There's no exciting story there."

"Okay," I say, nodding slightly.

I can't help but feel like I've been brushed off, but it seems like a sensitive topic and I don't want to push him.

"Sorry, Ava," he says with a sigh. "I didn't mean to be so…. I don't know. My human life was jus-"

A tap at the door interrupts our conversation.

"Are Zane and Kami back already?" I ask. "I thought they were going to be a while."

"Nah, it's your other babysitter," he says, giving me a teasing smirk as he gets up to answer the door.

I'm not all that sold on the idea of having to be watched, but if the situation were reversed, I'd probably insist Zane was safe too.

"Finn you stunning hunk of beefcake, you!" Kieran says as the door swings open.

"You big flirt," Finn says.

Kieran walks back into the living room with Finn close behind.

"You a'right, Ava?" Finn asks.

"Hey!" I say, standing to give him a hug. "If you're looking for Zane, he and Kami had to go check in with the council."

"No, actually, just here to see my favorite Incubus-human duo."

"Told ya," Kieran says. "Your boyfriend doesn't trust me to babysit alone."

Finn gives me an awkward smile and sits down on a nearby seat.

"How was the flight?" Finn asks. "You look a bit knackered."

"It was alright, actually," I say. "I'm just jet-lagged."

Technically, my body is punishing me for having the audacity to travel instead of staying home. And I'm also jet-lagged. But the jet lag is easier to explain.

"Well, uh… good to hea-" Finn is interrupted by another knock at the door.

"Don't tell me I have three babysitters."

"No," Finn says. He and Kieran both stand up, looking alert and confused. Kieran signals me to wait while he rounds the corner to get a look at the visitor through the window.

"It's just a delivery guy," Kieran says. "Anyone expecting a package?"

"Mmm…" Finn says, closing his eyes.

"Leave it on the doorstep, thanks!" Kieran shouts.

The delivery person seems to reply but I can't quite hear what he says. After a second, the door opens with a slight creak and Finn gives me an alarmed look.

"Don't make a sound," Finn's voice says in my head.

Crap. Who is it?

"Not a delivery man. Go to the bedroom and hide in the closet."

My heart begins to pound but I make my way toward the bedroom.

I hear Kieran shout and a loud bang shakes the walls of the house. I race faster toward the bedroom, colliding with a small table in my panic. The corner jabs into my side, sending a sharp pain through me as I stumble forward and reach the bedroom.

I quickly close the door behind me and rush to the closet.

"It's a demon," Finn says. *"Not sure what kind. They're looking for Zane. Arm yourself."*

Arm myself with what? I'm in a bedroom!

"Sharp… anything. Aim for the heart."

I look around and see nothing of any use until my eyes fall on my purse. I pull out the blue scarf and unwrap Zane's feather. For whatever reason, I just didn't want to leave it behind.

I remember him telling me it's sharper than it looks. That will have to do.

I hear a scream, but I'm not sure whose.

Shaking with fear, I make a beeline for the closet and close myself inside. The door is solid but I can see just slightly through the crack where it meets the frame.

Crap. This is bad.

I hear slow steps approaching the bedroom and I freeze, holding in my breath like the air is poisonous.

"Finn?" I call in my head. He doesn't respond.

The door slowly opens and I see a thin, black-haired man with a wicked smile.

"And this must be Zane…" the man says. "Leaving your friends to fight your battles while you hide? Not as impressive as the stories say, are you?"

He's looking for Zane?

Of course he is. This is Zane's house. They must've been keeping an eye on it in case he came home.

The man picks up one of Zane's shirts and inhales.

Is he smelling Zane's clothes? What a creep.

He tilts his head up, his nose in the sky, and takes another deep breath.

"There you are…" he says, snickering as his head swivels and his eyes land right on the closet door.

Crap crap crappity crap.

As he stalks toward me, I ready the feather in my hand.

Just aim for the heart, like Finn said. You can do this. Aim for the heart.

I'm screaming inside my head, but on the outside, I'm desperately trying not to make a sound.

In a flash, he opens the door and I leap out, stabbing the feather's pointed tip at his heart. I feel the feather connect with tissue and slice through it with surprising ease, but in the chaos, my instinct is to pinch my eyes closed.

I open my eyes to the demon staggering back with a feather sticking out of his neck.

Oh shit. I missed.

He collapses to the floor.

Is this a trap? This has got to be a trap, right?

Blood pours out of his wound as if it were a hose. In a split-second decision, I jump over the body and sprint out to the living room.

I spot Finn first, his face slightly bloodied as he writhes on the floor.

"I tried! I tried!" he mumbles as I kneel beside him.

"It's okay, Finn," I say, pushing a strand of red hair from his face. "I know you tried to protect me."

He doesn't seem to even hear me, so I return to my feet and search for Kieran.

I find him in the hallway by the door, curled into a ball and rocking back and forth.

"Kieran?" I whisper, dropping to my knees beside him and looking him over for wounds. He appears completely unharmed, but clearly something is wrong.

"Stop! No!" he whimpers. "No! Please!"

What is happening to him?

It's like he's having some kind of nightmare.

"He is…" a voice says behind me.

I panic and flip around, but it's only Finn.

"Where's the Shaytan?" he asks, scanning the room.

"The demon? I… I stabbed him in the neck."

"Neck, eh? That'll work."

"Did I kill him?"

"It's practically impossible to kill a demon, but you can bleed them out or slow them down. Maybe you caught the brain stem."

"What's wrong with Kieran?" I ask.

"He's living his own personal hell. It's what Shayatin do. They make you relive your worst memories—all the trauma from your past."

Kieran's face twists and he shudders over and over again. Tears fall down his face.

I hate seeing him like this.

"Can we help him?" I ask.

"We just have to wait until it wears off," Finn says with a sigh.

"Stop!" Kieran whimpers. "Please, Dad! No!"

At that, my heart shatters.

33

ZANE

My heart pounds as I shoot through the front door. I'm panting heavily from running here, but I still seem to be running off adrenaline.

I'm immediately met by signs of a struggle—splinters of wood on the floor, chunks of plaster taken out of the walls, drops of blood leading to the stairs.

Blood?

Fuck.

My heart sinks as I breathe in, hoping desperately that I don't recognize Ava's scent in the blood.

"Someone needs to call Zane," Kieran says from the other room.

"I'll call him," a soft voice says and I sigh in relief. It's Ava.

"Baby?!" I call, my voice more strained and frantic than I expected.

I round the corner to see Ava and Kieran sitting on the couch. They both whip their heads in my direction and I see Ava's face and neck covered in blood spatter.

I think I'm going to be sick.

"It's okay, babe," she says, standing up and walking over to me. "I'm fine. We're all fine."

I try to move but my limbs seem to be frozen in place. She wraps her arms around me and rests her head on my chest.

I step back, looking over her body for injuries. She seems fine, but she's soaked in blood.

"You're covered in blood," I say. "How-"

"She stabbed the fucker in the neck," Finn says, entering the room with a black feather in hand. He hands me the feather and I quickly recognize it as my own, but its shaft is coated in blood.

"You stabbed the attacker with… *my feather*?"

"I… I did. I'm sorry, I didn't have any other options and the-" I interrupt her by pulling her in and lifting her off the ground.

"Baby, you can take every feather I have if it means you're safe."

I set her back on her feet and take a real breath—the first time I've truly been able to breathe in the last fifteen minutes.

"Where's Kami?" Ava asks.

"She took the tube and I ran."

"You *ran* here? How far was it?"

"It was only five or six miles."

I lift one of my black boots to inspect the damage. There's a solid half-inch of wear and the tread is mostly gone.

I guess I'll need new boots.

"So who was it, then?" I ask. "Or what?"

"It was a Shaytan," Finn says.

Shit.

Shayatin are bad news. They creep into your mind and make you relive your worst memories. They're excellent interrogators—dangerously so—but they're evil. They delight in prying into the psyche and leaving their victims shattered.

If one got to Ava, I'll give this bastard a memory they won't forget.

"Where is it?"

"I cuffed him," Finn says, pointing to the broom closet. "He's in that cupboard over there."

I step back from Ava, but she gives me a scolding look.

"Zane," she says in a low voice, "you're not in the best mindset for this right now."

"For what?" I ask, feigning innocence.

"We need to be strategic," Finn says. "Use him for intel."

"We know everything we need to know. He's one of Leviathan's demons. You think that's a coincidence? I kill his brother and one of his demons comes for me. What else can we learn?"

The only thing left to learn is how to skin a Shaytan.

I smirk at the thought.

"Yep," Kieran says. "That's his evil smile. I'm out."

"He's unconscious anyway," Finn says. "Ava got his brain stem, so he's still healing."

"Fuck, really?" I look to Ava for confirmation and she nods. "Great aim, baby."

"Yeah, um… thanks," she mumbles.

"How did they even get to Ava?" I give Finn and Kieran a sharp glare. "You two were supposed to make sure that never happened."

"They caught us off guard, okay?" Kieran says.

I thought that Ava would be safe with an Immortal and a demon, but if there were more than just one Shaytan, this could have gone much worse.

"I honestly didn't expect Shayatin to be involved. This is a whole new problem."

"How so?" Ava asks.

"Shayatin are incredibly strong and very dangerous."

"He's right," Finn says. "Kieran and I just aren't going to cut it."

"It's not like we have a lot of options."

"I may actually have one option… it's a friend of mine. He does bodyguard work. I've seen him take on eight Immortals at once and walk away unscathed."

"Holy shit, what is this guy?" Kieran asks.

"Sorry, that's his private business."

What could he possibly be that would be that strong?

I look at Ava and the deep red stains on her skin and clothing, then back to Finn. "Set up a meeting."

AVA

We follow Finn along the walkway of the college campus where we're meeting his mystery friend.

"This is fucking ridiculous," Zane curses. "Why me? What's the problem with me specifically?"

"You're just gonna have to trust me," Finn says, his eyes soft and wide.

"I don't know." He crosses his arms and looks at me. "How do you feel about this, love?"

"I keep telling you I'm fine by myself," I say. "I can handle it. Besides, Finn vouched for him."

Zane nods begrudgingly.

"Where are we headed, anyway?"

"We're here," Finn says, gesturing to the impressive brick building to our left.

"The library?" I ask.

"He's a bit particular and he doesn't have a cell phone, so if you need to find him, you come here."

Sounds like a creep, but okay.

We head in through large double doors. The library is massive—at least four floors high, with a large opening in the center. There are books on every wall, filling every nook.

If there is such a thing as a sexy library, this would be it.

"Alright, mate," Finn says to Zane.

"Fine," he huffs. He kisses me on the cheek, then waves to Finn. "I'll be nearby."

I walk with Finn to the center area and he instructs me to sit at the end of a long wood table beside the Autobiographies shelf.

"I'm gonna look for him," Finn says. "You sit tight."

I nod, looking over at the bookshelf for something to entertain me while I wait. Most of these are about obscure historical figures I've never heard of.

I stand up and step into the aisle to see more choices and I find a chef's biography that has recipes in it. My interest probably has nothing to do with the fact that I'm really hungry right now.

A man down the aisle looks up at me and smiles slightly, revealing subtle dimples. He has short, curly, light-brown hair styled and a bit of a beard. He's wearing a dark grey, long-sleeve henley and dark-wash skinny jeans.

So far, my experience of British people is that they're all super attractive, like—obnoxiously so.

Is this what all of them look like?

I wander back to the table and sit down with my book, paging through and mostly focusing on the pictures.

Is that a tomato cake? Eww.

"Hello, gorgeous," a low, smooth voice says from over my shoulder.

I turn to see the handsome man from earlier, leaning on the table and giving me a knock-out smile.

Is this a sign that the Siren pheromones are acting up again? I mean, I'm cute and all, but this is getting a little ridiculous.

Jen did say there may still be some residual effects.

"Hi," I say quickly, trying to shut down the conversation. My eyes drop to my book and I pretend to read.

"Do you usually read cookbooks in the library?"

"I… uh…" I mutter, "only on Cookbook Thursday."

He chuckles quietly before gesturing to the seat next to me.

"May I?"

I nod, unsure what else to do.

As I look around, I catch Zane's silhouette. He's on the mezzanine above us, leaning against the railing with his arms crossed. Our eyes meet and he raises an eyebrow at me.

My best response is a shrug in which I attempt to convey the message 'Sorry, I'm dealing with it. It will be fine. I'm not interested.'

His green eyes narrow slightly but he remains stationary.

"You American?" the man asks, not getting the hint.

"Yep."

"I love your accent." He smiles, his dimples showing through.

"Thanks," I say.

"I'm Morgan."

"Ava."

He leans an elbow on the table and leans slightly toward me.

"Can I take you out sometime?"

Of all the things I expected him to say next, I really didn't expect that one.

"I don't mean to be forward, but I… I feel this incredible connection with you and you're absolutely beautiful and I just… This is coming off really stalker-like, isn't it?"

I nod awkwardly, giving him a polite smile.

"I never do this," he says. "I guess I'm making a fool of myself, I just…"

His expression morphs into one of sadness or maybe anger.

"Piss off, mate," another voice says.

Uh oh. Zane didn't stay upstairs.

"I don't believe I was talking to you," Morgan says.

"No, but you're talking to my girl," he says, his eyes getting greener by the second.

"That's *my* girl," he growls. My eyes go wide with shock and Zane jerks, as if the words physically knocked him back.

Why does this guy think I'm his?

"Excuse me??" Zane's voice is dark and gritty. He puffs up his chest and his eyes glow with fury.

"What are you?" Morgan asks, shaking his head and hitting it with his fist, like he's trying to shake something out.

"I could ask you the same."

"Morgan!" Finn says, hurrying over to us.

"Finn? What are you doing here?" He looks between a concerned Finn and an enraged Zane. "You brought a Siren into my library??"

Morgan begins to shake, taking multiple steps away from us.

"I'm sorry. He was supposed to stay away," Finn said. "Zane, please go!"

"He was trying it on with Ava," Zane says, clenching his fists.

"Please, Ava. This is going to get bad. You have to convince him to go, now," Finn pleads in my head.

I walk up to Zane and place my hands on his chest.

"He's threatened. He needs to know you're not going to leave him."

"I'm yours," I say, looking into his eyes. "Nobody can take me from you and I can handle this guy. I promise."

He sighs before jerking back and rushing out the front door.

"Okay, somebody tell me what the fuck is going on."

"I'm sorry," Morgan says, taking in a deep breath. "It was a mistake. Finn should know better than to have brought him around here."

Oh, thanks. That explains nothing at all.

"So you're like... anti-Siren? Why?"

"I'm not *anti-* anyone."

I look back and forth between them, hoping someone has a better explanation for me.

"Sod it, Finnegan," he huffs, stepping around a bookshelf to shield our conversation. He begins to whisper. "I don't fancy you, your boyfriend does. I got caught up in his ruddy feelings because... I'm an Empath."

Oh.

Wait—what does that mean?

34

Morgan leads Finn and me to a secluded corner of the library, taking heavy steps with his shoulders hunched and his hands balled at his sides.

I have very little idea of what's going on, but Morgan seems pretty pissed at us.

"It'll be okay," Finn says through my mind. *"Morgan is a bit of a grumpy blowhard but at the end of the day, he's a good guy. Remind you of anyone?"*

Now that you mention it, there is a certain familiar air about Morgan—a handsome, brooding, British immortal with a roguish attitude.

Morgan sits down at a table and reluctantly gestures to offer us seats across from him. He and Finn seem to be exchanging heated glances but neither says anything.

"It was a mistake," Finn says in a hushed voice. "I told him not to be around for the meeting. I didn't tell him why. He just didn't realize the proximity would even be an issue."

They trade glares for a moment.

"But you know I need a warning for something like that!" Morgan huffs.

What are they talking about?

"Hold up, are you guys having some sort of mental conversation without me?"

"Sorry, Ava," Finn says, taking a deep breath in. "Let's start over. Ava, this is my mate Morgan. Morgan, this is Ava."

"Hello," Morgan says, his eyes on the table as he extends his hand for a handshake. "I'm sorry about earlier—that wasn't me. I… It was my powers."

"It's okay. I know that stuff can happen," I say, shaking his hand. "Nice to meet you, Morgan."

"So you have a job for me, I assume?" he asks.

"We do," Finn says, tipping his head to me. "She's the job."

"Are you royalty or something? Someone important's daughter?"

"Do I have to be?" I ask.

"I don't usually do small-time protection gigs. I get the call when the client is incredibly powerful or has attracted the wrath of someone who is. Think of me as the nuclear option."

I thought his power was feeling people's emotions. It doesn't sound that dangerous.

"She's the latter," Finn says. "At least one Demon King and his horde of demons are after her. Well… technically, they're after her boyfriend, Zane, the Siren."

"So they're targeting her to get to him?"

"Sort of… um…" Finn pauses a moment. "We don't think they know she's alive. We're trying to keep it that way."

Thanks, Finn, that doesn't sound ominous at all.

"Does this have something to do with the murdered Sirens?"

"It was retribution."

"For what?"

"For killing Asmodeus."

Morgan straightens in his chair and leans forward.

"Bollocks," he says, his expression hard and serious. "Asmodeus is dead?"

"He is."

Morgan lets out a shaky breath and kneads his scruffy chin in his hand.

"How can you know for sure?" he asks, his eyes looking glossier. "Did he really do it? Your mate—Zane? Did he really kill Asmodeus?"

Finn stares a moment before answering.

Is he going to tell him that I killed him? Should we lie?

"No," Finn says, "but he's covering for the person who did."

"Wow."

Morgan leans back in his chair and crosses his arms.

"Finn, I want to help you—I do," he says. "But I can't work with a Siren. That's just too much of an ask."

What the heck is this guy's problem?

"Hey, douche," I say. "I don't know what your problem is with Sirens, but if you haven't noticed, that's my boyfriend you're talking about."

He looks at me stone-faced, his eyebrows lowered as we have a bit of a stare-off. The corner of his mouth turns upward until he's wearing a smirk. He explodes with a laugh louder than is probably appropriate for a library.

"I like you," he says. "I don't have a problem with Sirens. My powers don't interact well with their…state of being."

"What does that even mean?"

"Sirens are built to be intense, passionate," he says. "They're quick-tempered, lustful—they feel everything stronger than other beings. When I pick up on those signals… it's really hard for me to tell which feelings are mine and which are theirs. With everyone else, even strong emotions are just background noise that can be ignored. But it takes a lot of conscious effort to separate myself from the feelings of a Siren."

"Is it just Sirens?" I ask.

"Sirens and Furies. You really don't want to hang out with me when a Fury's around."

So that's what he does—he feels people's emotions. How does that help us?

"What are you?" he asks, staring into my eyes.

"What??"

Finn and Kami assured me that no one would ask me that because it was rude to Immortals.

Is this guy starting shit with me?

I mean, I'm not particularly tough or strong, but if I were ever going to be able to take an immortal in a fistfight, it's got to be the one with emotion powers.

Heck, I've been battling emotions since I was a teenager. Bring it, Empath!

"Human?" he asks, interrupting what I'm sure would have been a clever retort on my part.

"How do you know that?" I look down to make sure I don't have 'HUMAN' written across my shirt.

"Because you feel like shit." He smirks and raises his eyebrows.

"Okay, I know I'm not a fancy Immortal like you guys, but that was definitely rude." I give him a dirty look and he chuckles.

Finn, this guy is a douche.

"I mean… you're in pain. A lot of pain."

"Oh…" I grumble. "Yeah, so I'm human. Does it matter?"

"Wow," Morgan says, shaking his head from side to side. "You lot want me to guard a human who's clearly already falling apart, *and* work with her Siren boyfriend even though nobody knows the girl exists? No. You couldn't pay me enough."

"I wasn't planning on paying you at all," Finn says.

"Oh, you thought I'd do it for free because I hate Asmodeus?"

"I wouldn't bring them to you if I thought you couldn't handle it."

Morgan shakes his head again.

"Good try, Finn," he says with a chuckle.

I watch them stare at each other for a good few seconds, undoubtedly having some kind of telepathic conversation. They both look frustrated with each other.

"Would you help the person who did it?" I ask.

Both of their heads snap toward me.

"*You don't have to tell him,*" Finn says in my mind. "*It's your call.*"

We need the guy on our side. This would help.

"Are you saying your Siren did kill Asmodeus?" Morgan asks.

"No. But I did."

Morgan's eyes go wide.

"A human killed Asmodeus?" he asks, a smile growing on his face. "He would have loathed that."

"Brilliant, yeah?" Finn says.

"Fine. You have yourself a bodyguard, Killer."

"Good…" I say. "But um… can I ask… why are you such a particularly great bodyguard?"

He and Finn both instantly break into laughter.

"Do you know what an Empath is?" Morgan asks.

"I mean, you said you can feel other people's emotions."

"I don't just sense them," he says, "I channel them. And it's not just emotions."

"What else?"

"I can channel the powers of every Immortal in the immediate vicinity— all at once."

35

My hands shake as I pace in circles beside the rental car. The encounter plays through my mind on repeat.

Who does that wanker think he is?

It's one thing to try it on with Ava, it's another thing to do so right in front of me.

"That's my girl," he said. He called her his girl.

It's as if I can feel the blood boiling as it runs through my veins—filling with heat and irritation, frothing beneath my skin.

A couple of students pass me, giving me judgmental looks as they pass by.

I must look like a right nutter, mumbling to myself in a university car park.

I open the car and get inside, letting out a heavy breath as I lay back in the driver's seat.

Fuck.

Ava can handle herself—I know she can. But being challenged like that eats at me. This man didn't just threaten to take the love of my life, but he claimed her as his own. If any other Siren were in my shoes, the bloke's insides would be splattered across every book in that library.

I hate feeling so helpless, especially when Ava's safety is on the line.

Why is he so insistent on this no-Sirens policy, anyway? There are plenty of Immortals who judge Sirens for their particular gifts or because they have no real lineage, but this seemed different. He was angry that I was there—furious even, almost as much as I was.

My heart is still thrashing against my ribcage, readying my body for a fight. The urge to do something—anything—is crawling within me.

I could go back, knock him into next week and show him just what happens to someone who challenges me. But would that quell the anxiety or feeling of helplessness?

Probably not. It never has before.

The soft hum of Ava's voice shakes me from my thoughts. She walks up with Finn, who waves in my direction before heading over to his own car.

"Hey," she says, jumping in and closing the door behind her. She reaches across the seats to give me a hug and I breathe in the calming scent of her shampoo. "Are you okay?"

"Doing better now," I say with a smile. It must not be particularly convincing because Ava seems to be concerned.

"I appreciate you letting me handle it."

"Of course. I want you to know that I trust you."

She grabs my hand in hers and squeezes reassuringly.

"You're shaking," she says, her eyes wide and worried.

I look down at my hand. She's right, I'm trembling—undoubtedly a residual effect of the confrontation earlier.

"It's fine," I say, shaking my head. "I just got a bit worked up and can't burn off the energy."

"And burning it off would usually entail a fistfight?"

"Something like that," I say with an awkward, slightly forced chuckle. "I'll be fine, really. It just takes a lot of effort to fight my instincts sometimes."

"You know I love you, right? You don't have to worry about losing me."

I nod.

Sure, I know that, but convincing my constricted chest is another issue.

"Well," she says, placing her hands on the edge of my seat and leaning toward me with a glint in her eye, "I've got an idea for burning off a little energy."

Her soft lips meet mine before she takes my lower lip between her teeth and bites slightly.

Oh hello.

I pull away for a moment.

"You don't have to do this for me," I say. "You don't have anything to prove."

"And what am I proving?" she asks, nibbling at her lip while she looks up at me through her eyelashes.

"That you're... um... I... I dunno."

Fuck me. I can't think when she looks at me like that.

She smirks and starts to kiss my neck. A shiver runs down my spine and I lean my head back. I feel her fingers slowly lowering the zipper on my trousers.

"Fuu-uuck," I groan.

I can feel my brain shutting down as the blood travels to my groin.

Her tongue trails from my neck to my collarbone, pleasure radiating from her every touch. I feel the pressure release as the button on my jeans pops open. Her warm hand slips between my legs, freeing me from my trousers.

If it were possible to bite through my own lip, I surely would have done so by now.

I close my eyes, reveling in the sensation. My every muscle relaxes under her touch until I feel like I've melted into the seat.

I'm pulled back into reality by the feeling of warmth as she takes my length into her mouth. I shudder and my teeth dig further into my lip.

This woman could truly kill me. I'm completely helpless under her touch.

She moves up and down, slowly at first but with increasing speed, her soft moans sending vibrations through my skin that have me practically on the edge.

Her motions continue as her tongue swirls around, sending sparks through every nerve as it goes. After a few minutes, I feel a pressure building deep within me. My hips buck involuntarily and I let out a deep, guttural growl.

"Ba- baby, I…" I say between staggered breaths. "That's gonna… you.. I…"

She pulls away and looks up at me with a smirk.

"It's okay, I've got you," she says. "I'm yours."

She takes me back into her mouth, moving rhythmically up and down as the pressure becomes unbearable and tips over into a cascade of sensation. The noises that pour from my mouth are far from human, some even surprising me. My muscles tighten all at once before everything relaxes and my head drops back.

"Feeling better?" Ava asks with a giggle.

"Yeah…" I mumble.

To be honest, I don't even remember what I was upset about in the first place. In this moment, my entire world exists inside this car.

What was I even on about, anyway?

Oh. Finn's friend—I think he was called Morgan?

I smirk to myself in contentment. Leave it to my girl to know exactly how to dissolve my anxieties into nothing.

"How did your meeting go?" I ask, the fog clearing from my mind.

"Oh yeah, that," she says, blushing slightly. "Morgan agreed to help us. Finn is going to work out the details with him."

"Did he try it on with you any more?"

"No, that was actually you, I guess. I don't really understand the details, but I guess he's an Empath and he was sensing your feelings toward me."

I blink, taking in her words and slowly processing them.

He's an Empath?

I honestly didn't think there were any Empaths left. They're incredibly strong, so strong that Immortals and demons alike are terrified of them. That kind of power draws in enemies.

No wonder he didn't want me there—Empaths are especially sensitive to Siren emotions.

I rub my hand over my face and back through my hair.

I am such a bloody idiot.

"I'm sorry," I say, shaking my head. "None of that would have happened if I had just kept my distance. I didn't realize."

"It's okay," she says, leaning into my shoulder. "You didn't know."

"Yeah, but I could've done a better job of controlling myself."

"So? There are so many things I could've handled better in my life. I'm not going to fault you for being human."

"Except I'm not human."

"Okay, fine, then I'll start blaming you from now on," she says with a smirk. "Smartass."

I chuckle slightly, but my smile quickly falls when a new thought occurs to me: if Morgan agreed to help, that means we'll be seeing more of him.

Fucking fantastic.

36

As we step through the front door of Zane's house, we're confronted with a sweet, burning smell and a bit of smoke. Kieran emerges from the kitchen in nothing but a pink apron and socks. He holds out a tray of burnt pancakes and smiles.

"You guys want pancakes?" he asks.

"It's two in the afternoon, mate," Zane says, walking past Kieran into the living room.

We both follow him to the couch and sit around the coffee table.

"You look happy, Z-man," Kieran says. "Meeting go well?"

"Went shit actually," he replies, shooting me a subtle glance as he smirks.

"Oh dang, really? What happened?"

Zane shakes his head and sighs.

"There was a little power mix-up but everyone is fine now," I say, squeezing Zane's knee.

"Power mix-up, eh?" Kieran picks up an entire pancake on his fork and bites half of it off.

My instinct is to tell him about Morgan being an Empath, but it occurs to me that it might be inappropriate. Everyone seems pretty sensitive about the 'what flavor of Immortal are you' question.

"I think we ended things with an understanding," Zane grumbles.

"Sho what ish thish guy, shumshorta super-Immortal?" Kieran asks with a mouthful of pancake.

I raise an eyebrow at him as I attempt to decipher what he just said.

"Sort of," Zane replies. "He's about as strong as it gets. I'm sure you'll see eventually."

"You're no fun," he says, crossing his arms. "You guys didn't bring Finn back with you?"

"No, sorry. Your boyfriend went back to his hotel."

Kieran stabs another pancake and it flops around on his fork before he takes another oversized bite. He chews for a moment, then swallows.

"Well we gotta plan an Immortals' day out or something. I'm not coming all the way to London to hang out in your house all day and babysit Ava—no offense."

"We should," Zane says, looking at me. "Let's maybe go into the city tomorrow."

———

I'm curled up on the couch with a heating pad on my legs. My muscles are clearly not happy with me today.

"What's that for?" Zane asks, pointing to my legs.

"My legs have been cramping up on me. Trying to loosen up the muscles a bit."

"Figures."

"Figures what?" I ask, scrunching my lips.

"Just another thing, you know," he says with a sigh.

That's how chronic illness works—it's chronic. As in, it doesn't stop.

I nod, unsure of what else to say.

"It's just interesting, that's all," he says. "I didn't realize this was so serious. I just wish I had known before."

My head snaps to him and my eyes widen.

"What did you just say?"

"I just wish I had known before."

"No," I say, shaking my head and standing up. "You do not say that to me. You don't. You don't mean it."

"You're so dramatic," he says, huffing in a way that almost sounds like a laugh.

This isn't right. No.

"This can't be you," I say as I back away.

A sinister smile spreads across his face.

"Who says?" he asks, standing up. He takes a few steps toward me that I counter with steps backward.

He grabs the sleeve of my shirt and throws me down onto the floor. I scream for help as my heartbeat pounds faster and faster.

"Baby?" his voice calls and my eyes open to a dark room. "You alright? You were crying out in your sleep."

Uggh. I hate these dreams.

"I'm fine," I say, letting out a shaky breath. "It was just a bad dream."

Zane wraps an arm around me and pulls me tight to his chest. After a few minutes, he falls back to sleep, but I'm left wide awake in the dark.

I slip out from his grasp and head to the kitchen for a glass of water.

I tiptoe down the hall, stopping when I see a soft glow from the kitchen. As I round the corner, I see Kieran standing at the open refrigerator.

"Hey," he says softly. "You needed a late-night snack too?"

"No, I uh… couldn't sleep."

"Jet lag?"

"Something like that."

"Liar liar, pants on fire," he says with a smile.

"Okay, maybe I had a bad dream."

"I know." He grabs an apple from the fridge and takes a bite before closing the door. The room becomes much darker, so he flips the switch to a small lamp.

"How do you know?"

"I could hear you whimpering," he says. "I've heard it twice now. Besides, it takes one to know one."

What does that even mean?

"Huh?"

"Me too. On the bad dream front."

"Demons can dream?"

"Not exactly… but those thoughts and memories can still creep in and haunt you."

I pour myself a glass of water and we both sit at the dining table.

"Do you want to talk about it?" I ask.

"Do you?"

"Touché," I say with a snicker.

Maybe I should talk to someone.

"Promise you won't tell anyone?" I ask.

He mimes crossing his heart and gives me a smile.

"I've been having nightmares about Zane, or… kind of Asmodeus with Zane's face. It's complicated. It's just all my fears wrapped up in this trauma. Things will start normal and then suddenly he'll turn on me and say something strange, give me a creepy smile like Asmodeus, and then attack me."

"And you think I'm really Kieran?" he asks, looking up at me with a disturbing smile.

My heart sinks and my eyes go wide as I jump out of my seat.

"Shit, Ava," he says, leaping up and reaching out to me with puppy dog eyes. "I'm so sorry; that was such a dick joke to make."

The color has drained from his face and he sweeps his hair from his eyes.

"Not cool," I say, narrowing my eyes at him as I sit back down. "That was hard for me to talk about."

"I'm sorry, Ava." He shakes his head and sighs. "You really can trust me, I promise. I… okay… you were putting yourself out there. I appreciate that. So uh…"

He twists a piece of his hair in his fingers and looks down at it.

"I meant it when I said I was awake because of bad dreams too," he says. "Well, in my case, more of a memory. You remember the other day with the Shaytan?"

"How could I forget?"

"I'm not sure how much you could tell from the outside, but uh… it caught me off guard and was able to send me into a bad memory. That memory was of my dad."

"I did hear you say something, but I didn't want to pry. It seemed personal."

"It was," he says with a sigh. "When I was human, I had a family. I grew up in the sixties. My dad was one of those holier-than-thou types. He had this bullshit sense of masculinity and, as his only son, he wanted me to live up to that. I rarely did."

It's so hard to imagine Kieran as a child. He always seems like this larger-than-life figure, unaffected by everything—immovable.

"Anyway, he used to beat the shit out of me. Being a stupid kid, all I wanted to do was please him. I thought I could be the person he wanted me to be if I just tried hard enough. But there was no winning with him. There was no right answer."

"I'm sorry," I say softly, reaching out to give his hand a comforting squeeze. "Was that what the dream was? That memory?"

"Yeah. My friend came over and… while we were in my room… he kissed me. Turns out, my dad was watching in my window. He was gonna kill him for 'corrupting' me, so I said it was me who kissed him. I took the blame and I got the brunt of his wrath."

"Crap." I cover my mouth with my hand. "How old were you?"

"Nineteen. I guess the Shaytan stirred up some shit I had tried to bury."

"I'm sorry Kieran. You deserved better."

"We both do," he says with a sad smile. "Trauma gets to everyone. It builds a home and stays. You don't have to be ashamed that things have gotten to you. It's not about being strong enough to act like everything's fine all the time. It's about coexisting with the trauma and moving forward with it as a new part of you."

"That was surprisingly deep."

"That's what she said," he says, laughing as he holds up a hand for a high five.

Yep. It's definitely still Kieran.

37

We exit the tube station out onto a bustling city street flanked with grand brick buildings flying the Union Flag on every corner. Zane wraps his arm around my waist and leads me along the sidewalk as we pass fancy clothing shops and jewelers that just scream 'you can't afford anything in here.'

Kami follows close behind and Kieran quickly catches up after her.

"What's so special about this store, anyway?" Kieran asks, taking an oversized bite of the samosa in his hand.

"It's a tourist thing," Kami says. "Since we're taking Ava to do London-y things today, I suggested we stop here. It's famous."

"Famous for what, though? Do they have good two-for-one deals or something?"

"Pshhh," Kami scoffs, almost laughing. "You're definitely not going to get a good deal at Harrod's, no. It's more of an attraction."

"Zane said it's a really fancy department store," I say. "So I'm expecting like… a Bloomingdale's, but British."

"Is that what you told her, Z?"

"Well," Zane shrugs, "it's not technically wrong."

"That's it," she says, pointing to a massive brown building with impressive architecture. It looks more like a palace than a department store.

"Oh shit," Kieran says with a mouthful of food. "Does the queen live in this store, or what?"

"Royalty had to live here at some point," I ask. "Right?"

"Not that I know of," Zane says as we cross the street. "It's been a store for as long as I can recall. You remember when we came to see the escalator?"

He glances back at Kami, who nods.

"Hard to forget. There was a huge queue," she says, her English accent coming out slightly.

"You came to see the escalator?" Kieran asks. "How boring is England?"

"It was the first escalator in the country," Zane says, shooting Kieran a scowl.

"Ava," Kieran says, walking next to me, "is it weird dating a prehistoric dinosaur?"

I giggle slightly but Zane seems less amused.

Kami steps in front and opens a door to the building as Kieran scarfs down the remainder of his samosa and throws away the wrapper. We step inside and are greeted with a massive, gilded space with high ceilings and marble floors. There are ornate, Egyptian-style carvings on the walls and towering stone columns along the hallways.

"Oh daaang," Kieran says. His jaw goes slack as he scans the room in awe. "This is hella nice. This Harrod guy was fucking the queen, wasn't he?"

A nearby security guard glowers in Kieran's direction, clearly wondering who let the riff-raff in.

I look at my clothes and realize I'm wearing jeans, an oversized sweater, and flats. I opted for comfort since we were going to be sightseeing and doing a lot of walking. I'm far from properly dressed to be shopping inside what can only be described as a modern Egyptian tomb.

"I'm not sure I'm dressed appropriately," I whisper to Zane as we walk in. "Is there a dress code in this place?"

"No, love," he says with a smile. "You're fine as you are. Lots of tourists come here to shop and wear any old thing. Don't fret."

I nod, though I can't help but tug awkwardly at my clothes.

On the bright side, it's not like I can run into an ex-boyfriend in London.

"So did Helen get that information you were looking for?" Kami asks.

I passively listen to their conversation as I take in the scene around me. Designer bags and shoes, jewelry in individually lit cases—my $15 Payless flats are seriously outclassed here.

"Yes," he replies. "Belphegor is in London. We don't know for certain if he's involved, but it's unlikely."

"He's never been one to jump into a fight. He's more of a sidelines kind of guy."

"Dude!" Kieran calls. "Look at the chandelier. Those crystals are fucking giant. One of those things is as big as my dick!"

"So pretty small, then?" Kami asks.

"You wound me," he pouts, placing his palm to his heart.

"Truth hurts."

I giggle as he feigns injury.

"Zane?" a woman calls. We all turn in the direction of the voice.

Zane's eyes go wide and his posture stiffens as the woman approaches. She's gorgeous, with golden skin and brown wavy hair. It's clear from a brief glance that her dress, shoes, and handbag each cost more than my car.

"Tara…" he mumbles.

"Oh my god!" She runs to him and wraps her arms around his neck. "It's so good to see you."

"Hey," he says, his arms stuck uncomfortably at his sides.

The woman turns to Kami and runs to hug her as well.

"Kami! It's been so long! Are you lot finally back from America?"

"Hey Tara!" she says with a smile, quickly removing herself from the hug. "We're just here for a visit."

"I can't believe you didn't tell me you were in town on holiday!" she says, slapping Zane's arm playfully. "And who are your friends?"

She turns to Kieran and me.

"Er… this is Kieran, my American mate," Zane says, gesturing to him.

"Well hello, gorgeous," Kieran says, giving her hand a kiss.

"And this is my girlfriend, Ava."

"Oh wow! Girlfriend, huh?" she asks with a smile that doesn't quite seem genuine.

I reach out my hand to shake hers but she goes for an aggressive hug instead.

"You're adorable," she says, looking me over.

I suddenly feel very aware of my unimpressive outfit and messy hair.

I don't know who you are, but I already don't like you, lady.

Kami narrows her eyes and pinches her lips together. Maybe she feels the same way.

"She's gorgeous," Zane says with a slight growl, leaning over my shoulders and draping his arms over my shoulders as he kisses me on the cheek.

"Oh, of course, yes," she replies, her fake smile making another appearance. "So how long are you in town?"

Zane shifts uneasily.

"We don't have a lot of time while we're here," he says. "We're mostly here on business."

"Oh, that's a shame. Well, you'll have to make some time for me before you go! Do you still have my number?"

"I have it," Kami says curtly. "Speaking of which, we totally have to get going. It was nice seeing you!"

Tara says a quick goodbye as Kami rushes us through to the next department.

"What was that about?" Kieran asks.

"Which part? The run in or the fact that she was challenging Ava?"

"She was what now?" I ask.

"She's an idiot. Just ignore her."

"Wait, how was she challenging me?"

"Yeah," Kieran says. "I'm curious too. What did I miss?"

"Well, she's a Siren," Kami says. "In our culture, if you want to insult someone, you insinuate that someone isn't… sexually satisfying their partner. She probably was trying to figure out if you were a Siren. If you were, you would've reacted to that."

"What? How did she… what?"

That fucking bitch.

I'll show you satisfied. I'll be satisfied when I punch you in the face.

Okay, I really need to work on my trash talking.

"She wasn't that upfront about it, but… I certainly would never call another Siren adorable. That's just trying to start something."

"Well… I didn't know that. I feel like I need a do-over."

"You don't need a do-over, baby," Zane says, hugging me and giving me a kiss on the cheek. "You're my girl, she's not. She can fuck off."

"Why would she come after me, anyway? I don't even know her."

I'm hoping the answer is not what my mind is assuming.

"She's erm… she and I used to…"

"Okay, nope. Got it. That's enough."

I was feeling pretty confident I wouldn't run into an ex-boyfriend today. I guess I forgot about Zane's exes.

38

 AVA

Sitting on the living room floor with my laptop on the coffee table, I stare mindlessly at the screen. I can't tell if it's the jet lag or just more of my usual brain fog, but I've found it near impossible to get any work done since we arrived in London. Kieran's muffled voice in the other room only serves to distract me further.

Who is he even talking to?

Zane left a few minutes ago for a meeting, so it should just be Kieran and me in the house.

"Who are you talking to?" I shout to him.

"Your bodyguard!" he yells back.

Oh. Of course. I completely forgot about Morgan.

I turn to see him and Kieran walking into the room.

"Hi, Killer," Morgan says.

"Hey," I reply.

This is awkward. I've never had a bodyguard before. Are you supposed to hang out and make small talk or do they just stand in the doorway making a serious face?

Kieran hops into a chair, swinging his legs over the arm. Morgan takes a seat in the chair next to him.

"Are you alright?" Morgan asks.

"Uh, yeah, I guess so," I say. "You?"

"I'm fine, thank you."

"You didn't tell me your bodyguard was such a babe," Kieran says with a smile.

"I get that a lot," Morgan says, giving him a wink.

"Getting hungry, are we?" I ask.

"You know me," Kieran replies with a laugh, "I can always go for a slice of beefcake."

Oh god. Is he just going to be flirting with Morgan this whole time? I'm already prone to nausea and this isn't helping.

"How about we leave Morgan alone and let him do his job?"

"Buzzkill," Kieran says, crossing his arms. "Well, I guess I'll go grab a snack."

He stands up and starts walking away.

"You're leaving?" I ask.

I'd prefer not to be stuck here on my own making small talk with the Empath. Then again, it might be preferable to watching Kieran stare at him like a piece of meat.

"Just to the kitchen," he says. "A literal snack, Ava, jeez. Get your mind out of the gutter!"

He laughs and heads to the kitchen.

I continue attempting to work on my current design project. At this point, I'm mostly just hitting keys and pretending to do something so I don't have to come up with a conversational topic.

"Incubus, eh?" Morgan asks.

"Oh, uh… how do you know?"

"It's not that hard to guess. Plus, I could feel his thirst for me the moment I stepped in the door."

I chuckle a bit at the thought.

"That must be weird, right? Sensing when other people are attracted to you?"

"I'm used to it. Not people being attracted to me, I mean. Although…" He shrugs. "What I meant was that I'm used to sensing what other people are feeling. It's different than feeling it myself. Except, well… with particularly strong feelings, as you saw the other day."

"Ah yeah… because Zane is a Siren, right?"

"Yes. Two creatures in particular—Sirens and Furies—have unusually potent emotions. Most emotions are whispers, but theirs are screams. If the emotion is too strong, it drowns out my own. It can be a bit overwhelming and the line between myself and them begins to blur. That's why I arrived here after Zane left. I can handle it if I need to, but honestly, I'd rather avoid it. It takes a lot of energy to control that kind of intensity."

"What kind of intensity?" Kieran asks, walking back to his chair with a bag of chips in hand.

"Sirens," I say. "Oh, or… I mean…"

Crap. Did I just accidentally out him as an Empath?

"It's alright," Morgan says with a nod. "He's probably going to need to know eventually. From what Finn told me, he's around a lot. Let's get it out of the way, shall we? I'm an Empath."

"Oh shit! For real?" Kieran asks, his jaw slack. "Dayummn!"

Morgan just laughs in response.

"That's gotta be good in the bedroom, right?" Kieran continues. "Like, you can feel it on your end but you can also feel what they feel?"

"What did I say about harassing Morgan?" I scold.

"Yeah, yeah," he says. "Don't hit on Morgan. Don't ask Morgan about Empath sex. Don't leave Morgan alone with Ava. Y'all really have a lot of rules around this guy."

"What was that last one?" I ask.

"Yes," Morgan chimes in. "Aren't I supposed to be Ava's bodyguard?"

"Oh, that's just Zane," he says. "He's pretty possessive over Ava. You know how Sirens can get."

"Well, I can't blame him for that. Our first encounter was rather inappropriate. Again, I apologize for that."

"What happened?" Kieran asks.

"Oh, um… Morgan got Zane's… um…"

How do I explain this?

"I picked up on his rather intense feelings for Ava and I may have tried it on with her. When he confronted me," Morgan says, biting his lip, "I picked up on his anger and possessiveness, so we had a bit of a confrontation."

Kieran bursts into laughter, kicking his legs in the air.

"What I wouldn't give to see the look on his face! How many shades of red did Zane turn?"

"You're so mean!" I say.

"It's not my fault Zane is so entertaining when he's angry."

I glare at him before turning back to my work.

After an hour or so of chatting with Morgan, Kieran wanders off somewhere, leaving us sitting quietly while I work on my laptop and Morgan distracts himself with his phone.

My back and neck ache and I finally accept that I'm not getting any more work done today and close my laptop.

"Are you well?" he asks.

"Yeah, I'm just done for the day."

"No, I mean, if it's not too personal. It seems like you're in a lot of pain. You were in pain the last time we met. Did Asmodeus do something to you?"

"Ah no," I say. "That's just me. I have some health problems. It's fine."

"Is it? Because to me it feels… not fine."

I'm not used to people calling me out on it when I say I'm fine. Usually people prefer to hear that I'm okay. The truth is a lot more complicated.

"I've gotten used to it. I don't really have a choice, so I just have to live with it. At some point when things don't get better, you just… have to start living again anyway."

"I'm sorry."

"It ended up kind of working in my favor. Asmodeus underestimated the sick little human girl."

"It seems that was his mistake."

"I guess so," I say with a smile. "Why do you hate him so much, anyway? Asmodeus, I mean. Finn said you hated him."

"Ahh," he says, his smile falling and his eyes closing for a moment. He leans forward and rests his elbows on his knees, clasping his hands together.

"I'm sorry. Is that a personal question?"

"It's alright," he says, his eyes meeting mine. "This was bound to come up. It was a long time ago."

He takes in a deep breath and sighs before continuing.

"I don't know how much you know, but Asmodeus had a serious eye for women. Well, he and I happened to set our eyes on the same girl."

This story is awfully familiar.

"Her name was Elizabeth. She was beautiful and bright. Exceptionally kind, too. I was…" He pauses to clear his throat and looks out the window for a minute.

"You don't have to…"

He nods and gives me a sad smile, but continues.

"I was in love with her. But when Asmodeus has his eyes on someone, it's dangerous. So we devised a plan and we got married in secret. I was young and foolhardy. We knew Asmodeus respected marriage and we thought… that he would give up."

I feel my heart ache as my mind starts imagining endings to his story. None of them are good.

"He didn't, of course. He decided that… if he couldn't have her, no one could. He sent a demon to slit her throat. When I arrived home… I…"

He struggles to speak and sucks in his lower lip.

"I'm so sorry," I say. My heart twists in my chest at the sadness in his eyes.

"Don't be," he says, gathering himself and sitting up straight. "You did what many couldn't do—what I couldn't do—you killed him. He'll never hurt anyone again."

I don't know what to say to that. 'You're welcome' seems really inappropriate, so I settle instead for a nod.

Morgan's head quickly turns to the door and his brow furrows.

"Your Siren must be home," he says. "I can feel him. And I'm guessing his meeting didn't go well."

39

 ZANE

"This is not exactly what I expected," I say, eyeing the five-story glass building.

"Peor Energy Associates?" Kami asks, reading the sleek metal sign outside. "Are you sure this is where he's supposed to be?"

I nod. Helen said he had taken on some new business ventures, but I think we're both a bit surprised to find a Demon King running a hip startup in Central London.

We enter the lobby through a revolving door. The inside is sleek and modern, with bright green touches everywhere. There's a large green logo on the wall and drink machines lining one wall. Anything that's not green seems to be made of concrete and, for some reason, there's a green motorcycle in the center of the room. It looks more like the headquarters of a Silicon Valley startup that hasn't yet figured out what their product is.

"What does any of this have to do with an energy company?" I ask.

"They're not exactly an energy company," Kami says, pointing to the symbol on the wall. "That's the Konqr logo. They make energy drinks."

I'm trying to ignore the fact that they apparently spell conquer with a K.

"Belphegor makes energy drinks?" I try not to smile as I ask.

It's hard to ignore the irony of the Demon King of Sloth producing energy drinks.

"I know, right?" Kami chuckles as we approach the front desk.

"Hello," I say to the man at the desk. "We need to see your boss. It's a… er… family matter."

"I'm sorry," he says. "Mr. Belphus doesn't take walk-ins."

Kami reaches out and grabs his hand.

"Tell us where he is and we'll go meet him. It's fine. He's expecting us."

She looks at him tentatively, furrowing her brow as she tries to detect whether or not he's human—and if her charm is working.

"Of course," he says with a compliant nod.

I guess he's human.

He writes instructions to Belphegor's office on a piece of paper and calls us an elevator to the top floor. I charm our way past his personal secretary and we make our way into his office.

Every room we pass has glass walls, but the walls of Belphegor's office are frosted and opaque. I take a breath, then tap softly on the glass.

"Come in!" a voice calls.

Kami and I step inside. The décor is gaudy with a strange mix of ultra-modern furniture and opulent antiques. The walls are lined with priceless art in vintage frames and an avant-garde gold chandelier hangs from the ceiling.

It's difficult to spend this much money and end up with a place that looks so incredibly tacky. I'm almost impressed.

Belphegor is sprawled out on a fuchsia daybed shaped like a hand.

I'm not sure what I should have expected, but I didn't see that one coming.

He has rounded, soft features and short brown hair. He remains lounging in a white silk shirt and a pair of relaxed, slate-blue trousers with a tie belt.

"Oh, look at that!" he says, sitting up with a smile. "If it isn't the enemy of demonkind himself. I was wondering when you'd show up here. And you brought a friend."

He gestures to a pair of white chairs that look as uncomfortable to sit in as they are on the eyes. Kami and I each take one and seat ourselves.

"You were expecting me, then?" I ask.

"You're not about to go to my brothers, now are you?" he says, speaking slowly and clearly with a slight drawl. "Mammon and Beel aren't even on this continent. You know better than to ask Abaddon, and well…"

"Well?" Kami asks.

"I'm sorry," he says. "I don't recall getting your name."

"Kami." She sits rigid in her chair and pinches her lips together.

"Is this the girlfriend? I had heard that Asmodeus had put an end t-"

"Enough," I interrupt. Just hearing him speak of Ava makes me want to kill him.

How much does he know?

"Aww," he says with a growing smile. "Still sensitive about that? I guess the rumors must be true then."

"I'm a friend," Kami says, glaring in his direction.

"And you're both here to… what? Get me to turn on my brothers? Because that's a fool's errand."

"No. We're just looking for information. We know you prefer to not involve yourself."

"And providing you with information would be involving myself, now wouldn't it?"

He leans back and rests his hands behind his head.

"It will get us out of here faster," Kami says. "And get you back to your normal life. Isn't that what you really want?"

"Well, that's a clever way of looking at it." He smiles, scratching his chin and squinting as he seems to ponder his options. "What do you want to know?"

"Who are we up against?" I ask.

"Two of my brothers want to see you dead," he says. "Leviathan and Lucifer."

Shit.

"My brothers are always at odds with each other. That's in part why we each created our armies. But we still don't take kindly to anyone else coming after our family. Leviathan and Asmodeus were closer than the rest of us. He's out for your blood, if only to prove a point to those who wrong him. For Lucifer, on the other hand, it's a matter of pride—as it always is."

I've always been good at messing with the wrong people. But to have gotten on the bad side of three of the seven Demon Kings? I've really done it now.

"And that's why they're killing Sirens?" Kami asks.

"That was just an eye for an eye, so to speak. You kill one of ours, we kill a hundred of yours."

"But they didn't kill a hundred Sirens," I say. "Our best estimate is more like 30."

"Ah well… there may have been unintentional consequences of that."

"You mean our powers?" Kami asks.

"They figured out some way to keep the Sirens dead, but apparently that just made the remaining ones more powerful. That's not exactly a great strategy, and one they quickly decided against pursuing."

"So they didn't know?"

He nods and runs his thumb across his lips.

"My brothers can be ignorant. Many creatures operate from a shared power source. Honestly, I'm surprised Asmodeus's powers weren't absorbed by the remaining kings. But then again, there's no precedent here. A death among the family is new to us all."

"For someone who claims not to hold a grudge," Kami says, "you still seem to consider your brother to be family. Why don't you want us dead?"

"Did I say I don't?" he asks, a smirk growing on his face.

Fuck.

Kami and I exchange worried looks.

"Then why are you helping us?" she asks.

"One could say I'm helping," he says, "though I'm not a particularly helpful type."

We hear a bit of commotion outside the office doors, followed by the thumping of dozens of feet.

Whatever this is, it's not good.

"And what would you call it?" Kami asks.

The door bursts open to reveal a group of demons, their eyes completely black.

Belphegor's smile twists into a more sinister one.

"It's called stalling."

40

There's thumping and clamoring from the entryway and I turn to see Zane stumbling in, his arm supporting a limp Kami as he drags her inside. They're both disheveled, breathing hard, and covered in blood—though it's hard to tell whose. Kami is slumped over in Zane's arms and there's a large gash across her shoulder, so it's safe to say some of it is hers.

"Holy shit, Z!" Kieran curses. "What the fuck happened to you guys?"

"The meeting might not have been as harmless as we expected," Kami mumbles, hissing slightly as Zane guides her to the couch.

"Yeah, we can see that," I say. "What happened?"

"Someone got to him before we did," Zane says, setting Kami in her seat before stumbling to the chair beside me. "He was waiting for us. Somehow, he notified someone that we were there, and before we know it, we're accosted by demons—mostly Incubi and Succubi. Belphegor was apparently working with Leviathan."

"So the guy you went to see is working with the demons who are trying to kill you?"

"Yes and no," he says with a slightly pained grunt. "I mean, I don't think he's in on the larger revenge plan. But he seemed happy to help when it was convenient for him."

"So it's just the one Demon King, then. I guess that's good."

"Well," Kami says with a bit of a cough, "that's not entirely true."

"Lucifer," Zane says.

"Lucifer??" I ask.

Lucifer is real?

"He's a Demon King," he says. "Another of Asmodeus' brothers. He's bad, but he's not the bogeyman he's made out to be."

Lucifer exists and he's trying to kill my boyfriend. Sure, why not?

"Wh-" Kami begins to say, but instead lurches forward and violently coughs. A deep red stains her lips and I realize blood is spurting from her throat.

Kieran and Morgan both jump to their feet.

"Oh my god!" I yelp, looking to Zane in a panic. "Wha-, why isn't she healing yet?"

"Fuck," he says. "We need to get you venom right now."

"Well give her venom!"

"Venom from an injured Siren won't work," Zane says. "I keep a bottle in the bathroom cabinet."

Kieran fires out of the room and returns at lightning speed with the venom in hand.

Kami grabs it and screws open the bottle, but stops and furrows her brows.

"Zane, this isn't enough for both of us," she says with a bit of panic.

"I don't need it," he says with a shrug.

"Tell that to your punctured lung."

"What?" I ask, looking him over. He's in a black shirt so I can't see much blood on him, but his arms have smears here and there. He pulls up his shirt and turns around to reveal a major open wound through his back.

I had dismissed the sharp pain in my chest as more of my usual problems, but I should have been able to tell that it was something more.

For once, I was feeling Zane's pain.

"Holy crap, Zane!" I scold, jumping out of my seat.

"Take the venom," he says to Kami. His eyes meet mine and he smirks slightly. "You're in a much worse way than I am."

"We should split it," she protests.

"It won't help anyone if we're both half-healed. I'll be fine."

She looks at him with a slight squint, but downs the venom.

Wait. What does that mean? He needs the venom too, doesn't he?

"Okay, I'm so out of here," Morgan interrupts, taking a couple of steps toward the door.

"You can't leave now," Kami says. "We need you nearby in case anyone followed us."

"Well I'm sure as hell not sticking around for this," he says, cringing slightly as he gestures between Zane and me.

"This?" I ask, looking to Zane for clarification. I'm met with glowing green eyes and a look of hunger I wouldn't expect from him at this particular moment.

Um... what's happening?

Before I can speak, Zane scoops me up and pins me against the wall.

"That," Morgan says, closing his eyes tightly and pinching the bridge of his nose in his fingers.

Zane smiles at me and leans in for a kiss, stopping just inches from me.

"Guess we're gonna have to do it the old-fashioned way, baby," he says, his lips brushing mine as he speaks.

I forget for a moment that we're in a room full of people as his green eyes seem to bore into my own.

"Oh," I say.

That's actually the only word that seems to be in my vocabulary at this moment. His gaze has me completely tongue-tied. I can feel my cheeks flush and butterflies rise in my stomach.

He picks me up by my thighs and I wrap my legs around his waist. There's a gust of air around us and suddenly we're in his locked bedroom and I'm being thrown onto the bed.

Oh.

"Sexual healing?" I say with a chuckle.

He responds with a deep laugh that makes my whole body shiver.

"If you wouldn't mind, baby," he says with a smile, peeling off his shirt.

How does someone look so good even when they're injured? This is really just unfair.

"Well, I suppose if your life literally depends on it," I tease.

He growls slightly and leaps on top of me, but I roll over him and he lets out a groan.

"Oh, shit!" I say, backing off. "Your back, I'm so sorry!"

"It's okay, baby," he laughs, slightly coughing as he sits up.

"Would it help if you had a nurse to make it better?"

I can't believe that just came out of my mouth, but my sex brain has a mind of its own so I'm just gonna roll with it.

I bite my lip and grind my hips into him. He lets out a deep moan and his eyes flash a brighter green.

"You're my nurse, love?" he says with a playful smirk. "Fittest nurse I've ever had."

He leans in until his lips are on my neck, kissing and sucking greedily. He traces his tongue along the line from my collarbone to my jaw, his teeth nipping slightly when he reaches my earlobe.

He wraps his hands around my hips and tugs me down, sliding my body against him, before flipping himself on top yet again.

"You're being a very naughty patient," I say with a giggle. "I thought I was supposed to be the one taking care of you."

"You can take care of me all you'd like, baby." He winks and, with a quick ripping sound, I feel my panties being torn off.

His hand travels under my top, stroking his fingers across my skin as I unbutton his pants.

"Is this part of the exam, Miss?"

I lean in until my lips are just touching his ear.

"Only if you're good," I hum.

He growls in response and his wings spread wide, shadowing me beneath them. His pants and underwear fly off in an instant and, in a quick maneuver, he flips me back on top of him. I can't tell if it's all the rapid movement making me dizzy, or just the feeling of his touch, but I'm feeling very lightheaded.

Wait, if it didn't hurt him to lie on his back, does that mean this is working?

I'm distracted from that thought by one look at his sculpted chest.

What was I saying?

I slowly lower myself onto him as he curses and grabs the headboard. I collapse on top of him as the sensation of fullness overwhelms me. He thrusts his hips, slowly at first but picking up speed as he goes.

An inhuman roar leaves his lips, his chest vibrating beneath my fingertips.

"Does this mean I've been good?" he asks with a mischievous smile.

"I- I-," I try to answer, but my brain seems to be completely cut off from the rest of my body.

"Sorry miss, I didn't quite hear you," he replies. His grin has turned full-on cocky at the response he's gotten from me.

"I was going to say I don't know if you've been good enough."

"How can I be better?"

"Hmm…" I say.

I roll my hips in a circular motion and his eyes roll back as he moans my name.

"That's… that… I… you're…" he mumbles.

"Sorry, I didn't quite hear you," I say, rolling my hips again.

"Ch-cheeky girl."

His eyes are radiant and intensely locked with my own.

"You're about to pu- push me over the-" he says, interrupted when I drop myself down onto him and begin bouncing up and down.

A combination of a moan and growl erupts from his chest as he shudders before falling back onto the bed.

"Fuck!" he curses.

I fall onto his chest and sigh.

"Are you alright?" I ask through heavy breaths.

"I'm better than alright, love," he says with a contented sigh.

"Good."

It occurs to me that I'm still a bit worked up, but in this instance, I'm just glad to be able to help Zane.

"Could I ask you a question, nurse?" he says, kissing my neck softly. I feel the corners of his lips curl against my skin. "Do you think it's safe for me to engage in more physical activity?"

41

 ZANE

"Are you sure it's safe?" Ava asks, her eyes wide.

"Of course," I say. "Why?"

"Oh, I dunno, maybe the fact that a bunch of demons attacked you yesterday?"

Ah. That.

"That was different, love." I sit beside her on the edge of the bed and rub my palm along her thigh. "When we were attacked, it was because we went behind enemy lines, so to speak. This is just a night out at the pub. Contrary to how it may seem, demons aren't everywhere."

"Just everywhere we go."

Fair dues.

It's strange to know that she worries about me—the Immortal who has been alive for several human lifetimes. But when it comes to herself, she's ready to charge right into danger with no regard for her own safety.

My little human daredevil wants to keep *me* safe.

I fucking love this woman.

"I should come," she says with a resolute stare.

"You going to protect me if we run into a demon, baby?"

"Well…. No. Shut up, okay? I dunno. I just don't like the idea of you being in danger and me not being there to do something about it."

I wrap my arms around her and pull her into my lap.

"I kind of like the idea of you beating someone up for me," I tease.

"Wouldn't be the first time. I did kick Asmodeus's ass if you'll recall."

"How could I forget?" I give her a kiss on the cheek and she giggles.

I convince Ava that I'll be fine without her and she heads out to the living room where Kieran is waiting. I slip on a T-shirt and jeans before joining them. Ava is wrapped in a blanket on the couch while the two of them watch TV.

"You look good," Kieran says. "Could probably do with a looser T-shirt, though. I'm trying to get laid tonight, not you, remember? I'm supposed to be the hot one."

"You're supposed to be the hot one? Guess you should work on that, eh?"

I smirk and he shoots me a glare.

"If you weren't so gorgeous, I might be mad at you for that little comment."

"Ahh, but I am so…"

"Uggh," a voice groans from behind me. I turn to see Morgan standing in the corner with his arms crossed and his lips pinched into a thin line. "It's bad enough that I have to watch Kieran flirt with Finn all the time, but this? You're both attractive. Let's end it there, shall we?"

So I guess Morgan is here then. Great.

"Speaking of Finn…" I decide to change the subject rather than engage. "Is he here yet?"

"No, Finn called me, said he couldn't make it after all. Some sort of family thing, he said."

"F- Finn's not coming?" The words catch slightly in my throat.

"I told him I could handle anything that comes up. Not like Finn's powers are of much use in a fight, anyway."

My eyes narrow as I look between him and Ava. I know I can trust Ava, but I don't feel comfortable with this bloke at all. My first interaction with him is still burned into my memory.

I've never been so directly challenged for Ava before. I still kind of want to kill him.

Is it possible to kill someone just a little bit?

"You okay?" Ava asks, snapping me out of the thought.

Me? Oh, I'm fine. Just trying not to act like a jealous cunt.

"Yeah, baby. Why?" I lean down to give her a kiss. Morgan snickers, obviously sensing how I'm actually feeling.

"Your eyes are a little…"

"Ah… um… no, I'm fine. I was just thinking… maybe you were right. Maybe you should come with us. It would be more fun. Plus, you haven't been to an

English pub yet."

"Uhh… I love Ava, I do," Kieran says, "but when she's there, you just obsess over her all night. I'd prefer to not die of hunger."

"Piss off, mate. I'm not going to obsess over Ava. You'll still get your meal."

"He's right," Ava says. "You do worry too much about me. Besides, I don't want to intrude on your boys' night."

"I can join you," Morgan chimes in. "That's what I'm here to do, right? Look after you? Doesn't really matter to me where we go. I could go for a pint anyway."

Wanker.

"Well, I'm not too fond of inviting another ultra-smoking-hot dude to compete against," Kieran says. "But eh, why the hell not—the more the merrier!"

Ava agrees and retreats to the bedroom to change her outfit. After fifteen minutes or so, she emerges in a tight leather miniskirt and black sweater with leather boots.

"Is this okay?" she asks, looking down and straightening out her skirt.

I swallow hard as my eyes follow her curves.

Bloody hell. This woman lives to torture me.

We're greeted by loud music, raucous chatter, and the smell of beer and warm shepherd's pie. I spot an open table toward the back and I head past the band with Ava's hand in mine. We sit down and my eyes take a moment to adjust to the warm, dim light.

"So this is a real live British pub?" Kieran asks. "I'm not sure what I expected, but it's kind of just a bar with more exposed brick. I guess the Brits were the original hipsters."

Cheeky arse.

"I'm going to get us a round. Cider for you?" I ask Ava, who nods in response. "For you two?"

"Beer, whatever's good," Kieran says.

I turn to Morgan for his order.

"Newcastle," he says. "Cheers."

I make my way to the bar. The pub is lively with its usual Friday night crowd—university students, rowdy football fans, and a few regulars that I imagine are here during most times of the day. After a minute or so waiting at the bar, I order our drinks then make my way back to the table with a tray in hand.

"Thanks, dude!" Kieran says, grabbing his beer off the tray. The others grab their drinks and I take my own, taking a heavy swig of beer.

"Have you scoped out any targets yet?"

Kieran shoots me a knowing smile and tilts his head in the direction of a nearby table. A group of girls is sitting together in a booth, clearly all dressed for a night out.

"The hoop earrings," he says.

Only one of them has big, gold hoop earrings. She has voluminous curly brown hair and dark skin and is wearing a tight silk dress and heels. She's well overdressed for a pub.

Ava nods in understanding and Kieran and I approach the table. Kieran uses one of his usual lines, and before long we're seated amongst the women. Two of them seem particularly smitten with me, and I keep having to push their hands off of me. Neither seems to be receiving my message.

Hopefully it's not upsetting Ava.

I look over at their table, but Morgan is now sitting alone. He catches my eyes and smirks, but points toward the band. Ava is standing in front of the band amongst a crowd, dancing by herself to the music.

My heartbeat slows as I watch her dance. She looks so happy, bouncing up and down as she swings her arms and sings along to the music. I know she doesn't dance a lot because it causes her pain, but I'm glad she's feeling well enough to get lost in the moment—if only for a minute.

The girls seem to continue talking, despite the fact that I'm clearly ignoring them. I turn back to Morgan, whose face is mostly still, but his mouth is turned up slightly at the edge as he watches her dance.

I'd like to think he's smiling at Ava's less-than-coordinated dancing, but my gut churns at the thought that he could be smiling at her the way I do—with adoration.

Stop.

I turn my attention back to my table, where the conversation seems to be flowing seamlessly without my participation. A string of discomfort tugs at me, pulling my attention back to Morgan.

No. Ava is with you. Fuck this guy.

But I can't help it. I find myself turning toward him again, but this time his expression is different. His mouth has pinched into a thin, straight line. His brows are furrowed and his eyes are narrow and questioning. I follow his gaze to Ava, who has stopped dancing and is now talking to a dark-haired man who towers over her small frame.

Who the fuck is that?

I look back to Kieran, who has his tongue down the girl's throat in the corner of the booth.

Fuck it.

I quickly excuse myself from the table and speed over to Ava, but Morgan beats me there.

"Stupid American bitch," the man curses.

I'm not sure what has happened, but I've already heard enough to want to knock this man out.

"Take a big step back there," Morgan says, his voice low and threatening.

The man instead takes a staggered step toward Morgan, which only seems to make Morgan smile.

"I've got this," I say to Morgan, stepping forward as I sweep Ava behind me.

"This is what you hired me to do," he says under his breath.

He's right. I hired him to protect Ava. But somehow, the idea of him being the one to take care of her has me feeling sick.

"But I'm here now," I say, trying to situate myself between him and the man.

"And so am I." He glares at me and grabs the man's wrist. The man tries to swing for him but he grabs his other wrist in midair. "Apologize and go home."

The man blinks a few times before looking at Ava.

"I'm sorry. It was my mistake. I'm really drunk." He immediately turns and exits the pub.

"See?" Morgan says with a smirk. "Handled."

Did this bloody bastard just use my own powers to defend my girlfriend in front of me?

42

Zane left about twenty minutes ago to help Kami track down a new lead. Morgan, of course, showed up about a minute after he left. Morgan has always done his best to avoid Zane, but now they both seem to be actively steering clear of each other.

I use Zane's busy days to catch up on my work while Morgan and Kieran keep an eye on me like I'm a 25-year-old toddler who can't be trusted not to color on the walls.

Kieran has been in his room for a while, probably taking a nap. Morgan sits in the corner with his legs crossed so that his ankle is resting on his knee. He seems engrossed in his book—a thick red hardcover with gold lettering spelling out a title in what appears to be Russian.

I can't help but be curious. Is it some kind of magical Immortal book?

I squint in an attempt to work out the letters.

Epatbr… Kapamaeobbi?

"Staring, are we?" he asks with a chuckle.

Oops. Awkward.

"Sorry," I say. "I'm just curious what you're reading."

"*Brat'ya Karamazovy,*" he says with a slight smirk.

"Ahh…"

I have no idea what that means.

"It's *The Brothers Karamazov.* It's fiction. By the same author who wrote *Crime and Punishment.*"

"And you're reading it in Russian?"

"Nothing gets past you, does it, Killer?"

"So you're fluent in Russian and asshole?" I tease.

He jokingly scoffs before returning to his book.

A ringing sound from my computer startles me and I see a green notification bar pop up in the corner of my screen.

Incoming Call: JEN

I pick up my computer and step outside into the garden, setting it down on the patio table before accepting the call.

"Heeyyyy girrrll!" Jen's voice calls as she appears on my screen.

"Hey!" I say.

"I've missed you! You've hardly called me since you've been in London. You're a terrible best friend. Tell me everything! Have you killed any more demons or warlocks or whatever else you guys keep running into over there?"

"Jen!" I scold. "I'm not just going around killing everybody left and right!"

"Sure, Killer," Morgan says, appearing behind me as he waves to Jen.

"Excuse me, Mister Eavesdropper!"

"Just doing my job." He heads further into the garden and sits on a bench nearby.

"Who is that?" Jen asks. "You extended your superhero posse without telling me?"

"He's not… nobody is a superhero, Jen. We are *not* the X-Men."

"Oh, okay, sure. You just have a boyfriend with a British accent who can control people's minds and a demon who has horns and a tail and a girl with wings…"

"That… You're just… That doesn't count."

"Plus all of them are like, crazy attractive. What does this new guy do?"

Morgan stands up and walks behind me, leaning on my chair as he looks curiously at the screen.

"Who might you be?" he asks with a cocky grin.

"I'm Jen," she says. "Chemist, certified genius, plus-size hottie, and Ava's best friend. Unfortunately, human. Who are you?"

"Morgan," he says with a bit of a laugh. "Ava's bodyguard. Or, as you call it, 'the new guy.'"

"Oh! So you're the bodyguard? What are your superpowers?"

My eyes widen as I try to subtly signal to her that the topic may be inappropriate, but she seems undeterred.

"My superpowers?" Luckily, he seems to be more amused than offended.

"Yeah, Ava is trying to convince me you guys aren't the X-Men. So what do you do? Are you a shapeshifter? Do you have big metal claws? Are you super fast?"

"Well, you just get right to it, don't you?"

"Yes. Yes I do."

I let my head fall into my hands.

Oy. That's Jen, alright.

"Do any of your X-Men have the power to channel the powers of others?" he asks.

Oh boy. Here we go.

"What?" she asks, her mouth agape for a moment. "You're…. You're… Ava, he's fucking Rogue!"

Her high-pitched squeal nearly breaks my computer's speakers.

"I'm what?" he asks with raised brows.

"Rogue has that power and she's, like, super cool. I've always wanted her and Jubilee to get together, but apparently it's *'not canon.'* Unfortunately, you're a dude, which is disappointing, bu-"

"You find my gender disappointing?" he asks. "Don't think I've gotten that particular reaction before."

He takes a seat beside me, just outside of the camera's view.

"Oh, I'm sorry. I didn't mean it in a bad way. Did I offend man-Rogue?" she asks.

"Still here," he says.

"Well, my bad," she says. "Do you have any other powers?"

He leans back into the frame.

"I can feel what others are feeling—which makes it real easy to tell when I'm being lied to or double-crossed. I can also shift emotions or feelings between any two beings that I'm touching. Comes in handy during combat."

"How so?"

"Well, I can temporarily take pain away from anyone on my side and give it to whoever I'm fighting."

He can weaponize pain? I've definitely got plenty of ammo for him.

"That's awesome," she says. "They can't hurt you without hurting themselves. I like you, man-Rogue."

"That's sticking, is it?"

"Oh yeah."

He chuckles and shakes his head, moving back to his seat and returning to his book.

"Aannnyyway…" I say. "How are you?"

"Me?" she asks. "Who cares about me? You're in London, having adventures with the X-Men. I want deets!"

"It's not particularly exciting…" I say, trying to think of something interesting to tell her. "Oh! I know… turns out Lucifer is real and he's one of the Demon Kings after Zane."

"Lucifer? Holy shit… Does he have the horns and the pitchfork? The whole nine yards?"

I look to Morgan, who shakes his head side to side.

"Sorry, apparently not."

"Dang. That would have been cool. So is he like… really dangerous? Are you guys in trouble?"

"Zane and Kami seem to think we'll be okay. We've got the council on our side and they seem to think that's enough."

"Well that's good. But if you need me, you better tell me. I've been reading up on all the lore I can get my hands on and I've learned a lot about Immortal beings and stuff."

"Except you haven't learned that it's not okay to ask someone what their powers are…"

"Shit, it's not? Well… there's a lot out there, okay? There's not exactly a guide to Immortal culture out there."

"True," I say. "I wish there was. We ran into Zane's ex a little while ago and apparently she was super offensive to me and I didn't even know it."

Morgan peers up from his book.

"What did she say?" Jen asks. "Do I need to fight a bitch?"

"No, no. She just called me cute."

"Ooof," Morgan says with a slight hiss, not looking up from his book but clearly still listening.

"What?" I ask. "Is it that bad?"

"It's not good," he says. "Sirens are all about attraction, passion, sexual prowess. If you want to start a fight with a Siren, you question their attractiveness or seduction skills. Or you make a move on their lover."

"Pretty sure coming on to anyone's partner is gonna piss them off," Jen says, "Siren or not."

"Fair dues," he says with a nod, but he's still off-screen, so she can't see it.

"What a bitch! That's not even fair to you because you're human. What are you supposed to do? Swap punches with a superhuman?"

"I know, right?" I say. "Besides, I'm not even a full-strength human. The best I've got is the occasional snarky comeback, and I couldn't even do that because I didn't know she was insulting me at the time."

Morgan looks up from his book, scrunching his lips as though he's considering saying something.

"Do you have something to add?" I ask.

"Uh… technically you don't have to fight her," he says. "There are two options, really."

"Is one of them a magic potion?" Jen asks. "'Cause I fucking love a good magic potion."

"No," he scoffs. "Not a magic potion."

"What then?" I ask.

"You just defend your partner the old-fashioned way. Show your physical prowess with a bit of a… display of sorts. This is… ugh, what an awkward topic… you… uh…"

"Oh my god," Jen says. "He's talking about PDA."

"Oh…" I say.

I look to Morgan, who shrugs his shoulders and nods.

"I love it!" she squeals. "You show her who's boss with some good ol' fashioned making out and getting all up in there!"

"Eww. How do you always manage to say things in the grossest way ever?"

"It's a gift." She flips her hair and smiles proudly.

Part of me is creeped out by the thought. Another part of me is kind of hoping we run into Tara again.

43

I shift in my seat as I sift through yet another book from the Council archives. This one is mostly in French, which is fortunate because the last three I've found have been Greek or Latin, neither of which I'm particularly great with.

My eyes scan the pages for anything that might help us fix the issue of Sirens not being reborn.

Nothing. Fuck.

I flip to the next page and sigh.

"You alright, Z?" Kami asks from across the table, looking up from her own book.

"I'm fine," I say, combing my hair back with my fingers. "I'm just tired of dead ends. I'd rather be home with Ava."

"Aanndd you hate the fact that she's home with Morgan instead?"

My eyes shoot daggers in her direction.

"Thanks for the reminder," I say, grinding my teeth.

"Why are you so uptight about those two, anyway? You know Ava's crazy about you."

"I don't know. It's not Ava that I don't trust, but him…. He just… I don't like the way he looks at her. It's like… he's enthralled. Like he's lost in her, just like I am."

"And you don't see the irony in that?" She raises a brow and tilts her head.

What about that is ironic?

"Apparently not," I say. "What irony?"

"Listen to what you're saying. He looks at her as if he has feelings for her— like you do."

"Yeah, he…" I pause for a moment, taking in what she's saying. "Oh. Fuck."

She gives me a knowing nod.

"He's just channeling your feelings, Z. What you're seeing is a reflection of you. Those are your own feelings being projected into another person."

Up until I met Ava, I'd barely ever been jealous. I never let anyone get close enough to have a real connection—something I could fear losing.

Now I'm getting jealous of myself.

Well, that's embarrassing.

"You might be right," I say, dropping my head into my palms.

"I usually am." She smirks and grabs another book from her stack. "Have yo-"

The door opens and a man with black hair and a goatee walks in. He's wearing a grey suit, but his collar is loosened and he has no tie. Clearly an overworked Council employee.

He heads over to a bookshelf just behind Kami and peruses the shelves, grabbing a thick leather-bound binder before looking up and noticing us.

"Hey, you're Zane, right?" he asks with an unnerving, lopsided grin.

"Yeah," I say. "That's me."

"I'm Felix." He approaches me, tucking the binder under his arm and extending his opposite hand to shake mine. We shake and I give him a nod before turning back to the book in front of me.

"Everyone's talking about you. Did you really kill Asmodeus?"

Kami shifts in her seat and glances up at us. His question seems to have us both on edge. With everything going on in the world, it can be difficult to tell friends from allies, so any questions out of the blue are bound to set off alarm bells.

"I did."

"How?" he asks, leaning onto the table beside me. "Nobody has ever been able to kill a King. How does a Siren of all people end up finally taking him out?"

It's a question I've intentionally dodged up until now. In part, because I don't want to bring Kieran into it, but also because I didn't *actually* kill him. The last thing I want is to put Ava on anyone's radar.

I suppose 'fuck off' isn't the most appropriate response here, but I don't have another prepared.

"Those details aren't something that can be shared," Kami says.

She has always been better than me at giving diplomatic answers.

"Hmm…" he says, his face becoming more stern. He turns around and heads out of the room without saying another word.

Well, that's bloody suspicious.

"Thanks for handling that," I say to Kami. "I really need to get my story straight if I'm going to keep this up. We keep running into people with questions."

"Yeah, good idea," she says with a teasing laugh. "Speaking of running into people, I saw Tara again yesterday."

"I thought you were here yesterday. What would Tara be doing at the Council offices?"

"She came for a follow up of the shot."

"Shot?"

"Yeah, injection, jab, whatever. I told you the Council had their own version of Jen's cure."

"Oh, yeah."

"Honestly, I'm pretty sure she was trying her darnedest to run into you. She was pretty disappointed when I told her you weren't here."

"What a shame," I say with a laugh. "Considering how she was talking to Ava when we last spoke, she's probably lucky I wasn't here. I know she and I didn't part on the best of terms, but I'm not about to fucking let her get away with that rubbish again."

"I was kind of hoping Ava would punch her."

"She would've broken her hand!"

"True, but she has a punch or two coming. Especially after what she did to you."

"I've practically forgotten about it," I say with a shrug. "Tara is just… Tara."

"Well, I certainly haven't. I know you prefer that I just let it go, but sometimes being polite with that woman is impossible."

"With any luck, you'll never have to see her again anyway."

"Unless she keeps stalking you." She snorts in irritation and rolls her eyes.

Let's hope it was just a coincidence and she's not actually following me. The last thing I need is Tara chasing me around.

I arrive home later than I'd hoped. The fog has almost entirely blocked out the light of the moon and the sky is pitch black. It's just before midnight and there's a damp chill in the air.

I open the door to a mostly dark house, with the only light being the flickering blue glow of the living room TV. I follow the light to find Kieran on the couch, Morgan in a chair beside him, both watching Jurassic Park.

"Hey," I say in a low voice. "Has Ava gone to bed?"

Morgan nods, his expression rigid and tight. He squints and stirs uncomfortably in his seat. I seem to have that effect on him.

"You should too, dude," Kieran says. "You look tired."

He's not wrong. I'm fucking knackered.

I drag my feet up the stairs into the bedroom, taking care to avoid waking Ava. I strip to my boxers and slide under the covers, wrapping an arm around her waist. My face falls into the curve of her neck and I take a deep breath in, inhaling her scent. As I exhale, I feel my consciousness fade.

I close my eyes for minutes, or maybe hours—I can't really tell. But I'm startled awake by a deep feeling of wrongness and fear.

Ava tosses and turns in my arms, whimpering and twisting violently.

Another bad dream?

I prop myself up on an elbow and lean over her, stroking her face in an attempt to wake her up gently. She grimaces, her eyes still closed as she shudders.

I hate that she's reacting this way, but I try to remind myself that it's not me she's reacting to.

My hand moves to her shoulder, shaking her just enough to hopefully wake her.

"No," she cries softly. "Stop, please!"

Fuck. I hate hearing her like this.

"Baby, wake up. You're having a bad dream."

She thrashes more, weak sounds of pain leaving her lips.

"Please," she mewls. "Zane, stop! Stop!"

At that, an impossible weight crushes my chest and I feel the world crumble around me.

The monster haunting her dreams... is me.

44

Light peeks through the curtains as I slowly wake from sleep. My body aches and my stomach is in knots. Despite sleeping for hours, I feel more tired now than I did when I went to bed.

I stretch my arm out to find Zane, but instead I'm met with a cold, empty mattress.

Did Zane get up already?

He should've gone to bed later than me, so I expected him to sleep in today. The clock says it's only 7:30 am.

I hop out of bed and slip on a loose gray sweater and black leggings before heading downstairs. I follow soft sounds of movement to the kitchen, where I see a man's silhouette against the window light. As he turns around, I realize it's not Zane, but Morgan.

"Morning, Killer," he says, his voice hoarse and dry.

"What are you still doing here?" I ask. "Weren't you supposed to head home last night?"

"Yeah uh… after you went to bed, Kieran and I started watching a movie marathon and uh… well, about four beers and three dinosaur movies later, I ended up sleeping on the sofa."

"Oh, I guess that explains why you seem so tired."

"You seem pretty knackered yourself, love. Rough night?"

"Yeah um… not the best night's sleep, I guess. Hey uh… have you seen Zane this morning?"

He furrows his brow and looks deep in thought for a moment.

"No. It's unlike him to leave you alone, isn't it?"

"I'm sure he's around here somewhere," I say, peeking out the window to see if he might be in the yard.

"Mmm… sorry, I don't think he is."

"What?" I say, my heart pounding harder as anxiety begins to build in my chest. *What does he mean by that? Where could he be if he's not here?*

"If he were here, I would be able to sense him."

"But you said that you can't tell the difference between his emotions and yours. Are you sure you're not just getting your wires crossed?"

"I'm sure. When he's around, I can sense his feelings for you. You're brilliant, but uh, I don't feel *that* way about you when he's not here. No offense."

The uneasy feeling in my stomach twists and expands.

Where is he? Did he get home safely last night?

"He came home last night, didn't he?"

"Yeah, he got some time after eleven… maybe midnight? Relax, Killer," he says, stepping toward me and giving me a reassuring pat on the back. "He probably just ran out to the corner shop."

"Yeah…"

I don't even believe myself as I say it. This isn't like Zane at all. He wouldn't just leave without leaving me a note or something.

It just feels wrong.

"You don't believe that," he says, shaking his head.

"Not really," I say with a sigh. "Something feels wrong."

He pinches his mouth into a narrow line and looks into my eyes.

"Trust that feeling," he says, his voice deep and monotone. "You have good instincts. If you say something is wrong, I believe you. But if I can't feel him… you still can."

He's right. If Zane's in trouble, I should be able to feel it.

I close my eyes and concentrate on any sensation that might be able to tell me what has happened to Zane.

I feel anxiety, pain, fear… I'm pretty sure those things are all my own.

"There," Morgan says. "I could feel him for a second."

"You can? How?" I ask, opening my eyes. "All I feel is my own anxiety."

"It's not all yours. Concentrate. What do you feel?"

I close my eyes again and take a deep breath in.

"Fear. And pain."

"Get specific," he says.

Fear—it's a deep fear, but it's…different. I feel… inadequate. It's a deep self-loathing. A fear of… myself?

Why would Zane feel that way?

"He's in trouble, he's scared," I say. "He's… sad. He's upset with himself. He fears himself. I don't understand."

I open my eyes to Morgan's concerned face.

"It sounds like whatever's happening with Zane isn't supernatural… it's personal. I'll wake up Kieran and we'll go find your boy."

In a few minutes, a reluctant and drowsy Kieran shambles into the room in a distressed band t-shirt and jeans. His hair is a tangled nest that he has just barely swept from his eyes.

"So… Morgan said something about Zane being missing and I guess we're going to find him or something? I'm gonna be honest, I'm like… less than 12 percent awake right now. I'm not even entirely sure I'm not dreaming."

"Let's go," Morgan says, his entire demeanor shifting. When there's a task at hand, he becomes cold and focused.

We head out the door. The cool morning air hits me before I even realize I don't have any clue where to go.

"Where are we supposed to start?" I ask, turning to Morgan.

"This is up to you, Ava," he says. "You can feel him. But more importantly, you know him. You know how he thinks. He's afraid, he's in pain… where does he go?"

"I don't know!" I say with an exasperated sigh. "We've only been in England for a couple of weeks. I don't know the area at all."

"But you know Zane. His car is here, so he didn't drive anywhere. Did he take the train? To Kami's, maybe?"

"No." I shake my head. "He doesn't like asking for help. He always tries to handle things on his own."

"When you guys broke up, he got really drunk and trashed his house," Kieran says. "I mean, obviously he's not home right now, but maybe he's getting drunk?"

"I doubt it," Morgan says. "If there's one thing I've learned about this guy, he'd never get wasted while he's concerned about Ava's safety."

"Ahh, good point."

I wrack my brain for any idea of where Zane could be.

When he's not destroying things… how does Zane deal with panic?

"Water," I say. "He's always dipping his feet in the pool. When we broke up… he fell asleep sitting like that."

"Okay," Kieran says, tapping at his phone for a moment. "According to the map, the nearest water is a creek a bit that way. I don't see much else within walking distance, so we start there."

We walk a few minutes down a path through the nearby woods.

"Hey," Morgan says. "I'm picking him up. He's nearby."

I start walking faster until I'm jogging, then running until I spot a familiar silhouette beside the creek. Morgan and Kieran have stopped following, probably to give us space to talk.

I still don't know what has Zane so shaken.

"Zane," I call as I approach.

His head swivels around and I catch his defeated expression. His eyes are bloodshot and raw, his skin puffy and his cheeks damp with tears.

I run up to him and wrap my arms around him. He seems stunned by my sudden appearance, but lets out a sigh of relief and pulls me in.

"You had me so worried!" I say.

He blinks a few times before his gaze drops.

"I'm sorry," he says.

"What's going on? Why are you out here? Did something happen yesterday?"

"I…" He steps back and runs his fingers through his hair, grabbing a fistful and tugging in frustration.

"Talk to me," I say. "Don't hold out on me. What's up?"

"Really?" he asks, his expression turning slightly sour. "You want me to be open with you, then? You first, eh? Want to tell me about the dreams you've been having?"

I freeze.

I knew this reckoning was coming, but I was hoping I could put it off for at least a few more months. Or, in a perfect world, forever. Yeah, forever would have been ideal.

"Zane… I… Okay." I take a deep breath in. "I was having dreams about… you—sort of. It wasn't really you, though. It was more like when Asmodeus pretended to be you. It's just… it's my brain's way of dealing with everything that happened, you know? It's my fears and anxiety. It's not reality and I know that, and you should know it too."

"It is reality. You know who I am. You know *what* I am. And your mind—rightfully so—is telling you to run. It's trying to protect you. From me."

I watch as tears spill over from his eyes and he tries to hold back a sob.

"No!" I say, holding his face in my palms. "Look at me. That is just not true. I love you and I am *not* afraid of you. Not one bit."

"You were screaming, begging me to stop in your sleep. Not Asmodeus, me!"

I feel his sorrow radiating through my bones. He's in so much pain, and it's my fault. I should have found a way to tell him. He never should have found out like this.

"Do you trust me?" I ask. He looks deep into my eyes as if I've asked him the most ridiculous question. "Do you?"

"Of course."

"Then I want you to listen to me and do what I say. No questions. Just trust me, okay?"

He nods, wiping a tear from his eye.

I take his hand in mine and I bring it up to my neck.

"What are you doing?" he asks, his eyes wide with concern.

"No questions, remember? Trust…"

He takes in a jagged breath and nods.

I wrap his fingers around my neck and resist when he tries to pull away. I place both of my hands over his, holding it in place.

"You can feel me through the bond. Close your eyes." He follows my instruction reluctantly. "Can you feel me?"

He nods.

"What do you feel?" I ask.

"Concern," he says. "You're worried."

"Am I afraid?"

"I don't- I don't know. I don't like this. I don't want to be… I d-"

"Your hand is around my neck. You're a million times stronger than me. We're in the middle of nowhere in the woods. You could kill me right now, couldn't you?"

"Don't say that," he says, tugging at his hand slightly. "I don't like this. Don't."

"Am I afraid?" I ask, our eyes locking.

"No." He looks down and another tear falls from his eyes.

"Dreams are just that, Zane. They're not reality. My reality is complete and utter faith in you. It always has been and always will be. My subconscious can have a field day and come up with whatever worst-case scenario it can, but you—the real you—I will always trust with my life. You understand me?"

He reluctantly nods and chuckles slightly.

"You scolding me, love?" he asks with a smile.

"You bet I am. It's freezing cold and it's early and I just ran like half a mile. You're in big trouble and you owe me a pancake breakfast."

45

"You're not going to tell me where we're going?" I ask as Zane holds my hand and leads me down the sidewalk.

"You said you wanted to see *my London*," he says, "so I'm showing it to you."

I look around for a moment. I doubt this quiet neighborhood is home to any secret London attractions. The street sign reads: Royal Hospital Rd.

"And your London has something to do with… a hospital?"

"Good try, love," he says with a smirk.

He tugs at my hand and turns toward a modern-looking brown brick building. The words 'National Army Museum' are emblazoned over the door.

"Army museum?" I ask. He gives me a smirk and pushes the front door open, escorting me inside.

The doors lead to a large, open space with a high ceiling spanning a few stories. On every wall, there are murals of old war photos and pieces of memorabilia in glass cases. Considering the amount of artillery surrounding us, this may be the most American place in all of London.

"So you used to go here?" I ask.

"No, actually," he says, clearly enjoying how much he's confusing me. "This wasn't around when I lived here."

"Do you enjoy being cryptic?"

As if he's decided to be extra mischievous, he replies with only a wink.

He scopes out the room before leading me down a hallway lined with photos. I take in the photos as we pass—young men kicking around a soccer ball, the queen's guard marching in uniform, mustachioed men holding muskets, soldiers sharing drinks from a flask. It's a warm, human side of war that I really didn't expect.

Zane squints as he scans each frame, seemingly looking for something in particular. After a moment of walking, he stops in front of a black-and-white shot of soldiers casually lounging on the ground beside their guns. They're wearing brimmed caps and structured uniforms that I'm guessing were a classic military green.

He points to the photo and looks back to me.

Then I see it.

The familiar face of one of the soldiers in the background catches my eye.

My mouth drops as I lean in to examine the photo.

"Oh my god," I say, bringing my hand to cover my mouth.

It's one thing to know that your boyfriend is 200-years-old. It's another thing to see a photo of that boyfriend in a museum.

"An old friend told me this was here," he says. "Said I should check it out next time I was in town. You said you wanted to know more about my life in London, so I thought… maybe you'd like to see it?"

"Wow, Zane. This is…. Yeah, of course I want to see it. I kind of expected you to, I dunno, take me to the restaurants you used to go to. This is next-level."

"To be fair, I haven't lived here in ages. Most of the restaurants I knew back then aren't around anymore."

"This is really cool," I say, unable to tear my eyes away from the photo.

The man in this photo is so serious—stoic, sad even. His curly locks are chopped and tamed in a short military cut. He's a completely different person than the man who stands in front of me. If I wasn't so familiar with the curves and lines of his face, I wonder if I'd be able to recognize him at all.

"Were these men your friends?" I ask, pointing to others in the photo.

"These two were," he says, pointing to the soldiers standing beside him. "This one here is Immortal too."

"Was that a thing? Like… Immortal military units or something?"

"Not really, but most of us ended up in the elite units because we outperformed the humans. There were about six in ours."

Sometimes I realize there's so much about Zane and being an Immortal that I still don't understand.

"I want to learn more about Immortals… and Sirens. I want to know more about you and your life."

He wraps his arms around my waist and tugs me against his chest.

"You are my life, baby. This stuff, it's my past. The important parts of my life didn't happen until you showed up."

"Well, I want to know all of it."

"What do you want to know?"

"I don't know… you tell me. What do I need to know about Sirens?"

"I'm really the wrong person to ask about this. I spent a long time avoiding being what one might call a typical Siren. Uh… er… if you want, there is this thing…"

"What thing?"

"Alek and David are having a party this weekend. There are going to be a bunch of Sirens there, not just Alek. Kami is already planning on going but I figured we'd pass."

"Why? Don't you want to hang out with your friends?"

"I'm not exactly the most social bloke on the planet. I really just want to spend time with you, and I know parties tire you out."

"Way to make me sound like an old lady."

I scrunch my face in irritation.

Do I technically have the physical stamina of an old lady? Yes. But that's beside the point.

"Well, it may also have something to do with the fact that I don't love the idea of you surrounded by a lot of horny Sirens," he says, giving me a kiss on the forehead. "That, and I hate fancy dress."

"Fancy? Is it like, black tie?"

"Er, um, sort of…"

Why does that sound so ominous?

———

Following Kami around a shopping mall should be an Olympic sport. I can only imagine the amount of ibuprofen I'm going to need to get through this day.

"Where are we going?" I ask.

When Kami said she wanted to help me shop for this party, I didn't know I was agreeing to quite so much speed-walking.

"It's just down this way," she says, sauntering forward with ease like she isn't dragging a sluggish human in her wake.

"So why are we going to a special store, anyway? Zane said it was a special kind of dress code but he's not particularly great at explaining this sort of thing."

"It's a *Great Gatsby*–themed party. This store has a lot of fun, beaded dresses."

"*Great Gatsby*? Oh… I have no idea what that's supposed to be."

She stops and turns into an incredible dress shop, each rack full of intricate, beaded dresses with a bit of vintage flair.

"Wow!" I say, my eyes scanning the racks. "There's no way I can afford anything in here."

"Zane said you'd say that, so he gave me his credit card."

I walk up to a dress and flip over the tag. The price is £340, which I'm now realizing I don't actually know the value of—but it sounds like a lot.

I open my mouth to protest, but Kami cuts me off.

"Just try some stuff on," she says. "If you really don't want to buy anything, we can go somewhere else."

I begrudgingly nod and start browsing the racks.

Everything here is beautiful, but my eyes linger on a dark green dress covered in beaded fringe that swishes as it moves. It has slinky spaghetti straps and a low-cut neckline that would undoubtedly make my boobs look excellent. It's the perfect combination of that twenties vibe with a modern twist.

"Oh wow," Kami says. "You absolutely have to try that on."

"I don't know. It's really expensive."

"You said you'd try stuff on, remember?"

"I know but… don't you think it's a little risqué? I mean… it's really short and really chesty."

"All the better," she says with a wink. "Remember, this is a Siren party."

"It's a bit much, though."

"Oh, did I mention Tara is probably going to be there?"

My ears prick up at her mention.

"What?" I ask, trying to sound cool and relaxed.

"I'm just saying, if I wanted to show a bitch up, that's the dress I'd do it in."

I want to argue with her, but my petty inner self is dancing with delight.

I would look super bangin' in this dress.

"If I'm going to do this," I say, a smile growing on my face, "then we should probably stop at a lingerie store, too."

46

With Zane's hand rested on the small of my back, we follow Kami down the dimly lit street to a large, white concrete building with towering columns and dark, wrought iron doors. Kieran trails close behind. We step inside and a man in a fancy tux leads us down a corridor with white marble floors and light stone walls. As we walk, the low hum of music grows louder until we reach a sign that says '*Celebrating Alek and David.*'

Another man in a tux opens the door for us and the sounds of jazz piano and crowd chatter fill the air. Before us is a gorgeous ballroom lit with soft red lighting. There's a platform in the center of the room with a live jazz band playing. Above them hangs a large, gold chandelier where a half-naked man is performing aerial acrobatics. Ladies in feathered white showgirl outfits hold trays of champagne and men in top hats pass out hors d'oeuvres.

"Whoa," I say, taking in the spectacle before me.

"No shit," Kieran says. "This is fucking dope."

"Is this normal?" I ask Zane. "Are Immortal parties always this extravagant?"

"No," he replies. "This is all David. He's really into the themed party stuff and it's their anniversary so I'm sure he wanted to go all out."

"David is the heir to a pretty massive railroad empire," Kami chimes in. "Big fancy parties were the norm for him growing up."

"Dayum!" Kieran says. "You think they're looking for a boyfriend?"

"I think you might get your ass kicked if you suggest it," Zane says with a chuckle.

A man in a top hat approaches us and offers to take our coats. I slip off mine and hand it to the man as the others do the same.

"Wow," Zane says, his eyes flashing green as he passes the man his own jacket. Of course he looks flawless in his black tux and bowtie. "This dress is something else."

"You saw the dress before," I say, feeling my cheeks heat up under his intense gaze. He did see the dress earlier on the hanger while I was getting ready, but by the time Kami had finished my side-swept hairdo and pinned my peacock-feathered headband into place, he had given up on waiting and was hanging out with Kieran in the living room.

"I didn't see it on you. Probably a good thing, too, as we never would've made it out of the house."

My boobs do look pretty fantastic in this.

"Come on, let's find a table," Kami says. This is the first time I've seen her outfit, a stunning, floor-length, glittery silver dress with art déco detailing. She told me she was going to wear something she already owned, and from the looks of it, this dress may actually be from the 1920s.

We weave our way through the crowd, grabbing glasses of champagne on the way, and find ourselves an available booth close to the stage. The booth is probably wide enough to fit eight people, so it easily accommodates our group of four.

As we sit, we're greeted by Alek in an impeccable all-white suit and a gold tie. David is at his side in a three-piece tweed ensemble, complete with pocket watch. They may be the cutest couple I've ever seen.

At the very least, they're the cutest gay Immortal couple in complementary Gatsby outfits I've ever seen. That I'm sure of.

"So glad you could come!" Alek says in his low, buttery-smooth voice. Between his looks and his voice, he's so obviously unreal that it would be a miracle if he *wasn't* supernatural.

Alek and David exchange hugs with the group and Zane introduces them to Kieran. He seems to have gotten the message not to flirt with either of them, because he is surprisingly well behaved. After a few minutes of small talk, they excuse themselves to welcome their other guests.

We all sit and chat as we listen to the band and watch the aerial performer twist and contort in the air.

"How long is he gonna be up there?" Kieran asks.

"Aiming to shag the acrobat?" Zane asks.

"Look at him, Z-Man. His muscles have muscles. That man was sculpted by the gods. It would be a crime for me to not at least attempt to fuck that beautiful creature."

"You're a poet," he says sarcastically, laughing into his drink as he takes a sip.

"You guys want drinks?" Kieran asks. "I mean, other than champagne? I'm heading to the bar to grab something a little more demon-friendly."

"Beer, whatever's good. Cheers."

"I'm good," I say.

"Me too," Kami says. "I'm actually going to go mingle a bit anyway."

As Kami and Kieran exit the booth, Zane pulls me onto his lap. A devious smile spreads across his face as his eyes begin to glow.

"You look incredible tonight, love," he whispers into my ear, dipping into the curve of my shoulder to plant a kiss on my neck.

"You're not so bad yourself," I say. "Is this new or something you already owned in the twenties or something?"

"It's new. The gray houndstooth set that Kieran's wearing is an old one of mine, though. Lent it to him for tonight."

"Why didn't you wear it?"

His eyes shift and he looks down bashfully.

"Maybe I wanted to look good for my girl." He gives me a shy smile and I kiss him on the cheek.

I cuddle into his chest and listen to the jazz band play. My eyes scan the room and I'm almost overwhelmed by the sheer beauty of every single person in this room. I'm guessing there's a lot of Sirens here, because not only are they all absurdly gorgeous, but I also catch several eyes gleaming in the dark. One woman's eyes seem to even glow purple.

I guess I'm not in Kansas anymore. Or America, for that matter.

"Ten minutes," Kieran says as he hops back into the booth with drinks in hand.

"What?" I ask.

"Ten minutes till that stallion finishes up his routine." He gestures toward the aerial dancer. "I hope he hasn't used up too much energy, 'cause there's more gymnastics in store for him."

"TMI."

"Kieran is the human embodiment of TMI," Zane says with a laugh.

Good point.

"Heyyy!" a woman's voice rings, and I turn to match the voice to the face.

Tara approaches our table in a black mini-dress covered in gold, tinsel-like fringe. Her hair is slicked back into an immaculate ponytail and her golden skin glistens in the light.

Crap.

I was pretty sure I could handle this, but my insecurities are quickly bubbling to the surface. This woman is perfect, and I am *so not perfect.*

"Hey Tara," Zane says in a monotone voice, wrapping his arms tighter around my waist and resting his chin on my shoulder.

"Hey there," Kieran interjects, giving her a slight wave as she smiles back.

"Mind if I sit?" she asks. Kieran offers her a seat beside him and she joins us.

Traitor.

"How do you know Zane?" he asks, apparently oblivious to the drama going on beneath the surface.

"Oh, we dated for a while." She shoots Zane a smile and bats her eyes.

"Yeah?" Kieran takes a sip of his drink. "That's crazy—I've known Zane for, like, half a century and he's never mentioned you."

Okay, I take that back. He's not a traitor, he's a friggin' legend.

"Huh," she says, poorly masking her irritation behind a forced smile. "Well, it was a long time ago."

"So what do you do, Tara?" I ask, trying to play the role of nonchalant girlfriend who is definitely not intimidated by the ex.

"I'm a model," she says with a smirk.

Of fucking course she's a model.

This is my chance. I just need to be super sexy and seductive with Zane and show this bitch who's boss.

"Oh cool," I mumble, shuffling off of Zane's lap. "I'll be right back; I need to run to the ladies' room."

Or—I could run and hide like a wimp.

I step out of the booth and make my way to the restrooms.

Great. Good job, Ava. You are literally running away from your problems.

I lean on the sink and stare in the mirror for a moment.

My makeup and hair were perfectly done by Kami. My dress is killer and my boobs look amazing. This is probably the hottest I've ever looked—and I'm still self-conscious.

Damn it.

It's impossible to be surrounded by precisely sculpted superhumans and not notice all the little things wrong with yourself.

Okay, nope. You know what? I'm done with this. I can't control my body—lord knows that's a battle I've lost—but I can go out there and kick ass.

I just may need to grab a shot on the way back.

As I exit the bathroom, I run into Kieran with a knowing look on his face.

"Wha-… what are you doing here?"

"I'm checking on you," he says. "I kind of expected you to show that girl up, but you bailed."

"Yeah…" I mumble, my eyes falling to the floor.

"Ava, you're a million times better than that chick. You don't have to take her shit."

"I know, but I feel so awkward. Trying to be all sexy and 'claim my man' in front of a literal Immortal model? It's intimidating."

"Was that your plan?" he asks with a laugh.

"It's apparently what Sirens do to tell other Sirens to back off. It's either that or a fistfight, which is definitely not going to go in my favor."

He smirks and narrows his eyes in a way that tells me he has a devious plan.

"Well you're in luck, Ava. If you need seduction tactics, you've come to the right man. Now take a sip of my drink and head back into the bathroom."

"Wha-… why?"

"I figure you don't want to take your panties off out in the open."

———

I can't believe I'm doing this.

I take in a deep breath and head back to our booth.

Here goes nothing.

Zane is standing beside the booth while Kami and Tara are seated next to each other, chatting.

"Hey, baby," he says as I approach, grabbing my waist and pulling me toward him. "You okay? I was just coming to check up on you."

"Yeah, I'm fine," I say.

My heartbeat begins to quicken, so I distract myself by pulling him in for a kiss.

When I pull back, his eyes are a vivid green.

"Are you trying to torture me?" he asks, his gaze scanning my body. "You and this dress are certain to give me a heart attack before the night ends."

"Well, the dress isn't the only part of this outfit you'll enjoy." I bat my eyes at him and bite my lip slightly.

"Fuck," he hisses.

"Zane," Tara calls. "Come sit back down."

He doesn't respond and he takes in a shaky breath as his eyes stay locked on mine.

"You *are* trying to torture me." He smirks and licks his lips. "Naughty girl."

I reach my hand into his suit pocket and slip the lace thong inside, leaning into his body.

"Here's a preview," I whisper into his ear.

"Zane?" Tara calls.

He reaches into his pocket and looks down briefly at the fabric before his eyes go wide and snap back to mine. He grabs the back of my head and, in a swift motion, his lips connect with mine. I kiss him back with equal force, my tongue sliding teasingly between his lips. I feel his hands migrate to my ass.

That's right, Tara. Get a good eyeful.

I hear her voice, but it's muffled as if it's far away. Kissing Zane has taken away both my anxiety and my ability to hear anything this woman is saying.

"Wow, okay," she huffs.

"You doing okay there, Tanya?" Kieran says. "You seem a little flustered."

I tune them out as I grab Zane's lapels and deepen the kiss, hearing a whine and mumble from Tara behind us. He moans against my mouth and I take the opportunity to nibble at his lip.

With a loud, frustrated grunt, Tara storms off and I turn to see Kami and Kieran laughing hysterically.

I think that means I win.

47

 ZANE

Ten Minutes Earlier

Where does she find these dresses? Is there a special shop for boyfriend-torturing garments?

"Wow," I say, my eyes roaming across the landscape of her body. "This dress is something else."

That's a mild way of putting it.

"You saw the dress before," she says, batting her lashes as her cheeks flush pink.

As if seeing this dress on a hanger could compare to seeing it hugging her curves, dipping at the spot between her breasts to flaunt her cleavage, the hem just lower than scandalous.

"I didn't see it on you. Probably a good thing, too, as we never would've made it out of the house."

I lick my lips as I consider ditching the party entirely, but that would probably not go over well with the group.

Kami suggests we find a table, so we make our way through a sea of people to a booth beside the stage. Alek and David come by to welcome us to the party before shuffling off to tend to their other guests.

Somewhat predictably, Kieran's eyes remain glued to the shirtless man in tights performing acrobatics above the stage. Nothing says 'Kieran's Type' quite like being already half-undressed.

"Look at him, Z-Man," he says. "His muscles have muscles. That man was sculpted by the gods. It would be a crime for me to not at least attempt to fuck that beautiful creature."

"You're a poet," I tease.

"You guys want drinks? I mean, other than champagne? I'm heading to the bar to grab something a little more demon-friendly."

"Beer, whatever's good. Cheers."

"I'm good," Ava says. Kami declines and excuses herself to mingle with the crowd.

As they leave, my hands migrate to Ava's waist, as if on autopilot. I lift her onto my lap as my gaze traces the lines of the dress from her cleavage to her collarbone.

"You look incredible tonight, love," I whisper into her ear before lowering my lips to her neck.

This party is wild enough that no one would pay any attention to anything we do in this booth right now.

Fuck—no, behave yourself. You can do this.

"You're not so bad yourself," she says with a giggle. "Is this new or something you already owned in the twenties or something?"

"It's new. The gray houndstooth set that Kieran's wearing is an old one of mine, though. Lent it to him for tonight."

"Why didn't you wear it?"

Because I thought you'd like this better and I wanted to look good for you.

Don't tell her that; you'll sound pathetic.

"Maybe I wanted to look good for my girl," I admit.

She leans into my chest and I feel her heart beat a bit faster. In this moment, it's just Ava and me—and it's perfect.

"Ten minutes," Kieran says, sitting back down and passing me a beer.

"What?" Ava asks.

"Ten minutes till that stallion finishes up his routine. I hope he hasn't used up too much energy, 'cause there's more gymnastics in store for him."

"TMI." She twists her mouth into a tight knot.

"Kieran is the human embodiment of TMI," I say, chuckling.

"Heyyy!" a woman calls.

Fuck.

I know that voice.

It's Tara.

Tara walks up in a black dress covered in shiny gold strands. It's remarkable how hard she tries and how truly transparent she can be.

I knew there was a chance of running into her tonight, and odds are that's exactly what she was counting on. Knowing her, she wore this for me, but she's completely clueless if she thinks this is going to impress me.

"Hey Tara," I say, pulling Ava in closer, hoping she'll get the hint and move along.

"Hey there," Kieran says.

"Mind if I sit?" she asks. Kieran gestures beside him.

What is he up to?

"How do you know Zane?" he asks.

I'm not sure why he's asking that, as he already knows the answer.

"Oh, we dated for a while," she says, giving me a smile.

"Yeah? That's crazy. I've known Zane for, like, half a century and he's never mentioned you."

Ahh, yeah, that's more his style.

"Huh," she huffs. "Well, it was a long time ago."

"So what do you do, Tara?" Ava asks.

"I'm a model," she replies with a smirk.

The perfect career for Tara. She needs endless attention. I'm pretty certain the only reason she seems to want me now is that she's jealous someone else has become the center of my focus.

I feel Ava squirm slightly on my lap and begin to get up.

"Oh cool," she says in a soft voice. "I'll be right back; I need to run to the ladies' room."

What? Where is she going?

She quickly heads to the restrooms, but I can't help but think something else is up.

"So Zane," Tara says, "Have you been in America this whole time? You certainly haven't stayed in touch."

"Yep." I take a sip of my beer.

"Why-"

"Hey guys, hey Tara," Kami interrupts, sliding into the booth beside Tara. "Have you guys seen the stilt walkers in the back? It's crazy."

"Oh yeah," Tara says. "They're brilliant."

"Are they hot?" Kieran asks. She nods in reply.

He quickly hops over the back of the booth, presumably to chase down these stilt walkers.

"So why are you back in town?" Tara asks, turning back to me. "Is it about the Siren deaths?"

"Yeah," Kami says. "We're unofficially working the case."

"Have you figured it out? Do you know who it is? Can you fix it?"

"We know bits and pieces, but uh… we're at a bit of a dead end at the moment."

"You should try Syllek," she says. "He knows everything that goes on in the Immortal world."

That's a nice way of saying he has no morals or loyalties. He sells his allegiance to the highest bidder.

"That's actually not a bad idea," Kami says.

"It sure as hell is," I say. "Syllek is always out for himself. Besides, we can't pay the price he requires."

Syllek collects and trades in Immortals, demons, basically any creature that he sees as unique. We don't exactly have anyone like that, and even if we did, we wouldn't be willing to sacrifice them to a psychopath like Syllek.

Kami steers the conversation to other things, holding Tara's obvious flirting at bay.

Thank fuck for that.

My mind starts to wander to Ava and I wonder if she's doing alright. I decide to go investigate for myself and step out of the booth.

"Zaaanneee…" Tara drawls. "Where are you going?"

"I figured I'd just check on Ava," I say.

"Oh, I'm sure she's fine."

I turn toward the bathrooms to see Ava walking back to the table. Even just seeing her manages to turn my souring mood back to a relaxed one.

"Hey, baby," I say, grabbing her waist and tugging her into me. "You okay? I was just coming to check up on you."

"Yeah, I'm fine," she says.

I can feel her heartbeat quicken beneath her skin as she pulls me toward her and her lips connect with mine.

This must've been one hell of a bathroom break.

As she pulls away, I'm drunk on her and can hardly think straight.

"Are you trying to torture me?" I ask. "You and this dress are certain to give me a heart attack before the night ends."

"Well, the dress isn't the only part of this outfit you'll enjoy," she says, nibbling on her lower lip.

"Fuck."

That's it, I'm taking her to whatever side room I can find in this place and…

"Zane," Tara calls, interrupting my train of thought. "Come sit back down."

Hell no.

My body shakes as I stare into Ava's eyes, seeing the bright green of my eyes reflected in hers.

"So you *are* trying to torture me, then…" I say, licking my lips. "Naughty girl."

I feel her hand reach into my pocket as she presses her body into mine.

"Here's a preview," she whispers into my ear.

I hear someone call me, but it's weak and distant.

I reach into my pocket and feel a textured fabric, lace maybe. I pull it out slightly and look down—it's a black and red lace thong.

All the blood in my body immediately rushes to my dick and I'm so stunned that my ears are ringing.

In an instant, I grab her and kiss her needily. My knees shake when she slips her tongue between my lips, leaving a tingling sensation in her wake. My hands find their way to her arse and I can't help but squeeze.

"Um, Zane," Tara says, clearing her throat. "Getting a little over the top with the PDA, there, aren't we?"

Even when my girlfriend is clearly all over me, Tara still can't get the hint.

Bloody hell. Is Ava making a point?

She hums against my lips.

She's fucking claiming me right now?

Fuck that's hot.

"Wow, okay," Tara huffs.

"You doing okay there, Tanya?" Kieran asks. "You seem a little flustered."

I almost laugh, but Ava grabs my lapels and bites at my lip.

I hear Tara stomp away and Ava turns to a hysterical Kami and Kieran.

I'm so high on Ava that my vision is starting to blur, so I take the opportunity to pick her up and speed off to the restrooms. Luckily, they're unisex and there's no one else in here, but I'd probably risk it if they weren't. Ava giggles as I pull us into a stall and lock it behind us.

"I can't wait," I say, my voice low and breathy. "I need you."

She shyly nods and sucks in her lower lip.

God, she's perfect.

I kiss a trail from her neck to her collarbone, then further between her breasts, grabbing a handful along the way. In a quick motion, she wraps her legs around me and bites at my earlobe, pushing me back against the door.

FUCK.

I flip us around so that her back is at the door.

"Hold the top of the door, baby," I say.

She smiles and grabs it tightly. I hook her legs over my shoulders and kneel down with my head between her legs. Like a starved man, I lick and hum in ecstasy, slowly sliding a finger into her. She moans, but quickly stifles it, likely remembering we're in a public place. I can't help but take that as a bit of a challenge.

In just minutes, she's moaning and rolling her hips in time with the waves of an orgasm. I support her hips as her grip on the door falters a bit.

I stand and, with my free hand, unzip my trousers and free myself. I grab a condom from my inner breast pocket and roll it on.

"Hold tight baby," I say. She tightens her grip on the door, her gray eyes urging me on.

I sink into her, pinching my lips shut to hold back a flurry of curses desperate to escape. We both breathe heavily and shake. She tugs me closer by my bow tie, and I oblige, kissing her with everything I have.

We move in rhythm to the muffled beat of the music outside. With each thrust I fall further into a blissful oblivion until she moans loudly. I attempt to cover her mouth to quiet her but my own orgasm hits me like a train and I lose any sense of control, burying myself in her with three more quick jolts.

We both pant for a moment and I kiss the flushed skin of her chest and neck.

This woman is everything I've ever wanted.

I lower her back to the floor and fix up my trousers as she readjusts her dress. We hear the door open as two sets of footsteps enter the bathroom. Their masculine voices talk in low mumbles and we hear what sounds like kissing.

Ava and I exchange looks and do our best to hold back giggles.

"Yeah," a man's voice says. "Oh my god, you're so sexy, Kieran."

At that, we both burst into laughter.

48

I sit up in bed and take a moment to stretch out. My joints crack and pop like bubble wrap and my muscles are tight and uncooperative.

Ow.

Last night was fun, but I'm definitely paying for it today.

I wrap myself in a fuzzy robe and shamble out into the living room where Kieran and Zane are watching tv.

"Morning," I say. I was going for cheery, but it comes out as more of a groan than I intend.

"Not feeling well?" Zane asks. I nod in reply.

"Still?" Kieran asks.

"Yes, still, you daft twat. What do you think chronically ill means?"

"Honestly, I have no idea," he says. "I thought chronically meant sorted by date."

"That's chronologically," I say, holding back a chuckle.

"Oh shit, yeah it is, isn't it? I didn't think it made a lot of sense, but I thought maybe you had whatever Benjamin Button had."

"Benjamin Button isn't a real person," Zane says with a scoff.

"Demons aren't supposed to be real either."

Fair point.

"Chronically means it keeps coming back," I explain.

"Oh, that makes way more sense!" he says.

Zane pours me a cup of tea as I snuggle into the couch with a blanket.

"Where did Kami disappear to last night, anyway?" I ask.

"She went home with an extremely hot guy whose eyes were glowing red, so

I'm assuming she had some Siren-on-Siren sexy times."

"Oh." I take a sip of my tea as Zane sits beside me and drapes an arm around my shoulders.

"While you guys were having your little liaison in the bathrooms, you missed Tara having a total meltdown. She was asking everyone who you are and why she'd never heard of you before. I think someone let it slip that you were human because she went pretty ballistic and stormed out."

"I was wondering where she went."

"Well, my woman did a great job of claiming me," Zane says with a wide smile.

"You enjoyed that a bit too much."

"I think I enjoyed it the appropriate amount."

"Well," Kieran says. "I gotta admit, I enjoyed it too. I've never seen a tiny woman so furious. And the look on Zane's face—I thought he was gonna bust a nut right there."

"Fuck, mate—you have no filter."

"That's right. 100% unfiltered Kieran, 24/7."

"Unfortunately."

We're interrupted by a knock at the door, but Kami walks in before anyone has a chance to open it.

"Hey, Z!" she says. "Ava. Kieran."

We say hello and she grabs a seat in a chair next to the couch.

"So I heard you went home with a friend," I say with my best wink.

I can't really wink, but I keep attempting it anyway.

"That I did," she says with a smirk.

"It's pretty early. Did you ditch him already?" I ask.

"No, I just had to get to work. I'm an early riser anyway."

"Work on what?"

"I actually… uh… wanted to talk to Zane about that."

Zane sits up and narrows his eyes.

"About what?"

"Syllek." She turns back to me. "He's a… what would you call it…"

"Human trafficker," Zane says, "but he trades in Immortals. He's also a bit of a private collector. He's a psychopath."

"Oh… that sounds lovely," I say. "Why are you talking about this guy?"

"Because we might be able to use him," she says.

"The only language Syllek speaks is payment." Zane crosses his arms.

"Couldn't you ask the Council for, like… a stipend or something?"

He smiles and kisses me on the forehead.

"You're sweet, love, but he'd want something more valuable than money… or rather, someone."

"Oh. So you'd be giving a person in exchange for information."

"Well, maybe," she says. "I was thinking we could make him think we're giving him someone, and then double-cross him."

"Just what I need—more enemies," Zane says.

"He won't be able to come after you if he's dead."

"And who do we dangle as bait? We don't have a fresh supply of rare Immortals at our disposal."

"Well, that brings me to the next part of the pitch…" she says, twirling her hair and looking down.

It's rare to see Kami uncomfortable like this, so whatever she's going to pitch isn't good.

Another knock at the door interrupts the conversation.

"Speaking of," she says, running to the door.

She returns with Morgan trailing behind her.

"Hello all," he says. He leans against the wall with his arms crossed.

"I wanted to discuss this with everyone present," Kami says.

"Morgan?" Zane asks with a scoff. "You've got to be kidding. Sure, he's a rare Immortal, but Syllek would never deal in creatures that powerful. It's too much of a risk—especially an Empath."

"Well, actually, I agree with you. Morgan is a bad choice."

"Then wh-" Zane stops mid-sentence and his eyes go wide. "Fuck no. No, Kami. That's way too bloody far."

"What?" I ask.

"It doesn't matter. It's out of the question."

"You brought me here to tell me you lot are sacrificing Ava?" Morgan asks.

Wait…what?

"No!" Kami scolds. "We would not be sacrificing anyone. You would be there as Zane's 'bodyguard' to keep an eye on things and handle it if something goes wrong."

"But I'm not Immortal or rare—I'm just human."

"You're actually part Immortal, part human," Kieran says. "Which is pretty rare."

"So you guys would… pretend to sell me to this guy?"

"No, we won't," Zane says, his eyes glowing slightly.

"Well, come on now, let's talk about this."

"Talk about selling you to a psychopath? No."

"*Fake*-selling. I mean, you and Morgan would be right there if things were to go south. If it would help you find a way to restart the Siren birthing cycle, it might be worth it."

"Even if I would agree to that, which I won't," Zane says, "don't you think it would look a bit suspicious to be a Siren trying to sell a Siren's mate? He'd figure out she's mine."

"You can't see her mark," Kami says. "So we could just say she's some other kind of hybrid or something. Plus, you have both your wings, so he wouldn't suspect you could have a mate anyway."

"Do you have any idea of the kind of danger we could be putting her in?"

"Of course I do, Z, but let's be realistic—we have no leads. If someone comes after more Sirens, they die forever. They never come back. And the collective power will just keep getting stronger. We have to do something."

"And that something is using my girlfriend as chattel?"

"Okay, don't talk about me like I'm not here," I say. "We need to make these decisions together, and if we can do it safely, then I think we should seriously consider it."

"Why do you always seem to have a death wish?" he asks.

"I can't die. I'm immortal, remember?"

49

"Well," Kieran says, "you know I'm always down for a crazy plan."

"What about you, Ava?" Kami asks. "Ultimately, this comes down to you and Z… and I guess Morgan, too, since he needs to protect you if things go wrong."

"I'm open." Ava bites her lip anxiously as she turns to me. "I think we should discuss it, but I trust you all to keep me safe."

Kami turns to me and then back to Morgan.

"What about you two?" she asks. "You're both awfully quiet."

"No," I say. For a moment, I think there's an echo, but I realize that I've spoken in time with Morgan.

I'm surprised. I expected him to say yes.

"This plan is insane," he says. "My job is to protect Ava, and this idea does the opposite of that."

"You don't think you can do it?" Kami asks.

"Of course I can do it. But there has to be another solution, preferably one that doesn't involve putting Ava in the crossfire."

"Really?" Ava asks. "Why does everyone think I can't handle this? I know I'm human and all, but I'm not as incapable as you think. I trust you all, but you don't trust me."

She crosses her arms over her chest and pouts, with an expression that is equal parts hurt and furious.

"It's not that we don't trust you," I say. "But the risk is just too high. And even if nothing went wrong, we'd have to treat you like property, and I can't do that."

"You guys always underestimate me."

"I'm not underestimating you, love. If anything, you're *overestimating* me. You're overestimating my ability to risk you, hurt you—to live without you."

Her eyes soften and she sighs.

"Can you at least think about it?"

I reluctantly agree and excuse myself to the garden for a bit of fresh air.

What if something goes wrong?

What if she gets hurt?

Could I really pretend that she is nothing to me?

I hear the door creak behind me. Ava must have followed to check up on me.

Without a word, someone appears beside me, but it's not her—it's Morgan.

"Did they already change your mind?" I ask, shoving my hands into the pockets of my jeans.

"Not them… she did."

"Ava?"

"Yeah. She's right. That girl may not have any powers, but she might just be stronger than all of us."

"She deals with a lot," I say with a sigh.

"Can you feel it through your bond? All the pain she deals with?"

"I can." I run my hands through my hair and take a deep breath in. "I can tune it out more now. It doesn't hurt me like it hurts her."

"You wouldn't know by looking at her. She hides it well. You two are alike in that way."

"What do you mean?"

"She hides her pain; you hide your feelings. You are the *Iron Siren*, are you not?"

"So you found out about that, did you?"

"It's funny, really. You're known for suppressing your emotions, yet I certainly struggle to control them when I channel you. Sirens really feel everything so much more intensely."

He struggles to control my emotions? What does that mean? Is he talking about Ava? I swear I'll bloody kill thi-

"Calm down, that's not what I mean," he says with a frustrated sigh. "She's yours, mate. I know that. I'm not after your girlfriend. I just mean that your emotions are heavy to hold."

My shoulders relax and I give him a quick nod of understanding.

"So you think we should do it?" I ask.

"Maybe. If we don't have another option. But I don't think we should write it off because of Ava. If anyone can handle this, she can."

He's right. She can.

———◆———

I can't believe we're actually going to do this.

"You've been pacing for ten minutes," Kieran says. "What's got your panties in a twist?"

I shoot him a glare.

"I'm supposed to meet Morgan here and prep for this deal with Syllek."

"Prep how?"

"I don't know. I just don't like this entire thing."

"What thing?" Ava says, walking into the kitchen with a blanket around her shoulders.

"This plan, to use you as bait. I hate it."

"We've talked about this," she says, walking to the dining table and sitting down.

"That doesn't mean I have to like it."

I hear a tap at the door and Kieran goes to answer. Ava sighs and slumps into her seat.

"Are you feeling alright?" I ask.

"I'm fine."

Kieran walks in with Morgan following behind.

"Morning," Morgan says, leaning on the kitchen counter.

"Hey Morgan," Ava says.

I give him a quick nod. He turns to Ava, narrowing his eyes at her.

"Bad day?" he asks.

"Uh… yeah, I guess," she says.

"You told me you were fine, love," I say, raising my brow.

"I am fine. It's complicated. Fine for me isn't fine for everybody else."

"What is fine for you?"

"Fine means I'm not fine, but that I can handle it. It means… that I've got it. Even if I'm not fine, I can deal with it."

"Fine means not fine—that makes sense," Morgan says with a smirk.

"If you had to deal with the shit I do, you'd get it."

"So what's on the agenda today?" Kieran asks. "Zane says you're here to prep.

What are we doing? Are we gonna fight each other?"

"Not exactly," Morgan says, shaking his head. "I need to practice channeling Zane. If we're in this kind of situation, emotions are going to run high. I want to make sure we're prepared."

That's what we're doing? Fuck.

"Where do we start?" I ask.

"Let's go to the sitting room."

We head to the next room. I sit on the sofa and he takes a seat in a chair across from me. Ava heads back upstairs to take a shower. Kieran posts up in a chair in the corner, perched on the balls of his feet with a bowl of cereal as if he's about to watch a cage match.

"I don't like this," I say.

"You say that a lot," Morgan says with a chuckle.

"Let's get this over with. What do I do?"

"I need you to get angry," he says. "I assume that's the main thing we'll have to worry about."

"Ooh ooh! I can help!" Kieran exclaims. He raises his hand like a child in primary school.

"Bloody hell, mate," I say. "Why do you live to piss me off?"

"Because it's fun! Plus, it used to be much harder to get your goat before Ava came along, so I'm enjoying it now."

"Well, as much as Kieran is pretty good at making you angry, we're going to need you to dig deeper."

"How so?"

"I want you to think of something that has made you furious and focus on that."

Fucking Mike.

I look down at my hands and think for a moment—how he kept texting Ava when we were together, how he approached me in the bar.

I take in a deep breath and look up to see Morgan visibly shaking. He takes a shaky breath in and closes his eyes and the shaking stops. He reopens them and looks at me.

"Keep going," he says. "More."

I think of Krisztian and finding Ilen. I remember ripping him limb from limb. Then I remember the videos from Asmodeus—kissing Ava, hitting her.

I grip my fist so tight that my knuckles turn white. Now I'm starting to shake too.

"Control yourself," Morgan says through gritted teeth. "If you can't handle your emotions, how do you expect me to handle them?"

I growl in response.

Fuck this bloke.

"That's the bloody opposite of what I just said," Morgan says, his jaw tight and his eyes narrow.

"Come on, Z-Man," Kieran says. "You're the Iron Siren."

I take a deep breath in and my muscles relax slightly.

"Hold it in, but stay angry," Morgan says. "What about me? We all know you dislike me; I feel it every time we're in the same room. You're jealous of me, right? Because I chatted up Ava when we met."

My blood feels like it's boiling, but I don't give him the satisfaction of a response.

"What was it I said that made you so angry?" he asks. I hear Kieran chuckling in the corner.

The bastard is enjoying this.

I feel my muscles tense but I don't move. He wants the Iron Siren? That's exactly who I'll be.

I remember exactly what this tosser said.

"That's my girl."

My girl.

I can't let him win. He's trying to get me angry and I won't let it work.

"Okay, fuck!" Morgan shouts, jumping from his seat and running his hands through his hair. "Bloody hell… that was a lot. Fuck."

My anger recedes, replaced with a slight satisfaction over his distress. He breathes and shakes for a moment before sitting back down.

"Okay," he says with a sigh. "Let's go again."

50

After about an hour on the road, we pull into the parking lot of a run-down church. Its red brick facade is stained and crumbling and the property is overrun with sprawling vines and weeds.

"Well," Kami says, looking to Zane and me, "this is it."

I have to admit, the last place I expected to be meeting a human trafficker was at a church.

Finn's car pulls up beside us and he hops out with Morgan and Kieran close behind.

Zane lets out an exasperated sigh and gives my hand a squeeze before getting out of the car. Kami and I join the group, now standing in a half-circle in the empty lot.

"You lot good to go?" Morgan asks.

"Always," Kieran says with a smirk.

"We've got this," Finn says, looking to Zane as if he's talking to him in particular.

"Somebody's got to grab…uh…her," Morgan says, glancing in my direction.

Zane takes a heavy breath in and swallows hard, grabbing my forearm and closing his eyes for a minute. He looks at me with wide, sad eyes, as if to ask if I still want to go through with this. I reply with a small nod. Almost instantaneously, his expression morphs into a cold, lifeless one that I've never seen on him before. But I know this is him playing a role, one he knows all too well—the immovable Iron Siren.

He tugs me forward as we walk toward the entrance of the church. I know this is all just for show, but I'm surprised by how uncomfortable it makes me. It's not that my boyfriend is manhandling me, but rather than seeing them all acting so serious is just unnerving.

Kami knocks three times on the tall wooden door and a large, imposing man opens it. His broad shoulders fill the doorway. He looks like a bodybuilder, but his top half is twice as big as the bottom.

Somebody skipped leg day.

"We're here for Syllek," Kami says. "We have merchandise for him."

She tips her head toward me. I say nothing, since I've been instructed to say as little as possible and let her and Zane do the talking.

The man with the Hulk torso comes up to me and leans into the crook of my neck, inhaling my scent.

"Interesting," he says in a low, gravelly voice. "One moment."

He retreats into the church, shutting the door behind him as we wait.

"*You're doing great,*" Finn's voice echoes in my mind.

The door opens again and Mr. No-Leg-Day stands before us.

"Syllek will meet you," he says. "But only two."

The group exchanges looks for a moment while I attempt to keep my head down and play the role of prisoner.

"Then it's me and my bodyguard," Zane says, looking to Morgan, who nods.

The big guy steps aside and lets us pass into the church.

"*I should be able to reach your thoughts in there,*" Finn says in my mind. "*If anything goes wrong, tell me right away, and we'll bring the cavalry.*"

I will.

We're led past dusty church pews and stained glass windows to a dimly lit stone staircase that heads underground.

Yeah, this is definitely the kind of place in a horror movie where you know everybody is about to die.

At the bottom of the stairs is a system of wide archways and tunnels, lit by electric sconces.

Not gonna lie, I was expecting torches. This is a very torchy type of place.

We follow the man into a large room at the end of a corridor where a man sits on a plush sofa drinking wine. He's wearing a suit with a loose collar and no tie. He looks young at first, but his splotchy skin and haggard appearance seem to reveal a man far older than he looks. His cheekbones are sharp and his sunken, pale blue eyes are haunting.

"Syllek," the man says. "These are the guests who brought you a Siren's mate."

Uh oh.

The plan was to say that they didn't know what I was, only that I was both immortal and human, but apparently they already know exactly what I am.

"A Siren's mate," he says in a slight French accent, standing up and setting down his glass. "How did you get her away from her Siren?"

"He abandoned her," Zane says, his face stone cold.

"A Siren abandoned their marked mate?" he asks, raising a brow.

"Precisely why she's a rare creature."

Syllek steps toward me like he's inspecting a product. Then again—I guess that's exactly what he's doing. I feel Zane's grip on my arm tighten slowly, but he maintains composure.

"Why would your mate abandon you, beautiful?" Syllek asks, grabbing my chin between his thumb and forefinger.

"I…" I say. "Because I'm sick. It wasn't what he signed up for."

Zane's piercing eyes meet mine, but his expression remains still.

"Sick and immortal," he says with a smirk. "You are unique."

He grabs my arm from Zane and looks at the tattoo on my wrist.

"And you're decorated," he adds. I try to tug my arm from his grip, but it's no use. He smiles and his eyes roam up and down me. "She's very attractive… and feisty, too. Which is perfect. I have plenty of clients who prefer them… resistant."

Zane's jaw tightens, but he doesn't move or look at me again.

"And what are you looking for in return?" Syllek asks.

"Information," Zane says. "We want to know how the demons stopped the Siren birth cycle and how we can restart it."

"Well, you are correct in assuming I have your information, but why would I want to give it to you? A Siren—former Council, no less—brings me the abandoned mate of a Siren. This is an obvious setup. She has to be yours."

"No," Zane says. "She's not mine."

He pulls off his jacket and T-shirt and his wings unfurl.

"See? Two wings. If she were mine, I'd have none."

"Hmm…" Syllek says, tapping a finger on his lips. "Then prove it."

"I just did."

"Hit her."

My eyes go wide. Syllek smirks as he picks up his wine glass and takes a sip.

"What? No!" Zane says.

"You want me to buy her, you want that favor, then prove to me this is not a trap. Prove that she's not yours. Hurt her. I don't care how."

"I'm only here because I need your help. I don't like it, but I'm here. That doesn't mean I have to participate in your games."

Finn? Are you still hearing this?

"*I'm here,*" he replies in my head.

Tell Zane it's alright. Tell Zane he can hit me if he needs to sell it. I'll be okay.

"*Ava, he won't.*"

"Yet you'll sell her to me? What would make you think my plans for her will be any better?" Syllek asks.

"There's a difference between knowing what will happen and participating in it," Zane says through gritted teeth.

"Or you can't bear the thought of hurting your mate."

"I'll solve this," Morgan says, his eyes wide when they meet mine.

He grabs my hips and pulls me toward him in a quick motion. One of his hands goes to the back of my neck and his lips are suddenly on mine.

I'm completely frozen, my every cell locked in place.

What the flying fuck is happening right now?

Morgan leans into the kiss. His lips are soft against my own but all I can think of is how insanely awkward this moment is. This is not how I expected this mission to go.

Risk of potential death? Sure! Sign me up. Risk of Morgan kissing you while your boyfriend watches? Uh… no thank you.

Oh my god. Zane is watching right now. He's going to kill Morgan.

Morgan takes a step back, one hand still at my hip as he breathes heavily. His blue eyes are wide and unblinking.

His dear-in-the-headlights expression fades as he backs away.

"There," Morgan says. "You think a Siren would let me live if I kissed his mate like that?"

Syllek looks to Zane, who hasn't moved from his position. His face is cold and indifferent, but I can sense a sea of emotion behind his eyes.

"You have a point," Syllek says. "Fair enough, I'm convinced. So you want to know what Leviathan and his demons are up to and how you can undo whatever they've done to Sirens."

Zane nods.

"Well, it's simple enough. They've cooled the volcano—Thera—from which you are all born. I'm not exactly sure how, some sort of scientific apparatus beneath the surface, but I know it can be manually shut down."

"And you're sure of this?" Zane asks.

"I am," he says.

"*We're coming*," Finn says.

In an instant, I hear a loud bang and what sounds like wood breaking. Zane's arms are wrapped around me like a shield as Morgan fights off both Syllek and his top-heavy guard with ease. More guards come bursting through the door, but Morgan sends them flying with a wave of his hand. Two more guards suddenly burst into flames.

Before I can even process what's happening, another guard is on the ground and a smirking Kieran appears on top of him.

"That's right," he says. "Cavalry's here, bitches!"

51

 ZANE

"I think that's everyone," Kami says, returning from a quick search of the corridors with Morgan. "I'll call the Council to clean up the mess."

My skin is still burning and my chest feels tight. Now that the chaos has subsided, my rage is at the forefront of my mind.

I stalk up the stairs and into the church. Soft warm light pours through the stained glass, illuminating the dust floating in the air.

Ava, Kami, and Kieran follow me up. In a moment, Finn and Morgan surface.

Just seeing Morgan's face brings back the memory of him kissing Ava. His hands gripping her waist, caressing her neck…this motherfucker. I'll kill him.

My vision narrows and focuses on him alone. In an instant, I lunge at him but am brought down by someone tackling me from the side. I struggle against them as they attempt to pin me to the ground. Long black hair falls into my face.

It's fucking Kieran.

"Get your bloody hands off me!" I curse. He's holding his own surprisingly well, considering I've been the stronger one lately. "What the fuck are you doing?"

"Sorry dude, Finn told me to," he says. I kick him off me but he lands on his feet between me and Morgan.

"Get the fuck out of my way, Kieran."

"What the hell happened? Why are you trying to kill Morgan?" He huffs and brushes his tousled hair from his face.

"Zane's going off on one," Morgan says, rolling his eyes and crossing his arms across his chest.

"You fucking kissed my girl, you maggot!"

Kieran's eyes go wide and he glances between me and Morgan.

"Holy shit," he says. "What? You didn't…"

He looks back at Morgan, who has a smug grin plastered on his face.

"I'm sorry, dude," Kieran says, stepping to the side. "I like you, but I'm not about to die for you."

"Zane," Ava cautions, stepping behind me and putting a hand on my back. "He was trying t-"

"I know what he was trying to do," I say through gritted teeth. My fists are balled tightly at my sides and my muscles are so tense they feel like they're about to burst through my skin.

"What would you have preferred? Did you want me to hit her?"

"I'll kill you, you bloody bastard!" I scream, rushing at him and belting him in the jaw. He staggers back slightly and smirks.

I reach for his neck, but am pulled back by Kami and Finn, one on each arm.

"It was tactical, you jealous ape," he snaps.

"Real bloody convenient, that. Of all the options, it just so happened you had to kiss her. I knew it. I knew you fancied her. You son of a bitch."

"I had to sell it."

"Was there a reason you took so long with your tongue down my girl's throat? Was that all 'to sell it' too, mate?"

"I had to make it convincing," he says with venom in his voice.

"Then well done you—I'm bloody convinced."

I break loose from Kami and Finn's hold and charge at Morgan, slamming him through a row of pews as they snap and splinter. He kicks me backward and my skull cracks the hard stone floor.

Fuck.

I leap back up, readying myself for more.

"Zane, don't," Ava says, running up to me.

Morgan looks her way and brushes his hair back.

"Don't look at her, prick," I snarl.

"You really think I'm here to get a leg over?" he scoffs. "You lot asked me to help you, remember?"

"I also distinctly remember you coming onto my girl."

"What if I did? You afraid she'd like me better?"

I pull an oversized stone from the church's dilapidated wall and pitch it at him.

It hits him square in the chest and knocks him back several feet. He collapses to his knees and wheezes, gasping for breath and coughing.

I launch over the pews and debris, landing just feet in front of him.

"Zane, this is not worth it," Ava says.

Morgan pulls himself to his feet and smirks.

"I've got this, Killer," he says.

A guttural rumbling sound erupts from my chest as I stare into his eyes.

"If I hear that fucking pet name out of your mouth one more time…" I growl.

"You'll what, Siren? You think you can take me?"

I jump on top of him and we roll, exchanging punches as we both fight for the upper hand. He lands several centered on my face before my hands lock around his neck.

"You didn't even deny it. I should've paid more fucking attention. You said she was mine and you knew it. Not 'I don't want her.' Not 'I don't have feelings for her.'"

He rips my hands off his neck and I swing at him again, but find myself being pulled back by Kieran and Kami.

"Z, stop!" she says, pushing me away from him. "You need to calm down."

Kieran steps in between us and sighs, turning to Morgan.

"I better get a fucking medal for defending your ass, you know that?" he says.

"Zane," Ava calls. I turn to see her concerned face as she stands just a few feet behind me. "You're pissed off, okay, I get that. But right now you're not in a good headspace, which means he's in the same headspace. You're both spiraling."

She walks up to me and wraps her arms around me, burying her head into my chest. My heavy breaths shake my body, but she doesn't move.

I sigh and tuck my face into her neck, kissing her skin as I let calm radiate through me.

"Let's go," Ava says. "You and me, let's go outside right now. Don't focus on him, focus on me."

I nod, which sends a pounding pain through my skull.

She grabs my hand and I follow her out the front door into the car park. The sun peeking through the clouds is a stark contrast to the bloodshed inside the church.

"Fuck!" I curse, running my hands through my hair.

"Listen," she says, pulling me into a hug, "what happened in there happened, but nobody is taking me from you. Not now, not ever, okay?"

"But he disrespected you, Ava. Both you and me. Do you have any idea how offensive it is to do something like that in front of me?"

"I assume pretty offensive?" she asks softly.

Serious understatement.

"I can't think of anything worse he could do."

"Maybe he didn't know."

"He did. That's exactly why he did it. He knew that it was the one thing no Siren would let pass, so he used it to make a point."

"But you handled it," she said. "He knew you could deal with it. He knows that you're strong enough."

Well then he should also know that I was going to eventually gut him for it.

"That arsehole just knows exactly how to get under my skin."

"Don't let him," she says, placing a hand on my chest. "He has nothing on you."

"Doesn't he?" I tug at my hair with my fingers. "He's substantially more powerful than me. With his gifts, he could help your pain."

"You're an idiot sometimes, you know that?" She gives me a knowing glance and smirks. "I don't choose my partners based on their supernatural abilities."

"Is that so?" I asked, smiling slightly as I realize she's right. It sounds so absurd when she says it out loud.

"I choose based on personality, intellect, and of course—how good they are in the sack."

I can't help but let a laugh slip.

"Well then," I say with a mischievous smile. I scoop her up so that her legs wrap around my waist. "I guess I should get some more practice."

52

"I don't have to go today," Zane says, combing a hand through his hair as he paces across the bedroom. "I could wait."

"It'll be fine," I say. "I won't be alone. Kieran will be here too."

"Kieran isn't the one I'm worried about."

"I know who you're worried about. But he's fine, really. Morgan just takes in your energy when you're around. You two are just bad for each other—like oil and water, you don't mix."

He nods and sweeps a hand across his face.

"Alright," he says with a sigh. "I'm going to have a shower."

He pulls off his T-shirt with a swift motion, exposing his hard chest and perfectly carved abs.

Dammnn.

He walks into the bathroom and a moment later, I hear the water turn on.

I lay back in bed, staring at the ceiling as I try to distract my mind from the thought of the incredibly gorgeous naked man being drenched in water in the next room. Part of me wants to stay comfortable in bed, but another part of me has a sudden urge to take a shower.

Well, you know that they say—if you can't beat 'em, join 'em!

I jump out of bed and head straight for the bathroom. The door is cracked open slightly so I can sneak in easily. The room is filled with warm steam and I can smell Zane's rosemary shampoo in the air.

If I surprise him, would that be sexy or would I just get a Siren kick to the face?

"Need something, love?" he asks.

"How did you know I was here? I thought I was being so quiet."

"Quiet to human ears, maybe. Plus, I can smell you."

That's never going to not be weird.

"That's such a creepy thing to say."

"Sorry," he says with a chuckle. "What are you looking for?"

Before I have a chance to back out, I slide my panties down and pull off my shirt.

"I'm looking for you," I say, pulling back the curtain just enough to slip in behind him.

He turns to look at me over his shoulders. His eyes are wide with surprise, but quickly narrow and darken as he takes in my naked form. The green begins to fill his irises as a smile grows on his face.

"Is that so?" he asks, turning around and sweeping his hair out of his face.

Tiny water droplets coat his body and trace the contours of his muscles as they drip down his torso. His curls are even darker and dripping wet.

Oh yeah, this was a good idea.

"Well you've found me, baby," he says with a devious expression.

I wrap my arms around his neck and pull him into a kiss, his warm chest pressing into mine as he returns it with fervor. His tongue sweeps over my lower lip and his hands reach my hips, turning me around in a quick motion.

He starts to kiss the back of my neck as one of his hands makes its way to my breast, pinching my nipple between his fingers and rolling it as I moan.

…a very, very good idea.

He bites at my neck with a bit of a growl and my head falls back into his shoulder. I feel his bulge straining against my backside. His other hand heads lower and in minutes I'm biting my lip and holding back an orgasm to avoid my legs collapsing beneath me.

He takes a step back and guides me forward slightly so that my palms are against the wall of the shower. In an almost torturously slow movement, he sinks into me and I'm overwhelmed with a sense of fullness.

His fingers continue to bring me closer as his thrusts have my legs shaking. He scoops an arm around me to help support me as he continues, his own movements becoming increasingly erratic.

My skin is coated in beads of moisture and I can't tell what is my own sweat or water from the shower. My breathing gets heavier as the pressure builds in my core. In seconds, I come undone, most of my weight falling onto Zane's supportive arm as he rides the waves of his own release.

After a moment of heavy panting, we both sink to the floor of the shower in bliss, chuckling. My legs are jelly—or maybe just mush.

Yep. Officially a good idea.

After another hour or so of sleep, I make my way down to the living room, where I can hear Kieran and Morgan chatting.

"Good morning," I say, rubbing my bleary eyes.

"Sounded like it," Kieran says with a schoolgirl giggle.

"Oh shut up."

"I don't want to know," Morgan groans, putting a palm to his face. "Why are you wearing a hoodie that's twelve sizes too big for you?"

"Oh," I say, looking down at Zane's sweatshirt loosely hanging over my black t-shirt. He's right, I am swimming in this thing. "It's Zane's. I dunno why, but I couldn't find any of my sweaters this morning. I brought, like, three of them. You would think I would be able to find one."

Morgan scoffs and rolls his eyes.

"Of course," he says. "I'm sure it's a coincidence."

Kieran seems to be smirking to himself over whatever this inside joke is, but neither of them seems to want to tell me.

"Where did Z-Man go this morning, anyway?" Kieran says. "I mean, after *Pound Town*, that is."

Morgan cringes at Kieran's comment while I choose to just ignore it.

"He and Kami are talking to the Council people about the next steps. It sounds like the Council is going to help them assemble a team to head to the volcano in Greece and fix everything."

"Well, that's good news, right?" Kieran says.

"I think so. I'm sure we'll hear more when they get back."

I take a seat next to Kieran on the couch and join in watching whatever they're watching. It seems to be some kind of British sitcom with teenagers.

After grabbing some breakfast and watching about a lifetime's worth of British TV, Kieran decided to set up a game of croquet in the yard. It's hilarious to watch him try to figure out how to place the wickets as he curses under his breath.

"He has no idea what he's doing," Morgan says with a chuckle.

"No, no he doesn't," I say, shaking my head. "But it's the only game Zane had in the house and I think he's bored."

"He's pretty docile for an Incubus," he says. "Far less sex-crazed than most. Certainly doesn't seem to need to feed as often."

"Kieran?" I ask, almost choking on air. "You think Kieran is *docile*?"

"I've met plenty of Incubi and Succubi," he says. "In comparison, Kieran is quite reserved."

"Wow. I feel like I need to meet other Incubi now."

"Pretty sure your Siren would blow a blood vessel."

He's not wrong.

"So what's your deal, Morgan? What do you do when you're not defending badass demon-king-killers?"

He laughs and smiles at me.

"Nothing too interesting, honestly. I spend time at home, I garden, I drink with friends in the pub… most of my time is spent in the library."

"Why is that?" I ask. "Why are you always in the library?"

"Well, I like the quiet. I'm usually surrounded by other people's emotions. But in the uni library, most people are studying. There's not a lot of depth of emotion happening during studies—besides boredom, that is."

"I guess that makes sense. What's the opposite of that, then? Where are people most emotional?"

"Hmm…" he says, pausing for a moment as he scratches his chin. "Airports are big ones. Government buildings. Ikea."

"Ikea?" I ask, laughing.

"People are at their worst when shopping for furniture."

"So you garden, drink, read… kind of sounds like my grandpa's dream life."

"Oi," he says, feigning hurt. "I may be 287-years-old, but that doesn't make me a grandpa."

Whoa.

"Wait, you're seriously 287?" I ask.

"Yeah. Finn's older than me. What's Zane at, anyway?"

"Oh, uh… 200."

Every once in a while, I realize how weird these conversations are.

"See? For an Immortal, it's not that old. I still feel like that small-town boy."

"Born and raised in South Detroit?" I ask, snickering.

"What?" he asks, his brows furrowed.

I grab the TV remote and start to sing the next line of Journey's "Don't Stop Believin'."

He smirks and raises his eyebrows in surprise.

I continue as he starts to laugh and I hear Kieran singing along from outside.

Morgan's eyes catch mine for a moment and he smiles a genuine smile, which for him can be few and far between.

"I uh…" he says, interrupting my singing. "I think your Siren is home."

"Oh, really?" I ask.

"Yeah." He clears his throat a bit.

In a flurry, Kieran bursts through the door singing.

"…to that feeeeeeliinn'!"

He looks between us and sighs.

"Aww," he whines. "Did I miss the sing along?"

"Sorry mate," Morgan says. "I think Zane is almost home. I should get going."

"Huh?" Kieran squints and tilts his head. "No, I just got a text from him. They literally just left, should be back in like, forty minutes."

"Oh," Morgan says, his eyes flashing briefly with confusion but settling quickly. "My mistake."

53

In hindsight, I should never have mentioned to Ava that Immortal clubs are a thing. Now we're waiting in the queue outside Sempre, London's Immortal nightspot. The problem with Immortals is that I can't charm my way past lines like I usually would. Instead, Finn, Kami, Kieran, Ava, and I are all bundled in our coats outside the gray stone building.

"This is awesome," Kieran says. "I'm so excited. Are you guys excited? I'm fucking stoked right now."

"I think you may be more excited than Ava," I say with a laugh.

"Well, it's a first for both of us," he says. "Plus, I get to hit on hot Immortals. What's not to like?"

"Can you…" Ava asks, "you know… feed on Immortals or whatever it is you do?"

"No," Kieran says. "Sadly, I can only feed on humans. But I don't have to feed to have a little taste, if you know what I mean."

"We always know what you mean," Finn says.

The bouncer signals to our group to head inside. We follow the line to a small window where a woman at a desk checks our IDs.

"How many?" she asks. Kami steps forward to answer.

"Three regulars, one lite, one extra strong."

"What does that mean?" Ava asks.

"They give you wristbands based on what you drink, so the bartenders can give you the right strength of alcohol," I explain. "Regulars are for most Immortals, lite means human, and extra strong is for demons or certain other types of Immortals."

"Oh, so it's a code of sorts."

"Exactly."

Kami hands me a purple band, plus a green band for Ava. We put them on our wrists, check our coats, and head inside. The club has multiple levels, all lit in vibrant purples and blues, with a light-up dance floor in the center. Kami finds some open seats in the back corner and the rest of us join. A waitress comes by to take our drink orders before leaving to fill them.

"So, everyone here is an Immortal?" Ava asks.

"Everyone except the people with green wristbands like yours," I say. She scans the room, clearly trying to pick out the humans from the Immortals in the crowd. Most of the wristbands I can see are purple—Immortals—with a handful of orange for demons and those with higher tolerances. I spot a couple of green bands too, but the humans are definitely outnumbered here.

The waitress returns with our drinks and she sets our glasses down in front of each of us. Kieran's glass has an orange rim, probably to delineate the stronger liquor.

"Look who it is!" a voice calls over the music. We turn to see Alek in grey trousers and a black tee that reads *Lads on Tour*. It's far from his usual tailored and pressed attire.

"What are you doing here, mate?" I ask, standing to give him a hug.

"I could ask you the same. I'm here for a stag do."

"That explains the shirt," Kami says, hugging him as well. "Good to see you again!"

"Same to you! Small world, eh?"

Alek says hello to the rest of the group and sits down to chat. I sit back down and Ava joins on my lap.

"So, are we gonna get to have one for you soon?" he asks with a wink.

Shut up, Alek.

The last thing I need is someone selling me out to Ava.

"No time soon," I say, giving him a glare and taking a sip of my drink.

My expression doesn't have its intended effect as he doesn't seem to plan on dropping it.

"You sure you haven't been eyeing one of these?" he asks, pointing to his gold knot bracelet.

"What's that?" Ava asks, looking to me for an explanation.

Thanks, Alek.

This is not exactly how I planned on bringing up the topic.

"It's a… er… it's like an engagement ring but for Sirens," I say.

"Oh."

"It's the Hercules knot," he adds, holding out his bracelet so she can get a closer look. "Aka the love knot. If your mark wasn't under your tattoo, it would look something like this."

"Why do you have the bracelet if you already have the mark?" she asks.

"Well, it's mostly just tradition. It started because the human partners of Sirens were marked, but the Sirens themselves wanted to show that they were taken in some way too. Some got a tattoo in the shape of the mark, but over time, bracelets became more popular. Now Sirens wear them even if they don't have human partners. It's the Siren equivalent of an engagement ring."

"Oh."

"Zane didn't tell you this already?"

Bloody hell, he's calling me out. I was going to get to it, goddamn it. I've been kind of busy if you haven't noticed.

Finn snickers and gives me a knowing look.

"It hasn't come up," I say, this time with a more intense scowl.

"I'm gonna run to the restroom," Ava says, scooting off my lap.

The last thing I want is Ava running off alone in this place.

"I don't want you going alone," I say. "Especially not in an Immortal club."

"Actually, I need to hit the jacks anyway," Finn says. "I'll come with you."

AVA

We weave through the crowd toward a set of double doors with a sign for the restroom.

I'm trying to get my mind off of Zane's dismissive attitude.

"No time soon," he said.

Wow, okay, pal. Don't be too excited about marrying me or anything.

I mean, we're already soulmates and literally bonded together forever; is it really that unappealing to be married to me?

"I don't actually need to go, I just wanted to chat," Finn says. "I heard your thoughts before and I could tell you were a bit upset. You know he wants to marry you, don't you?"

Oh yeah. Can't hide anything from a telepath.

"Nope," he says with a smirk. "He's just awkward, I promise. The man is crazy about you. If you asked him right here and now, he'd say yes."

"How do you know?"

"Telepath. Remember?"

Oh yeah.

"Well, thanks," I say, feeling a bit better. "Okay, I'll be right back."

"I'll be here," he says with a nod.

I open the door to a long, well-lit hallway. The contrast between the dark club filled with booming bass and the bright, relatively quiet hallway is jarring. The walls are painted black and the floor is concrete. There's a man leaning against the wall flirting with a blonde in a black dress. At the end of the hallway is the women's room to the right and the men's to the left. I turn right and open the door to about three women waiting in line for five stalls.

After I finish in the restroom, I step back out into the hallway. The man seems to have the blond woman pinned against the wall and she looks slightly uncomfortable.

His hand is on the side of her neck in such a way that I can't quite figure out if it's romantic or threatening.

"Shut up," he whispers to her, just loud enough that I'm able to pick it up.

Okay, that's definitely threatening.

"Are you okay?" I ask, walking up to the couple.

She turns to me with a look of panic in her eyes, but says nothing.

"Do you want to go back to the club?"

The man gives me a dirty look and the woman nods, then takes off sprinting for the doors. I follow quickly behind her, but the man grabs my wrist and tugs me back hard, wrenching my shoulder slightly.

"Get your hands off of me!" I shout, now realizing that I'm in a possibly dangerous situation.

I need to get out there to Finn.

He pulls up my wrist and looks at the green wristband with a wicked expression.

Oh shit.

I look at his own arm, hoping to see a green band that tells me I have some chance of fighting this guy off.

It's purple.

Crap.

He grabs my face in his other hand.

"Don't scream. Don't make a sound," he says in a low, sinister voice.

I would scream if I thought someone might hear me, but the music out there is impossibly loud and if Finn can't hear me, it'll just piss the guy off even more.

I decide for the safer option: screaming in my mind. If that's even a thing.

Finn! Help! I'm in trouble!

"Since you scared off my date for the evening, I think it's only fair that you take her place," he says. He licks his lips and smiles. "Pull up your skirt."

Uh, how about I pull my knee up between your legs instead, creep face?

I go to knee him where the sun don't shine, but he blocks me with his knee and pushes me against the wall.

FINN! FUCK! HELP!!!

54

 ZANE

"Did I say something I shouldn't have?" Alek asks.

Do you think?

"Why'd you have to bring up marriage in front of Ava?" I say.

"I mean, you already marked her. Is it really that unexpected of a question?"

"No, but…"

"Z already bought the bracelet," Kami says with a big smile.

"Holy shit, dude," Kieran says, nearly choking on his drink. "You told Kami, but not me?"

I cover my face with my palm.

"I didn't tell Kami either," I say. "She found it in our apartment."

"Well, that's exciting!" Alek exclaims.

"Not if you ruin the surprise. I haven't had a chance to explain the bracelets yet, let alone figure out a way to ask."

"Sorry, I didn't know," he says with an apologetic grimace.

"It's alright, mate, I know you didn't mean anything by it. I re-"

I'm interrupted by a strange uncomfortable feeling in my chest.

Something feels wrong, but I can't tell why.

I look around the room to see if anything has changed or if anyone is watching me, but everything seems normal.

"You okay there, Z?" Kami asks, raising a questioning brow.

"Yeah, something just… uh… distracted me."

"Is everything okay with Ava?"

Shit. Ava. That didn't even occur to me.

I try to focus on what I'm feeling, but can't quite make heads or tails of the sensation. I stand up to look for them and spot Finn standing in the corner outside the entrance to the restrooms. He catches my eye and gives me a curious look.

"What's going on?" he asks from across the club.

Where's Ava? Is she okay?

He pauses for a minute as his eyes glaze over before they shoot open.

What? Is she alright?

"No," he replies before flipping around and slamming through the double doors behind him.

Fuck.

I'm on my feet in an instant and take off running toward the restrooms.

———•———

AVA

FINN! FUCK! HELP!!!

The door swings open, its hinges nearly warping with the force, and the man turns around with a shocked look on his face.

Finn appears in the doorway with his chest inflated and a concerned look on his face. As he stares at me pinned beneath the creep, his expression morphs into one of anger and disgust.

"What in God's name?" he huffs, walking toward us. "Are you okay, Ava?"

"We're just having a bit of fun," the creep says. "Tell him we're just having fun." He looks into my eyes with his hand still tight around my wrist.

Yeah, sure buddy.

"I found this guy intimidating some girl and he came after me instead," I shout, ripping my hand out of his grasp and pushing him back.

He stumbles back with a look of shock on his face.

"What the…" the guy mumbles before recovering. "Is this a fucking setup?"

I walk over to Finn, shaking slightly. When the door swings open again, this time the top hinge literally snaps in half with a loud crack.

"Ava," Zane says through heavy breaths, grabbing my shoulders and looking me over as if he's expecting me to be injured.

"Hey lads," the creep says with his hands raised, palms facing outward. "I don't know if this American bird is your girlfriend or what, but she came onto me."

Zane looks up at the man, his eyes a vibrant green.

"Wills?" he asks, a mix of shock and fury on his face.

Wait… does he actually know this guy?

"Zane?" the man replies, a look of relief on his face. "Thank fuck, mate. Your friend and I are having a disagreement here. This bird-"

Zane erupts in a loud, thunderous growl as he steps in front of me.

"Wills, is it?" Finn asks, stepping toward the man with a menacing expression I've never seen from him. "You think we're thick, eh?"

"Whoa, this is all a big misunderstanding."

Zane begins to shake as he turns to Finn.

"What happened?"

"He was trying to… errgh," Finn says, wincing. "It's pricks like this that make me really wish I couldn't read thoughts."

Zane launches at the guy—Wills, I guess—and pins him to the wall by his shoulders.

If we tell Zane what actually just happened, he might kill the guy right here and now.

"What did he do, Ava?" Zane asks, his voice low and menacing.

"He was, um… he was bothering this girl, so I asked her if she was okay and then she ran away and he got mad at me."

"Did he hurt you?" Zane asks me, stepping forward until he's almost nose-to-nose with the man.

"Calm down," Wills says. "What happened to the Iron Si-"

Zane throws a fist into the wall beside his face, sending scraps of drywall crumbling to the floor.

"Fucking finish that sentence, I dare you."

Wills swallows hard and looks to Finn, as if he finally realized Zane isn't on his team after all.

The doors behind me open and Kami, Kieran, and Alek walk into the hallway.

"Damn," Kieran says. "What did I miss?"

"Wills?" Alek says with wide eyes.

"What the hell is going on?" Kami asks. "Ava, you're shaking."

She wraps her arms around me and pulls me in for a hug.

"That guy attacked me," I say. "He was trying to get me to… uh…"

"He didn't," she says, her lips pursing into a thin line. She looks at Finn, who seems to be communicating with her telepathically.

"Did you…" Zane asks, his eyes brightening. He turns to me with a concerned expression. "Did he tell you to do anything? This is important."

"He uh… he told me not to call for help… and to tell Finn everything was fine."

Zane's fist collides with Wills's face faster than I can process, leaving a large dent in the wall behind his head as he slumps to the floor.

"You motherfucker!"

Kieran runs to Zane and pulls him back, but Zane shrugs him off.

I guess it's a good thing I didn't tell him about the part where the creep told me to pull my skirt up.

Finn turns to me with a look of horror on his face and covers his mouth with his fist.

"He's a Siren, yeah?" Finn asks Kami. She nods in response.

Oh. That means… when he told me to do something… he was charming me? *OH GOD THAT IS SO MESSED UP.*

Kami rubs a hand reassuringly along my back.

"I'm so sorry, Ava, I should've heard you calling me," Finn says telepathically, frowning as his head hangs low.

"She's lying," Wills says from the floor.

Zane responds with a heavy kick to the man's abdomen.

Kami, Alek, and Finn stand watching as Zane pulls the man upright and twists his arm backward, an unholy snapping sound radiating from him as he shrieks in pain. Kieran cringes and looks away.

"Aren't you going to stop him?" I ask Kami. She bites her lip as if she wants to say more, but instead shakes her head.

She lets me go and looks to Finn for a moment before walking over to Zane.

"I want you to tell me the truth," she says, stepping forward to take Zane's place. She grabs the man's collar and twists it in her hand. "Tell me what you really did to Ava here."

"I'm… telling you," he says between coughs. "She was trying it on wi-"

He takes a swing at Kami mid-sentence, possibly thinking he can take her instead of Zane.

The man has a death wish.

She pulls a knife from somewhere under her dress and stabs through his hand, pinning it to the wall behind him as he screams in agony.

"Kheru knife," she says with a smirk. "Made of demon claw. You wanna try me again, prick?"

Someone attempts to exit the women's restrooms behind her, but goes right back in when they see everything happening in front of them.

Probably a good call on their part.

Zane stands behind her, fists balled at his sides but smirking slightly.

"Alright," Kami says with a sigh. "Last chance. You want to come clean and tell us what happened, or you want this knife between your eyes?"

"I'm telling the truth," he says.

"Well, that's unfortunate. See our pal over there?" she says, gesturing toward Finn. She leans in to his ear to whisper. "He's a Selkie."

In a swift motion, she pulls the knife from his hand and jams it into the side of his neck and he falls to the ground.

Zane walks over to me and pulls my head into his chest. I look over at the others in an attempt to understand what's happening. Kieran's eyes are wide with shock but everyone else has their heads lowered.

What the hell just happened?

55

 ZANE

The cool outside air is a welcome change from the hot, humid club.

"So much for having a nice night out as a last hurrah before Greece," Kami says with a heavy sigh as she slumps against the outside wall. "I called a Council contact for cleanup. They should be here soon."

Finn stumbles, leaning on the wall with one hand, and heaves forward, throwing up on the sidewalk. He's pale and holding his stomach tight. I can't tell if he's gotten more averse to violence or is just repulsed by the thoughts he's just been subjected to.

"Fuck," he curses.

"Is someone gonna explain what the heck just happened?" Ava asks, looking between Kami and me with questioning eyes.

"Yeah, I'm a little lost too," Kieran says, twisting his hair between his fingers. "It doesn't help that I'm also legit wasted off that drink I ordered. They weren't kidding when they said it was demon strength."

"You're lost because you're not an Immortal," I say.

"In our world," Finn chimes in, "what he did in there is a capital offense. Immortals don't have many laws, but we have a couple big ones. Most of them are to keep anyone from drawing too much attention to the community. The others are against the worst atrocities. This one… is a bit of both."

"What exactly is it?" Kieran asks.

"Immortals with powers of body or mind control can't make a person complicit in their own victimization. So you can't use your powers to convince someone not to fight back while you assault them. You can't force them to kill themselves, and you can't encourage them not to report abuse."

"Because it's sick and cruel," I say, gritting my teeth as I wrap Ava tighter in my arms.

"Forcing a person to participate in their own assault," Kami says, shaking her head as her eyes glow gold. "It's despicable. Not everyone agrees on how to treat humans, but we all know there's a line. It's preying on the weak and using psychological torture to do it. If I didn't kill him, the Council surely would have… or worse."

"Why did he come after you in the first place?" I ask, feeling bile rise in my throat. "Just because you interrupted things between him and some girl?"

"Well um… I think he was trying to do the same thing to her when I got involved."

I turn to Kami, whose face holds a mixture of rage and disgust. Finn must've told her something I didn't get to hear.

"I think he was trying to charm someone into having sex with him," Ava says softly. "He didn't know I was immune."

What?

A tremor creeps from my fingertips to the rest of me until my entire body is shaking. I knew something more was going on than a small physical altercation, but I didn't want to think about it.

"That's fucking wrong, dude," Kieran curses. "I'm kind of disappointed that he's dead now; I would've liked to have killed him myself."

He kicks an empty can across the street and huffs.

"How did he even know you were…" I start to ask, but I look down at her hand in mine and am confronted with the answer: her wristband. "…human. You're wearing a human wristband."

"That bloke had a whole system," Finn says, still hunched over. "Sick fuck has been doing this for a long time."

I feel sick to my stomach too. Wills was only a minor acquaintance in the Siren community, but I had no idea what was lurking underneath.

A roar rips through my throat and I punch a chunk of cement loose from the nearby wall.

"Oh my god, Zane," Ava says grabbing my upper arm, "your eyes are bright white."

I hiss at the unexpected touch.

"It's just me," she says. "Come on, don't hurt yourself!"

My shoulders rise and fall rapidly with every breath. My ribcage feels tight around my lungs.

"The problem is solved, Z," Kami says, taking a step toward me.

"Are you guys going to be in trouble?" Ava asks.

"For killing him?" she asks. "No. We're both deputized to act on behalf of the Council right now. They probably won't love that I did it in a hallway in the back of a public nightclub, but they'll be okay with how we handled him. The Council is hardly known for their leniency in matters like this."

———•———

I hardly slept at all after what happened last night, which is ironic because Ava seemed to sleep fine. It only sours my morning further when I open the door to a familiar smirk and dark blond curls.

"Morgan," I grunt. "You're early."

I begrudgingly welcome him in and close the door behind him.

"Good to see you, too. Still got your knickers in a twist?"

"Don't start with me today," I grumble. "I'm hardly in the mood."

"Your night out was that much fun, eh? Sorry I missed it."

"Trust me," Kieran says, walking in wearing just his flannel pajama bottoms. "You should be glad you weren't a part of that."

"What happened?" he asks, his expression hardening as his lips press into a thin line.

"Ava almost got assaulted," Kieran says.

"She what?" Morgan's shoulders straighten and his eyes burn with intensity. "This is exactly why she has a bodyguard."

"It was a fluke, unrelated thing—we solved it, guy's dead," I say. "End of story."

"How was-… Wait, he's dead? How serious are we talking?"

"He tried to charm her…" I look down at my hands as I lean on the kitchen counter.

"Fuck," he hisses, sitting at the dining table. "You lot are magnets for drama, aren't you?"

"Wish we weren't."

"Is she okay?"

"She's alright," Kieran says, joining him at the table. "Honestly, I think Finn handled it the worst. Have you talked to him?"

"No." He shakes his head and sighs. "When you get insight into a dark mind like that… it messes you up for a bit. It's hard to see the worst inside people. I get their emotions, but Finnegan… he gets all the details. I wouldn't want to trade places with him, that's for certain."

"You didn't wake me," Ava murmurs groggily as she rubs her eyes and walks into the kitchen in her pajamas. She stops when she spots Kieran and Morgan sitting at the table. "Oh, morning!"

They both greet her before quickly moving to small talk.

"You were supposed to wake me," she says, giving me a hug.

"I was going to wake you before we left," I say.

"This is the last I'm going to see you for two days. What if something happens to you?"

"I told you, the Council has a good team built for us. You have Morgan and Kieran here to protect you. From our early reconnaissance, it seems like the volcano isn't even a priority for them—it's barely defended. This is an easy win."

"That's what people say just before something goes horribly bad, Zane. You might as well have just said, 'What could possibly go wrong?'"

I chuckle and pull her in closer, giving her a kiss on the forehead.

"We're prepared. I'll be back before you know it."

"I just hate that I'm leaving you to do this alone."

"No offense, love, but a tiny human girl is hardly going to be the lynchpin in a team of elite Immortals."

"You don't know. Maybe I'm the chosen one. I did kill Asmodeus after all."

"Which is the exact reason you need to stay home. We need to keep you off their radar. We can do this. Kami would never let me fail on one of her missions—trust me."

As if on cue, I hear the front door jingle as Kami lets herself in. She walks into the kitchen with her usual early-morning pep. On an average day, her energy would be an annoyance, but on travel days, it's downright exhausting.

"Hey, Z! You all packed up?" she asks.

"All ready," I say.

Ava chews on her lip worriedly.

"Are you alright?" Kami asks her.

"I'm just nervous," she says. "I don't want you guys to get hurt."

"We're just helping out, really—we're not even the main people on the job, we're more like backup. This one will be a piece of cake. We go in, shut down some big machinery, and get out. We'll be back before you know it."

She nods reluctantly.

"Okay," Kami says, "let's get your bags out to the car."

I grab my small leather carry-on and swing it over my shoulder.

"That's all you're bringing?" she asks.

"I pack light."

I follow her to the front drive and she opens her car. I throw my bag in the back seat and lean a hand on the top of the car.

"Do you really think this is all as safe as you told her?" I ask.

"I don't know," she says with a heavy breath. "Everything we're doing right now is in uncharted territory. Is it safe for us to go on this mission? Probably. Is it safe to be on the hit list of two Demon Kings? Almost certainly not. Is it safe for Ava to be involved in this? No. But in terms of safety, this is probably the least risky part of our current situation."

Not exactly the pep talk I was hoping for, but she's not wrong. Everything from here on out is going to get a lot more dangerous.

56

 ZANE

Kami slips another gun into the holster around her waist before strapping a set of silver daggers to her upper thigh.

"Did you get any sleep on the plane?" she asks as she pulls on a set of black tactical gloves.

"None," I huff. "Three separate flight attendants insisted on chatting me up. Be glad you had the window seat."

"It's probably because we killed another Siren. We've tipped the power scales again. Hopefully, what we do today will solve that."

"Here's hoping."

I add a pair of hunting knives to my belt and tuck my vest into my jeans.

Another man from the team walks up and throws a metal box into the helicopter. It's Blake, a towering brick of a man brought in by the Council to help handle any trouble that comes our way. He's a Cusith, a fiercely strong fighter with absurdly quick reflexes and rows of sharp fangs in place of a smile. The man probably never had much of a career path as a model, but he seems a perfect fit for special ops.

Our other team member, Valentina, is a small but serious woman and a healer of some sort, in case of unexpected trouble.

After a few minutes of loading up, we get into the helicopter and the pilot starts the blades rotating. We each put on a headset and slide the doors closed. The copter heads up and before we know it, we're several thousand feet above the Mediterranean Sea.

"The rest of the team should already be on the ground by the time we get there," Blake says, his voice humming through our headsets. "With any luck, we should just be air support confirming that we can see around the volcano. All you lot will need to do is confirm any effects you may be sensing as Sirens."

"What is the ground team doing?" Kami asks.

"We know there's some kind of device installed off the shore of the volcano," Valentina explains. "It seems to be relatively straightforward tech. Human geologists have used similar techniques to manage magma flow in active volcanoes. The main goal is to shut it down, possibly remove the equipment entirely."

"How defended do we think this place is?" I ask.

"Not at all, as far as we can tell. Initial reconnaissance showed no defenses."

"Yet we're still armed to the teeth," Kami says, raising a brow.

"We don't expect a fight," Blake says, "but we are prepared for it."

"You're always prepared for a fight," Valentina jokes.

He snarls at her slightly before turning to look out the window.

"We can't all be hippie flower-child types, going into battle armed with love and positivity."

"It's fine. I know you're not used to using your brain."

Kami shoots me a subtle smile, likely pointing out the familiar dynamic between them.

I watch the ocean outside the window. From here, the surface looks simultaneously rough and still, one wave blurring into the next in the light of the sun. There's no land in sight now, and there probably won't be until we reach the island.

———·———

"We're here," Blake says as the helicopter approaches a group of islands, jarring me from a near-sleep against the window.

"This isn't really how I remembered it," Kami says, looking over the shallow hills surrounded by cerulean bays.

She's right—none of these look like a volcano. But then again, it's been almost a lifetime since we were last here. I can't actually bring to mind a single memory of the place.

"It's in the middle there," Valentina says, as if preempting our question. "The previous eruption sank it lower into the sea, but it's still active."

The island is encircled in black sand beaches and doesn't come to a clear peak, but its dark gray, jagged terrain surrounds a small crater at its center.

"Connect me to the ground team," Blake says to the pilot, who gives him a quick nod. We make wide circles around the island as Blake mumbles into his headset.

"I'm was seeing a lot of bubbles in the water just south of the volcano," Kami says, "but they seem to be dissipating. Is that us?"

"Yes," Blake says. "That's expected. They've turned off the machine, now, meaning that a lot of the lava that was being diverted underwater is now going back to where it's supposed to be."

We watch the crater at its center in nervous silence for a moment as smoke begins to build. After a moment, a projectile shoots up from the haze. Black wings sprout from a naked body, stretching outward into immediate flight.

"Whoa," Kami says. "Seems like a pretty good sign, right?"

"Yes, mission success," Blake says. "We just need to refuel and head back to the mainland. Do we have a-"

We hear a series of loud bangs and see chaos and fighting erupt on the island beneath us. From this height, it's hard to make out who is who, but it looks like our team is being surrounded.

"Get us on the ground, quickly!" Blake shouts to the pilot, who nods and takes the helicopter quickly down as we see another Siren emerge from the volcano. Blake fires several shots out the door of the helicopter, but the mob seems barely affected. "They're all demons—they have to be. Not sure which kind, but they're not going down easy."

Kami grabs a knife in each hand.

"Well," she says, "we prepared for a reason, right?"

I grab my knives as well, since guns aren't much help against demons and I'm more comfortable with hand-to-hand combat anyway. If only we hadn't just weakened ourselves by restarting the Siren birth cycle.

We land in the closest clearing and immediately jump out, all four of us armed and ready. We duck beneath the blades and run to the beach where we had seen much of the commotion. Valentina sees two ground crew members lying on the ground and rushes to tend to them. The rest of the team is further ahead, fighting off a horde of demons.

Blake is already far ahead of us, ripping into one demon after the other with surprising ease. He tears one in half at the waist, tossing him aside as if it were nothing before he bites into the next.

As we catch up, an ally calls to us.

"Don't let them touch you," she groans. "Some of them are Shayatin."

"Wasn't planning on letting them get the chance," Kami says to me with an assured nod, before launching into the chaos.

Her newly sharpened knives slide through a demon's legs in an instant, dropping him to the ground. Several more surround her and I join to help, sweeping my knife across the throat of one, and then another. In just moments, we're huffing and covered in blood as more demons approach.

I suddenly feel a cold, hard object against my throat. I look at Kami, who seems frozen in place. A pinch of pain confirms what I had hoped wasn't the case: this is a Kheru knife, and it can pierce my skin.

"Hey there, pretty boy," a man says behind me. "You're surprisingly difficult to get in touch with, you know that?"

"Is that so?" I ask. "Did you ever try giving me a ring?"

The man lets out a laugh that tells me he's teetering on the edge of sanity. Fighting has mostly stilled around us, the remainder of our team clearly unsure of what to do.

"Why would I? The Kings knew you would come to us; we just had to wait for you. And here you are."

"Okay, I'm here," I say. "So you don't need them. Leave them be."

I see Kami dart forward with a look of panic, but my vision blurs before going black, and only echoes of voices remain.

57

 AVA

"Okay, your nervousness is making me nervous," Jen says through my cell's speakerphone.

"How do you know I'm nervous?" I ask, marching back and forth across the kitchen.

"I can feel you pacing."

I mean, I am pacing, but there's no way she knows that.

"How can you tell?"

"That's your pacing voice."

"Well, I can't help it, okay? My boyfriend is off somewhere fighting Lucifer and he really should've called by now."

"Did he give you a time he'd call by?"

"No, he said he didn't want to give me a specific time in case he was late. He said he didn't know when it would be and he didn't want me to worry."

Jokes on him, 'cause I can worry like a crazy bitch with little to no provocation.

"Then you shouldn't stress," she says. "Zane and Kami can handle themselves. Is Man-Rogue there? Man-Rogue, tell Ava not to stress!"

"He's not in the room," I say with a chuckle, sitting down at the dining table. "And his name is not Man-Rogue."

"What *is* his name?"

"Morgan."

"You're kidding," she says with a laugh. "That's basically an anagram of Man-Rogue. I was hella close."

I hear Kieran laugh in the other room, but I'm not sure if he's eavesdropping or laughing at something else entirely.

"So tell me something interesting," I say with a sigh. "I need a distraction."

"Okay interesting… it's early in the morning over here, so give me a minute. Well… actually… I do have some kind of interesting news to share. Wasn't sure if I should tell you in person or not."

"Exciting? Good exciting?"

"I think so."

"Good, I need exciting. Spill."

"Okay so you know how I told you Deb and I were fighting a lot and she was being all weird with me since the reunion?"

"Yeah…"

"Well, I thought she was on a diet because the one time I tried a diet, I was soooo moody. Cutting back on food makes people lose their minds, okay? I started wondering if I could eat my scented erasers…"

"Erasers?"

"They taste like dirt. Not that I tried. Okay, I licked it. But regardless, you cannot eat erasers and diets make people grumpy so I *thought* that's what was going on with Deb. And then the other night I said I was texting you and she asked about Kami and I'm like, 'oh my god what is your deal with Kami, like, I get that she's hot but you keep bringing her up,' and she was like, 'no, *you* keep bringing her up,' and I'm like, 'no, it's definitely you,' so she goes—'I'm still in love with you.'"

"Oh shit," I say.

"Yeah, I know, right?"

Deb and Jen were crazy in love when they were together back in high school, but they ended up going to college in different states, so they broke up after graduation. They stayed friends, but I always did wonder why they never gave it another go.

"Wha-, what did you say? Do you still have feelings for her?"

"I was a badass, Ava. I walked up to her and I kissed her. It's by far the smoothest thing I've ever done. I wish I had it on tape."

"So that's a yes, then? You do have feelings for her?"

"Oh, yeah, anyway, we're dating."

Leave it to Jen to just drop the most important detail like an afterthought.

"That's great!" I say. "I'm really happy for you. Di-"

I feel a sudden sharp pain in the back of my head. It's not entirely rare for me to have a random headache, but this feels weird—different.

"Ava? Are you there?"

"Yeah, sorry. I just felt something weird."

"What kind of weird?"

"Just a stabbing pain in the back of my head."

Morgan appears in the doorway with a concerned look on his face.

"Are you alright?" he asks. "Seemed like something happened."

"Did it?" I ask. "Yeah, I got a weird headache. I guess maybe you felt it or… wait…"

Did something happen to Zane?

My heart is straining against my ribcage, thumping in my ears.

"Sorry Jen, I need to go," I say, quickly ending our call and standing up from my chair.

"Okay, calm down, killer," Morgan says, grabbing my shoulders and placing me back in my seat.

"I need to help him."

Kieran walks in, clearly concerned over the commotion. His eyes narrow as he takes in my panicked expression.

"We don't know anything for sure, do we?" he asks. "I mean, it's possible you just had a normal headache or something, right?"

"Exactly," Morgan says. "We stick to the plan, wait to hear from Kami and Zane. Even if he did get injured, he's a Siren—he's probably alright."

"Did Finn have any updates for you?"

"He's reaching out to some Council contacts but as far as we know, there's no news."

"No," I say. "I know something is wrong. I can feel it. We need to go find Zane."

"In Italy or Greece or whatever island he was headed to? We wouldn't even know where to start," Morgan says.

"We'll just have to figure it out."

"If something happened to Zane—*if*—we still couldn't just get on a plane and find him. And if you did, what are you going to do? You may have killed a Demon King once, but you're still human."

"Then… you can come with me."

"Really, Ava?" he scoffs, rubbing his face in his hands. "Did you forget why you hired me? Why I'm here? It's not to protect your boyfriend."

"You're here because you wanted to help the person who killed Asmodeus—that's me."

"Help you. Not get you killed. This is a suicide mission."

"I'm immortal."

"And just how far are we willing to go to test that?"

"As far as necessary to make sure Zane and Kami are safe."

"You're mad. You buzz toward danger like a moth to a flame, as if you won't get burned."

"Fine. You don't want to help and no one's going to force you. But I'm not going to let my friends get hurt when there's something I could do."

"Bloody stubborn woman," he huffs, throwing his hands up as he steps outside onto the patio.

—◆—

KAMI

A cold drop of water hits my face and I'm startled awake. I'm laying across the floor beside Valentina, the Council healer. She seems to be unconscious but her chest continues to rise and fall.

We seem to be in some kind of underground structure, possibly the foundation of an ancient building—with stone walls and dirt floors. There are heavy iron bars across the door. Naturally.

I hear soft male groans and peek my head through the bars. We're in a corridor of similar cells, with a large open space at the end. A shirtless man is slumped over and possibly unconscious or dead, chained to the floor in the center.

This is far from ideal.

Two women walk by and approach the man in the main hall, paying me no attention. They yank him upward with surprising strength—demons, no doubt.

That's when I see his face: it's Zane.

He's dirty and disheveled, but it's him. One of them takes a bag of powder and empties it into his mouth. He tries to fight them, but doesn't seem to be fully aware of where he is or what's happening to him.

What are they doing?

They wouldn't go to this much trouble to poison Zane.

If anything, they're going to a bit of trouble not to kill us. They could've found us before instead of waiting for an ambush. They could've killed us all instead of knocking us out. Demons, and especially the Kings, aren't known for their squeamishness.

And now they're forcing something down Zane's throat?

"Shayatin," a voice beside me says. I turn to see Valentina slowly waking up and taking a look around. "That one got me earlier. Nothing quite like a Shaytan's touch."

"Do you know what they want with Zane?" I whisper.

"No, but it's safe to say they're trying to uncover secrets."

"Secrets?"

"Shayatin can use your memories against you, but they can access them too. Does he know something? Or do they think he knows it?"

My stomach churns.

The only secret I can think of that Zane would be keeping is the one we've been trying to hide—that he didn't really kill Asmodeus.

58

We walk along the dirt path towards town, Kami swinging her empty basket back and forth. A crowd murmurs up ahead, but it's not quite clear where the sounds are coming from. As we round the corner past a group of trees, we see dozens of people gathered at the end of the road outside a large home—the Schauberg estate.

Ilen.

Almost in unison, Kami and I take off into a sprint for the estate.

Did Asmodeus finally kill Count Schauberg?

I can't help but smirk a little at the thought. Krisztian Schauberg is a typical pompous, arrogant rich man, but I have no good reason to wish him dead. He could give Ilen a good life, and that's what I want for her.

The crowd continues to swarm around the steps as we approach, but they still manage to give a wide berth to whatever they're looking at. Gasps and shouts fill the crowd. A woman buries her face in her husband's chest, sobbing. That's when it hits me—the thick, unmistakable smell of death.

I turn to Kami, whose eyes are wide and frozen with concern.

I inhale deeply.

Her smell is here—Ilen.

I push past the crowd to find a battered woman's naked body draped on the steps, blood trailing from the house's front door to her body.

No. It can't be her. It can't.

I run up the stairs and drop to my knees beside her body. I delicately turn her head toward me. Her face is swollen and covered in blood, unrecognizable, but her scent—it's her.

This can't be happening.

"No, no, no," I say, cradling Ilen's cold, naked body in my hands.

Tears pour uncontrollably from my eyes as I shake her.

"Ilen, please, darling. Wake up!"

My own voice sounds unfamiliar through my sobs.

This doesn't feel real. It can't be that this lifeless, bruised, and bloodied body is the girl I know. No twinkle in her eye. No bashful smile. No contagious laugh. My Ilen is so full of life—or, was.

But I took that from her.

"If this is where we've started, I can't wait to see where we end up," a voice says.

I look around for its source but find no one, just the huddled crowd watching from afar.

"Try again," another voice says.

Where are these voices coming from?

—◆—

I push past the crowd to find a battered woman's naked body draped on the steps, blood trailing from the house's front door to her body.

No. It can't be her. It can't.

I run up the stairs and drop to my knees beside her body. I delicately turn her head toward me. Her face is bruised and bloodied, but even with her hair caked in blood, I can make out the unforgettable shade of bright purple—*no*.

No. No. God please no.

A blood-curdling scream erupts from my chest and I collapse on top of her, sobbing into her shoulder.

My heart feels like it's been ripped from my chest, snapping my every rib. Every time I breathe, my lungs feel like they're on fire.

"Please, no, no, no," I cry, holding her to my chest. "No, this wasn't supposed to happen. Baby, please, no…"

—◆—

KAMI

Zane's pained screams echo through the walls of the dungeon.

"What are you doing to him?" I scream, but the demons just laugh in reply.

He's still chained to the floor, his eyes closed as he howls in agony. His wings rip through his shirt as he thrashes against his chains.

"No, no, no," he cries.

One demon has her hands on either side of his head, following him as his body flails.

"If this is where we've started, I can't wait to see where we end up," the other demon says with a laugh.

"What are they doing to him?" I ask Valentina. "He's clearly in pain!"

"They're looking inside his mind, triggering his worst memories," she says. "Be prepared. It'll get worse from here."

"But she's touching his head. Why?"

"They can manipulate your mind—your memories. Their touch will push you, guide you where they want you to go. It's usually to torture you, but sometimes they'll do it for information."

"They can make you see what they want you to?"

"Not quite. They don't have complete control. They rely on your own brain to access those bad memories—to turn them against you, make them more painful. I guess the brain is pretty good at that."

"How can we help him?"

She shakes her head and sighs.

"If I knew, I would try," she says. "But there's not a lot we can do to save him from his own mind."

ZANE

I pace at the foot of Ava's hospital bed as she lays unconscious, hooked up to an IV and a few beeping machines.

"Acute hepatic failure," the doctor mumbles, flipping through her medical chart on a clipboard.

Jen pinches her lips together and looks down at the floor.

"What does that mean?" I ask.

"Her liver is failing," she says. "We have a hepatologist coming to look at her shortly and we'll know more then."

"Is she gonna be okay?" Jen asks.

"I…" the doctor says. "I'm not a specialist, so I wouldn't want to give you any information until-"

I grab her wrist and she looks at me with wide, frightened eyes.

"Tell me the truth. Is she going to be alright?"

"It's fifty-fifty at this point, but it's certainly not looking good. I… I'm sorry."

My chest clenches and I feel as if all the blood has drained from my body. I can't even look back at Ava as she lays in her hospital bed. If I see her, I might just fall to pieces.

———————

I down the last bit of a bottle of whiskey and pitch it at the wall. It shatters, the glass shards gathering along the baseboard.

Fuck.

I pick up the phone and call Ava.

What am I doing?

"Hey," she answers.

"Hey," I say weakly.

This feels wrong.

"Everything okay?" she asks.

"Uh. We need to talk."

No. What are you doing? Stop.

I try to correct myself, to say something—anything at all—but I can't speak. I can't even move. I'm trapped inside myself.

"Uh, okay," she says, her voice shaking slightly. "That sounds really ominous."

I say nothing in response.

Fuck this. Say something. Tell her you love her. Say fucking anything.

"Do you wanna come over?" she asks.

Say yes. Please.

"No," I reply. "I… we… this isn't working out."

My heart is collapsing in on itself, endlessly crushed under its own weight.

Every second of her silence is breaking me in ways I didn't know I could be broken.

"You're… you're breaking up with me?" she asks. Her voice is soft and trembling, dragging me further into a wretched agony that burns my chest from the inside out.

I did that. I hurt her.

"Yeah," I force out, nearly choking on a sob.

"Wh-… Why? I mean, I know I went a little crazy last night, but I think that the alcohol just really got to me more than usual. I don't know if-"

Stop. Fuck. You're hurting her.

"No, it's not about last night. I just can't."

"I don't understand," she says. I can hear the tears in her voice now. "Can we talk about this in person?"

I can't stand the sound of her crying. It's ripping me apart. My lungs are on fire and my head throbs.

"No. I'm not changing my mind."

"If you're going to break up with me over the phone, I at least deserve to know why."

"Because, I…" I start to say, but I feel myself gag on the words.

Don't do this. Stop, please. Fuck! Why can't I stop?

"Can I just come over and we can talk? This doesn't make any se-"

"Because I don't want to be with you anymore."

I hit the End Call button and drop my phone to the ground.

Bile creeps up my throat and, in a violent lurch, I collapse to the ground, emptying my stomach into a bin as the room spins around me.

"He's in bad shape," a voice says. "What have you got?"

"I'm not sure yet," another voice says. "There's more here—I can sense it. It's almost like he has another memory beneath the surface."

Who is that? Where is that voice coming from?

"Right… here…"

———•———

Suddenly, I'm in Ava's apartment. I can't quite remember how I got here… the details are hazy and my memory is a blur.

Ava is sitting on the couch talking on her phone. Her eyes are watering and she bites her lip as it quivers.

"What's wrong, baby?" I ask, but she doesn't look at me. "Baby?"

She doesn't react, as if she can't hear me. I take a few steps closer.

"You're… you're breaking up with me?" she asks.

"No, never baby, I-" I say as I walk over to her, but I catch the name on her phone—Zane.

"Who are you talking to?" I ask, reaching out to touch her shoulder. I see my hand on her shoulder but I can't feel it.

"Wh-… Why?" she says into the phone, a tear falling onto her cheek. "I mean, I know I went a little crazy last night, but I think that the alcohol just really got to me more than usual. I don't know if-"

Fuck. What's happening. This is… how am I here?

"I don't understand. Can we talk about this in person?"

The tears start to spill more freely and she clenches her eyes shut.

"Baby? Please, listen to me," I beg, but she doesn't react. "Baby? Can you hear me? I love you, please just…"

"If you're going to break up with me over the phone, I at least deserve to know why."

I hate seeing her cry. I hate that I'm the one that did this to her. I can't handle it. My heart is tearing at the seams.

This is hell.

"Can I just come over and we can talk?" she asks. "This doesn't make any se-"

She looks at her phone and the screen reads 'Call Ended.'

I collapse to the floor and scream, in both desperation and pain, until my throat burns.

She doesn't hear me.

59

I feel an intense pang of sorrow in my stomach and double over at the sensation.

"What's wrong?" Morgan asks, crouching beside me with a look of concern.

"It's Zane," I say. "He's in pain. Something's wrong. It's this… intense feeling of sadness—grief."

Kieran runs into the room with his brows furrowed.

"What's happening?" he asks.

I clutch my stomach and groan.

"Probably Shayatin," Morgan says. "Ava is feeling Zane's pain. She said it feels like grief. She's probably right—they hone right in on loss and pain."

"They're making him relive his worst memories?" I ask. "Like they did to Finn and Kieran?"

Morgan crosses his arms and nods.

"We've got to help him," I say. "What do I do?"

"Ava," Morgan says with a sigh. "You can't help him. We don't even know where they are."

"But he's in pain. He's suffering. If I can feel him, can't he feel me? Can't I, like… I dunno, send him good feelings or something?"

"I'm not exactly an expert on the Siren mating bond," he says. "I'm the wrong person to ask."

"Well we don't exactly have a Siren to ask right now," Kieran says.

"We could call Alek," I suggest.

"Do you have his number?"

"I- Crap, no, I don't have it." I huff in frustration and sit myself on the floor.

"I hate this. Why can't I help him?"

Morgan sits in front of me and sighs.

"I know you want to help him," he says, "and we will. But right now, there's no way to help him. Not in this way. We'll find him and we'll find Kami and we'll make sure we get them out of there in one piece. But right now, he's on his own. He can handle this."

I'm overwhelmed by the emotions coming at me—fear, grief, sadness, guilt. I can't imagine what he's dealing with right now.

We sit for a few minutes in silence. I have no words for this situation.

In a flash, I'm overwhelmed with the intense memory of the moment Zane broke up with me. It's vivid, surprisingly so, almost like a waking dream. I gasp in shock.

"What was that?" Morgan asks.

"I- I don't even… a memory, I think, but I…"

"You could see Zane's memory?"

"No, it wasn't Zane's. It was mine, I think."

"Yours?" Morgan asks, his eyes popping open wide. "What do you mean?"

"It was me, in my house. It was something… from my past."

"You're remembering something from your past?"

"I guess so. I don't know… it was more intense than usual."

"Fuck," Morgan mumbles under his breath.

"What?" Kieran asks. "What's happening?

"They're somehow accessing Ava's memories," he says. "Through the bond no doubt."

"Is that bad?"

"If they can access her memories, then they can know what she knows, and more importantly—they know she's alive."

ZANE

I'm in a car driving down a road near Pike's in Port Charlotte.

But I'm not in the car so much as I am seeing inside the car. It's as if I'm seated where the dashboard should be.

Ava sits in the passenger seat and Mike in the driver's seat.

What is happening?

I can't talk or move other than to look side to side—I can only watch.

"The only reason I came there was for you," Mike snaps. "And then you start flirting with these guys that you mysteriously seem to know and it comes out that you had a hospital appointment that you didn't tell me about—I felt totally blindsided by the whole thing!"

Fucking prick.

If I could, I'd punch him in his smug fucking face.

"I only know them because I showed one of them how to find his friend's hospital room," she says, "and I wasn't flirting with them."

Wait… she's talking about me?

This is the night that I picked her up on the side of the road. I had no idea their fight had anything to do with me.

"I'm sorry I didn't tell you about the appointment," she continues. "I honestly didn't think you would have wanted to know. I promise. Nothing was going on. There's no conspiracy."

"Okay," he huffs.

What a bloody prick.

"So what was this appointment for?" he asks.

"Just another round of tests. They did an MRI and took more blood."

"And? What did they find?"

"It's too quick to tell. I think it's mostly to eliminate a few worst-case-scenario things. I doubt they'll come back positive."

"Worst-case scenario? Like what?"

The fucker looks more irritated with her than he is actually concerned for her wellbeing.

"Um, brain tumors, cancer, the big dangerous things. I think they're just trying to cover their asses."

"Mmm…" He pinches his lips into a tight line as if she's just offended him in some way.

"What?"

"It's just interesting, that's all," he says, acting aggrieved.

"What about it?"

"I just… I didn't realize this was so serious."

As if he gives a shit about Ava's health. If there's one thing I've learned in interacting with Mike, it's that the only person he cares about is Mike.

"I don't know… I hope not," she says, looking out the window. "I just want to find out what's going on at this point. If it's serious, I guess I'd rather know than be ignorant. I just need an answer."

"I just wish I had known before," he says with a sigh. "I wish you had told me."

"What do you mean? I am telling you."

"I mean before all…" He gestures between them. "…this."

What?

That… this… this is why they broke up? Because he didn't want her to be sick?

"What do you mean by that?" she asks.

I struggle desperately in an attempt to say or do anything. Ava's trying to hold an unaffected expression, but I can see how much he has hurt her. I want to comfort her and I want to throttle him for hurting her.

"I mean, I wish I had been able to make an informed decision. When we started dating, I didn't know you were sick. You didn't tell me you had all these problems."

Fuck.

I hate this motherfucker.

"Why?" she asks. "Do you not want to be with me?"

"I'm not saying that. I'm already in love with you. It's done now."

My gut churns and heat fills my lungs. I knew this guy was an asshole, but I didn't know just how stupid he was. Ava has always been better than he deserves, and here he is telling her that she wasn't good enough because she's ill?

"You would have chosen not to love me?" she asks.

"I dunno… Maybe… Yeah, I probably would have."

The broken look on her face nearly breaks me too.

"Fuck you!" she screams at him.

That's my girl.

"That isn't what we're looking for," a voice says. "Move along."

———·———

I don't recognize where I am—it's a narrow hallway in a small house with beige walls and dark green carpets. A door opens and Ava steps out into the hall. Her usual purple hair is a dark brown and she looks different, younger.

She walks to another door that opens as she reaches for it. A teen boy nearly collides with her as he steps out.

"Hey Ava," he says, licking his lips.

"Hey," she mumbles.

I don't like how uneasy she looks.

"You looking for me?" he asks, stepping closer to her.

She crosses her arms and looks at the floor.

"Just trying to go to the bathroom," she says.

Another boy steps into the hallway, this one more familiar—her brother, Dylan. He has fewer tattoos and appears younger too, but it's definitely him.

"Jake, stop trying to fuck my sister," he says with a laugh. "You'll probably catch a disease."

"Fuck off, Dylan," she says, holding up her middle finger.

"Ava!" a man's voice calls from the end of the hallway. "What the fuck did you just say?"

"Dylan started it."

"Get in here!" the man shouts.

She walks down the hallway with her shoulders slumped, emerging in the living room where her father sits in a reclining chair.

"What have I told you about starting fights with Dylan?" he says.

"I didn't start anything, he did!"

"You're just difficult. It's like you live to make problems."

"I'm not difficult. I was just trying to use the bathroom and Dylan started making jokes about me," she says with a sigh.

"Are you laughing at me?"

"What? No, I'm not laughing."

"Do you think I'm fucking stupid?" he asks, sitting up in his seat. His pupils are wide and he's covered in sweat.

"Dad, I'm no-"

"Shut up!" he shouts.

I feel my muscles tense. I want terribly to rip his limbs from his body. He's scaring her, intimidating her.

"It's no wonder people don't like you, Ava," he says. "You're a mouthy bitch."

I can't handle this. I try to close my eyes, but I can't.

"I wasn't laughing," she says.

He rips the phone from the cord connecting it to the wall and whips it at her. It hits her in the arm as she attempts to dodge it.

"Go to your goddamn room Ava!" he shouts. "I don't want to see your face again tonight!"

I'm going to kill this bastard.

———

I'm in the penthouse with Ava, holding out my phone to take a video of her.

"Faith in what?" I ask. "The whole thing…"

"I know that you will never hurt me," she says. "I trust you."

I look back up at Ava and suddenly my arm swings out, hitting Ava across the cheek and knocking her to the floor.

No. No no no.

"Ava, fuck, that… I didn't want to do that," I try to say. "Please believe me. I don't know what just happened."

But I can't hear the words come out. It's like I have no voice.

"What about now?" I ask, my voice speaking without my mind's permission. "Still so sure?"

No. This is all wrong. Someone stop me, please!

"I…" she mumbles, sitting on the floor and holding her cheek.

"Oh, come on, Ava," I say, chuckling. "A moment ago, you were so sure of me. So much faith. Where did all that go?"

How can I fucking laugh right now?

"Whatever's happening, Zane," she says. "This isn't you. We can fix this."

As always, Ava has faith in me. It's her faith in me that has built my own faith in myself.

"Oh really?" I ask, opening the video on my phone to send it to an unsaved number.

Wait… Isn't that my number? Am I sending it to myself?

"What's wrong with you?" I ask.

"Well, you did just hit me in the face and stuff, so I'm pretty sure I'm not feeling too great about that."

"Is this what we're looking for?" a voice says.

Where did that come from?

"What gave me away?" I ask, suddenly speaking in an American accent.

Fuck. It's Asmodeus.

"Asmodeus," the voice says. "It's him. He has the girl, but he's not killing her."

"This is it. We have it," another voice says. "Just let it play out from here."

60

The doorbell rings and Kieran gets up to answer it while I stay on the couch wrapped in a blanket.

"How are you doing?" Morgan asks, sitting in the chair next to me.

I don't even know how to answer that question. It's been about 24 hours since Zane was supposed to come home and we haven't been able to reach him or Kami. I haven't gotten any sleep—partially due to anxiety and partially because every time I close my eyes, random memories from my past are playing on repeat.

"Tired," I say.

"I can imagine," he says, his eyes dropping to the floor. "The uh… memories haven't stopped?"

"No. They're kind of in the background at times but when I close my eyes and try to sleep, they're more vivid."

"Are they bad? I mean, I know they target your worst memories, but…"

"They aren't my worst memories," I say. "I mean, some of them, maybe. They're not great memories, but they aren't necessarily the worst."

"Really? Wh-"

"Hello," Finn says, walking in with Kieran. "How are you, Ava?"

He takes off his coat and sets it on a nearby chair.

"Been better," I say. "Did you find anything?"

Finn shakes his head and frowns.

"My council contacts say they don't know anything more than we do. The whole team has been missing since the mission, including the helicopter pilot."

"Did… did they crash?" My chest clenches at the thought.

"No," he says. "That's the only thing I was able to learn. They found the helicopter landed safely on the island. Not sure how they got off the island without it, but they seem to have done."

Should I be relieved or even more worried? I can't even tell anymore.

"What do we do?" I ask. "We don't know where they are or what kind of trouble they're in. All we know is where they were last."

"We know a bit more than that," Morgan says. "We know Zane was attacked by a Shaytan. It could be classic torture, but I suspect that they're looking for information."

"Why's that?"

"Well, you said that the memories you were reliving weren't your worst ones. I'm thinking maybe they weren't looking for the worst."

"Or they weren't looking for *your* worst," Finn says.

Oh god, he's right. Those memories—of our breakup, of Mike, of my dad—they're precisely what would hurt Zane.

"Oh," Morgan says, biting his lip. "That could be. What do you think, Ava? Where are your memories now?"

"They seem to be looping now. They have been for several hours."

"What was the last one before they started looping?"

"Um… it was when I killed Asmodeus."

All eyes in the room are suddenly on me.

"Fuck," Finn says, placing his palm across his face.

"So they know," Morgan says with a scowl. "Brilliant."

"That must have been what they were looking for. They wanted to know if Zane really did it."

"Why?" I ask. "What reason would they have to doubt him, anyway?"

"It's a good question," Morgan says. "They should have just taken him at his word. It's not like they have any problems with executing an innocent man. There must be more to this than we understand. Can you think of any reason they may be curious about the details of Asmodeus's death? Anything you haven't shared?"

"No, it wasn't particularly impressive. I wheeled Kieran into him. It hurt like a bitch standing on my broken leg, and then I fell down and he went poof."

"I can't help on this front," Kieran says. "Unfortunately, I was unconscious for all the fun parts."

"So you have no idea what they're looking for?" Morgan asks.

"No, how would I know? I'm not an expert in evil villains and their master plans."

"Actually, that's not a bad thought," Kieran says. "We should ask an expert."

"Who?"

"An expert in villains and their master plans of course," he says, lifting his phone. After a moment it begins to ring on speakerphone.

"Tell me you have good news," Jen's voice says on the other end of the line.

"Hey, everyone's here and you're on speaker. You've been getting my texts, right?"

"Yes, of course. I take it that means you have no news on Zane and Kami?"

"Not since my last text a minute ago," he says. "I thought you should be here to brainstorm."

"Okay. What do we know?"

"They've been looking into Asmodeus's death," Finn chimes in. "They probed Zane's memories, and through him, Ava's. They now know that Zane didn't kill Asmodeus. We can only imagine they'll be coming for Ava soon but we don't know why. They shouldn't be this concerned with the truth."

"Oh crap on toast!" Jen says.

"Yeah, that was our reaction," Kieran says.

"Ava, are you okay?"

"No," I say.

"Aww honey, I'm so sorry. Okay, okay… I'm on it. So we've got creepy nightmare-causing demons, they've kidnapped our peeps somewhere in the Mediterranean, and they're working for the Demon King guys and they want to know who really killed Asmodeus because… why?"

"That just about sums it up, yeah," Kieran says.

"Because… maybe they can bring Asmodeus back from the dead by sacrificing the person who killed him or something?"

"Except the Demon Kings all hate each other," Morgan says. "In some ways, they're probably glad he's dead. They just feel obligated to avenge him out of pride."

"Okay then… maybe they want to make sure he's really dead or maybe… Wait, Ava, is it possible you absorbed his powers when you killed him?"

"I'm pretty sure not," I say.

"Easy to test," Kieran says. "Give me a command."

"Um… tell us something embarrassing about yourself."

"Yeah, no, sorry Ava. I don't think you have Demon King powers."

"Damn," Jen says.

"It doesn't even matter if it's a conspiracy or not," I say. "The real problem is that we don't even know where they're keeping Zane and Kami."

"Can't any of your guys' superpowers help with that?" Jen asks.

"Yeah, wait… Finn, you can contact him telepathically, can't you?"

"Sorry, love," he says, shaking his head. "I can only communicate with people who are in the immediate vicinity."

"I don't know of anyone who can reach people over long distances," Morgan says.

"None of you have some kind of magical mojo that will let you talk with Zane?" Jen asks.

"Actually," Morgan says with a slight smirk, "that's not *entirely* true."

———◆———

ZANE

I collapse to the floor beside Ava's hospital bed.

I need to do something. Need to help her. Somehow.

"Z-Man?" a voice calls.

I turn around to see Kieran standing behind me.

"What are you doing here?" I ask. "Did Jen tell you we were here? Ava, she's not doing great. They sa-"

"Dude, it's okay," he says, giving me a pat on the back. "None of this is real."

"What are you talking about? Are you high?"

"No, I… Uggh, listen Z-Man, this is a memory. You got hit by a Shaytan's touch. Ava is at your house with the rest of us."

This doesn't make any sense. What is he saying?

I search my mind for some kind of logic to what he has said, but I find nothing. The edges of my consciousness are blurry and I can't seem to remember much outside of this moment.

"No," I say, shaking my head. "I'm dreaming. I've got to be dreaming. Maybe I fell asleep at Ava's bedside."

"God damn it, Zane, you stubborn mother fucker," he curses.

Before I can respond, he smacks me across the face. The shock snaps my mind into focus.

"You better snap out of it," he says, "or next time, it'll be a kiss."

"Bloody hell, mate, calm down."

"Are you with me now?"

"What do you want, Kieran?" I ask.

"I need you to see that none of this is real. This is a memory."

"If this is a memory, then why are you here?"

"Well, the memories that are triggered by the Shayatin are kind of like dreams. Morgan realized I might be able to talk to you through them. I guess he was right. Honestly, I'm pretty impressed with myself that I was able to target you from so far away. I've never done it before, but apparently I'm just that good."

"So you're visiting my dream, or… memory? Why?"

"Ava needs your help."

Now he has my attention.

"Wha-… how?"

"A Shaytan is probing your memories and they've gotten into Ava's too through the bond. You were kidnapped after your mission on the island. Do you remember?"

I nod as the memories slowly work their way back into my mind.

"Do you know where you are?" he asks. "Where did they take you?"

"Fuck, I don't know."

I try to tune into my senses. There's a musty, earthy scent in the air and I feel hard stone against my skin.

Memories come back to me in tiny scraps.

"Underground…Catacombs maybe?" I say. "I'm not sure where. Must be relatively close to the island because it couldn't have taken us long to get here. I'd say forty minutes, maximum."

"How is Kami? Is she with you?"

"I… I don't know. She was fine when I last saw her. I don't know where she is now."

"She's probably alright. They haven't killed you, so that's a good sign."

"What about Ava? Is she okay?" I ask.

"She's uh… yeah, she's okay. She's worried—we all are."

"But she's safe."

"She's safe. Just stay put. We're coming for you soon."

61

 AVA

"Are we serious about doing this?" Morgan asks. "You think we can find and infiltrate an underground hideout, undoubtedly crawling with Shayatin, Incubi, and Succubi, so that we can rescue Zane and Kami from not one but two actual Kings of the underworld?"

Wanting to save them and thinking we actually stand a chance are two very different things.

"Do you have a better plan?" I ask.

"Yeah, how 'bout we not risk everyone's lives by embarking on an impossible mission with a sex-crazed demon bro, a crippled human, a seal, and an Empath," he says, turning to Kieran and Finn with an apologetic look. "No offense."

"Definitely offended," Finn says, crossing his arms and narrowing his eyes.

"Not me," Kieran says with a shrug. "You pretty much have me pegged there."

I can't really bring myself to be offended right now when we have so many other problems going on.

"Honestly, I'm not sure I can help anyway," Finn says.

"Why?" Kieran asks. "You don't think you can slap them with your fish tail?"

"Oi! Why is everyone on my arse today?"

"You're right, bro. Sorry. Why can't you help?"

"Well… I told Marella I wouldn't get myself into too much trouble. It uh… turns out we've got a little one on the way."

"Oh wow," I say. "Congratulations. You're right, you shouldn't be involved in this."

"I'll help in whatever way I can."

"You can watch Ava while Kieran and I find Kami and Zane," Morgan says with a stern expression.

"But I can help," I protest.

"How? You plan on pushing a chair at them? Let's face it, you'll be more of a liability than an asset."

"So we stay at some hotel while you guys go rescue everyone?" Finn asks. "It's not a bad plan, honestly, but are we sure this isn't exactly what they want? Get Ava isolated with little protection. This could all just be a diversion to target Asmodeus's real killer."

We all exchange glances but no one says anything for a moment.

"He's got a point," Morgan finally says with a sigh. "But what's the alternative? Take her with us? That's precisely what they want. Might as well bring her in on a silver platter."

"Listen, I don't pretend to know battle strategies or what is best here," I say. "I'll do whatever you guys decide is best, but I have to go somewhere."

"I know," Morgan says, running a hand over his face. "Have we considered the alternative? That we *not* do this? I'm sorry, but someone needs to say it—Kami and Zane are just two individuals. Should we be sacrificing so much to save them?"

"Why would you say something like that? They're not *important* enough to you? You don't think they're worth saving?"

"I'm not saying that," he says, shaking his head. "I'm saying maybe the price is too high. Do you think either of them would want you risking your life to save them?"

"I really don't give a damn what they want me to do, Morgan. I'm going to do whatever I need to do to bring them home safe."

He lets out a heavy sigh.

"I'm gonna get more tea," Finn says with wide eyes, clearly feeling uncomfortable as he steps into the kitchen.

"I don't mean to be cold," Morgan says softly. "He's lucky, you know… to have so many people in his life who are willing to fight for him. To have you willing to risk your life for him. What did this guy do to earn such devotion?"

He looks almost sad with his head hanging low.

"Zane comes off harsh," Kieran says, "but he's not that guy on the inside."

"I know. I always thought it was interesting how he and Kami were polar opposites. Zane with his cool exterior and the fire inside; Kami burning hot on the surface, but calm and cool underneath. It's no wonder their souls were reborn together—they're yin and yang."

"Not a lot of people see that."

"Most people aren't Empaths."

"I want to tell you a story," Kieran says, sweeping his hair out of his face. "This gorgeous Succubus started sleeping with me-"

"Okay, we don't need to hear your sex tales…"

"This isn't a sex story," he scoffs. "She was the one who recruited me. She brought me to Asmodeus, who converted me—made me a demon. And then they left. I was on my own."

"Oh."

"So here I was, totally lost, trying desperately to get by. I was starving all the time, and when I fed… the only way to get enough sustenance was to drain them dry. The first time I killed someone… it was brutal. I didn't mean to. But I still remember their face—completely pale—and they weren't breathing. I must've cried for a week."

He twists his hair anxiously between his fingers and keeps his eyes on the floor.

"I was living in a small enough town that I ended up drawing the attention of the cops," he continued. "It was bad. I would've definitely been in deep shit. But outside of a bar one day, this guy jumps me. He takes me by the collar and he pins me up against the wall and he asks me who the hell I am and why I'm killing people. And I just… started sobbing. Not gonna lie, it was not my most badass moment. I didn't know what to do. I was young. My family had kicked me out years back and I was living on the streets. I had nobody."

"I'm so sorry," I say. "I didn't know about all of that."

"It's okay, Aves. I was lucky. That guy who confronted me—it was Zane. He took pity on me. He listened to my story and he understood. He took me inside and he helped me get a meal for the night. His venom worked to boost the effects of the target's sexual energy and I was able to satiate myself without hurting someone for the first time."

He nods and smiles slightly.

"The thing is," he continues, "he could've just left it at that. He could've left me on my own again, but he didn't. He kept helping me. And a lot of Immortals wouldn't have; they see demons as beneath them. Kami was certain I was taking advantage, but Zane stuck by me. He had no reason to—I was this huge burden on him—but he didn't want to leave me alone to suffer. Zane has a good heart. He walks around in his leather jacket and boots like he's all tough and hardcore but he's a teddy bear inside, one who feels and cares and takes pity on little demons who have nowhere to go."

"I know he means a lot to you all," Morgan says. "We'll get them both back. I just… I wish it didn't mean we had to risk both of your lives to do so."

He looks at me with soft eyes and a bit of a frown and sighs. It's obvious he's worried this is going to go horribly wrong.

I am too.

———

I drop my bag on the hotel room floor and fall forward onto the bed.

Between all the stress and the physical toll of traveling to Greece, I'm exhausted and every part of my body is sore.

"Get settled and try to get some sleep if you can," Morgan says as he walks in. "Kieran will be on the couch and I'm in the other bedroom if you need anything."

"Thanks," I say. "What time are we leaving tomorrow?"

"I'm gonna play it by ear. We don't want to go off at half-cock and show up tired. Get some sleep. We'll need to be fresh if we're taking on two Demon Kings in the morning."

"I'm still coming along, right?"

"Yes," he says, shaking his head slightly. "I don't think we have another option. You're going to have to stick close to me."

"I can always ride on your shoulders like a human backpack."

He raises a brow at me and tilts his head.

"I'm joking!" I say.

"It's not a bad idea," he says with a smirk, heading back to the living area. "Goodnight, Ava."

"Goodnight."

62

 AVA

I latch onto Morgan's back as he scales the high, brown stone wall with incredible ease. The wall is covered in red warning signs reading "ΑΠΑΓΟΡΕΥΕΤΑΙ Η ΕΙΣΟΔΟΣ", which I don't need to know Greek to realize means something like "stay the heck out of here."

With a firm thunk, his feet hit the ground on the other side and I slide off his shoulders.

The building in front of us is made of the same brown stone, cracked and decaying.

"Are we sure this is the place?" Kieran asks in a hushed voice.

"There are only two known catacombs within 40 minutes of the island," Morgan whispers. "The other one is open to the public, so yeah… pretty sure. Now be quiet and follow me."

Morgan gestures for us to follow as he walks up to the entrance, which is just an open archway where a door may have once stood. He steps inside as I walk close behind with Kieran at my back.

After a moment, he finds the entrance to the catacombs and signals for us to join him. We tiptoe delicately behind. A narrow stairway leads down to an even narrower passage that looks too slim to be intended for fully grown people. My jeans rub against the stone as I do my best to fit through the tiny gap. I'm not typically bothered by tight spaces, but this has me completely creeped out.

I exhale as we make it out of the passage into a larger corridor with arched ceilings. The stone walls are rough and discolored from decades of water damage and decay. There's modern lighting installed all throughout the space, with tunnels shooting off in every direction.

I start to feel a bit dizzy, so I lean on the wall to stabilize myself. I feel the surface crumble beneath my fingertips and send tiny rock pieces falling to the floor with a clattering sound.

Morgan flips around in a fast motion and the pebbles go flying behind me, just missing Kieran.

"Sorry," I whisper to a wide-eyed and tense Morgan.

He looks around for a moment before looking back at me.

"This isn't good," he says softly. "That power—telekinesis—no demons have it. Only the Demon Kings. They must be nearby. Stick close to me. And Kieran, watch the rear."

"I'm pretty sure Zane would kill me for that," Kieran says in a hushed tone.

Morgan shoots him a glare before continuing to move forward.

After a few feet, he stops in his tracks just before an opening to the next corridor. We hear voices arguing in the distance, but I can't tell what they're saying. He nods—indicating that we're about to encounter trouble—and swivels around the corner.

We can't quite see the sources of the chatter, but nearly run into a woman with long black hair and a leather vest. It's pretty safe to assume she's not on our side, as a smile stretches across her face when she sees me.

She grabs Morgan by the wrist, but she must be a Shaytan because she seems shocked when he doesn't succumb to her powers at her touch. He flips her around and locks his arm around her neck, putting a hand over her mouth.

"Where are they keeping the Sirens?" he whispers.

He lifts his hand so she can speak, but rather than respond, she screams.

"They're here!"

She manages to slip her arm loose and reaches out to touch me, but Kieran intercepts her and in a flash, Morgan snaps her neck.

"You okay mate?" he asks Kieran.

Kieran nods.

"I think you got her before she was able to hit me with her powers," he says. "Thanks."

A horde of demons appears at the end of the path, rushing toward us. Morgan throws his arm forward and sends three of them flying back into the others, knocking them down like walking bowling pins.

"Shit," one of them curses.

Most of the group gets to their feet and begins charging forward again, while Morgan yells for me to stay back. Kieran turns to watch the other entry so that his back and mine are touching.

Morgan was right... I'm definitely a liability in this fight. Maybe I should've stayed at the hotel.

With a few more flicks of his wrist, Morgan has managed to throw the demons from one side of the cavern to the other, sending them flying into walls as the ceiling cracks and large chunks of rock whip through the air.

After a moment, the dust clears and nearly a dozen demons are scattered across the ground.

"Is anyone on our tail?" Morgan asks.

"No, we're clear," Kieran says.

"Are they all Shayatin?" I ask.

"A few of these guys are Incubi or Succubi," Kieran says as we step over their unconscious bodies. "Not sure about the others. Probably a mix."

We walk for several minutes, not encountering another soul as we wind through what seems to be an endless underground maze.

"Alright, Ava, we're lost here," Morgan whispers. "I'm gonna need you to tap into that bond. Can you sense Zane anywhere?"

"Wha-... how do I do that?" I ask.

"I don't know. That's for you to figure out."

I close my eyes and take a deep breath in, but all I can sense is the constant heavy beating of my heart and the ringing in my ears.

"I'm sorry, I... I don't know. I can't tell."

"Okay," he says softly. "It's okay. We'll find him."

"Find who?" a deep voice says over Morgan's shoulder.

We all turn to see a man with a wide build, five-o'clock shadow, and a wicked smile. He's wearing a slick grey suit with an unbuttoned white shirt.

"Looking for me?" the man asks.

"That all depends on who you are," Kieran says.

"Excuse my manners," he says, looking me directly in the eye. "My name is Leviathan. And I don't know if you've been looking for me, but I've certainly been looking for you."

Morgan scoops me behind him and puffs his chest before knocking Leviathan back with a wave of his hand. Leviathan staggers back into the wall, but the blow wasn't nearly as effective as it was on the demons before.

Leviathan looks up with a mix of surprise and concern in his eyes, but his smirk doesn't waver.

"Interesting power, there, son," he says. "Who might you be?"

Morgan replies with a swift fist to Leviathan's face. The two begin exchanging blow after blow as Kieran does his best to keep me out of the fray. Morgan is managing to hold his own surprisingly well against the Demon King.

"Don't worry about me," I say to Kieran. "Help Morgan."

He nods and launches into Leviathan, forcing him down to the ground. The two of them successfully manage to pin him.

"What are you doing, Kieran? I got this guy," Morgan grunts as he struggles to hold Leviathan down. "Protect Ava!"

"It didn't look to me like you had him," he says.

"Protect Ava, huh?" Leviathan asks Morgan, his lip corner twisting upward. "Who is the girl to you?"

Morgan pushes his knee harder against Leviathan's chest to silence him.

"Should I-" I start to say, but am interrupted by the feeling of an arm wrapping around my neck and an unfamiliar voice from behind me.

"What do we have here?"

Morgan and Kieran both look at me with wide eyes, frozen in place.

"You want to let me go?" Leviathan asks Morgan. "Or do you want to watch him snap your pretty little lover's neck?"

"She's not my lover," Morgan snaps.

"You're better off telling lies like that to someone who can't sense your desires."

"Fine," I say. "Snap my neck then."

Part of me is really hoping that this immortality business will get me out of this, but another part of me is willing to risk whatever I have to in order to get my friends out of here alive.

"Ava," Morgan scolds. "We don't know how this will go. We can't risk it."

"I brought you guys into this. I can't have you fight all my battles for me."

"What should I do with her, brother?" the man behind me asks.

Brother? Oh shit… so I'm being held captive by… Lucifer?

"Kill her," Leviathan says.

I can't help but shudder as I await my fate.

"Stop!" Morgan shouts. "If I surrender… I have your word that neither you, nor anyone working for you, will hurt her or my demon friend here?"

"You do."

Morgan lifts his hands and Kieran takes his cue and does the same. They both stand and Leviathan rights himself.

"It's okay," Morgan says with a solemn look. "Leviathan keeps his word."

I feel the grip around me loosen and can finally turn to see my attacker—a sharply dressed, handsome, young-looking man I now know to be Lucifer. He has tanned skin, a sharp jawline, and short curly brown hair. He looks more like a male model than an icon of evil.

Leviathan calls for more demons, who rush in and cuff Morgan and Kieran, taking them away down one of the many corridors.

"Where are you taking them?" I ask.

"Shouldn't you be more concerned with where we're taking you?" Lucifer asks, grabbing my upper arm and pulling me in another direction.

"Fine. Where are you taking me?

"Well, I assume you're here to see your Siren. So why don't I take you to him?"

63

Lucifer leads me down the musty corridor with Leviathan following behind us.

"Your friend is quite strong," Leviathan says. "Where did he get that power?"

"What power?" I ask.

"He managed to move me with a wave of his hand. That's not a common power among Immortals."

"I dunno," I say with my best clueless shrug. "I'm a human; I don't really understand all that Immortal stuff."

"And yet you managed to kill Asmodeus," Lucifer says, "one of the strongest Demon Kings, beside me of course."

"I'd be impressed if I weren't so envious," Leviathan says with a chuckle.

I hear noise and chatter up ahead as we enter a new section of the tunnel. There are demons everywhere—or at least, what I assume are demons. Several of them lean up against the walls, chatting amongst themselves, while others congregate in a large open space at the end of the hall.

As the passage widens, we start to pass cells filled with prisoners. Thick iron bars cast long shadows across their faces.

"Ava!" a familiar voice calls.

My eyes find a disheveled Kami leaning against the bars of a nearby cell.

"Oh my god, Kami!" I yell. "Are you okay?"

"I'm okay," she says as we walk closer. "What are you doing here? Why are you alone?"

"They took Morgan and Kieran somewhere else." I lower my head with guilt. When it came down to it, I had no way of defending them.

"That's enough chatter," Lucifer says with a smirk. "Besides, aren't you here to see your boyfriend?"

He jerks me forward past Kami's cell.

"Ava! Be careful!" she shouts. "Zane—He's not himself! They gave him Tamarix, way too much. He's… he's not… he's not in control."

All I really know about Tamarix is that it's some sort of Immortal drug. It made Kami act a little drunk, but I have no idea what happens if you take too much.

As we walk further, I see a large black shadow on the floor ahead, but in the low light, I can't quite identify what it is. Several demons stand around the shadow but keep a distance.

The shadow stirs as we approach and suddenly launches at us with incredible speed. I let out a yelp and nearly jump out of my shoes. The shadow is a chained man with eyes glowing green from edge to edge, black wings extended and thrashing in the air.

Zane.

He lashes out at us again, a cougar-like growl emerging from his throat. His chains prevent him from reaching us, holding him just ten feet from me.

I just want to run up and hug him, but I barely recognize the person in front of me. He snaps and rails against his chains like a vicious animal.

What did they do to you?

My heart sinks as I consider what they put him through. I can't decide if I want to cry or crush the skulls of the bastards who hurt him.

Both. I want to do both.

More footsteps behind us draw my attention, and I turn to see Kieran being held by two demons.

"Why are you here?" Leviathan asks. "There's far more room in the other dungeons."

"The other one is an Empath," the demon says. "He let it slip while we were taking them to the cells. Figured you didn't want us housing an Empath near anyone else."

How could he make such a mistake?

"Good call," Lucifer says. "Put him in here, give him a front-row seat."

He points to a cell just beside us with another man inside, lying on the floor. The demon brings Kieran over and unlocks the cell with a key off the wall. Kieran gives me a wink as the other demon throws him inside and locks it again. He hangs the key back on the wall, almost within my reach.

"I wouldn't," Leviathan says. "Everyone here is much, much faster than you. Your neck would be snapped faster than you'd be able to reach the lock."

Well, okay, maybe not the best plan then.

"I thought you promised not to hurt me," I say. "Morgan said you're a man of your word."

"That's true." He scratches his chin and smiles. His teeth seem almost sharpened behind his lips. "I did promise that I wouldn't hurt you—nor would anyone working for me."

"Pretty sure you promised not to hurt me either," Kieran says.

"True. And I won't," he says, his eyes wandering back to Zane. "But I can't be held responsible for anything he does."

Lucifer pushes me forward and I stumble a few steps closer. Zane shoots forward, his arms swinging in all directions as he snarls and tugs at his chains.

"You're wrong," I say, my voice shaking slightly. "He's not going to hurt me."

"He's killed three of my best demons since he's been chained here," Leviathan says. "You so sure this is still your beloved Siren? Step closer, then."

I shake slightly.

This is still Zane, right?

I look over to Kieran for reassurance, but his expression is uneasy—he's not so sure either.

"What are you waiting for?" Lucifer teases.

He pushes me again, and this time I fall to the floor just feet from Zane's reach.

Zane lets out a violent roar and scrambles to reach me, his wings thrashing through the air. The demons surrounding him take another step back.

I look up at Lucifer and Leviathan, both watching with a mix of curiosity and delight. Lucifer slides his tongue along his lips before laughing.

I turn back to Zane. There's no sign of his deep brown eyes beneath the overwhelming glow. His skin is covered in dirt and the vein in his neck is bulging as he fights against the chains.

I've spent a long time telling Zane I'm not afraid of him—that he's not a monster. Here's my chance to prove it.

I stand up and take a step closer, so that I'm just a foot away from his grasp.

In the corner of my eye, I see Lucifer grab a metal crank on the wall and quickly turn it.

Zane's chains suddenly extend, loosening enough that he launches toward me, tackling me to the ground. I cringe, expecting the harsh collision between my head and the ground, but it never comes.

I open my eyes and see mostly dark. It's Zane's wings, wrapped over our bodies. His hand is cradling my head, protecting me from the impact.

He tucks his head into my neck and inhales before peppering me with kisses.

He looks up at me, his eyes still a vibrant green as he mutters. I can only make out one word.

"Baby."

64

I hear gasps and shrieks around me.

"What is he doing?" Lucifer asks.

"Is he biting her?" Leviathan asks. "Why isn't she screaming?"

I can hardly sift through the clutter of my mind. My limbs are heavy and my vision is blurred at the edges. I take a deep breath in, inhaling her familiar scent, allowing it to fill the chambers of my mind, clearing the fog that fills every corner and replacing it with the only thing that could bring me clarity—Ava.

She's my connection to the world when I've fallen through the cracks. She pulls me to the surface when I'm drowning.

Ava's eyes find mine and she smiles slightly. My eyes roam across her face, looking for any sign of harm or injury. I let out a sigh of relief when I realize she's okay, but the relief is short-lasting.

We're surrounded by demons—Shayatin, Incubi, and Succubi—and two Demon Kings. If I broke Kieran and Kami loose, we might stand a chance, but even then it's a likely suicide mission.

And where did they say Morgan was? Another cell somewhere? Did they say he admitted to being an Empath? But why?

"She certainly didn't defend herself," Lucifer says. "Does this mean it's time to cut our losses?"

"It does," Leviathan says. "It would seem Asmodeus was killed by a human. Just a human. How boring. He'd be positively mortified. Time to clean up, I'm afraid. Kill them all."

That gets my attention. I leap to my feet, positioning Ava behind me and spreading my wings.

"Oh, talk about boring," Lucifer says with an eye roll. "He didn't kill her after all."

"Oh well," Leviathan says. "We'll have to handle it ourselves."

I swing my arm toward him, but something is wrong—my limbs don't seem to extend fully.

Fuck. I'm still in bloody chains.

I try another sharp tug, but it's clear I can't break through.

If I'm in chains, I can't protect Ava.

"Cute," Leviathan says before looking at his Shayatin. "Kill everyone."

"Hey hey, wait!" Ava says. "I thought you promised we'd be okay."

"Oh that's right," he says. He pulls a kheru knife out of his belt and throws it to a Succubus next to me. "They're the ones who killed your king. It's your choice what to do with that. Shayatin, kill the rest—leave the Incubus."

The Succubus smiles and begins walking toward me.

"No!" Kami calls from the cells. "Don't you touch them!"

I hear the rapid footsteps of someone running down the corridor and I recognize their sound. Morgan runs at full speed into the room and, with a quick arm motion, sends the Succubus flying backward.

Of course—Morgan wouldn't just give himself up as an Empath without a reason. He was looking for an excuse to separate the demons and get them alone. Then he just follows Kieran back to us.

Lucifer and Leviathan both ready themselves to fight before charging at Morgan. Lucifer flies into the ceiling before crashing down with a loud thud. Leviathan hits the bars of a nearby cell, then stumbles forward, throwing a knife at Morgan. With another motion, Morgan pushes the knife back at him.

I turn around to find Ava, but she's no longer behind me. She's grabbing for the key on the wall and is tackled to the ground by an Incubus.

I reach for her, but find myself helpless in these chains.

Fuck.

"Morgan!" I shout. "Ava!"

The Incubus shoots backward with the keys in his hand.

Ava has a large claw scratch across her chest and struggles to stand up.

"I'm fine," she says, looking me in the eye. "I'm fine."

She's not fine, but she's her kind of fine. She's letting me know she can handle it.

Morgan manages to temporarily incapacitate both the Kings and runs over to us.

"How do I undo these chains?" he asks me.

"I don't know; it doesn't matter," I say. "Take Ava, get her out of here."

"What? No!" Ava protests.

"And Morgan?"

"Yeah?" he replies.

"Take care of her."

He nods and runs to Ava, scooping her up over his shoulder. She kicks her legs and fights him, but she's no match for his strength on a good day.

Before he can make it out of the room, he's stopped by two very angry Demon Kings. Lucifer creates a large fireball in his palm and throws it directly at Morgan. He contorts to prevent it from hitting Ava, but it hits him in the side.

He falls to the ground and Ava manages to land on her feet.

"Morgan!" Ava calls.

"I'm okay," he says, rising to his feet. He creates his own fireball and throws it back at Lucifer.

"Zane!" Kami screams. "Look out!"

I turn just in time to catch the Succubus with the kheru knife in hand, raised above my head. I grab her wrist and do my best to resist, but she's surprisingly strong. Another demon grabs me from behind, trying to restrain me while the Succubus lowers the knife.

An object whizzes past my vision and hits the Succubus in the eye. She stumbles back and I manage to tear myself free from the other demon's hold. I look for the source and find Ava with a handful of rocks, clearly gathered from pieces of the crumbling walls.

"You threw a rock at her?" I ask, yelling over the commotion.

She nods.

The Succubus approaches me again, but is taken down by another swift motion from Morgan. I pull and kick against my chains to no avail. I see Kieran beside me, growing increasingly frustrated. With a kick, he manages to slightly bend one of the thick steel bars.

"Keep going, mate!" I shout.

He kicks again at the bar and it bends a bit more.

"How are you doing that?" I ask. "I can't make these budge at all."

"I'm just that good," he says with a smirk.

The ground begins to shake and the floor beneath us begins to crack. It grows into a deep fissure that leads back to a furious and battered Leviathan.

"Ava! Watch out!" Kieran shouts.

A Shaytan appears behind her and grabs her neck. She seizes and falls to the dirt floor, her face contorting in pain.

"No!" I shout. I tug against my chains and this time, my left arm breaks free, a foot of chain dangling from my wrist.

I try to reach for Ava, but it's no use. I'm still too far away to help her.

"Zane!" Kieran shouts, louder than ever, but I'm too distracted by Ava's pain. "Zaaannne!!"

I turn to see the Succubus with her kheru knife, plunging down straight toward my heart.

"Nooo!!" Kieran shouts.

Her arm freezes in midair and she drops the knife to the floor. Her eyes are wide with a mixture of shock and fear. The whole room seems frozen for a moment as our eyes all fall on Kieran in his cell.

Every Succubus and Incubus in the room drops to their knees in deference.

To the new Demon King of Lust.

65

 ZANE

"What's happening?" Kami asks from her cell. "What's happening? Why did everyone stop? I can't see from here! Somebody tell me what's going on!"

Lucifer awkwardly clears his throat and looks at Leviathan.

"So…" Leviathan says with a soft voice, "it appears we may have gotten off on the wrong foot."

He walks toward Kieran's cell and pulls a key from his pocket. He unlocks and opens the door, letting Kieran free.

"No shit," Kieran grumbles.

"You're a sensible, attractive man…" Lucifer says. "Can't you let bygones be bygones?"

"That depends," Kieran says.

"On?"

"What are bygones?"

Lucifer raises a brow and smirks. With a cue from Leviathan, the Shayatin quietly file out of the room.

"He's calling for a truce, I think," I say.

"What the heck is going on out there?" Kami says.

"It would appear there is a new Demon King of Lust," Morgan says, scratching his head and looking at Kieran.

"What? Who?"

"Only the sexiest Demon King ever!" Kieran says.

"Oh lord… seriously?" she rests her face in her palm.

"You know it, babe!"

"What does this mean?" I ask.

"Well…" Leviathan says, "The Demon Kings have existed for eons. None of us have ever been killed before. We suspected his powers may have transferred somewhere but… this was unexpected."

"As Kings, we really do try to get along," Lucifer says, taking a couple of defensive steps back with his hands in the air. "So you can see how this is all just a mistake."

"Get along?" Morgan asks. "You all created armies of demons to fight each other."

"Technically, Abaddon created his demons for war—the rest of us were just trying to build our defenses."

"We're all pretty evenly matched," Leviathan says. "That's why we try to keep peace among ourselves. Nobody wins when the Kings go to war."

Leviathan walks over to me and unlocks my cuffs with another key from his pocket.

"And why shouldn't we just kill you now instead?" I ask.

"Well, you tell me. How did killing a King go for you last time?"

He's got a point. Not sure I want to draw that kind of attention again.

I walk over to Ava, still in the throes of a Shaytan nightmare, and lift her in my arms. She shivers and whines softly.

"So we have this truce, then what happens?" Kieran asks. "My friends are off-limits and we all just go about our business?"

Leviathan nods. Kieran looks at each of us and sighs.

"Okay then. Release everyone from your cells and we have ourselves a truce."

———·———

"Wh- what… where am I?" Ava mumbles as she comes to. "What happened?"

"You're alright, love," I say, my voice slightly hoarse. I pull her tight into my chest as I follow the others out of the catacombs. "We were fighting the Demon Kings. It's okay, it's all over now."

I'm a bit unsteady on my feet with the Tamarix still coursing through my system, but I manage to weave through the tight corridors without hitting the walls.

"Did we win?"

"Hell yeah we did," Kieran chimes in as we step out into the daylight. "Thanks to the world's most handsome demon. You missed it, Aves. I was a total badass."

Ava taps my shoulder to let me know she wants to walk on her own, so I set her on her feet. She has a few scuffs and scratches on her arms and the side of her face is covered in dirt, but I'm grateful that she's relatively unharmed. That's more than I can say for the rest of us.

Kami's hair is frizzy and matted with dried blood. Valentina is disheveled and bruised, supporting a bandaged and bleeding Blake limping beside her. Kieran is coated in dirt and sweat. I haven't had a chance to see my reflection, but I imagine I look like hell.

The only one of us that doesn't look like they've just lost a fight with a blender is Morgan, who appears more or less unscathed, minus a few smudges of dirt. But he doesn't seem like someone who just won a battle. He trudges yards ahead of the group with a stern expression and his eyes trained ahead.

"I don't understand," Ava says, huffing as she walks through the brush. "What happened?"

"I'm the new freaking Demon King!" Kieran exclaims, doing a bit of a celebratory dance as he walks. "Some crazy sumbitch was trying to stab Zane and I fuckin' brain-controlled the fucker!"

She looks at me wide-eyed, as if she's ready for me to refute his claims. I shrug and she looks toward Kami, who sighs.

"Unfortunately, it's true," she says, scrunching her face.

"Damn right!" he says. "I guess when you stabbed me into Asmodeus, his powers transferred into me. When I was able to control the Succubus, everyone realized I had absorbed his powers. Good ol' Levi and Lucy were all 'oh shit, we didn't wanna fuck with the new Demon King' and they let us go."

Ava's brows are raised to their limit as her eyes dart between us. She obviously thinks this is some kind of wild tale—but for once, Kieran isn't exaggerating.

"So you're the new Asmodeus?" she asks him. "What does that even mean?"

"Hell if I know. I didn't even know I had the powers in the first place." He chuckles as we reach Morgan, leaning against a car parked at the side of the road. "Hey, why didn't you know I had new powers?"

Morgan shrugs and lets out a huff.

"I'm not a bloody power-detector," he says. "Half the time I don't even know what power I'm calling on when I go to use it, it just happens. It's all instinct. You're the one who didn't notice you were a Demon King."

He holds a middle finger out to Morgan, who just shakes his head.

"So what other powers do you have?" Ava asks.

"I have no idea," he says with a tilt of his head. "Lemme try."

He stares at a nearby bush for a moment, squinting and tightening his muscles. After a minute, he throws his hands forward, first one at a time, then both at once. He spins around and points his palms outward, but still nothing happens.

"Fucktarts!" he shouts. "How do I make them work?"

Out of nowhere, a wad of paper whirs past me toward Kieran's face and he lifts up his hands to shield himself. As he does, the wad bursts into flame and falls straight down.

I turn to see a smirking Morgan.

"That's how," he says with a slight chuckle.

"Oh shit!" Kieran says. "I mean, I knew I was hot, but damn!"

"Oh lord, here we go," Kami says.

"I guess you could say I'm smokin'!"

Everyone groans.

———◆———

We follow Morgan into the hotel suite. Ava walks into a room and lays down on the bed. She hasn't said much since the car ride back.

"Are you alright?" I ask.

"No," she says, sitting up. "You told Morgan to take me away. I should kick your ass for that."

"You could try," I say with a smirk.

"Smirk at me again and see how that goes."

Her face is serious enough that it wipes the smile off my face.

"I'm sorry, love. I wanted to be sure you were safe. Things were getting bad. We were losing. I thought it was the only way you'd be okay. What would you do if you were me?"

She ponders for a moment before nodding, then she jumps up and wraps me in a hug.

"Your eyes have dimmed a lot," she says. "Has the Tamarix worked its way out of your system?"

"I think so. The adrenaline probably helped, but more than anything, it was just having you there."

"What do you mean?"

"If there's one thing that can always guide me through the fog, it's you."

She tightens her arms around me and rests her head on my chest.

Kami appears in the doorway with an exasperated expression.

"Can I room with you guys?" she asks. "Kieran has been singing 'Who run the world—Demon King' since we got in. I'm going to pull my hair out."

"Nope," I say. "He's your problem now."

"You suck," she says, stomping away.

Ava laughs and pats my chest as she steps away.

"I'm going to take a shower," she says. I raise a brow and she smiles back. "—alone. Sorry."

She heads into the bathroom and I begrudgingly join Kami and Kieran in their adjoining room. Kieran is doing a choreographed dance to his new song and Kami is burying her head under a pillow on the sofa.

I turn to see a closed door that I assume leads to Morgan's room. He's been awfully silent since the catacombs, but I owe him more than I care to admit. Morgan saved everyone in there, and when it came down to it, he was willing to take care of Ava even if she fought him.

I walk over and knock at the door. Morgan opens it, then leans in the doorway, crossing his arms.

"Hey," he says with a brow furrowed, almost asking it as a question.

"Hey mate," I say, resting my hands in the pockets of my trousers. "Could we talk?"

He nods and waves me in. I step inside and lean against the dresser.

"What's on your mind?"

"I want… to thank you."

His eyes meet mine for a moment and his head tilts slightly.

"For saving your arse? You're welcome, but if it were up to me, I would never have gone. So you should really thank your girl and your mate." He forces an awkward smile and shrugs.

I want to hate him. Until now, all I saw in Morgan was someone who wanted my girl. But now, I see someone who protected her when I couldn't. Someone who saved me and my friends. Someone who was willing to take care of Ava if I couldn't.

"But you did it. And you kept her safe."

He shrugs.

His eyes never quite reach mine and his shoulders are slumped. It's a look of defeat that I recognize well.

He loves her.

Deep down, I should've known. She's always been easy to fall for.

I can't help but feel bad for him.

"I'm sorry," I say.

"Nothing to apologize for." He smirks and I give him a knowing look.

"Sure."

"Just make her happy or I'll kick your arse with your own powers."

66

We've been back in Zane's house in London for almost a week now, but I'm still aching from our battle with the Demon Kings.

Of all the dumb reasons my body decides to ache, this one actually kind of makes sense.

I guess I can check 'Fight with Lucifer' off my bucket list now.

Tonight, Zane has talked me into going out on a late-night date. That date turned out to include a very long hike.

Great.

I don't know what about me screams 'I would enjoy exercising in the cold', but he is very, very mistaken.

We come to a still pond sparkling in the moonlight.

It's pretty, but not worth the leg cramps.

"You like it?" he asks.

"It's pretty," I say.

"Just wait."

"Huh?"

He steps behind me so that my back is touching his chest and wraps his arms around my waist.

"I told you I had a surprise for you."

"This isn't the surprise?" I ask.

"Nope. Ready?"

"I guess so…"

He jumps, lifting me up in the air with him, but our feet don't return to the ground. We're lifting higher and higher until I realize we're flying over the pond. We go higher still, over treetops. The wind in my hair is cold, but the feeling is exhilarating. I giggle as we soar over forests and rivers.

"Bend your knees," he says.

I do, and he descends. A building appears in a small clearing ahead—a real-life stone castle. We land on the roof, overlooking the hills below.

"Wow," I say. "That was amazing. Why have we never done that before?"

"It's hard to find the right unpopulated areas," he says with a laugh.

"What is this place?"

"An old castle. It's a historical monument now."

"I like it."

I sit down on the stone rooftop and he sits beside me.

"Ava," Zane says with a serious voice. He's shaking slightly and chewing on his lower lip. "I want you to know that I love you more than anything. When I imagine my future, you're the only constant."

"I love you too," I say.

"You and I are… messy and imperfect and yet… we make sense in the most honest way."

He pulls out a small box roughly the size of his palm and my heart nearly skips a beat.

"There is no part of me that doesn't love every part of you. Will you be my wife?"

He opens the box to reveal a gold knot bracelet like the ones other Sirens wear—the marriage knot.

I take a deep breath in, unsure what to say.

Does he really want to be with me? Forever?

"Can I ask you something?" I say.

"Su- sure," he says.

"If you knew back then… about my health… and all my baggage… would you have chosen not to love me?"

"I never had a choice," he says with a smile. "I loved you from the start. But would I choose you all over again? Of course. I will always choose you. Every single time I get the chance."

"Yes," I say. And he pulls me in for a kiss.

We walk back to the house hand-in-hand, my new bracelet on my wrist. There are lots of lights on inside and I hear loud chatter and music.

"I guess everyone is still awake," I say.

We open the door and head to the living room, where we are greeted by a loud cheering crowd of our friends and a sign that says 'Congratulations.'

"I hope you said yes," Kieran says, "'cause otherwise this would be really awkward."

"And I would have come all this way for nothing," Jen says, popping out from behind Kami.

"Jen!" I scream, running up and giving her a big bear hug.

"Okay, okay," she says. "Don't squish the goods!"

I laugh and release her.

"She's wearing it!" Kami squeals.

"Congratulations, boo!" Jen says.

Finn and Morgan hand us each a champagne glass.

"Congratulations, Killer," Morgan says with a smile.

"You know, as Demon King, I'm pretty sure I could be your officiant," Kieran says.

"Oi!" Finn says. "We get it, you're Demon King! You have a kingdom of Incubi and Succubi to do your bidding and you're very impressive."

I laugh and Kieran scowls.

Right here, right now, I have everything I ever wanted. Zane was right—we never had a choice.

Zane was a decision my heart made for me, right from the beginning.

There was never a question. Only an answer. Only a line from my heart to his, ever tugging us closer. To our future. To this moment. To us. Forever.

THE END

A Note from the Author

Thank you for reading my book and supporting me as an indie author. It means the world to me that you've taken this journey with me and my characters.

If you enjoyed this book, I would be so grateful if you left a review! Reviews help indie authors like me get our books into the hands of more readers. They make a huge difference in visibility, recommendations, and even future opportunities to keep writing the stories we love. Even just a few sentences about what you liked can mean the world!

In regards to the ending: Some readers have asked why Ava's illness wasn't cured. The truth is, not all illnesses have a cure or a magical fix. As someone who is chronically ill myself, I wanted to write a romance heroine that my fellow sick girls could relate to—someone whose happy ending didn't depend on becoming healthy.

For many of us, chronic illness is lifelong. It's something we live with every single day, knowing that it won't just disappear. But that doesn't mean we can't find joy, love, and fulfillment. A happy ending doesn't have to mean being cured—it can mean being loved exactly as you are.

So for those who, like me, are navigating life with a body that doesn't always cooperate, I hope this story reminds you that you are worthy of love, happiness, and your own version of a happy ending.

If you enjoyed these books and would like updates on my future releases, I hope you'll consider following me on Instagram or visiting my website to sign up for my newsletter. Every tiny bit of your support matters.

Instagram: @LuxRavenWrites

Newsletter: LuxRavenWrites.com/newsletter

About the Author

LUX RAVEN writes paranormal romance with brooding bad boys, strong-but-vulnerable heroines, and a heavy dose of spice. As a chronically ill writer, she got tired of never seeing heroines like her in romance—so she created her very own disabled protagonist who goes on adventures, has hot sex with a winged bad boy, and finds the swoon-worthy love we all deserve.

Lux first unleashed her stories online on Wattpad, where they racked up over 3.5 million reads and even won a Watty Award in 2022. Now, she's bringing her debut duology to print, ensuring more readers can escape into a world where love always wins (because if it doesn't have a happy ending, it's not romance, and she will absolutely die on that hill).

A lifelong paranormal fangirl, Lux spent her teen years obsessing over *Charmed, Sabrina the Teenage Witch*, and *Big Wolf on Campus*, so naturally, her books are full of supernatural drama. These days, she lives in Los Angeles with her partner and their dog, where she's living her best basic-millennial-bitch life going to weekend brunches and drinking her body weight in green tea.

You can find her on Instagram at @LuxRavenWrites or at LuxRavenWrites.com, where she's probably rambling about book tropes or raging against the patriarchy. (Probably both.)

LuxRavenWrites.com

www.ingramcontent.com/pod-product-compliance
Lightning Source LLC
Chambersburg PA
CBHW011129190726
48289CB00012B/2959